Nicaraguan Gringa

ALSO BY JOHN M. KEITH

Complete Humanity in Jesus: A Theological Memoir

*True Divinity in Christ: A Testimony of Faith
and Hope with Four Short Stories*

Canebrake Beach: A Novella and Four Short Stories

NICARAGUAN GRINGA

Claiming a Home

John M. Keith

NewSouth Books

Montgomery

NewSouth Books
105 S. Court Street
Montgomery, AL 36104

Library of Congress Cataloging-in-Publication Data

Keith, John M.
Nicaraguan gringa : claiming a home / John M. Keith.
pages cm
Includes bibliographical references.

ISBN 978-1-60306-359-3 (pbk.) — ISBN 978-1-60306-360-9 (ebook)

1. British Americans—Nicaragua—Fiction. 2. Coffee growers—Nicaragua—
Fiction. 3. Nicaragua—Politics and government—1979-1990—Fiction. I. Title.
PS3611.E3685N53 2014
813'.6—dc23

2014013957

Printed in the United States of America

For the members of
St. Francis Episcopal Church
and
The Union Church
Managua, Nicaragua
1966–71

Contents

Author's Notes

A lthough real political figures in both Nicaragua and the United States are mentioned in the novel, all of the characters that actually speak and appear in the narrative are fictional. Places that are mentioned in the novel pose a more complicated mixture of real locations and imagined settings. Quinta Louisa, the coffee factory, and the village are all fictional. Although the names of actual barrios in Managua are used, the descriptions of them may be somewhat fanciful composites of several areas of the city.

The time-line that follows these notes offers a context for the larger national and international events within which the story is set. Some of these events are noted in the narrative so that the reader is reminded of the historical time and situation. Other events are included in the time-line as a general historical background.

Italics are used to indicate the dialogue in Spanish, and regular type is used when English is being spoken. On occasions the actual Spanish word or phrase is printed when no English translation seems adequate for its meaning at that point in the story. In conversations where English predominates but a Spanish word is "thrown in," the actual Spanish word is printed in the text followed by its translation in parenthesis. Bilingual characters often use "Spanglish," a mixture of the languages within a single sentence or phrase. A suggestion of the syntax and rhetoric of the Spanish conversation is attempted in the English italicized translation, such as the omission of contractions and possessive nouns, although a strict word-for-word translation would render the dialogue too stilted. Italics are also used on occasion in the usual manner for emphasis.

In all these matters the reader's discernment and judgment will be needed.

Time Line
of Nicaraguan Events

1912–37   U.S. Marines intermittently occupy Nicaragua.

1934   Augusto César Sandino assassinated.

1936   Anastasio Somoza "Tacho" García takes control of the country with complicity of U.S. Marines

1937-56   Somoza elected president in 1937, serving effectively as dictator until his death in 1956. His sons, Luis Somoza Debayle and Anastasio Somoza "Tachito" Debayle, follow him as presidents/dictators.

1961   National Liberation Front is founded at the University of León by Carlo Fonseca, Silvio Mayorga, and Tomás Borge.

1962   National Liberation Front name is changed to Frente Sandinista Liberación (FSLN).

1967   January 22: A coup is attempted in Managua.
April 13: Luis Somoza dies of a heart attack.
August 27: Silvio Mayorga is assassinated in Matagalpa.

1968   October 23: Volcano Cerro Negro begins erupting near León.

1972   December 23: Managua is destroyed by an earthquake.

1973   President Anastasio Somoza embezzles money from relief funds provided by the United States. It is later revealed that he controls 40 percent of the economy.

1974   U.S. Marines are again sent to support Somoza's regime.
November 8: Carlos Fonseca dies in combat in the mountains.

1978	April 30: Pedro Joaquín Chamorro, editor of *La Prensa,* is assassinated.
1979	FSLN intensifies the uprising against Somoza. July 17: Anastasio Somoza flees Nicaragua. July 19: Commandante Cero (Edén Pastora) leads FSLN troops into Managua, and the city falls to the Sandinistas.
1980	March 24: Archbishop Oscar Romero is assassinated in El Savador. September 17: Anastasio Somoza is assassinated in Paraguay.
1981	Ronald Reagan is inaugurated President of U.S.A.
1982	Boland Amendment in U.S. Congress prohibits U.S. funds to be used for overthrow of Nicaraguan government.
1983	"Iran Contra Affair": U. S. funds go to Nicaraguan opposition fighters via sale of ballistic missiles to Iran with payments diverted to Nicaraguan Contras. Civil war in Nicaragua is estimated to have killed 60,000 people at a cost of 178 billion dollars.
1984	Daniel Ortega (FSLN candidate) is elected President of Nicaragua. Ronald Reagan imposes an embargo on Nicaragua.
1985	"Iran Contra Affair" is exposed publicly.
1986	Daniel Ortega goes to Soviet Union seeking funds.
1987	Hurricane Hugo devastates Nicaragua.
1990	Violeta Chamorro, widow of Pedro Joaquín Chamorro, is elected President of Nicaragua.
1991	Coalition government (National Opposition Union) cuts social programs (health, education, etc.) and land reform.
1997	Armando Alemán is elected Presidents of Nicaragua representing the Constitutionalist Nationalist Party.
2007	Daniel Ortega is again elected President. Sandinistas control government once more.
2012	April 30: Tomás Borge, last surviving founder of FSLN, dies.

Nicaraguan Gringa

Tuesday, August 26, 1980

Sarah Rutledge experienced no strong feelings in the lobby of the Nicaraguan Ministry of Justice in Managua, neither repulsion at its drabness, nor anxiety in anticipation of what might happen, just impatience. She didn't like sitting and waiting for the Chief Minister to see her and thought of leaving. The minutes seemed even longer because they were empty, because she was empty, ready to give up and give in. At least her wait didn't stretch into hours. Within a half an hour a secretary called her into the office of Aldolfo Castillo López.

There were few signs of privilege and power in Castillo's office—an old battered metal desk, three wooden armchairs and four straight chairs and one comfortable padded swivel chair for the minister, not even a carpet on the floor nor curtains over the windows. At the side of the room a table was piled high with maps and blueprints. On the minister's desk were stacks of papers and a stapler. A very large, exquisite pre-Columbian jade carving served as a paperweight on top of a high pile of rumpled pages. It was insecurely balanced and could have fallen off and broken, even though it was probably worth hundreds of dollars.

"*Buenos días* (Good morning), *Señorita Rutledge Lloyd. Please have a seat.*" Castillo López shook Sarah's hand and stared at her. His hands were cold against her palm as she thought the metal of the pistol on his hip would feel if she were to touch it. Her heart also felt cold inside her chest.

"*Gracias* (Thank you)." Sarah sat in one of the straight wooden chairs without an armrest.

"*What do you want me to do for you?*"

"*I want to get a final decision about the disposition of my property.*"

"*Do you plan to stay in Nicaragua permanently and live on the finca* (farm), *or do you intend to sell it and leave the country?"*

Weariness overcame Sarah. She could no longer pretend and deceive Castillo, perhaps because she could no longer pretend and deceive herself with tentative possibilities and illusions of happy resolutions. She had already collapsed and given up within herself, and there seemed no reason to maintain any outward resistance to the government's program of confiscating foreigners' property, no matter how much they might protest.

"When I came back to Nicaragua, I did not think I would stay permanently. After the revolution and the death of my father it has been difficult to operate the finca and the factory; but since I have been back, almost three months now, I have found it hard to think of leaving for good, forever. This is my home. I am a citizen of the United States, but I have always thought of Nicaragua as my real home. Quinta Louisa has been the home of my family for almost a century. I have not been able to decide whether to sell it and give it up or to stay. Right now I think I will leave, but I just do not know."

Against her will Sarah was forced to dab away tears from her cheeks. Castillo's face softened, almost as if it might show a human expression. She thought that telling the truth moved him more than her tears. His lancing stare had penetrated to the center of her ambivalent sentiments.

"If it is difficult for you to decide, you can imagine that it is also difficult, much more difficult, for the government to decide what is right in these matters. In times of great change not all matters are easily adjudicated fairly and justly."

"What do you think my chances are for keeping Quinta Louisa at this point?"

"I cannot speculate. It will be decided on the basis of what this ministry and other officials think your true rights are. Some people want to curry the good favor of the United States government and make that a part of the issue. I do not personally think the issues of property settlement should be influenced by the international climate. I believe each case should be decided on its own merits."

"Even if I decide to leave Nicaragua, surely I have the right to receive something in compensation for Quinta Louisa."

The cold mask returned to Castillo's face, and he made no reply. Sarah understood that rights and values were defined differently in the two worlds in which they lived, one socialist and the other capitalist.

Tyranny and Colonialism: 1964–72

Who Belongs Here?

S arah was nine and a half years old, almost nine and three quarters, as she calculated her age for anyone with the patience to listen to her, when she ran down the hall of Quinta Louisa on the Feast of the Epiphany, January 6, wearing the homemade crown with two quetzal plumes attached to its sides. It was constructed from cutout cardboard and gilded with gold paint whose long drips had dried into permanent globs under the feathers, and Sarah believed it endowed her with magical powers.

"*Have much care, Sarita,*" Don Martín called from the patio door. "*Have much care not to break the feathers.*"

"*I am going to wear the crown to the . . . party at the church . . . for the three kings.*" Sarah couldn't remember how to say Epiphany in Spanish, even though it was almost the same as in English, *Epifanía.*"

"*You may not take the crown away from the forests. The quetzal belongs in the forests.*"

Sarah knew that she would lose the battle if she appealed to her mother and father to overrule Don Martín. Even if he hadn't seen her, permission to wear the quetzal crown to the church would have been a long shot at best.

"*Then you must tell me the story again.*"

"*You know the words exactly. It is not necessary for me to repeat them.*"

"I want to hear you say them."

"Well, come outside to the patio."

"No. You come in here."

Martín laid his machete on the edge of the stone patio and sat down beside it and waited. Sarah carefully took off the crown and placed it on the table behind the English Sheridan sofa that had been shipped from England by her great-grandmother—she knew that Don Martín wouldn't allow her to wear it outside—then opened the screened door. Sarah had grown almost as tall as Don Martín, but his body and arms and legs were strong and firm under his ginger colored skin. His face was smooth and round, but in the sandals he'd made with leather thongs and soled with treads from old automobile tires his feet were scarred from cuts and bruises.

As he told her the story for the hundredth time, Don Martín's black eyes twinkled and rolled like a little boy relating a secret.

"Long ages ago when the world was young, before Jesus was born of the blessed Virgin, there was a handsome prince in our land. His skin was golden, and his hair and eyes were as black as the night but glistened with light like the stars and the moon. He loved the forests, the animals and the flowers and the butterflies, but he especially loved the birds. He found the feathers from the tail of the great blue and green quetzal on the forest floor, and his sisters wove them into beautiful robes for him. Then the quetzal had no red breast." Don Martín paused. It had been a long, wearying day. *"He began to trap the quetzals . . ."*

"No, no, Don Martín. Tell about the little boys. You're leaving that part of it out."

"¡Como no! (As you say!) *Those were evil days when men killed each other in war. Their priests came and told them that the king must choose a child, a male child, a beloved son, the most beautiful boy of the tribe and kill him. Every year a little boy had to be killed, so that the warriors would have success in war. The prince did not have to worry about the evil priests or about war while he was young. He played in the forest with his friends, the animals and the birds. He gathered flowers, and he brought the beautiful feathers of the birds and butterflies that had died and put them with his flowers in the temple. The*

priests laughed at the feathers and flowers and dead butterflies that he stuck in cracks of the temple walls, but he was the prince and just a little boy, and they didn't scold him. No one ever scolded him, and he grew up thinking that he could do whatever he wanted to do, because he was the prince. He became spoiled and vain, but his heart was good, deep inside. He did no work and walked around in his robe of gleaming green feathers like a proud bird."

"Would they have killed me if I had lived back then, so they would win the war?"

"Of course not. You are a little girl. They never sacrificed little girls, only little boys."

"I think Pablo is like the little prince, because nobody ever scolds him or makes him do anything he does not want to do."

"Maybe. Maybe so. Once the little prince captured five quetzals and put them in a cage; but within a week they had died, for as you know the quetzal cannot live in captivity. He took the feathers from the dead birds and asked his sisters to make him a new robe, more beautiful than any of the others. And then his luck began to change, perhaps because the sacred birds had died and lost their plumes, perhaps because he had grown older and could no longer play in the forest and do as he pleased in the temple with the flowers and feathers and butterflies. He swore that he would never cause anything beautiful to die again. Then his father, the old king, died, and the young prince became the king. He was no longer a boy. Now he was a young man. The time for the great feast of war arrived, and the priests came to the young king and told him that he must choose the most handsome male child in the tribe and cut out his heart and offer it to the gods. He did not believe that the gods who had made the flowers and the butterflies and the birds would want a child's heart cut out of his body. After the quetzals died he had promised not to kill anything beautiful. He refused to choose a little boy to be sacrificed, but the priests told him that he must do what they commanded."

Martín paused, as he always did at this point in the story and looked down at Sarah's expectant, impatient face that reflected how she was annoyed by the delay. "Go on. What happened then?"

"You finish the story today. I am tired. You tell the rest of it. You know it as well as I do."

"*I do not want to. It is not the same as hearing you tell it. Even Daddy is not able to tell it like you do. When he speaks in English, it does not seem real. It seems like it really happened when you talk in Spanish.*"

"*Very well. The day of the festival arrived. The young king was very unhappy. Somehow he knew that one life must be given for another. It is something people have always understood, but this was a long time before Jesus came to tell people about a loving God. He was very confused and sad. He could not decide whether to obey the priests or to keep his oath never to kill anything beautiful. When the hour for the festival arrived, the young king had been persuaded to choose a boy from the tribe. He chose a child—how old are you now?*"

"*You know very well that I am almost ten years old, and I am in the fourth grade at the* American School."

"*The young king chose a ten year old boy, but they did not have schools then, so he was not in the fourth grade, and the priests brought the boy up to the high altar at the temple. A sword was standing beside the altar with its sharp tip pointing up to the sky. The priests planned to take the sword and cut out the heart of the little boy. He cried and screamed when they pulled him toward the altar. It took three strong men to hold him.*"

"*Just like Pablo.*"

"*Then, just as they placed him on top of the altar and were reaching to pick up the sword, the young king rushed forward and threw himself onto its point. It pierced his heart, and the red blood ran out all over the golden skin of his chest, but none of the blood touched the green-feathered robe. Not even a year had passed when people began to see the red breasts on the quetzals. No one was allowed to kill a quetzal or a boy again. Now the quetzals are the sacred birds of the forest that guide people into all truth.*"

Martín stood and picked up his machete. Sarah hopped up from the edge of the patio like a bird herself and hugged the peasant laborer around his waist and put her cheek against his naked, sweaty, brown belly. "*I love your stories. Thank you, Don Martín. I really do love you.*"

A COUPLE OF MONTHS later when Mary Rutledge asked her daughter what she wanted for her birthday, Sarah said she wanted her bedroom floor strewn with orchids.

"Really, Sarah, how foolish! They'd just wilt in a few hours. Think what a waste it would be!" Mary spoke in her Southern-lady tone of voice. "I've never heard of anything so silly and impractical. It's outrageous!"

But Martín had overheard her; and when Sarah came home from school the afternoon of her birthday, tiny mountain orchids were scattered across the floor of her bedroom. "Mother! The orchids! How beautiful! Where did they come from?"

"Martín gathered them in the forest for you. Who else would humor you with such foolishness!"

"Oh, I should have guessed. I should have known Don Martín would pick them for me if I'd asked him to." Sarah paused, afraid her mother had misunderstood. "I didn't ask him to, but he must have overheard me talking to you. He understands us when we speak in English, I think, even though he won't say a word to us except in Spanish."

"Martín overhears everything we say in this house. It's impossible to keep anything private." Mary Rutledge pursed her mouth as she often did when she was annoyed.

Somehow Sarah knew that Don Martín had gathered the orchids for her as a compensation for refusing to let her wear the quetzal crown to the Epiphany party at the church. She put the orchids in a round fish-bowl on her dresser, and they didn't wilt for almost a week, which went to show how much Don Martín knew about beautiful things that lived in the forest and how little her mother knew.

After Sarah's birthday George Rutledge told his daughter that she could no longer ask Don Martín to ride piggyback around the house and garden. "It's too hard for him to carry you, now that you're a big girl, and you're too old for that sort of thing."

Sarah believed that Don Martín would still be glad to give her rides on his back. He seemed to enjoy them as much as she did and laughed even more than she did, but she knew her father's command was unimpeachable and unwavering. It must be obeyed absolutely.

The next day Martín brought Sarah some little brown melons. "*Don Jorge said I must not carry you on my back any more, señorita; but I brought you some fruits from the forest."* The wild melons had no names in dictionaries nor even in the market because they were too sparse and perishable to sell, with tough hard dark skins and soft deep pink insides that made her blush to look at them for reasons she couldn't explain. They were very, very sweet, so that she needed almost as much lime juice as pink flesh to cut the nectarous honey. Although Don Martín would know the Indian names for them, she'd ceased asking what they were called long ago, because she quickly forgot; and the next time he would bring a different variety with yet another name but just as sweet.

QUINTA LOUISA WAS A rather ordinary adobe house with a red tiled roof and beautiful polished tile floors. It was furnished with one or two nice chairs and the English Sheridan settee. The appliances had come from the United States, especially the refrigerator and kitchen range. The rest of the furniture had been handmade from beautiful Nicaraguan wood, like the wooden furniture in humbler Nicaraguan homes. There were two extraordinarily primitive bathrooms with beautiful tiled walls and another toilet and shower with rough concrete walls in the servants' room next to the kitchen.

Martín and Flora lived in a little house in the village with their three sons, Julio, Guillermo, and Pablo; but sometimes Martín or Flora would spend the night in the room next to the kitchen. They never used the bathrooms in the other part of the house, although Mary Rutledge had told Flora that she was welcome to use them when she was working there, but Flora had looked at her with the gaping incredulity that she often expressed at things Sarah's mother said.

When Sarah refused to eat anything after being sick, Mary Rutledge's pleas were unheeded and ignored. "Won't you take a few sips of soup, dearest? Just a few spoonfuls?"

"I'll try to eat a little bit if Don Martín will come inside and eat with me."

Mary called Martín in from the garden and related Sarah's request.

"No, señora. I am sorry very much, but I cannot do such a thing. It is very improper."

"*You know that you and Flora are welcome to join us for lunch at our table. I do not understand. You are always welcome.*"

"*No. Never, señora. We will eat at our own table in the kitchen. You do not understand these things. It would be very wrong. A sacrilege.*"

Mary Rutledge didn't know the meaning of Martín's final word and went to the study to look it up in her Spanish-English dictionary. "*Sacrilego.* What nonsense!" She spoke so loudly that she thought he could have heard her from the dining room, but he'd already returned to the garden.

Julio and Guillermo were six and two years older than Sarah respectively, but she rarely saw Julio and hardly knew him. He didn't work on the *finca* (farm) except during the coffee harvest when he helped to pick the beans. Guillermo often helped his father in the garden, but he was shy and rarely spoke and never played with Sarah. George Rutledge had arranged for the two older sons of Martín and Flora to attend a school in Managua after they graduated from the village school, and he paid for their tuition and school uniforms and books. Pablo was almost seven years younger than Sarah and often followed Martín around the garden. When Sarah turned twelve, she thought of Pablo as a baby always needing attention, even though he was really a little boy of six who came and went as he pleased.

Avocados were George Rutledge's favorite fruit, and it annoyed him that the trees at Quinta Louisa had done so poorly that only three or four pears a year were harvested from his garden. He told Martín they ought to be able to do something about it.

"*I am going to take care of the problem, Don Jorge. You will have plenty of avocados when the rainy season comes again.*"

"As if that ignorant peon has the competence and training of a horticulturalist and can improve the yield of temperamental fruit trees," Sarah heard her father mutter as he entered the house.

Several days later George saw Martín cutting a ring of bark around the trunk of the avocado tree. "*What are you up to, my good man?*"

Martín uttered some long word that Sarah didn't recognize. "*What was that word you used?*"

("Who else in Nicaragua has an Indian peasant working for him that spouts out ten syllable words like some Cambridge don ... in Spanish, of course," George had said as he related the story to his wife that evening.)

George went into the study to look up the definition in the Spanish-English dictionary to be sure he understood it. *Circumcidante* (Circumcising).

Sarah read the entry on the page where her father had left the dictionary open on his desk, but the words didn't refer to fruit trees and confused Sarah and made her blush. "Circumcising: cutting circularly a portion of the skin around the male virile organ."

She heard the patio slam once again as her father went back to the garden.

"*Martín, tell me one more time what you are doing to that tree?*

"*I am circumcising it, señor.*"

Martín was cutting a strip of bark around the trunk of the tree. "*What are you doing that for?*"

("It really did look like some primitive circumcision ritual," George told his wife that evening.)

"*To change the sex. It is a male. That is why it will not bear any fruit. I am making it into a woman.*"

"*My good man, circumcision is not the way we go about changing the gender of things.*"

"*It is for avocado trees, señor.*"

George told Mary at dinner that the tree would be dead within the month but he might as well let Martín have his way. "You can't tell these bull-headed *campesinos* (peasants) anything. They'll just walk off and start sulking and do no work at all. You might as well let them have their way in little things and save your arguments for urgent matters. The tree is perfectly useless anyway if it bears less than a half-dozen pears every year."

To George's surprise the avocado tree didn't die. It produced more buds that season than it had borne in all the previous seasons added together, and there were even more pears the following season; but the next season after that, the year that Sarah turned thirteen, the tree put out almost no buds again.

"Martín has some crank theory about virgins. Perfectly ridiculous. These fool peasants are obsessed with superstitions about virgins. I don't believe a word of it. He told me an avocado tree won't bear fruit if a virgin climbs on its limbs after she begins to menstruate."

"Father! Really!" Sarah got up and threw her napkin on the table without inserting it into its ring, as she'd been trained to do, and ran to her room and slammed the door.

"You really shouldn't talk so freely around Sarah now that she's becoming a young woman, George. She's easily embarrassed." Mary's eyes twinkled, and she wrinkled up her lips. "But you might pay more attention to Martín's folk remedies. Remember how the tree began to bear fruit after it was circumcised a couple of years ago."

George forbade Sarah from ever climbing in the avocado tree again. He told her that she was too old for such behavior, just as he'd told her when she was ten that she was too old to ride on Don Martín's back.

The next season the trees produced even more fruit, and the next year they showed more buds than George had ever seen on a tree, with the promise of a prodigious crop of pears until Pablo's outrageous behavior ruined them. From the time that he was still in diapers there had never has been a child at Quinta Louisa who could make mischief like Pablo.

Pablo's troublemaking was partly Mary's fault. She hadn't objected to having Julio and Guillermo in the house before Sarah was born or even to having them play with Sarah as older boys when she was little, but she'd refused to have another baby under foot when Pablo was a toddler. He'd seemed always to be at the patio door or yelling in the garden, and Flora would have to run out to care for him.

Pablo was eight years old when Mary saw him high in the avocado tree, breaking off pears and tossing them to the ground. She rushed into the garden. *"You get down from there right now and stop picking the avocados."* For a moment he looked at her, and then he began pulling off all the pears with frenzied flings, even the green ones and those hardly out of the bud. *"Stop it! You hear me, stop it right now, you wretched boy!"* Mary ran under the tree and began shaking the trunk, although she herself was shaking more violently than the tree, while Pablo was scurrying around above her, pelting her with green avocados, giggling and bouncing them off her head and shoulders like some evil monkey. She screamed until everyone appeared in the garden—Sarah, Flora, Guillermo, and various other workers. Finally George heard her yelling hysterically even from where he was drying coffee beans in the sorting shed. (Martín was in Costa Rica taking the training course to run the new coffee-processing factory that George Rutledge planned to build.) One of the workers helped George get the rebellious little imp down out of the tree.

"*Why did you do such an awful thing to my avocados, you horrible, wicked boy?*" Mary's voice was raspy after her screaming and from her lingering anger.

The plump, brown little brat put his hands on his hips and looked Mary straight in the eye. "*My Papá planted the tree, and my Papá waters the tree, and my Papá gathers the fruit, so why do you call them your avocados?*"

George emitted one of his single puff-pops of laughter in spite of himself at the boy's audacious courage and spirit. No one else would dare talk to his wife like that.

"What are you laughing at, George Rutledge? You're the one who's crazy about avocados. I'm just trying to protect them for you, since you think they're the most delicious food that ever was."

Flora assured Mary that she would buy avocados for them at the market and replace every piece of fruit that Pablo had destroyed.

Mary was still trembling and breathless, near hysteria. She turned red-faced and bent over in an inelegant squat that must have been inherited from some long-dead North Carolina mountain ancestor. "*I do not want avocados from the market. These were mine, and they belong to no one else, and that wretched boy destroyed them, and I do not want him ever in my sight again.*"

"Mary, Mary, now let's keep things in perspective."

"*Get that child out of my garden, and do not ever allow him to come inside the garden wall again unless you stay with him. Not ever!*"

THE FOLLOWING DAY SARAH saw her father sitting on the bench in the middle of the garden after he'd gathered the limes that the family used to marinate meat and flavor their drinks. She slipped out of the house without her mother seeing her leave.

"Daddy, why was Mother so mean to Pablo yesterday? We can always buy avocados at the market, and Doña Flora offered to replace them."

As her father rubbed his chin Sarah recognized the gesture that often accompanied his reluctance to respond to her questions. "Well, Susi, you have to understand something about your mother. She is the most generous person in the world to those who are less fortunate. For too generous for her own good sometimes, I fear. But when someone takes something away from her that she thinks they have no right to, something that belongs to her and is important to her ... well, you saw how she acted yesterday."

"But why is Mother like that? She doesn't act that way all the time."

"Most assuredly not. She's usually the most kind and generous ..." George Rutledge rubbed his chin again. "I don't know. Perhaps it goes back to her early life on the farm in North Carolina. After the tenants all left for better jobs, and the Lloyds had to give up growing row crops and convert to timber and cattle; and people started taking advantage of them, encroaching on their land and filching things ... I don't know. It may go back to some of that."

"It's too bad. Pablo's not really so awful, not for a little boy his age."

"I know. And your mother does a great deal to help Don Martín and Doña Flora and their sons. I think it would be best not to mention any of our conversation to your mother. Don't you agree?"

"I understand, Daddy, and I promise never to climb in the avocado tree again either. I wouldn't want Mother to yell at me the way she screamed at Pablo."

"That would never happen, Susi. Not ever. But let's keep this as a secret just between the two of us."

George Rutledge took pride in telling whoever would listen to him that his tree bore more avocados than any others in the region after Martín circumcised it. Following her father's strict orders Sarah never climbed the avocado tree again, and except for the season when she entered her teens and a year later when Pablo broke off the buds of fruit, Quinta Louisa never lacked for avocados. George could never determine which had caused the larger dearth of fruit, Sarah's climbing on the limbs as a teenager or Pablo's vandalism. As a rational man he wondered if Pablo hadn't surreptitiously destroyed the buds on the tree the same year that Sarah had climbed it as a menstruating virgin.

About a week after Pablo's escapade in the avocado tree Martín came home from Costa Rica for a visit and told George that he wanted to quit the apprenticeship for running the coffee-processing factory.

"Now look here. You must not let that business between Doña Mary and Pablo bother you. You know how riled up she gets over little things from time to time. It will all blow over and be forgotten in another week or so."

"I miss my family, Don Jorge. I do not like living in the city."

"It's only for a few months. You're much too intelligent to spend the rest of your days as a servant or a common laborer picking coffee. I want to give you a better chance in life. You deserve it. Besides, a smart fellow like you can be extremely helpful to us in running the factory, if I decide to build it."

"I just want to come back to the campo (countryside) *and live in the mountains where I know the trees and the flowers. Please don't send me away again. Let me stay here with my wife and children in the village. I'll die in the city. I'll grieve myself to death. I belong here."*

George had been unable to persuade Martín to return to Costa Rica, and he never left the *campo* again for more than a couple of days at a time.

When Pablo was sick the month after he'd been banned from the garden, Flora had to care for him; and Martín spent several days doing Flora's cleaning chores inside the Rutledges' house, where he found the broken shells from wild birds' eggs in Sarah's room.

"Did you take eggs from the nests of the birds in the forest?"

"No, Don Martín. I just found the broken shells on the ground. They must have fallen out of the nest."

Don Martín swiped his index finger inside the shell and held the sticky albumen close to her nose. His eyes squinted, and Sarah was terrified.

"*I am sorry.*" She wept and tried to swallow her sobs so that her parents wouldn't overhear her.

"*They are the quetzal's eggs. Destroying the quetzal's eggs is a great sin against Nature, and lying is a great sin against God. You must go into the forest with me and do your penance.*"

When Mary Rutledge saw Martín leading Sarah toward the forest, she asked her husband what was going on; and George made the mistake of telling her what he'd overheard. Mary saw Sarah's tear-stained face and horror-strickened eyes when she returned with Martín.

"*You have no business punishing my child, Martín. It is no concern of yours, and you must not do it again.*" Mary spoke calmly, rationally, without any expression of emotion in her voice or on her face, but Martín's black eyes glittered like lightning reflected on obsidian. His jaw was clenched.

"*You can send me away if you want to, Doña María, but as long as I have responsibility for your finca and your family and your forest and your daughter, I have to do what is right.*"

"*Now Martín, I did not mean to imply that you were wrong, but I think parents ought to be in charge of punishing a child. I am sure Sarah deserved to be reprimanded. Please just inform us when she needs to be corrected, and tell us what you propose.*"

"*She can tell you what I did. That is up to her, not up to me. Then if you want me to leave the finca, I will go; but I have to do what is right with the children in my forest, just as you must do what is right with them in your house and garden when they steal the fruit.*"

Sarah told her mother that Don Martín had rubbed a bitter herb over her mouth to remind her how ugly lying was, and Mary laughed and said that she could remember how her grandmother from Virginia had washed her mouth out with homemade soap for lying. Several months later Sarah told her father what had really happened, how Don Martín had rubbed the ordure of wild birds over her lips.

EVERY SUNDAY MORNING THE Rutledges traveled up toward Managua on the Pan American highway for the English-speaking Anglican service at the little stone church that Sarah's great-grandfather and other British expatriates had built. St. Francis Church appeared like a chapel on a meadow in Kent with its narrow lancet windows that provided little ventilation in the stifling tropical heat. A new missionary priest had arrived from somewhere in the mid-West, and Sarah had overheard her father muttering to her mother. "I wonder if he'll fit in or be as much a disaster as the last one," (who had fled back to the United States in less than six months.)

"What's his name, George?"

"Father Richard Sims, I believe. I should have driven out to welcome him this week I suppose, but ..."

"We'll just have to wait and see. Give him a chance. Maybe it will turn out better this time."

Even though Father Sims was younger and taller than Sarah's father, he was somewhat stooped and very thin so that he appeared to be shorter. He seemed distracted by the insects flying around the church. His eyes glanced back and forth from one of the lizards crawling up the wall to a moth flitting around the chancel. The small congregation of forty-odd people was almost equally divided between North American and British expatriates and English-speaking Nicaraguans of Caribbean ancestry from the East Coast of the country. When a dark *costeño* (resident of the East Coast of Nicaragua) stood up to read the Old Testament lesson, Sarah began giggling.

George smiled and glanced at Sarah whose tittering laughter was almost out of control, but her mother was not amused and had no sympathy for such misbehavior, especially in church.

"Stop that, Sarah, or I'll thrash you within an inch of your life when we get home."

Sarah bit her lip and pinched her thigh, but she couldn't stop. "I can't help it, Mother."

"You must stop." Mary gave Sarah a stare that could have frozen even the sweltering inside of St. Francis Church. The reader paused and looked at them and frowned—an unusual expression on his usually broad smiling face.

After the service Mary Rutledge was shaking Sarah by her shoulders and screaming at her in a whisper, as only her mother could do. "Making fun of people who are different from us is the worst thing a person can do. I will not have you looking down your nose and laughing at the Negroes."

"I wasn't doing that, Mother. I wasn't making fun of him. I just got tickled at how he talked, and I couldn't quit."

During the coffee hour after the service on the brick patio beside the church Father Sims found Sarah standing by herself close to the wall in the shade. Only a few younger *costeño* children worshipped with their parents at St. Francis, and none of them was Sarah's age.

"I find the British-Caribbean accents a little amusing, too, although quite charming. A reading from Isaiah . . . ." He poorly imitated the flat monotone and long "*I*" of the reader. "Do you know Taylor? He's quite a nice chap."

"Not really. The *costeños* usually hurry off before the coffee hour to catch their bus downtown. I guess they're staying late today to welcome you."

"Are there any activities for young people here at St. Francis? A youth group or Sunday School?"

"No. There aren't any children except for me."

"Well, we'll have to remedy that. You stay there. I have something for you to take home." Father Sims scurried with his cassock flapping against his legs across the parking lot toward the small vicarage where he lived. He brought out a hand of bananas to offer Sarah in order to placate her and perhaps bribe her to behave better in church. Perhaps he'd heard during his first week of cultural orientation that bananas didn't grow well at higher elevations, and he had several heavily laden trees at the back of the vicarage garden.

"No thank you. I really don't like bananas at all."

As her mother approached them, Mary Rutledge overheard Sarah and shot her a withering look. In the parking lot, Mary read Sarah another diatribe. "You must always accept gifts graciously, Sarah. Refusing people's gifts is almost like rejecting them personally. Just say, *thank you*, and smile and be pleasant and gracious. It's almost as bad to spurn people's freely offered, friendly gift as it is to make fun of them.

I really don't know what's gotten into you today. I've tried to teach you to be polite and lady-like. Surely you understand that people's feelings are the most important . . . ."

"That little priest will soon learn to take off his cassock before the coffee hour, or he'll burn up." Sarah knew that her father was attempting to change the subject and alter her mother's focus.

"He'll learn, George. It's quite an adjustment for him, I'm sure."

"We should invite him to Quinta Louisa for a meal, Mary. Maybe Beatriz and Armando could join us for a little dinner party."

"That's a wonderful idea, dear. I'm glad you're going to give him a chance."

EVEN THOUGH ARMANDO AND Beatriz Chulteco were Nicaraguans from old aristocratic families that belonged to the Conservative Party, they had both attended college in the United States; and most of their close friends were North American and British expatriates. Beatriz's mother had been the closest friend of Sarah's grandmother, and Armando's grandfather had befriended Sarah's great-grandfather when he'd first arrived from England. Mary Rutledge often referred to Beatriz as her closest Nicaraguan friend; and when she was being honest with herself, she admitted that Beatriz was her closest friend in the world.

Whenever she talked, Beatriz raised her arms and jangled her multiple bracelets and flicked her long, tapered fingers with manicured nails that testified that she had never washed a dish or pushed a mop in her life. "Come sit by me, Sarita." Armando and Beatriz Chulteco did not have children, and Sarah was more than a goddaughter, more than a niece could have been to them, especially to Beatriz. "How do you like the new *padrecito* (little priest)?"

"He's nice. A little gawky maybe. Sort of like a scarecrow in his cassock."

"Wicked girl!" Beatriz hugged Sarah tightly against her. "We'll have to get him started on the right foot."

Even before dinner was announced, with Sarah still sitting beside her, Beatriz had beckoned Father Sims and begun instructing him about how he must employ a housekeeper in addition to the part-time gardener that cleaned the church and lived in the little house behind the parking lot in order to guard the church.

"I'm afraid I can't afford servants on a missionary's salary."

"Oh, *Padre!* A live-in maid costs only a hundred *córdobas* a week—that's just fourteen American dollars. Surely you can afford that!"

"Really? But I'm not sure I need . . ."

"Of course you do. You can't buy ready-to-eat food at the supermarket down here. Someone has to cook for you, and you can't leave your house unattended. *Ladrones*, sneak thieves, will carry off everything. They're not violent. They won't hurt you. You are perfectly safe from harm in Nicaragua. Do not let me scare you, but they will get inside while you're gone and strip everything bare."

"Perhaps I should consider it."

"I will take care of everything for you. I will line up some girls for you to interview. Do you speak Spanish well enough, or would you prefer a *costeña* that speaks English?"

"I can get by in Spanish. I don't think it would be appropriate to have a *costeña*, so many of them are members of my parish and even the Moravians all have family members in the parish."

"*¡Como no!* (As you say!) I always think of the Episcopal vicar as just the chaplain for my North American and British friends, but you have to care for them, too." Doña Beatriz began speaking in her giddy, silly little-girl voice and tugging at her dangling gold earring.

"Mrs. Rutledge says you know the American and British community better than anyone else in Managua. How can I meet them and invite them to church? I'm especially anxious to get something started for the children."

"*¡Claro que sí!* (To be sure!), Armando and I are Catholics, of course; but I'd be delighted to help you. What did you have in mind for the children?"

"A Sunday School for the younger ones. Some kind of youth group for the older young people."

"I'll get you their addresses so you can drop them a note. I'd suggest setting up a meeting one afternoon at the American School when the parents pick up their children. They all go to the American School, of course."

"Even the Nicaraguan children?"

"*Claro que sí* (To be sure), all those of a certain class, but most of them are Catholic."

"Would that make it impossible for them to be involved in a youth group, even a social sort of thing?"

"Oh no. That might be quite feasible, if it wasn't too religious."

"And then there would be the young people from St. Francis. The *costeños* as you call them."

"Now that might be a bit more difficult. They're from a quite different social class, you know."

George Rutledge approached them. "Am I interrupting?"

"Of course not, George. Do join us."

"I need Beatriz's advice and counsel." George scowled at Sarah in a teasing way.

"She's been very helpful to me, Mr. Rutledge."

"Please call me George. Shoo, Sarah, I have something to ask Doña Beatriz in private."

Sarah scurried away but stayed close enough to overhear her father's conversation. As an only child often left alone in the company of adults, she'd developed the skill of acute hearing for eavesdropping.

"Sarah's been feeling a little isolated and lonely lately. I was thinking of organizing something . . . a party or some such . . . for some of the children her age."

"That fits right in with what the *padre* and I were discussing. We might kill two birds with one stone, as you North Americans say. Don't you think so, *Padre?*"

Father Sims nodded in agreement.

"You know Halloween is coming up. I realize it's not a Nicaraguan custom; but I remember how thrilling it was for me when I first went away to boarding school in the States. I'd never experienced anything like it. Do you think we could have a costume party for the children here at Quinta Louisa? Would you be willing to help Mary organize something like that?"

Beatriz clapped her hands and shook her head so violently in her excitement that her bracelets and earrings jangled together in a tinkling chorus. "Of course! ¡*Ciertamente!* (Certainly!) It will be great fun!"

"Perhaps you could help get some costumes for Martín and Flora's boys and some of the other children from the village and some of the *costeño* children from the church."

"¡*Dios mío!* (My God!) George, that's just what I was trying to explain to *Reverendo* Sims. That just won't work. You can't treat your workers as equals. Even Mary knows people of different classes can't socialize together. You should know better. You've lived here all your life. Sometimes I think Mary knows more about handling servants than you do. Bless her heart! I love her better than ripe sugarcane with that North Carolina drawl." Beatriz's voice had once again risen in pitch to a little girl timbre.

THE LOGISTICS PROVED TOO difficult for transporting the *costeño* children who attended St. Francis from the central city to Quinta Louisa, but George Rutledge insisted that Martín and Flora's boys and the children from the village should come to the Halloween party. Beatriz Chulteco would have nothing to do with their costumes. Mary Rutledge had to find something for Flora's boys to wear and searched for scraps of cloth for costumes that Martín could take to the village for the coffee workers' children, but Beatriz provided all the decorations and many of the refreshments for the party.

The Chultecos came for an early supper before the party at Quinta Louisa. Some of Sarah's classmates came at dusk, but it was dark when the workers' children arrived in masks carrying torches. As the villagers entered the garden in their frightening costumes with painted faces and masked eyes, she clung to her father and was not in the least delighted with the pleasant feeling of squeamish awe that he had told her he had enjoyed as a boy during his first experience of Halloween.

One of the boys from Sarah's class came over to comfort her. His name was Carlos Vargas Allen. His mother was a North American friend of her mother, although his father was Nicaraguan. Carlos was shy and smaller than the other boys in her class, and she'd rarely paid any attention to him. He patted her on the shoulder. "It's all right, Sarah. I'll take care of you. I won't let anything bad happen to you." For the first time Sarah noticed his soft, gentle voice; and even through her tears she saw his beautiful black eyes sparkling in the darkness.

After everyone left that night, Sarah came whimpering and sobbing to her father's bed; and he clasped her and held her tightly in his arms for almost an hour despite Mary's protests in the twin bed beside them. He told her that she was safe and secure and that no phantoms of the night would ever be able to hurt her.

THE WEEKEND BEFORE SARAH's fourteenth birthday her mother asked her how she would like to celebrate. Sarah was aware that her father still blamed himself for the Halloween fiasco and that her mother continued to be preoccupied about her lack of social ties and friendships with her peers; and Sarah intended to take full advantage of their guilt.

"I'd like to go down to the Eskimo on Saturday night."

"Saturday is impossible, as you know very well. I'll talk with your father about Sunday evening when there are fewer rowdy people on the streets." Since George Rutledge's parents were killed in an automobile accident on the steep mountain road coming back from Managua, he'd resisted driving into the city at night, especially on the weekend, unless it was an emergency.

When Sarah and Mary allied in a united front to persuade George, he protested as usual. "You know we don't go into the city at night. Besides with the elections coming up, a political rally is scheduled in the central plaza."

As his wife and daughter persisted and his feelings of guilt about the Halloween fiasco were recalled, he relented. "I'll call someone at the American Embassy and see if they think there's any problem because of the rally." George's friend at the American Embassy told him that no inflammatory demonstrations were anticipated and that in fact a large dinner party with many American guests was planned that night at the Gran Hotel. George had forgotten that he and Mary had been invited and had declined to accept the invitation to the dinner party, but he did agree finally to honor Sarah's birthday request.

A few years earlier the Eskimo ice cream parlor had been built within sight of the National Cathedral but away from the Central Plaza where the Conservative Party was scheduled to hold a rally opposing Anastasio Somoza Debayle's candidacy for President of the republic. The plate glass windows and plastic covered seats and chrome-plated metal strips around the counter and stools and table edges seemed even grander and more elegant than the pictures of such places in the United States that Sarah had seen in magazines. The North American and British teenagers, who were several years older than Sarah, came here for a soda or sundae after their dates at the movies. Chic Nicaraguan boys, especially those who attended the American School, also brought their dates to the Eskimo.

Sarah didn't have a boyfriend, and no boy had ever tried to sit beside her even when a large group went together to a movie on a Saturday afternoon. She hoped that some teenagers might be at the Eskimo on that Sunday night, January 22, 1967, although they would have been more likely to be encountered on a Saturday night. At least she could fantasize about someday having a date and being accepted by the "cool kids" and luxuriate in her imagination at the only place in Nicaragua that felt like a part of the youth culture of the United States. (Even though her father often told her, when she babbled rhapsodically about the Eskimo, that the American Embassy and the ambassador's residence were actual properties of the United States, they certainly felt to Sarah more like any other big Nicaraguan office building and mansion.)

George Rutledge finally found a parking space on the street and hired an urchin to guard the car with a payment made more for extortion than for security. They began walking toward the Eskimo when they heard the noise. Firecrackers and backfires from old buses and trucks could be heard in the night several times every hour in Managua, but careful practice had taught George to distinguish their sounds from gunfire.

Sarah felt her father grasp her upper arm so tightly that it hurt and saw him reach his other hand toward her mother. "Back to the car, as fast as you can walk!"

George might have chosen any of a dozen routes out of the city; but habit took him on his customary route to the South Highway through narrow lanes with high curbs and extraordinarily high sidewalks, hardly wide enough for a single person to balance against the tiny wooden structures. The houses in the old neighborhoods were constructed from wood rather than from the concrete and stucco used for houses built later in the city. The walls and shutters were unpainted; but from the bright green or yellow or blue or red doors, now all open, soft light splashed into the street.

There were no street lamps, and the middle of the road was dark; but people crowded onto the narrow sidewalks and spilled off into the edge of the street, laughing, singing, drinking, and shouting. Women and girls in tight dresses and high heels stood alone or in pairs, never more than three together. Occasionally one of the bright doors would bang shut with a squeal and a high-pitched laugh. It was a prostitutes' district. Even young teenagers like Sarah felt a giddy amusement and delight knowing that it was the *putas'* (prostitutes') neighborhood without their parents' awareness of their comprehension of such things. Riding down the middle of the street, she imagined being involved in the bawdy joy and lascivious pleasure, as if she were standing on the sidewalk with the revelers.

"I'm sorry, Susi (her father's baby name for her), we'll make it up to you. Maybe we can take some of your friends to dinner at Los Ranchos next week."

"That's all right, Daddy. You tried. I shouldn't have insisted so much."

Suddenly they heard shots and saw people run from doorway to doorway. The merry voices became shrill with fear and then muted into whines and cries as the doors closed and the crowds thinned and darkness transformed the street into a black tunnel of terror. Only the headlights of the old Austin picked out a few cringing figures, no longer dancing, now staggering into some opening before it was locked against them. A woman ran across the street in front of them carrying a young child in her arms with another young child who held her hand. The older child couldn't keep up with her, and she dragged him by the arm. Then he fell. She paused for only a moment and bent down and tried to lift the fallen child, but she could not manage both children, and she ran into one of the last open doorways abandoning the injured child in the street. They could see now it was a little boy. George swerved to avoid running over the small body and then accelerated.

"George! Stop!"

"We've got to get out of here. They'll shoot us!"

"Stop!" Mary was screaming and opening the door of the car as if she intended to jump out while it still sped along. "We have to see about the child."

George stopped and put the car into reverse. Even before he had stopped again, Mary had leapt from the already opened door and was running toward the fallen child in the street. George followed his wife immediately out of the car, and Sarah slipped out behind her parents and saw a wound and bloodstains on the little boy's shoulder and realized he had been struck by one of the bullets. He was small, only three or four years old, with a dirty, flat, sweet Indian face. Sarah could smell the big chocolate stains around his mouth and thought of the chocolate soda she had been prevented from ordering at the Eskimo. She began to cry.

"Sarah, get back in the car. Right now!"

Sarah obeyed her father, but from the car window she looked down at the little boy in the street. He was wearing a ragged shirt but new shorts. He was barefooted. Sarah's mother put her head down close to his face and chest. "He's breathing, but he's unconscious, maybe he fainted or is in shock." His eyes were closed, but little bubbles of saliva gurgled out of the corner of his mouth. Blood ran down his right arm. His right hand twitched. Sarah could hear gunshots still striking and ricocheting in the distance.

George knelt beside his wife. He was shaking. "*¿Tu madre? ¿Dónde está? ¡Vámanos con prisa!*" (Your mother? Where is she? Let's leave quickly!) He mumbled, almost whined incoherently. Mary appeared calm, almost clinical, without feelings, without fear. She looked around for the mother of the child, who had disappeared in the darkness; but there was no one on the street to tell them which door she had entered.

"George, you carry him to the car." Sarah's father didn't respond, so her mother picked the child up herself. He was heavy for her. He was bleeding badly, and blood had soaked through Mary's sweater and blouse and moistened her shoulder. "Can you drive?" George nodded and followed his wife blindly, almost staggering, as the older child had followed the mother across the street. "George, can you drive? Answer me."

"*Sí.*" They got into the car, where the motor had been left running. Mary took off her scarf and tied it tightly around the child's shoulder and cuddled his head on her bosom. George seemed to be heading down his usual route toward the South Highway.

"No, George. To the hospital."

"*El Retiro?*"

"No, Baptist. The Baptist Hospital, George. *Hospital Bautista.*" He still seemed to be driving toward the site of the public hospital, *El Retiro*. "No, no, George. The Baptist Hospital." He didn't seem to respond to English. "*El Hospital Bautista, Jorge. A la Clínica Bautista.*"

When they reached the hospital, George carried the child inside; and Sarah followed them without receiving any protests or instructions from her parents. Mary knew some of the missionary nurses and communicated the situation to them immediately. Even though the child had lost a large amount of blood, the wound didn't seem to be critical, and Mary's scarf had stanched the flow of blood to some extent. A Nicaraguan doctor thought that the little boy would survive and recover. Mary told him that they would return soon to see about the child and promised to cover all his expenses. They would try to locate his mother tomorrow, if the shooting and violence had ceased in the besieged *barrio* (neighborhood).

"Let's go home now, George." He was silent. His terror had passed. Now he was silent out of shame. He was pulling at his fingers, popping the joints.

Sarah had never seen her father behave in such a frightened way before, and it terrified her more than the gunfire.

Mary turned toward George on the long, silent drive to Quinta Louisa. Once she reached out to him but withdrew her hand just inches before her fingertips touched his arm. "It's all right, dear. It's all right. Everything will be fine." The whispered words were intended as much for Sarah as for her father, but Sarah didn't believe anything would ever be all right again, and nothing would ever be fine for her in Nicaragua again.

Sarah's mother tucked her into bed late that night, but for the first time in her life Sarah's father didn't come to give her a goodnight kiss; and his absence frightened her even more than seeing the wounds of the injured child, more than the bloodstains on the street and on her mother's blouse, more than the words of her mother and the silence of her father in the car on the way home to Quinta Louisa.

BECAUSE ARMANDO AND BEATRIZ Chulteco lived in the center of Managua, in one of the old homes just off Roosevelt Avenue, Sarah's parents invited them to spend several days at Quinta Louisa until order was restored in the city. Although a few shots were fired back and forth on Monday, the Nicaraguan army had established complete control by Tuesday morning; but with stores still shuttered and tensions high, Mary and George believed their friends would probably be safer and would certainly be calmer on the *finca* (farm) with them.

The newspapers reported fewer than twenty people killed, but family members of coffee workers from the village counted almost sixty friends and acquaintances known to be slain, and the count must surely have been even higher. Sarah sat with rapt attention listening to her parents and the Chultecos narrate the facts and rumors about what had happened.

Both political parties customarily rounded up *campesinos* (peasants) from the rural villages during the election campaigns and brought them into the city on big trucks and offered them a drink and a sweet. The outing was a rare and coveted celebration for the peasant laborers, who paid little attention to which political party was sponsoring the rally.

Now at the peak of the cotton harvest, trailers of raw cotton packed outlying streets on the weekend, waiting to be the first in line to be drawn into the gins on Monday morning. Underneath the cotton, rifles had been hidden; and communist guerrillas from Colombia retrieved the guns and stationed snipers on the roofs of some of the taller buildings along Roosevelt Avenue. They set cars on fire along some of the side streets. The snipers then fired into the crowd of *campesinos* from both directions, so that they were trapped in panic on the central street.

Some of the leaders of the Conservative Party were arrested and jailed, although Armando swore that they had played no part in the riot and had no knowledge of the plot by a few Nicaraguan communist sympathizers and foreign terrorists to destabilize the country. Some Conservative Party leaders had rushed into the Gran Hotel and held the guests hostage at the dinner party to which the Rutledges had been invited but had declined to attend. The hostages were confined until the opposition political officials were assured that they would not be executed by the Somoza regime. Anastazio Somoza, the younger brother of the former President and now a candidate for the Presidency himself, was the Chief of the Nicaraguan army. He surrounded the hotel with tanks whose cannons were trained on the entrances.

"He would have blown the building down in a quick moment if his older brother had not been more level headed." Sarah looked at Don Armando with wide eyes and a gaping mouth.

"Really?"

"*Sin duda* (without doubt), Sarita. Most certainly."

"Tachito is an evil man." Everyone called Anastasio Somoza Debayle, Tachito or little Tacho. His father, the first dictator of the Somoza regime, was called Tacho, which was a word for a large kettle used for boiling cane to make sugar, although no one knew how the General got that nickname.

"One of my friends at school told me he had his soldiers throw some men who were saying bad things about him into the Masaya volcano."

"Sush! Do not say such things out loud, Sarita." Doña Beatriz held her long thin fingers with their four bejeweled rings across her lips. "You must not say such things except to friends you trust *absolutamente* (absolutely). Who knows what the servants may hear and repeat, or some of the coffee pickers that may be communists . . . ?" Doña Beatriz's eyes were wide with fear. "Especially for you as a foreigner."

"We've been here for four generations, Beatriz. This is our country, too." Armando's and Beatriz's faces reflected the fear that was present on Sarah's father's face in the *barrio* on Sunday night, but now George Rutledge looked calm, even brave. "We belong here."

"Don't be too sure who belongs here. If there's a revolution, I'm not sure even Beatriz and I would belong. At least you have to give the Somozas credit for maintaining order for four decades." Now Don Armando looked more sad than frightened to Sarah.

"This is all very tedious, and you're scaring Sarah. We've never had any trouble here on the *finca*. The people who work for us, the people in the village, would protect us from any danger. They always have. They always will. They love us, and we love them." Mary Rutledge stood and smoothed her skirts to show her objection to their conversation.

"Nevertheless, my dear, we walk a narrow line. Armando is right. We are foreigners, even after four generations. This is the only country Sarah has ever known, the only one I've ever called home for that matter. But we must be careful never to take sides . . . or undue risks." Sarah's father now looked as sad and serious as Don Armando.

"Sometimes risks are necessary. Now let's have some tea and talk about something more pleasant." Mary wiped her palms across her skirt again. "Come help me with the biscuits, Sarah." Mary Rutledge had learned to refer to cookies as biscuits, just as George's English grandmother Louisa had insisted that they should be called. After all, Quinta Louisa was named for her, and her spirit still pervaded the *finca*.

Eventually the Papal Nuncio negotiated an agreement between the leaders of the Conservative Party in the Gran Hotel and the Somozas. Some of the foreign visitors who had been staying in the Gran Hotel were taken to the homes of the expatriates and their friends in Managua until they could arrange flights out of the country. Armando and Beatriz Chulteco returned to their home and welcomed a German businessman as their guest. After his two terrifying nights as a hostage in the hotel he was sleeping soundly in the Chultecos' guest room, when Beatriz's perverse Siamese cat pounced onto his stomach in the middle of the night. His anguished scream was imitated as the story was told over and over at dinner parties over the next several months while Nicaragua settled back into its normal life, or what appeared on the surface to be normal.

THE FIRST ORDER OF business for the Rutledges after they were able to drive back into the city was searching for the mother of the injured boy. Remarkably the telephones had never stopped working during the tense days while the *Guardia* (National Guard) restored order in the city. (Telephones were controlled by the military; and permission to have one in a private home required proving that it contributed to military security, which in practice simply involved making one of the many customary bribes that foreigners as well as wealthy national citizens paid to a bureaucrat.) Mary had called the Baptist Hospital every day to check on the condition of the child and to give assurances that the hospital would be paid for his care and room accommodation.

Mary, or occasionally George, when she had an appointment, always drove Sarah to the American School each morning and picked her up each afternoon. It required more than two hours out of every day, but the only alternatives were a boarding school in the United States, like George had attended, or one in England, like the one where his father had been sent. Mary believed that long drives each day were worth her time and effort so that Sarah could remain with them at Quinta Louisa for as long as possible.

On the first day that the American School reopened, however, George planned to drive Sarah to and from school. Mary wanted to return with him to pick Sarah up in the afternoon and try to find the injured child's mother in the *barrio*. George wanted to bring Sarah home and then return alone to search for the mother by himself, but Mary insisted on accompanying him when he picked Sarah up. Then George wanted to bring Sarah home and return to the city with Mary, if she insisted on going with him.

"That's foolish, George. We don't need to make two separate trips into the city. Sarah can go with us after we pick her up."

"Well, how's this? We can go early and make our inquiries before school is dismissed."

"We can't predict how long it may take us to locate the child's mother in the *barrio*. It might take a few minutes. It might take hours. Besides it will be a good experience for Sarah."

As usual in such differences of opinion, Mary's plan prevailed, although Sarah was aware from the sour, pained expression on her father's face that he didn't believe it would be a good experience for her at all.

Barrio Arbolito was a rather notorious neighborhood. Directions in Managua were given from old landmarks—*two blocks north and a block and a half west from where the little tree used to be*—where the little tree used to be also gave the name to the *barrio, Arbolito*, little tree. The little tree had disappeared years ago, but the name stuck.

The doors of most buildings were closed against the afternoon light and heat. All of the old downtown neighborhoods would be closed and shuttered when the sun was brightest and the dust and smoke from traffic heaviest; but the confinement was even more pronounced in Barrio Arbolito than in other poor neighborhoods, because prostitution was the principal business. Those who work at night must sleep in the daytime. Poverty and squalor were also more evident in the daytime than they had seemed on Sunday night, even in the midst of the gunfire; but the memory of the child in the street and the sounds of the gunshots still echoed in Sarah's memory, like bullets ricocheting in her mind.

George Rutledge approached an older boy sitting on a doorstep. "*Young man, we are looking for the mother of the little boy who was shot Sunday night. We are the people who took him to the hospital.*" It was harder to find anyone in a prostitutes' district, because people living there were trained not to give out information.

"*I don't know who she is.*"

George looked at him with a stern, unbelieving stare. He probably knew. Perhaps he could be intimidated into supplying information. He would not be coaxed. Children here were too hardened by the time they were ten or twelve for gentle persuasion. If all else failed, he could probably be bribed. "*You know, of course, that a little boy was shot here last Sunday.*" George used the firm, almost angry voice of interrogation.

"*Yes, señor.*"

"*Do you know which house he lived in?*" George took some change out of his pocket and began rattling it in the cup of his left hand.

"*I do not know where they lived.*"

"*Maybe you can take us to talk with someone who would know something.*" George held us fifty centavos between the thumb and forefinger of his right hand. The boy didn't extend his hand. He waited for the money to be offered first, the ritual etiquette from a pubescent son of a whore, without a shirt, whose hands were black with layers of dirt and whose face was streaked with brown grit and stains. A younger boy appeared from inside the house and stood with them, as if he belonged to the party. *"Is this a friend of yours?"*

"He's my brother."

"Can I guard your car?" The younger boy hadn't heard the questions about the wounded child.

"Here's fifty centavos for you, too. I'll give you another córdoba if the car's all right when we return and a córdoba for your big brother if he takes us where we can get some good information." The younger boy also waited for George to hand him the coin. Even though they would have stolen everything from the car if it had been left unlocked and unwatched, they wouldn't violate the code of proper behavior, not with a gringo patrician.

The older boy led them in the direction of the local *pulpería*, a small, one room shack where candy and bottle drinks and tortillas and cakes and cigarettes were sold. It would be the obvious place to take them, the obvious place for them to begin making their inquiries even with his help. George wrinkled his chin at Mary and Sarah.

"You do not get any more money unless we receive some good information." George then turned to Mary and Sarah. "Are you sure you want to come? It would be better for you to wait in the car."

"We're coming with you. Here, take my hand, Sarah."

They passed the *pulpería* and turned down an alley between the tightly clustered houses on the street. Sarah saw a family living under a plastic and tarpaper tent inside the corner of a crumbling building with only two walls left. Such a degraded hovel was not allowed in sight of the street; it must be hidden from the slightly more respectable poor dwellings. The boy stopped at a door even rougher and cruder than the others, made from unpainted boards that were uneven at the bottom with cracks between them.

"Open up. Open the door, old woman. These North Americans gave me a córdoba to lead them to someone who could tell them about the boy who was shot on Sunday night."

The old woman who appeared at the door might have been eighty or ninety or two hundred years old. She possessed an ancient frame rarely seen in Nicaragua. The thick muscular body that made the age of poor women indistinguishable from forty to seventy years of age had shriveled. The thin, leathery, solemn face had crumpled into a thousand creases. The small hard hands and feet once like crude tools had twisted and contorted. The black hair had turned to a hoary mass of white that few women with predominantly Indian features ever lived to display. She leaned with both hands on a stick and wore two ragged sweaters and a shawl, even though the temperature was close to a hundred degrees. Her hut was like a dark, dank cave. The dirt floor at the back was rutted. The ground in the front had been leveled, and tiles had been laid over the bare earth, but they had not been grouted together. A *tijera* (canvas cot) was folded against the wall. Crude benches and stools were scattered among various jars and pans and pots and glasses, some turned over, many lying randomly on the bare earthen floor at the rear. There was no window, not even a hole covered by a shutter. The stench that came through the open doorway was sickening; and Sarah felt and tasted the darkness, a damp forbidding darkness.

"Bueños dias, señora. I am Señor George Rutledge. We took a little boy to the hospital when he was shot on Sunday night."

"What do you want, gringo devils? We don't have any money to pay you and give the hospital. I don't know anything about all that trouble."

"We don't want any money, señora." Mary's voice was soft and gentle unlike her husband's stern tone. Sarah thought that her father wouldn't have spoken so gruffly if he hadn't been embarrassed by exposing her to this seedy neighborhood. *"Please, señora, we're looking for the mother of the little boy who was shot, so that we can tell her that he's getting well."*

"His puta (prostitute) *mother lives at the back of the barrio by the field where we throw our garbage, since she moved from Casa Fuqui."* Another reference point for directions was Casa Fuqui, the whorehouse used by the U.S. Marines that had occupied the country during the 1920s and 1930s until they'd put Anastasio Somoza García into power. Casa Fuqui itself, like the little tree, had also disappeared long ago; but the stories

about the U. S. Marine occupation were frequently revived and retold, especially by the secret, subversive groups that wanted to overthrow the Somoza regime. *"The boy will show you, if you give him another córdoba. He is my grandson."*

The boy led them to a house that was even shabbier than the old woman's hovel, with a dirt floor and another rough, unpainted door and a thatched roof, also without windows. A pit for cooking, like a primitive barbeque grill, was dug outside in the yard. A toddler hugged the leg of the woman who opened the door. The little girl was also filthy, like the other children Sarah had seen in Barrio Arbolito. Her mother was a light-skinned woman with Spanish rather than Indian features. Her blouse and wrap-around skirt were dirty and ill fitting. The space lacked any walls and was divided into places for eating and sleeping by a blanket hanging from a rafter and a woven reed mat. The house smelled sour with the same odor of the old woman's house.

The Rutledges introduced themselves to the woman presumed to be the injured child's mother. Mary asked her to tell them her name. *¿Como se llama?* (How do you call yourself?)

"Me llamo Blanca. (I call myself Blanca: my name is Blanca)."

"The little boy who was shot is your son?"

"Yes, señor. Do you know if he is alive? I was told some norteamericanos (North Americans) *took him away."*

"Our family drove him to the Baptist Hospital. He is recovering well." Mary's tone continued gently and consolingly.

"How old is he?" Now George also spoke to the mother more softly.

"He has four years." Clinging to her was the little girl that she had carried in her arms the night of the attempted coup who seemed to be about two or three years old.

"What is his name?"

"He is César."

"Did you know that he had been taken to the Baptist Hospital?"

"Yes, señora, I knew that someone had taken him to the hospital."

"But you haven't been to visit him?"

"I thought that someone would bring him home if he did not die. I was

afraid they would make me pay money at the hospital if I went to see him."

"We are paying for his care. Would you like for us to take you to the hospital now to see him?"

"I cannot leave his little sister, señora. Will you bring him back to me when they make him well?"

"I don't think . . ."

George was interrupted by Mary who also responded to him in English before replying to Blanca in Spanish. "Never mind, George. *Of course we will. We will go to the hospital right now and see how he is recovering."*

"Mary, it's late. It'll be dark by the time we get home."

"There's time, George. We must do what we can to help these poor people."

When they inquired at Baptist Hospital, they learned that the little boy was ready to be discharged. By the time they finished the paperwork and paid his bills it was growing dark even in the city; and by the time they left César with his mother the night was totally black without any streetlights to guide them on the primitive roads through *Barrio Arbolito.*

"We must do something about that little boy, George. We can't leave him in that condition."

"You can't take care of every poor urchin in Nicaragua, Mary. It's impossible."

"I can take care of those that God drops into our lives, like little César."

"Mary . . . Mary." George's voice was exhausted. He knew better than to argue. He knew that he had already lost another battle. "Are you all right, Sarah?"

"I'm fine, Daddy. Thank you for letting me come with you. I'm going to do everything I can to take care of poor people in our country when I grow up."

"It's not our country, sweetheart. We're just guests here in Nicaragua. We try to take care of the people entrusted to us, like those in the village that work on the coffee *finca* for us, and Don Martín and Doña Flora and their boys; but we can't take care of everyone. It's not our responsibility."

Sarah knew that her father's words were actually directed to her mother through her, to whom he was ostensibly speaking.

As they drove through the gate at Quinta Louisa the headlights of the old Austin illuminated Martín wringing his hands as he paced on the front veranda.

Sarah had not even stepped out of the car before Martín began upbraiding her parents as if they were children and he were their parent. *"What do you mean coming home so late? I thought you had suffered an accident on the highway, and evil people had done terrible things to you as they did to your parents."*

Sarah didn't know what terrible things evil people had done to her grandparents, although she knew they had died in an automobile accident when her father was still in college; but she was too weary to ask what Don Martín had been talking about. She was too tired even to study her homework, a task she almost never neglected as a dedicated, conscientious student. Immediately after supper she dropped into bed and instantly fell asleep, but she dreamed about the poor people and shabby houses in Barrio Arbolito and then had a nightmare about evil people dragging her out of the car and beating her on the side of the Pan-American Highway.

It was late on a Sunday afternoon three weeks after Easter when Sarah overheard her father speaking on the telephone. What drew her attention was the tone of his voice, not quite panicked or alarmed, but disturbed. She soon realized that he was talking with Don Armando. She wondered if Don Armando or Doña Beatriz were ill—she knew they hadn't died or her father would have been more greatly distressed.

As soon as he hung up the receiver, she asked, "What is it, Daddy? What's the matter? Are Don Armando and Doña Beatriz all right?"

"They're fine, Susi. Luis Somoza died. A heart attack. It was very sudden."

"I thought we didn't like the Somozas."

"You can't paint everyone with the same brush, Susi. Luis was a good man. When he was President, he pushed through legislation to prevent him from succeeding himself and any member of his family from following him immediately. Only a dictator can end a dictatorship without bloodshed. He did many good things."

Mary Rutledge had entered the room during George's lecture to Sarah. "So Luis is dead. We'll miss him. He was an honest man, a good leaven for the country; but I wonder if he didn't undo all his progressive efforts by supporting Tachito's candidacy for President. He won't even be there to see him inaugurated in a few weeks."

"And he won't be there to rein him in over the weeks and months and years to come. If Luis hadn't stopped him, Tachito would have leveled the Gran Hotel and killed everyone inside during the coup. God help us!" George scowled and bit his lower lip as he often did when he was upset.

"Will we be all right, Daddy? Will Tachito hurt us?"

"Of course not, Susi. None of this affects Quinta Louisa very much. No one pays much attention to us up here on the ridge. Our lives will go on as usual, but God help Nicaragua!"

MARY RUTLEDGE LEFT ABRUPTLY for a trip to North Carolina. She usually made her plans weeks, even months in advance. She hadn't been feeling quite herself, she told Sarah and George; and she wanted to have a medical check-up by the doctors at Duke University Hospital. When she returned, she looked gaunt and pale, but she told her daughter and husband that she was just a little anemic and had been given a tonic to build her up.

Mary also brought a collie puppy from North Carolina for Sarah, who hadn't mentioned wanting to have a dog or even thought of asking for a dog. Sarah suspected the puppy was another response to her mother's concern about what she perceived to be Sarah's loneliness and isolation. The puppy was cute and fun to play with for a few minutes; but Sarah never had much interest in pets. If she'd chosen any pet, it would have been a bird; but she actually preferred to watch the wild birds that flew into the garden or see them with Don Martín in the forest rather than to put one of the local macaws or green parrots into a cage as many Nicaraguan families did.

Even though Guillermo was in the second year of study for his *bachil-lerato* (a diploma somewhat more advanced than a high school graduate's in the United States), he took the bus from the city every afternoon to the village, ostensibly to help his parents, Martín and Flora, with their chores, but partly to care for the collie puppy, Laddie, and to play with him in the garden at Quinta Louisa.

Pablo still attended the local village school supported by the Nicaraguan government for education only through primary years. Julio didn't visit Quinta Louisa often. He wrote long, obsequious thank-you letters to George and Mary Rutledge expressing how grateful he was that they were paying for his education, but he seemed ashamed of being the son of servants and even ashamed of Martín and Flora themselves, although he meticulously observed filial duty toward his parents.

Mary had effectively banned Pablo from the garden as an incorrigible child, but Guillermo enjoyed helping tend the flowers and fruit trees with his father, and after Laddie arrived Guillermo was present almost every afternoon.

Sarah conversed with Guillermo more during the first weeks of Laddie's residence than they'd ever talked before. She felt that she was obliged to spend some time with him, because he was caring for what was supposed to be her dog. Guillermo told her that he was fascinated by the dog with long silky hair and white and tan markings. Sarah could understand how exotic he might appear in comparison to the yellowish-brown, short-haired, bony, mangy curs that cowered on every street corner in Managua, just as the macaws and parrots fascinated their North American visitors and even Sarah herself compared to the drabber wild birds in the United States. As Laddie grew, he chased Guillermo around the garden. They wrestled in the grass as if Guillermo were a little boy Pablo's age, and Sarah found herself talking to Guillermo more because she really enjoyed his company than out of obligatory appreciation for his care for her dog.

"What are you going to do when you finish at the colegio (secondary school), *Guillermo? Are you going to the university like Julio? I'm sure Daddy would still pay your fees."*

"I am not smart like Julio. He wants to be a big businessman. I like to make things. I would rather live here in the village than in the city."

"Just like your parents, Don Martín and Doña Flora."

"I would like to go to the technical institute. Do you think Don Jorge would pay fees for me there?"

"I think so. I will ask him. He would probably like it if you could keep the machines at the processing plant running. Those are the only times I have ever heard Daddy curse—when they break down."

"You know he sent Papá to Costa Rica to learn about machinery . . ."

". . . and he begged Daddy to let him come back and work in the garden because he couldn't stand that dark place that smelled bad with all those loud noises that hurt his ears."

They both laughed.

When Sarah asked her father about Guillermo's plans, he said that he was sorry Guillermo didn't want to attend the university if he was able to meet the qualifications.

"A university education would give him many more opportunities in life. I'd like to do as much as I can to prepare him to help his people."

Mary arched her eyebrows. "He's a typical middle child. Such a sweet boy. Not like his brothers, that snobbish Julio or that imp Pablo, the little terror. Let him find his own level, George. Besides he'd be such a help to you if he could manage the machinery in the plant."

Before Laddie was even a year old, he developed a taste for the neighbors' chickens. George scolded him and beat him with a rolled-up newspaper and even whipped him with his leash until he made sounds that Guillermo couldn't stand to hear and ran with his hands over his ears to the village. Don Martín tied a dead chicken around his neck for days until he pawed at his head and scraped against the wall and rolled on his back like a rabid creature, but none of their efforts discouraged him from chasing the neighbors' chickens.

"We must do something about that dog, Mary. We can't put it off any longer."

"Those shiftless people ought to keep their chickens penned up. We're responsible for keeping our dog off their property, but they're responsible for keeping their chickens off the road in front of our house. When those chickens wander all over our yard and garden, I can't help what my dog does to them."

George Rutledge looked woefully at his wife. "You don't know how much a chicken means to a poor *campesino*, Mary. It has an enormous value in their scale of things."

Mary Rutledge was not moved. "Don't be absurd, George. A chicken is nothing compared to a beautiful purebred collie. Besides, if those *campesinos* think so much of their chickens, they should keep them penned up."

"I'm sorry, my dear. I shall have to see that Laddie's taken away. I'm especially sorry for Guillermo's sake."

Sarah was sad about Laddie, but she never asked her father what he'd done when he took the dog away. She felt even worse for Guillermo than she did about Laddie. She and Guillermo never spoke about what happened to Laddie or even mentioned him to each other again, but they continued to talk together often in the garden and on the back patio.

"Mother, I think Guillermo has become one of my best friends."

"I do wish you'd try to make more friends at school, Sarah. We are very fond of Martín's family, but they are different from people like us. Of course, Guillermo's my favorite of Martín and Flora's children, but you belong to two different worlds."

Sarah's mother continued to treat Guillermo with a mixture of affectionate admiration and condescension, not altogether differently from how she had treated the purebred collie, Laddie. When Sarah told her father how her mother had talked about Guillermo, he said that his wife acted toward people in Nicaragua as she'd been taught to behave in North Carolina and that Sarah should understand that her mother might never really understand the way people related to each other in Central America.

Ever since the Rutledges had visited Barrio Arbolito searching for the mother of the little boy that had been shot, Mary Rutledge had been campaigning to provide better housing for the coffee workers that lived in the village and especially better quarters for the temporary seasonal workers that came from other regions of the country to gather the coffee beans during the harvest. Last season many of them had fallen ill with flu-like symptoms.

Mary had stayed at the harvesters' camp from dawn until dusk for days that stretched into weeks, and George believed that she had become overly involved and obsessed with their problems. After the epidemic had long since passed, she continued to nag him about erecting what he considered to be elaborate houses to shelter the pickers at harvest time.

"They're little better than chicken coops, George. We've got to provide something more adequate."

"My dear Mary, they're only needed for a few weeks every year, and the combination of weather and illness last year happens only once a century or so. I know they're cramped and uncomfortable, but they do all right for the few weeks of harvest time under ordinary circumstances."

"I think they're sorely lacking in the minimal standards of basic hygiene and sanitation."

Sarah was always concerned when her parents argued, as if it threatened the security of her world, although their voices were usually quiet and calm with her father's British reserve and her mother's Southern gentility.

"I think you're more concerned about appearances than you are with the basic standard of life for poor Nicaraguans. You've been in a tizzy ever since your sister-in-law came down here and began ranting about having never seen such dreadful poverty as there is on our *finca*. I know the shelters for the harvesters don't look very attractive, but I've told you a thousand times that my resources are limited and the resources of this country are limited, and we have to take care of critical health problems and year-round living conditions first. We can't be distracted by appearances."

"I'm not talking about appearances, George Rutledge. I'm talking about contaminated water and a lack of available necessities that very nearly brought on a plague at our *finca* last year."

"Haven't I done more to alleviate poor people's problems than any coffee planter in Nicaragua?" He sniffed, as he often did when he felt he was being unfairly criticized. "This is not our country, Mary. We do what we can to help our own, our workers in the village; but we can't change this country."

"Your family has been here for three generations. Sarah is a fourth generation Nicaraguan, George."

"She's not a Nicaraguan. She's an American of British ancestry.

You're being more sentimental than practical. What do you know about contaminated water and conditions that cause a plague? What do you even know about how poor Nicaraguans really live? You've always had everything you needed and most of what you wanted in life."

"I'm a woman, and I have the feelings of a woman, and I see the poor women of this country spending half their lives carrying wood and water. I see them on the road, barefooted and ragged, with a stack of wood on their heads or a pot of filthy water on top of a rolled-up rag to balance it and protect their skulls. You're not a woman. You wouldn't understand what it means to gather wood and carry water ten hours a day, day in and day out."

George left the room and made no reply to his wife, but that very afternoon he sat down at his desk and began to work out the plan that would bring potable water to the village and extend the pipes to the harvesters' camp, where he decided to erect new, larger shelters. The new shelters would be simple and rude, certainly not what his wife had envisioned; but they would be safer and drier during storms than the old ones and larger and more adequate for the families that stayed there for the harvest.

SARAH DIDN'T USUALLY NOTICE how her parents looked or felt; but after her mother returned from North Carolina, Sarah couldn't avoid seeing her mother's pallor and loss of weight when her clothes seemed to droop from her shoulders as if they were hanging from wires in the closet.

"Mother, are you all right? Are you feeling bad?"

"I'm fine, dear. I'm just a little run-down. They gave me some tonic to build me up."

Soon Sarah's concerns about her mother were displaced by anxiety about her own situation. At fourteen her focus was most often on her social standing in her peer group, and her preoccupation was not alleviated by her mother's concern. Even when Mary Rutledge didn't pepper Sarah with seemingly benign questions about with whom she ate lunch, what the girls in her class were talking about, whether any boys had spoken to her, Sarah was aware of her mother's unspoken fretting. Sarah was at least half a head taller than the boys in her class and a full head taller than most of the girls. Both mother and daughter chased each other in circles of unspoken worry as the date for the end of the school year dance approached.

Finally, Mary broke the silence. "Are you going to the school dance, Sarah?"

"No one has asked me."

"Surely there's a boy from your set who would escort you as a friend. You don't have to be sweethearts."

"Carlos Vargas is my only friend."

"He's a lovely boy. I play bridge with his mother at the Gran Hotel every Wednesday. Nancy is rather shy and doesn't talk much, but she's very nice."

"They say his father is a revolutionary, a member of the FSLN." (Frente Sandinista Liberación National)

"Oh, I hardly think so, dear. If that were true, he surely wouldn't be married to an American. I could whisper a word in her ear."

"Mother! Don't you dare!"

"I'll be discreet. Carlos would never even know I've spoken to her."

"I don't want to go to the dance with him. I want to go with a boy like me, an American or English boy. Isn't that what you said you wanted me to do, mother, make friends with people like us?"

"He's half American, dear; and he goes to your school and even attends the church youth group sometimes, doesn't he?"

"What's this all about?" George Rutledge came through the patio door from the garden mopping his brow.

"Mother's trying to fix me up with a Nicaraguan boy for the school dance, but it's crazy. I want to go with someone like us or not go at all."

"Nicaraguans are more like us than you may think, Susi. Someday you'll understand that."

"Oh, Father! Really!" Sarah rushed from the room. Only when she was very upset did she call George Rutledge *Father* rather than *Daddy*.

Mary did discreetly mention Sarah's lack of a date to Nancy Vargas. Carlos did ask Sarah to go with him to the dance, and Sarah accepted with great trepidation. Nancy Vargas confided to Mary that Carlos had wanted to ask Sarah but had been afraid she would refuse him and even laugh at him. Sarah was self-conscious dancing with Carlos, who was even shorter than most of the other boys in their class, but they had found it easy to talk with one another. Carlos made her laugh. She felt almost happy with him; and when the other boys left their dates and moved off together to the back of the gymnasium, Carlos stayed by her side.

SARAH WAS SITTING CROSS-LEGGED on her bed studying the assignment for her history class when her mother called her from the hall and asked her to join her parents in the parlor. They almost never gathered as a family in the parlor unless they were entertaining guests. They often lingered around the dining table after supper and discussed the day's events and later would move to the back patio where the soft velvet blackness of the tropical night caressed them while they talked about things far removed from Nicaragua in time and space. Sarah wondered if she were in trouble, if she'd unknowingly broken some parental rule; but when she saw her father's anguished face, she knew that something was terribly wrong. Her mother's face rarely revealed anything. Mary Rutledge appeared most placid and serene when she was most troubled or frustrated unless she was angry; but as Sarah saw her father glance back and forth at her mother, she knew that the problem concerned her mother.

"Sarah, we have something very serious to discuss with you." Mary Rutledge's voice, which sometimes betrayed her true emotions, was as calm and tranquil as her face.

"Did I do something wrong?"

"Oh no, dearest. Your father and I have decided that you need to know something about me."

Sarah wondered in her first panicked thought whether her mother might want to divorce her father and return to North Carolina to live; and she immediately resolved to stay and live with her father in Nicaragua if that should prove to be true.

"What is it? Please tell me."

"You remember that I made a rather sudden trip to North Carolina a few months ago."

Her mother's impulsive trip to North Carolina had puzzled Sarah. As she recalled its out-of-character nature from her mother's meticulously planned routine, Sarah felt certain that her mother was leaving her father. Sarah nodded. "Un-huh." She wished her face could conceal her emotions as easily as her mother's did.

"I went to see some doctors. I went to Duke, because they're the best. The doctors here suspected something was wrong, but they didn't realize I had cancer. It's very bad." Mary Rutledge's tranquil face suddenly shattered like a rare crystal vase filled with water that has fallen to the floor and broken into scores of pieces.

"Mary."

"Mother!"

George and Sarah moved simultaneously to each side of Mary's chair and held her in their arms between them. George's face also flooded with tears, but Sarah was too stunned to cry. Then Mary dabbed her face with one of the handkerchiefs she always kept under her belt or in a pocket of her dress; and her face was restored to its perfect serenity, as if time were reversed and a broken vase came back together in unblemished wholeness.

"Now, my dears, sit back down. We have a lot to talk about." George and Sarah obeyed Mary, as they always did. "I was given some medicine that helps with the pain. I may have to return to Duke for a further palliative regime, but I'm not going to have chemo or radiation. Your father and I have discussed this."

"Mary, there's still time . . ."

Mary Rutledge held up her hand. "There may not be that much time, my dear. The cancer is very advanced. We'll review the situation as we go along and make whatever adjustments . . . seem appropriate. But, yes, dearest George, there is still time; and I want to spend it here with the two people I love most in all the world, in the home I love, and with other people . . . whom I care about very deeply."

Now Sarah's tears began to flow at last, too; and she and her father rushed back to the arms of Mary's chair and cuddled her like an infant, as if they were her parents, not her husband and her child. This time Mary indulged them and didn't push them away for a much longer time but finally patted them gently back in the direction of their chairs.

"There's one more thing. I've made your father promise to fix up the workers' houses in the village. You know how it's bothered me, and I want to move the family of the little boy who was shot up to the village and give his mother a job in the factory. Your father and I have agreed to all this. I hope you'll help him, Sarah, even if you have to give up certain things for yourself to pay for it."

"Of course, Mother."

"You know I'll carry out your intentions to the fullest . . . but . . ." George hesitated like a little boy who knew he shouldn't mention such things but couldn't help himself. ". . . when the time comes, do you want your final resting place to be in your family's plot in Burlington? Do you think they'd allow me to be . . ." He could not say the word *buried* ". . . with you there, too? You'd need to discuss it with them before . . ."

"No, my dear. I want to be buried here in Nicaragua. Here on the *finca,* out on the cliff, beyond the garden, on the other side of the forest. This is my home. This is the place I love. I think it's ridiculous to be taken back to the States like your parents or to England like your grandparents. Don't you think this is the place we belong, George, after all these years?"

"I do, Mary. I do indeed with all my heart. Thank you."

"Please stop talking about all this! I don't want to hear any more about all these things right now. Please! Please! Please!"

"Of course, Susi." Sarah's father reached out his arms to her, but she ran to her mother.

"Come here."

Sarah curled up in her mother's lap like a child that had grown as large as the parent but needed to be a baby again. Mary stroked Sarah's hair, and Mary's face was as peaceful and even as joyful as if they had just shared some wonderfully blissful experience together.

MARY RUTLEDGE LIVED LESS than three months after Sarah learned about her mother's cancer. Mary didn't appear to be in significant pain, although with her calm, stoic demeanor it was difficult to discern her true physical suffering. Although Sarah had usually preferred her father's company in the past, during those months she enjoyed talking and sharing drives in the car and baking bread and cakes and sewing clothes with her mother, as if they were meeting as new friends for the first time. They often laughed together. Sarah accompanied her mother to the village several times every week to survey plans for improving the workers' houses. They often stopped to visit with Blanca, the mother of the little boy who had been shot.

George Rutledge worked in the garden with Martín for longer hours than he'd ever done before. He never sat with Sarah on the back patio after supper while Mary and Flora put away the food and tidied the kitchen as they'd often done in the past, as if his pain were greater than his wife's and it was too much to inflict on Sarah.

Mary Rutledge died on a Wednesday afternoon while Sarah was at school, as if she'd planned the moment of her demise to spare Sarah the agony of her final hours. Sarah couldn't remember who the people were from the hoards that came to Quinta Louisa and to the funeral at St. Francis Episcopal Church and couldn't recall what they'd said to her. She did remember Doña Beatriz Chulteco and Carlos Vargas Allen's mother because they didn't try to talk to her and say things that would make her feel better. They hugged her in just the right way and released her at just the right time. Father Richard Sims was the only person she could remember talking to her. Even though she couldn't recall his exact words, she remembered that he'd made her feel, if not better, at least somewhat less terrible. Later she felt comforted as she remembered his gawky appearance and jerky movements when he'd spoken to her.

It was late in the afternoon following the funeral when they lowered Mary Rutledge's coffin into the hole at the top of the cliff. Martín had arranged for the grave to be dug, and he and some of the workers used ropes to let the coffin down slowly. Sarah thought how remarkably level they kept it with a rhythm that almost seemed like a stately dance. She could see far out across the mountains. The parrots chattered more noisily than usual. She watched a scarlet macaw fly into the trees at the edge of the forest. She wondered if she would ever see a quetzal. Then she thought that someday her father would be buried here beside her mother, and a long time from now she would also be lowered into the earth at the top of the cliff.

ALONG WITH THE CONSTRUCTION on the workers' houses in the village George Rutledge had a small house built at the back of the garden, so that Martín and Flora would be closer in order to care for Sarah. Pablo lived with them. Guillermo visited several times a week. Julio now worked in Costa Rica and came to Nicaragua only every other month or so. Flora did everything physically for Sarah that her mother had done—preparing her food and fussing at her for not eating properly, arguing about what clothes she should wear to school, waking her up in the mornings and reminding her to go to bed at night, asking her if she'd finished her homework—but Sarah never felt that Flora was like a mother to her in even the slightest way. When Sarah saw Flora embracing Pablo and laughing and talking with him, she remembered what it had been like to have a mother, especially during the last months of Mary Rutledge's life; and she felt a great weight of sadness enveloping her and had to walk into the forest so that the parrots and other birds would drown out the pulsing beats of her thoughts.

FATHER RICHARD SIMS STEADFASTLY pursued his plan for organizing a youth group. He had followed Beatriz Chulteco's suggestion of meeting with the parents of teenagers at the American School in the afternoons after classes were dismissed. A few enthusiastic parents came the first week and fewer returned the second and third weeks, but by the fourth week they realized his intentions were serious, and they brought other parents. After two months of meeting with the teenagers and their parents Father Richard began a Sunday afternoon gathering at St. Francis Church. Only Sarah and a younger girl, not yet a teenager, and a much older boy came. By the second week only the two girls arrived, and by the third week only Sarah appeared. None of the *costeño* children who attended St. Francis Church for worship on Sunday mornings remained for the youth group, even though Father Richard offered to give them lunch. For a couple of weeks the next month Father Richard tried a weeknight gathering, but only Sarah came, and George told him that it would not be possible for him to drive Sarah regularly from the *finca* on a weeknight evening.

Then Father Richard gave up his dream of bringing the poorer Nicaraguan children together with expatriate teenagers and relinquished his illusion of having a gathering at St. Francis Church. He began meeting at the American School on Wednesday afternoons with whoever showed up. The half-dozen or so teenagers that came the first month—Sarah was the only consistent member—grew to a group of twelve or fifteen the second month and by the third month reached an average of twenty-five to thirty regular participants that met faithfully every week.

It was neither scintillating discussions nor exciting outings that attracted the students but rather Father Richard's dogged consistency and dedication to the group, the same qualities that drew Sarah into regular conversations with him after her mother's death. Unlike other people who gave pat answers and slick euphemisms and polite advice to Sarah, Father Richard's embarrassed silences and incoherent mutterings and gawky movements seemed to break open Sarah's own inchoate thoughts and stifled emotions.

Father Richard and Sarah usually met at the American School on Thursday afternoons after classes were dismissed. Sarah knew that the afternoon, like the youth group meeting on Wednesday, took her father away for a longer time from the *finca* and the construction of the new coffee-processing factory that would grind and package the coffee for export as well as wash and dry the beans like the old plant had done. She felt badly about asking him to stay late on two afternoons a week and for creating difficulty for him, but he never complained. When she mentioned her concern about imposing on his time, he told her that it was all right. "Your happiness and well-being are my major concerns, Susi. What's the point of the rest of it if I don't take care of you?"

At the school Father Richard always wore a clerical collar without a coat. Sarah once teased him and asked if he wore his collar to bed. Father

Richard blushed deeply and raised his arms in his familiar scarecrow pose and smiled but didn't reply.

"Do you, uh, think about your mother very often, Sarah?"

His patient silence drew her out, a silence without anxiety, without frustration. The question elicited a string of memories that Sarah related for almost half an hour. She stopped talking only because she was sobbing too greatly to form words.

On another day he asked, "Do you, uh . . . visit your mother's grave very often, Sarah?"

Sarah began to talk again in an endless stream of words but not about her mother's grave nor about her feelings related to her mother but rather about listening to the parrots and other birds that she saw in the forest on her way to the cliff and sometimes seeing the squirrel monkeys and iguanas in the trees and how Don Martín had promised her that one day she would encounter the quetzal that she'd never seen. She wondered why she found it easier to talk with Father Richard than with anyone else, even than with her father.

There were only five Episcopal teenagers in the youth group—Sarah and the son and daughter of a British consular officer, who attended only sporadically, and the younger girl and older boy who had come to the very first meeting. The other members of the youth group were the children of American Embassy personnel and children of American business representatives as well as an odd selection of children of evangelical missionaries and children whose parents were Nicaraguans married to foreigners, two Germans, and a few Nicaraguans from wealthy families who sought to emulate *gringos*. Most of them were Protestants with a few nominal Roman Catholics. The strict Roman Catholic families refused to allow their children to participate.

Sarah was attracted to the muscular German boy and the tall, blonde English boy and hoped that one of them would notice her. Although both of them were almost painfully polite to her, neither of them ever paid any real attention to her. She had no close girl friends. A Nicaraguan girl named Carmen made her laugh and was easy to chat with, but Carmen applied such heavy make-up and wore such tight dresses that

Sarah alternately admired and feared her, simultaneously repulsed by her and envious of her. Sarah's only real friend was Carlos Vargas, the boy who had escorted her to the dance at the end of the previous school year before her mother had died.

"If only he wasn't so short," she told herself. Carlos looked more like his Nicaraguan father than his North American mother. His dark face and arms glowed with luminous Indian gold just below the surface, but his shiny black hair, through which he obsessively ran his long thin fingers every few minutes, was curly, not straight like an Indian's locks. Sarah wondered if somewhere back in his ancestry he had a drop of black, a *gota de negro*, as the Nicaraguans said, that made the passions smolder and flame.

On one of the youth group outings to the beach at Pocho Mil, Carlos Vargas rode with Sarah in her father's car along with Carmen and the young English girl whose parents had requested that she ride with George Rutledge. Carmen's vulgar chatter seemed to be inhibited in the presence of Sarah's father and the younger English girl. Even Carlos, who was usually easy to talk with, and Sarah herself were self-conscious in the company of her father and Carmen. They drove all the way to the beach in almost complete silence.

After a short swim the girls all sat and lay on towels and sunned themselves while the boys tossed a Frisbee back and forth on the black volcanic sand closer to the edge of the sea. The larger boys bumped against Carlos and knocked him down again and again. Sarah could see the bruises and scrapes on his elbow and a cut running with blood over one knee. She wanted to rush down and tell them to stop picking on Carlos, but she knew her words would bring him more embarrassed pain than his scruffs. She glanced up at Father Richard, but he seemed oblivious or perhaps only helpless to know what to do. Her father walked down behind her from the crude palm covered *cabaña* where the adult chaperone drivers were seeking shade.

"That Carlos Vargas Allen is a brave lad." Sarah was aware that her father was teasing her about her reluctance to allow Carlos to escort her to the school dance.

"I know that, Daddy. I know very well what you're referring to. You don't have to shame me. He's become a real friend, but just a friend."

"He's more a man than any of them down there."

"I know that, too. You don't have to tell me that either, but can't you do something to stop them picking on him?"

"I'm afraid not, Susi. Things have to run their course."

Then a thunderstorm blew up suddenly without warning. The adults ran from the *cabaña* to take shelter in their automobiles, and the teenagers ran to occupy the place of their chaperones in the *cabaña*. (People unfamiliar with the tropics don't realize how quickly the temperature can fall from blazing heat to chilling cold, as felt by those whose blood is thin.) Sarah and Carlos found themselves huddled together under a big beach towel apart from the others.

"I thought you played better than anybody else. You wouldn't take any of their crap, not from anyone."

Carlos laughed. His voice was deep, especially when he laughed, not like the girlish giggles of some of the other boys. "Watch your language, *gringa*. You're just prejudiced because you like me."

"I do like you, Carlos, very much, but . . ."

"But not as your boyfriend . . . ."

"Just as a friend," they said together and both laughed again.

"I wish you could . . . Sarah, there's something I have to tell you. Something very serious."

"Oh, no! He's going to tell me he loves me, and it will ruin our friendship," she thought. "What Carlos?"

"You better start calling me Charles. I have to get used to it. My father is sending me to a military school in the States to finish high school. He thinks I need the discipline, and I believe he's scared of something happening to me because of all he's messed up in."

"Carlos! Charles." Sarah laughed, but her laughter wasn't like her laughter before. Now it covered her pain and her sadness. "I can't get used to that . . . *Charles.*"

"I know. Me neither."

"Will we ever see each other again?"

"I'll be back for vacations, and I'll come home for good when I finish school. Will you still be here then?"

"Maybe. I might be away at college."

"Yeah. Me, too. But I mean, are you coming back here to live in Nicaragua?"

Sarah paused. She wanted to be honest, but she wasn't certain. "Sure, I suppose. Are you?"

"Of course. This is where I belong. I'm a Nicaraguan."

"You're half *gringo*. Your mother is a North American. She was Nancy Allen from Florida before she married your father. That's why you're Carlos Vargas *Allen*."

"But neither of your parents is Nicaraguan. You're not half anything, unless you're half North American and half British. You'd have to choose to be a *Nica*."

"I think I'll choose *Nica*. I don't like being a *gringa* very much."

"Good. Then we'll live here together until we're very old." Carlos grinned.

"I don't want you to go away. I'll miss you so, so much."

"I know. I don't want to go away either. I'll miss you, too, Sarah, more than anything else."

"Carlos! You'll always be Carlos to me."

"I . . ." Carlos never finished his sentence, and they moved closer and hugged each other more tightly under the beach towel. Sarah wondered if maybe she liked Carlos as more than a friend. She wanted to cry, but neither of them cried as they listened to each other's deep breaths and sighs. They didn't speak again at the beach, and the sun came back out, and Father Richard walked around the *cabaña* and told them to pack up their belongings to head back to the church. They rode home in her father's car sitting side by side on the back seat without ever saying another word to one another.

Although he lived with his parents in the little house that George Rutledge had built for Martín's family across the garden from Quinta Louisa, Pablo rarely came into the yard. Perhaps he'd internalized Mary

Rutledge's warning to stay out of her garden and feared being haunted by her ghost if he disobeyed her prohibition from beyond the grave. Sarah thought it was more likely that he was too lazy to toil in the dirt with his father and probably also wanted to disassociate himself from peasant labors like his older brother Julio had, at least in his own mind. Flora had always babied him, and she doted on him even more ardently after her two older sons left home. Pablo had nicer clothes than Julio or Guillermo had ever worn as boys. Martín acquiesced to Flora's indulgences, and Sarah suspected that her father gave them extra money for Pablo partly as an inducement to make them contented in the little house behind the garden away from their friends in the village.

Pablo was even given a boom box that he carried on his shoulder, and he played music so loudly inside his house that it could be heard all the way inside Quinta Louisa. George Rutledge, who found it difficult to reprimand Martín or Flora or any of his workers or his daughter, marched across the garden on at least a half-dozen occasions to tell Pablo to "*turn that damned thing down.*" Three times that Sarah could remember, Pablo had come up to Quinta Louisa to speak with his mother as he played the boom box on his shoulder and wiggled his hips toward Sarah in a way that made her blush, even though he was only an eleven-year-old boy.

Occasionally Pablo would help his father carry baskets of fruit and vegetables from the garden at Quinta Louisa to their house across the garden with pouty lips and squinted eyes after a threat from Martín. Although Julio came up dutifully from Costa Rica every month or two to visit his parents, Guillermo came every week and spent the day working with Martín in the garden. Late in the afternoon Sarah saw him sitting shirtless on the bench in the middle of the garden, mopping his brow with a bandana, and she walked down to talk with him.

"*Doña Sarah!*" Guillermo reached for his shirt and tried to cover his chest as if he were embarrassed out of modesty. His torso and arms, like Martín's, seemed to be molded from brown clay without any definition of the muscles on the surface of his skin, so that his vibrant strength was concealed, also like his father's.

"Do not doña me, Guillermo. I thought we were friends, equals."

"Friends, sí . . ." He smiled at her shyly and said with his eyes, *"but not equals, never equals."*

Sarah thought that Guillermo was a typical middle child and recalled her mother's analysis. Julio was the first-born successful son. Pablo was the pampered baby. Guillermo was the reliable, loyal, affectionate middle child, always trying to please and gain favor without calling any undue attention to himself.

"When Daddy and Don Martín are no longer able to manage . . ." Sarah looked away to conceal the tears forming in her eyes. *". . . who is going to help them manage?"* Despite trying to control her voice, it cracked. When Sarah looked back at Guillermo, she saw him also wiping his face again with his bandana, this time not to dry sweat but the tears that echoed Sarah's. *"Of course Daddy was grooming Julio after he had no son to take over."* Sarah looked back and smiled at Guillermo who mirrored her smile discreetly. *"But we know that is never going to happen."* They both began to laugh.

"You know I am going to be here and am going to do what I can."

"Will you, Guillermo? Will you really? If I am . . . if I am left here alone will you help me?"

"Of course. You know so. Of course so."

"You are more like a brother to me than . . . well, than anyone else; and if that doesn't make us equals . . . Shit! ¡Caramba! I don't know what would . . ."

"Watch your mouth!" Suddenly Guillermo looked stern and paternal and sounded almost like his father, like Don Martín, when he reprimanded her.

DURING MARY RUTLEDGE'S TERMINAL illness and after her death George had relinquished his custom of sitting on the back patio with Sarah after supper, as he had abandoned several other rituals that he'd shared with his wife and daughter during Mary's final illness before she died. Sarah assiduously maintained the familiar traditions, almost obsessively, as if not observing them every day would cause her to forget her mother. Gradually George's pain brought on by remembering and Sarah's fear of forgetting abated as they lived through the first stages of their fresh grief; and they came together again, adapting old practices and inventing new ways to be together.

THE FRONDS OF THE tall palm trees that lined the perimeter of the garden looked almost black in the moonlight, and the gentle breeze rustled them with quiet, soothing sounds that allowed George and Sarah to sit quietly together in silence or to talk to each other comfortably, without any repressed feelings of guilt.

"Daddy, are you going to send Pablo to school like you did Julio and Guillermo?"

"I don't think so, Susi. He's a poor student. I don't know whether he doesn't have the intellectual ability or just won't apply himself. In any case I'm not inclined to waste my money for no good reason."

"I think that's a mistake."

"Why?"

"If you did it for the others, you should do it for him. You ought to treat them all alike."

"I might pay for him to go to a technical school, but not the *colegio*."

"You really should consider doing the same for him as for Julio and Guillermo. You let Guillermo go to the advanced technical institute after he finished the *colegio*."

"The primary technical school is good enough for Pablo. He wouldn't achieve anything attending the *colegio*. He's not my son. If they were my children, I'd try to treat them equally; but I have no obligation to help him. The money I spend on their education is as much for the country as for them personally—to provide needed skills and future leadership."

Sarah sighed. "He is something of a rebel."

"Something! With those ridiculous clothes, that attitude, his infernal loud music . . ."

Sarah reached over and clasped her father's hand. It would have been a familiar gesture if he had reached for her hand; it was as if they were reversing roles of parent and child. "Pablo has lots of spirit. He may do something remarkable one day."

"Maybe so. Maybe so. But not on my shilling."

IN LATE OCTOBER JUST after the peak of the rainy season Sarah and her father were sitting together on the back veranda when she noticed a red glow in the sky to the northeast.

"What's happening, Daddy? It surely can't be a forest fire with everything so wet from the rains."

"I don't know. It's rather peculiar. Maybe it's some strange meteorological phenomenon."

The following day at school Sarah learned that the volcano Cerro Negro was erupting. Later she heard that several villages near León had to be evacuated; and as the winds blew over León, ashes piled up in layers over houses and automobiles in the city.

On several evenings some of Sarah's friends drove toward León to see the fiery boulders and lava hurled into the night sky, and Sarah pleaded with her father to let her ride along with them. George Rutledge adamantly refused to allow his daughter to put herself into such danger.

Finally one night her father agreed to drive her closer to the eruption himself, but only as far as he deemed an appropriately safe distance. He didn't trust the judgment of teenagers' daring recklessness.

"It should be a good experience for you to see such an event of Nature. You may never be able to see anything like it again."

When Martín heard about their plans, he went around the entire afternoon wringing his hands and muttering, *"Take care. Be very careful. You must not go too close to the vomit of the gods."*

George Rutledge stopped the car several kilometers farther away from Cerro Negro than what his careful inquiries over several days had informed him was a safe distance and even farther away from it than Sarah's friends had driven; but Sarah still shuddered when each explosion rumbled, causing the old Austin to vibrate. She thought that the fire in the sky was the most beautiful and most terrible thing she'd ever seen.

On the drive home her father was silent and seemed morose. Just before they left the main highway to take the steep, winding road to Quinta Louisa, George Rutledge began speaking in a soft monotone, as if he'd forgotten that she was sitting beside him and was musing alone to himself.

"This is a violent land. I wonder whether it will be destroyed by Nature or by its people when their anger is unleashed."

"Daddy?"

"Oh, Susi!" Her father turned toward her as if he'd been suddenly reminded that she was with him in the car. "I'm so sorry. I was just thinking out loud."

"That's all right. Thanks for taking me tonight." Sarah started to say something else and ask her father why he was sad. She thought that he'd descended into a moment of anguished mourning for her mother, as he often seemed to do briefly before he recovered his usual placid, positive demeanor; but this time he didn't emerge from his dismal funk.

Sarah wanted to say something more to him, but she didn't know what to say. She looked over at him and smiled; but he glanced away out the side window of the car turning away from her, as if he were afraid of her seeing something in him that he'd divined from the fire of Cerro Negro.

SARAH CONTINUED HER PRIVATE conversations with Father Richard Sims almost every week and continued participating every week in the youth group that he led, but it didn't seem the same after Carlos Vargas left. She'd hoped to see Carlos during his school's summer vacation and at Christmas, but his family had almost always visited his mother's family in Florida for Christmas, and they continued to do so after Carlos was in the military school. His mother spent more and more time in the United States, especially during his summer vacation, as if she were trying to keep him away from Nicaragua. Some of Sarah's Nicaraguan classmates whispered that Carlos's father was more and more involved with the Sandinistas. Perhaps Carlos's mother wanted to shield him from danger or from humiliation if his father was imprisoned by Tachito or suffered an even worse fate. As Sarah advanced through her final years of high school she thought of Carlos, like her mother, as someone cherished in memory and affection that she would never see again.

One evening near the end of her senior year Sarah and George Rutledge were sitting side by side on the back patio as they usually did after supper, looking at the garden beneath the blazing stars after the moon had set. Sarah had been accepted at Elon College in Burlington, North Carolina, where her mother had gone to school and close to some members of her mother's family. She wasn't sure whether her anxiety was induced more by her fear of living in what was to her a foreign land or her concern about leaving her father alone here in Nicaragua.

"Do you think I'll like it up there, Daddy? Do you think I'll fit in?"

"Of course you will. Your mother reveled in her college years at Elon. That's where we met, you know." Sarah knew very well. She'd heard the story recounted many times, but she didn't speak because she knew her father wanted to tell her again; and even if she had objected, he would have gone on narrating his memories.

"I was asked to speak at a forum about Central America at Elon. I'd just graduated from Duke, and Mary was a senior. From the first time I saw her, I knew she was the woman I wanted to marry.

Then George Rutledge continued with a long monologue about things Sarah had never heard before, perhaps things her father had never said aloud before. "I was so worried about how Mary would fit in down here, like you're worrying about fitting in up there in North Carolina, I suppose. But she was at home from the moment she got here. Not that she ever went native. Mary was always a North Carolina belle, as Beatriz Chulteco so often reminds us, to the day she ... left us. She always saw people down here as a reflection of North Carolina castes and classes, blacks and whites, cotton mill workers and old Southern families. But still, she was different from my mother and my grandmother. Mother never really left North Carolina. She was sort of a perpetual visitor in Nicaragua, and my grandmother ... well, Louisa was a whole other story. She tried to make everything she touched in Nicaragua British, from the furniture to the servants to the coffee finca workers, even to the garden. You've heard how she tried to plant an English rose garden."

"I've heard Don Martín laugh about it." Sarah chuckled at the story, especially the way Martín told it.

"Yes, just ask Martín about *la Dueña Louisa*. He was just a little boy, but he never forgot ... Mary was different. Mary felt a kinship with this country, with the people, with the *finca*, with the birds, damn it all, even with the volcanoes. That's why she wanted to be buried here, I suppose. She belonged . . ." George's voice broke, and he sobbed.

"Daddy, are you all right?"

"Yes, yes, of course. You know, of all the things I've done in my life, what I'm most proud of is what we did in the village for the workers . . . the potable water, the electricity, the renovation of their houses, even moving Blanca's family here. That was all Mary. That was her idea. Her passion. I only wish she could have lived to see it completed."

"I'm very proud of both of you. You know that."

"I know, Susi. I'll miss you very much, but I want you to have a wonderful time in college, as I did, as your mother did."

"I will, Daddy; and I'll miss you very much, too. You know that."

"I hope you'll come back someday . . . to live; but if you find your place in North Carolina or somewhere else in the States or somewhere else entirely, that's all right. You have to find your place where life takes you."

"Of course I'm coming back to Nicaragua. This is my home. This is where I belong."

Flora died in the middle of the night from a fever, perhaps typhoid, and Martín came to the front door of Quinta Louisa tapping softly and then speaking apologetically for waking them so late at night to tell them that his wife had passed away and asking helplessly like a little boy what he should do. Martín had always known what to do and told them what must be done at such times and so George Rutledge was flummoxed at first by his queries. George and Sarah had both noticed at odd moments over the past several days that Flora didn't seem to be feeling well, but they were so preoccupied with their own concerns that they were distracted from inquiring seriously about her health; and Martín and Flora had not wanted to burden the father and daughter for whom they worked with their problems and pain.

The next day Martín had asked George Rutledge if he could bury his wife atop the cliff beyond the forest close to Mary Rutledge's grave, rather than in the village cemetery beside the little church.

"*Of course. Of course you can, my good man. Where we will all be together someday.*" It was one of the few times that Sarah had seen her father weep openly in Don Martín's presence, and she wished that he would reach out and embrace Don Martín, but they never touched, not even their hands.

On the third day they buried Flora at the top of the cliff. The workers from the *finca* carried her casket though the forest, just as they had carried Mary Rutledge's casket; and all the people from the village followed them. Father Richard Sims helped them with the service at the grave. They couldn't find a Roman Catholic priest who was willing to come up from Managua for a *campsina's* funeral. George said the Catholic priests couldn't be blamed; it was estimated that there was only one Roman Catholic priest for every ten thousand of the faithful in Nicaragua. The people from the village and Martín and Guillermo and Julio and his wife and children seemed touched and grateful for Father Richard's words and prayers in broken Spanish; but Pablo ran screaming back through the forest before the service was finished.

"*Mamí! Mamí! Do not let that foreign devil priest take you away!*"

For the first time in her life Sarah felt a loving tenderness for Pablo and wanted to take him in her arms and comfort him like a little brother, but she remained standing beside the grave as if some force beyond her control anchored her there while the women from the village chased after Pablo through the forest.

Earthquake and Revolution:
1972–1979

Where Do You Belong?

International flights from the United States arrived in Managua in the morning and returned in the afternoon so that anyone traveling beyond New Orleans or Miami would usually schedule a connection to arrive at a final destination late at night or else stay in one or the other port city overnight. Not only would George Rutledge need to schedule a domestic flight for Sarah after clearing customs in Miami or New Orleans, but she would have to change planes again in Atlanta before flying into Greensboro, where college officials would meet her. It would be almost impossible to do in one day. George pondered and fretted over Sarah's itinerary. He wanted to accompany her, but it was a difficult time to leave the new coffee-processing plant unattended.

After dithering for almost a week George decided to call an old college friend who lived in Miami to ask if he would meet Sarah's plane and let her stay with his family and take her back to the airport the next morning. The telephone call took almost three hours to complete over the landlines from Central America through Mexico. "I know it's a terribly lot to ask, but . . ."

Before George could finish his request his friend had enthusiastically agreed to the plan. He was one of the few friends from George's college years who had kept in touch with him and the only such friend who had sent condolences after Mary's death. He seemed to be genuinely pleased to be able to do something to help George and delighted to be able to meet his daughter.

Of course Sarah protested vehemently and assured her father that if she was old enough to go away to college she was old enough to change planes or even take a taxi to a hotel for the night, but secretly she was relieved that someone would meet her and take care of her. She had never visited the United States without one or both of her parents beside her. Her anticipation of going to college and leaving her father and Nicaragua both thrilled and terrified her, although she confided none of her feelings to anyone except Guillermo.

It was raining when George and Sarah arrived at the airport, but the shower was typically brief. The sun came out and the sky cleared as the airplane rose over Xolotián (Lake Managua). Sarah had seen Momotombo and Momotombito from the air on previous flights; but looking down on them now she was shocked at how ordinary they seemed. Momotombito looked like a toy boat in the middle of a pond floating beside Momotombo like sloop moored on the shore. On their frequent drives home from Masaya, Momotombo always seemed magical looming ahead of them, as if the highway would crash into the base of the huge volcano with wisps of smoke blowing from its peak to complete the eerie effect. Sarah felt an aching desire to look up at them at sunset from the Masaya highway and wondered how long it would be before she saw them again. *"Will I go to Masaya during my Christmas holiday?"* she wondered and immediately swore to herself that she would. It seemed to be ages in the future, already in a distant land, the land she had just left.

George's college friend and his family in Miami were kind and solicitous as if she were some exotic bird that had flown into their patio. Their small talk was polite, but she found nothing of interest in their conversation. She struggled to remember the names of the two younger children and how to spell them, so that she could write the requisite thank you note prompted in her conscience from her mother beyond the grave.

The officials from the college who met her plane in Greensboro were equally kind and polite and unmemorable, and Sarah began to wonder if her imagined adventure of college would continue to be pale and insipid compared to her life in Nicaragua.

Then she met her roommate.

"So you're the foreigner they assigned to room with me" were the first words she spoke to Sarah. "You do speak English, don't you?" were the second words out of her mouth.

"Yes. My mother was an American from nearby here in North Carolina. My father's British. I went to an American school in Nicaragua where the classes were all taught in English."

"Is that where the pigmies come from? Nicara . . . Whatever?"

"I believe you're thinking of Nigeria. Nicaragua is in Central America, although I don't believe Nigeria is the part of Africa where pigmies live either. By the way, I'm Sarah Rutledge." Sarah extended her hand, which the large girl grasped limply.

"I'm Bebe. Bebe Jones. My real name's Barbara, but everybody calls me Bebe. I'm glad you're not a Negro, 'though I guess that would've been aw'right, too, the way things are going nowadays."

Sara felt a chill rundown her spine. Bebe was perhaps the plainest girl that Sarah had ever seen. Although she didn't feel any innate sympathy for her, Sarah resolved to befriend her and be as kind and understanding as possible.

"Are there any black students at Elon?"

"I don't know. Not that many, I guess. I've seen a few walking around. They started coming to my high school last year. I don't think any of them are here at Elon though. I didn't know any of them very well. We never talked much."

"I don't know anyone at all here. I didn't have a single name to write on the application where they asked for roommate preferences. Is that how it was for you?"

"Oh, I know plenty of girls in my class that came here, but none of 'em wanted to room with me. I just told 'em to put me with anybody. They asked me if I'd be willing to room with somebody from outside the

United States, and I said *sure*. I just wondered whether you'd be able to speak English and if you'd be white or not."

Sarah and Bebe kept very different schedules. Sarah preferred early morning classes, and Bebe slept late. Often Bebe was still asleep when Sarah returned from her second or even third period classes, and Sarah tried not to wake her. Sarah studied at night in the library; and Bebe studied in their room, although Sarah wondered whether Bebe studied very much at all.

By the end of the second week of classes Bebe had been accepted into a group of friends—Sarah overheard a wag in the cafeteria refer to them as the *ugly sisters*. They gathered in Sarah and Bebe's room almost every evening while Sarah was at the library. Whenever Sarah returned to their room, Bebe's friends usually left. Sometimes Bebe left with them. Sometimes she stayed and fiddled with things on her desk. Sarah tried to ask Bebe leading questions about her classes and her friends, but Bebe's laconic responses didn't lead to an extended interchange.

Sarah enjoyed some pleasant conversations with various students in the cafeteria, but none of them led to real friendships. She didn't feel that she was a member of any social group. One evening using the payphone in the student lounge and aching from loneliness she tried to call Carlos Vargas at the college where she'd been told he'd matriculated; but when she failed to track him down from leads by people who recognized his name and after several calls and running out of change, she gave up the effort.

Several times Bebe asked Sarah if she wouldn't prefer to room with someone else; and Sarah always replied that she was happy with Bebe as a roommate—however unhappy she actually was—because she felt sorry for Bebe and didn't want to be rude.

Then one evening after she returned from the library, Sarah found their room completely rearranged. Bebe and her friends were nowhere in sight. Sarah's desk had been shoved into a corner where it was almost inaccessible, and her books had been piled underneath it. Her dresses were hung in a different order in her closet, and even personal items in her chest-of-drawers had obviously been rummaged through. It suddenly dawned on Sarah for the first time that Bebe wasn't seeking reassurance in asking if Sarah wouldn't prefer another roommate. Bebe wanted to room with someone else. Until that evening the thought had been inconceivable to Sarah, who had believed that rooming with Bebe was an act of pitying mercy on her part.

Because it was only a few days until the Thanksgiving holiday, Sarah decided to wait until she returned to campus before taking any action about her roommate situation. If only she could have flown to Managua and talked with her father and Don Martín and Father Richard and Doña Beatriz, Sarah would have known what to do; but the time was too short and the expense too great for such a trip. Sarah also believed that if she should go back to Nicaragua now she would never return to the United States.

Sarah had been invited to spend the Thanksgiving with her mother's older brother and his wife, her Uncle Walter and Aunt Beth, on the family farm between Burlington and Durham where her mother had grown up; but she didn't think that she could talk to them about the horrible situation with her roommate. When Uncle Walter and Aunt Beth had visited them at Quinta Louisa several years ago, they sat with their hands folded in their laps and said very little. Their eyes wandered around the room like people waiting in a strange bus station unsure of their schedule for departure. Perhaps if she could wander by herself in the woods and listen to the birds and see some wild animals as her mother had told her that she used to do, the land itself would offer her some answers; but Sarah knew that the birds would not be as beautiful as those in Nicaragua and that the animals would be secretive and quiet, unlike the chattering of her impudent monkeys.

Sarah's Uncle Walter picked her up from the Elon campus late Wednesday afternoon. He drove his wife's car rather than his pick-up truck and had difficulty turning on the windshield wipers when it began to rain, because he was unfamiliar with the car he seldom drove. Walter was thin and gaunt like Sarah's mother and even more taciturn than she had been. After his warm smiles and greetings as they departed, he said almost nothing to her on the drive; and Sarah found the silence comforting. She was tired from studying for her tests before the holiday and even more exhausted from her anxiety about her roommate dilemma.

Aunt Beth was as talkative as her husband was mum. Her chatter was interrupted only by her broad grins and frequent hugs. Sarah had never seen her aunt frown except during her visit to Nicaragua, when she'd sat somberly for hours at the time like an animal that had been captured and transported to a foreign land.

"Can I help you do anything?"

Beth paused before responding and wrinkled her brow but never stopped her lips from smiling. "I can see how worn out you are. Wouldn't you like to get some rest? There'll be plenty for us to do tomorrow."

Sarah sighed with grateful relief. "That would be so very nice." She hadn't finished unpacking before she fell asleep on the bed and didn't awaken until almost eight o'clock the next morning despite the farmyard noises cascading through the window with the streaming sunshine.

Sarah's cousin Roger, Uncle Walter and Aunt Beth's single son, had arrived before Sarah had dressed for breakfast. Roger was six years older than Sarah, Julio's age. He looked even more like her mother than Uncle Walter did, much more like her mother than she did; and he talked even less than his father did. Uncle Walter and Aunt Beth's daughter and husband and two children arrived around ten o'clock. They sat down in the living room and began talking about people Sarah didn't know and things she didn't understand. Beth came and went to the kitchen, wiping her hands on her apron and entering the conversation as if she'd been there the whole time, perhaps because she'd heard it all before. Sarah tried to smile pleasantly and appear interested.

"Sarah, would you help me for a few minutes in the kitchen?"

"Of course."

"Can I do anything, Mama?"

"No, sweetheart. You stay here and keep the men company. I just need Sarah right now."

When they entered the kitchen, Sarah asked her aunt, "What would you like me to do?"

"Peel those sweet potatoes, if you don't mind; but mostly I was trying to get you out of there before they bored you to death."

Beth chuckled, and Sarah impulsively gave her a hug. "Oh, thank you!"

"What's the matter, honey? I think there's something bad wrong."

Sarah began to tear. "Aunt Beth! How did you know?"

Beth nodded and continued to stir a pot without look up. "You want to talk about it?"

"Yes, so, so very much, but not now, not on Thanksgiving Day. Can we talk tomorrow?"

"Course we can. We will. We'll take us a long walk in the woods."

"Oh, Aunt Beth, thank you, thank you, so, so much." Sarah sighed deeply and felt an enormous relief, as if half her problems and more than half of the burden of her worry had been removed, just by Beth's noticing.

Sarah enjoyed the Thanksgiving feast and ate ravenously until the skin on her stomach felt as tight as a drumhead. Her male cousin ventured one of his rare comments. "I reckon they don't feed you much over at Elon. Looks like you're starving."

Everyone laughed, including Sarah, who felt included rather than embarrassed by his taunt.

"I need to walk off some of this food. I wonder if anyone can show me the way to the creek?" Sarah arched her eyebrows and glanced back and forth at her five and eight year old cousins.

"I will!"

"I will!"

"Can we, Grandma?"

"Can we go with Sarah, Grandpa?"

The woods were silent in the winter chill. A few hearty birds chirped occasionally high in the treetops, and a couple of squirrels scampered up a tree trunk. Sarah felt tears running down her cheek.

"What's the matter, Sarah?"

"Oh, nothing. I'm just missing the parrots and monkeys in the forest behind my house."

"You have monkeys where you live?" The older boy asked in open-mouth amazement.

"And parrots?" echoed the younger boy.

"Yes, but we don't have a creek. I'll be fine when we get to the creek."

And when they reached the creek, she did inexplicably feel better.

Uncle Walter and Aunt Beth's daughter and family left late Thanksgiving Day afternoon. After their son drove away on Friday morning Sarah and Beth retraced the steps to the creek that Sarah had taken with the little boys on the prior afternoon.

Sarah poured out the frustration and pain of her roommate situation to Beth, culminating with an account of the rearrangement of the room and the jumbling of her things.

"That's outrageous! What time does your last class finish Monday morning?"

"Ten fifty."

"I'll meet you and we'll go have us a little discussion with the dean. They can match you up with a better roommate or give you a single room."

"I'm not sure I can afford a single room."

"Don't you worry your pretty little heard about that. Your Uncle Walter and I will pay for it, if we need to."

"There may not be any single rooms available, Aunt Beth; and everyone's probably already matched up with roommates."

"This is intolerable. With all the money our family has given to Elon College, they damn well better do something."

"Aunt Beth!"

"Pardon my French! I don't speak Spanish."

They laughed and hugged, and for the first time since Sarah landed in the United States she felt that everything would be all right.

ON MONDAY MORNING IN the dean's office Sarah rarely spoke except to affirm her aunt's account when the dean would ask her, "Is that right?"

Sarah would never have believed that a small plump farmer's wife could be as assertive and intimidating as her Aunt Beth.

The dean assigned a single room to Sarah with no additional charge, "until the end of the semester, if you can find an appropriate roommate for the spring term or until the end of year if necessary." He would arrange for members of the staff to help her move her clothes and books that very afternoon.

As Sarah and Beth left the dean's office, Sarah heard the chimes from the Elon Community Church that always rang at Noon. Usually they saddened her by reminding her of John Donne's words: ". . . for whom the bell tolls . . .", but today they sounded joyful, even hopeful.

Outside the administrative building Sarah blurted out, "Oh, Aunt Beth, how can I ever thank you?"

"No need to thank me, honey. We're your family, and we want to take care of you. Don't you ever let something like this go on so long again. We want you to feel at home here in North Carolina."

Buses and vans were arranged to transport students from the campus to the Greensboro and Raleigh-Durham airports following the afternoon classes on Friday, December 15, before the Christmas break began. Sarah had a better connection out of Charlotte to Miami, where she would spend two nights once again with her father's college classmate. He would drive her to catch the early Monday LeNica flight to Managua, because LaNica did not offer weekend flights from the United States. The dean's office offered to arrange for a car to take Sarah to Charlotte—partly as penance for her disastrous roommate assignment, Sarah thought—but Aunt Beth insisted on driving Sarah herself. Sarah didn't protest her aunt's offer, because she thought a visit with Aunt Beth would be a helpful transition from one of her worlds to the other.

She feigned weariness so that she wouldn't have to attend church services with the family of her father's friend in Miami and wouldn't have to make idle conversation and paste on a perpetual smile. Her thoughts and emotions had already arrived in Nicaragua, twenty-four hours ahead of her body. In the comparable temperature of Miami she could close her eyes and almost imagine that she was sitting in the parlor at Quinta Louisa.

George Rutledge had arranged for Sarah to bypass customs and passport control for the most part, so that she hardly stopped walking between the airplane and her father's arms. His eyes were misty and his cheeks damp with tears rather than tropical sweat as he kissed her.

"I'm so very glad you're home."

"Me, too. I love you, Daddy." Her greeting released George's last stoic barrier as tears ran down his cheeks. "What's the matter? What's wrong?"

"Nothing at all, Susi. I just missed you and am so happy . . ." He lost all control and buried his face in her shoulder as if once again she were the parent and he the child.

They spoke very little during the drive out of the city. Even as the car climbed into the hills they enjoyed a comfortable silence without any strain to force words.

"Is there any news down here?"

"Not much that I haven't written to you." Their weekly multiple-paged letters conveyed myriad details from her about the campus and from him about the *finca* and Nicaraguan friends; but they took several days in transit, and Sarah wondered if anything of note had happened during the previous week or if her father had concealed any bad news, as she'd omitted any reference to him about her roommate trauma until after Thanksgiving. "Oh, yes, Guillermo is going to be married."

"Guillermo! To whom?"

"I haven't met her. A student at one of the universities. León, I think. She's training to be a teacher. I hope she'll accept a position at the village school."

"¡*Caramba*! (Damn it!) Who am I going to marry then? I always thought Guillermo would marry me."

"Susi, don't be ridiculous." George looked over at her as he mouthed his wife's words and then laughed. "Not that I'd mind, you understand; but your mother would haunt you from beyond the grave."

Sarah laughed, but neither of them found George's caricature of his late wife very amusing, however accurate it may have been.

During the following week Sarah and George enjoyed going into Managua to shop for Christmas gifts for each other and for Martín's family and the workers at the coffee-processing plant. They made one quick side-trip to Masaya for locally made craft items, and Sarah remembered her vow as the airplane had left Managua in September as she saw the outline of Momotombo dimly in the mists ahead of them, although their schedule didn't allow her to see the mountain at sunset. She told herself that she should have bought gifts in the United States where they would have been cheaper, but she didn't "get the Christmas spirit" and hadn't felt like shopping until she arrived in Nicaragua.

While her father took care of business one morning in Managua she enjoyed a visit with Doña Beatriz in order to catch up on gossip, both personal and political. Most of it was idle banter with no new substantive information, but the familiar complaints and exaggerations were somehow comforting to her.

Her father allowed her to drive the car to St. Francis Church for a visit with Father Richard. Allowing her to drive alone on the South Highway was a major milestone, although George Rutledge still refused to let his daughter drive into the city. She was able to relate the events involving her roommate and her visit with Aunt Beth to the dean's office more fully to Father Richard than she been able to express them to her father. It was closest to how she might have related the story to her mother. The sudden realization that she could never again talk about such things with her mother brought a resurgence of grief and a sense of her absence that Sarah hadn't felt since leaving Nicaragua in September.

Late Thursday afternoon Sarah saw Guillermo enter the back of the garden, as softly and gently as a forest animal slinking toward the pond to slake its thirst in the dry season. She knew he was coming to see her. She knew he wanted to tell her about his fiancée and his forthcoming marriage. She knew he would sit on the bench in the middle of the garden and wait for her as long as need be without announcing himself. She hesitated and sighed deeply, attempting to sort out her feelings more than her thoughts. As she watched him from the window she felt a warm glow of affection rise up through her body. After perhaps a quarter of an hour she went out the patio door and waved to him. He rose, but neither of them spoke until she reached the bench.

"Guillermo, I hear you are going to be married."

"I wanted to tell you or write you, but . . ."

"You could not wait for me."

"I had to tell your father on account of Papá. I should have asked Don Jorge not to tell you."

"*I mean you just couldn't wait for me to marry you.*"

"*¡Doña Sarah!*"

"*¡Caramba! Do not doña me! You know I love you like a brother, as much as I could love any flesh and blood brother. When's the wedding to be?*"

"*We have not set a date. After Easter sometime.*"

"*If you'll wait until I get home in June I will give you the biggest party that has ever been seen at Quinta Louisa.*"

"*We will wait for you. Not because I want a party, but because I want you to be there.*" Guillermo sprang to his feet and enveloped Sarah with a hug, a real Nicaraguan *abrazo* that took her breath away. It was the first time he had ever dared to touch her beyond the polite handshake that she had always initiated. Then he began to tell her about his fiancée. Sarah realized her sadness came from jealousy that Guillermo had found a mate while she hadn't even dated anyone seriously. She tried to appear interested and to concentrate on what he was saying, but she was thinking mostly about her memories of their childhood and whether she would be able to rely on Guillermo in the future and trust him with her secrets, no matter what might happen.

ON FRIDAY NIGHT, HALF asleep, half awake, Sarah pictured the midnight service to be celebrated at St. Francis. This year it would be even more special than usual since Christmas Eve fell on a Sunday. It was the only time during the year that her father would drive down the South Highway late at night, because it had been his wife's favorite church service of the year. It was Sarah's second favorite celebration, next to Epiphany when people wore gilded paper crowns and ate the "Three Kings' Cake" after the Eucharist.

Twice during the night, about a half-hour apart, Sarah felt her bed shaking. The second time the bed was jostled across the floor for a few feet and wakened her enough that it took another half-hour to go back to sleep.

Earthquakes were common in Nicaragua, and she was accustomed to the strange sensation almost like being slung around by a huge dog. People who visited Nicaragua were often terrified when they felt a *temblor* (quake), but those who were at home in the country took it for granted and paid little attention, even though considerable damage often resulted.

The banging on the patio door before dawn on Saturday morning roused Sarah before her father had awakened. Martín's indistinguishable words and anguished voice through the closed door had sounded like this before only in speaking about death, the death of her mother and the death of Doña Flora. Sarah had begun to unlatch the bolt of the front door in the hall when George Rutledge stumbled out of his bedroom door still rubbing his eyes. He looked at her in her short, transparent nightgown. "Go get on a robe before I open the door."

"No, Daddy. Open the door and let Don Martín in. Something's terribly wrong."

George Rutledge meekly obeyed his daughter. *"What has happened, my good man? Is something the matter with one of the boys?"*

"The end of the world. Everything is gone. The city is destroyed."

When they calmed Don Martín, he told them that a terrible earthquake had leveled Managua shortly after Midnight. Someone in the village had heard a report on a battery-operated radio, and a boy came to tell Don Martín the news.

After George had said, "No, no, it can't be," none of them spoke again for a long time.

"Thousands and thousands and thousands are dead, Don Jorge. I do not know if Guillermo and Pablo are dead, too."

As the painful silence penetrated their bodies in the darkened room Sarah realized that Don Martín was sitting down beside them without even having been asked, something he had never done before, as if he were at last a member of the Rutledge family. Finally Sarah said, *"They are all right. I know Guillermo and Pablo are safe. I know it."* Her consanguineous father and her spiritual father looked over at her as if they believed her words, as if she'd made a solemn promise to the two men who looked years older than they'd appeared the day before, as if she now possessed wisdom and secrets that gave them faith and hope.

BY MID-AFTERNOON ARMANDO AND Beatriz Chulteco arrived in a car they had hired by paying a driver an enormous sum of money to transport them to Quinta Louisa over back roads. (Doña Beatriz always kept several thousand *córdobas* and even several hundred American dollars in her purse to use for an emergency, and Armando had often chided her and told her that carrying such a huge amount of cash made her far more vulnerable to danger than might befall them by some hypothetical disaster, but now Beatriz's cache was providential and allowed them to flee from the doomed city.) Their home had been demolished. They saved only the clothes they wore and a few precious items snatched from the rubble, primarily some of Beatriz's gold bracelets and earrings. They didn't ask for refuge, and George Rutledge didn't bother to tell them they were welcome to stay as long as they wished. It was understood and unspoken on both sides.

The Chultecos didn't speak about the destruction of Managua except to say that the Gran Hotel and the Cathedral were lost, which seemed to symbolize the devastating damage to all the prominent buildings in the central city. They had heard about a few friends. An elderly British woman who lived in an old mansion on the lakeside had fallen in her bed from her second story bedroom through the first floor into the cellar, thinking it was just a dream, and survived with no significant injuries. Her grandson, in his twenties, had died. Because the telephone lines were all down the only communication was by word of mouth from terrified people roaming the streets.

After the Chultecos related the few snippets of news about people they knew—those who had survived, those who had died, all of whom had lost their homes—they spoke no more and wandered around Quinta Louisa like phantoms whose souls had been separated from their bodies. Even Sarah and George and Martín walked through the house and garden like exiles from another world in spite of being at home in the place where they had always lived.

Late in the afternoon as the sun was setting Guillermo and Pablo arrived. They had walked beyond the suburbs of the city and finally hitched a ride on the back of a bus to the intersection of the road leading up the hill to Quinta Louisa. When Sarah saw them come through the gate, she burst into tears and felt an overwhelming sense of relief, as if the world, her world, would not end on Christmas Day.

"Daddy, do you think there will still be a Christmas Eve service tonight at St. Francis?"

"I don't know. We can't call Father Richard. We need to save petrol. Who knows when we can buy it again?" George saw Sarah bite her lower lip. "But I think we should go down to pray . . . formal service or not. I think we must."

Only a few communicants had arrived at St. Francis by eleven o'clock. Only three *costeños* who worked as servants in nearby homes were present. They had some reports about Nicaraguan members of the parish that had perished in the city. A dozen foreigners who lived in the Becklin Colony or other nearby homes on the South Highway arrived by eleven thirty. (On Christmas Eve the church was usually filled with regular members as well as expatriates, Roman Catholics and German-speaking Lutherans, who didn't usually attend Episcopal services.) The church was dark, lit only by candles, since there was no electricity. The altar guild had arranged the flowers on the brass stands in their usual places at the back of the church where they were hardly visible tonight. The aroma of the flowers mingled with the beeswax scent of the extra candles that had been added to provide as much illumination as possible.

In the darkness Sarah recalled the words of Dame Julian of Norwich that Father Richard often quoted, "*All will be well, and all manner of things will be well.*" Despite the destruction of much of the world she had known for her entire life, she thought that they would survive as St. Francis Church had survived.

People came and prayed and left. A formal liturgy did not seem appropriate. Father Richard gave the blessed bread and wine from the reserved sacrament to communicants individually when they approached the altar. Other than the words, "This is my body . . . this is my blood," nothing else was spoken. After nearly an hour Sarah and George returned to their car and took a back road to Quinta Louisa, again bypassing the Pan American Highway because a fissure had opened in the pavement during the earthquake.

The next morning, Christmas Day, Sarah went into the garden and sat on the bench and watched the hummingbirds flit and dive between the hibiscus blossoms. She could almost imagine that nothing in her world at Quinta Louisa had changed or been touched by the horrendous natural disaster until Don Armando and Doña Beatriz came out on the patio before breakfast and she looked at their faces.

After their Christmas dinner of roasted chicken and dressing from Mary Rutledge's family recipe brought with her years ago from North Carolina, all of which had been planned and prepared before the earthquake, Sarah saw Guillermo in the garden trimming bushes and digging around the trunks of the fruit trees. He didn't stop to look at her as she approached him, even though in the past he had always interrupted whatever he was doing to talk with her.

"Guillermo?" As he turned toward her he looked even more frightening than Doña Beatriz and Don Armando had, whose faces made Sarah think they'd seen ghosts; but Guillermo appeared dead, as if she were seeing the face of a corpse. It suddenly occurred to her that Guillermo's fiancée might have been killed in the earthquake. When she called his name again, it was in a different, softer tone, "Guillermo?" He tried to smile, but failed to move even his lips upward. *"Are you all right? Is your fiancée . . . ?"*

"She is well. She was in León. But Sarita, all the dead people, hundreds and hundreds and thousands and thousands of people who lost their homes, tens and hundreds of thousands who lost their children and parents and grandparents and uncles and aunts . . ." Guillermo began to weep, and Sarah was somehow relieved to see the tears streaming down his cheeks that restored a human countenance, resuscitating the corpse.

"You will be all right. You will be fine."

"Oh, I know. My apartment is gone, where Pablo and I were staying. My job is gone. The factory is demolished. The school where Pablo attended was crushed. We will move back with Papá, and Don Jorge told me this morning that he will give me a job at the coffee processing plant for as long as I want to work there. Yes, of course, we will be fine; but all the others, the thousands and thousands and thousands of others . . ."

He wiped the tears off his cheeks, and once again his face took on the appearance of a corpse.

"It is awful, terrible. I will let you get back to your work." Sarah knew it was only busy work, nothing that was necessary to be accomplished, especially on Christmas Day, but something to occupy his hands and perhaps a small part of his mind. *"We will talk again later."*

But they didn't talk again, and a week later her father drove her to San José, Costa Rica, to fly back to North Carolina. Sarah had insisted that she did not want to go back to college and leave her father alone at Quinta Louisa, but he'd been even more adamant that she must return to her classes and what he called "a normal life". Then she protested about using their precious resources driving to San José—if he'd pondered driving to the Christmas Eve service at St. Francis, how could he think of driving to Costa Rica? The coffee-processing plant had a gasoline tank, which George Rutledge always referred to as "the petrol barrel" for the trucks and the generator; and he told her that even though they must preserve the petrol, the trip to San José was fully justified. They wouldn't need the trucks or even the generator at the plant in the foreseeable future. Only Martín had realized that their valuable resources must be protected. He sat with a rifle across his knees beside the tank the first few nights after the earthquake, and one of the workers took his place every night for weeks thereafter until the tank was almost empty and gasoline was once again available to be purchased in the country.

Sarah did not see the devastation in the central city. The closest she had come to the earthquake zone was on a suburban street on the periphery of Managua where she and her father had driven around the former city in an attempt to reach the airport to learn if there was the possibility of an international flight before they'd given up the effort as being futile and decided to go to Costa Rica. Even on those outskirts the throngs of people carrying bundles of bottles and cans and ragged clothes, everything they owned, horrified her. She was accustomed to seeing people in extreme poverty, but she'd never witnessed anything like these starving, hopeless refugees before. Even there on a suburban road she could look toward what used to be a great city, now leveled like the photographs of German and Japanese cities bombed in the war. Like Hiroshima, she thought.

IN THE DAYS AND weeks and months that followed, the destruction of Managua seemed to Sarah more like a dream, a horrible nightmare, than a real event in her life and in her world, as she read about more than 20,000 people killed and over a quarter of a million people homeless, jobless, hungry, almost naked, nearly starving.

Armando and Beatriz Chulteco stayed at Quinta Louisa with George Rutledge for almost a month after the earthquake before they moved to Miami where Beatriz hoped that they would settle permanently.

George flew to the United States for a short visit with Sarah at Easter and a longer visit the following Christmas. On both occasions George and Sarah visited at the family farm with Sarah's uncle and aunt. Sarah began to realize that her father's financial resources were strained, and he couldn't afford both international airfare and hotels for frequent visits. She refrained in her letters from her plaints about missing him and being lonely and wanting to see him.

BETWEEN HIS VISITS TO the farm George made one trip for a short visit between Sarah's summer semester and just before her college courses started again the fall. They met in Miami and stayed together in the Chultecos' little house where George and Sarah were cramped together in a tiny bedroom, the closest physical proximity overnight that the father and daughter had ever experienced. George's gentle snoring was comforting to Sarah when she awoke during the night. At bedtime and when they rose in the morning she hugged him, and once again felt that she was acting as the parent and he the child and remembered how he had always tucked her into bed when she was little, after her mother had left her room to prepare herself for bed, and how she had always felt safe and unafraid sitting in her father's lap. The days were more difficult than the nights. George worried about his daughter, and Sarah worried about her father; but neither of them could express their concerns to one another, although they could read each other's anxiety in their faces.

Armando spurned the out-of-doors and preferred to sit in the barely lit house smoking his cigar. George Rutledge felt obligated to keep Armando company in the small dusky living room, which gave Sarah the opportunity to escape her father's self-accusing countenance and to join Beatriz on the tiny patio, swathed on three sides by walls of vines to conceal the view of the street and the next door house only a few feet away, so unlike Quinta Louisa with its open view from the patio of the garden and the forest beyond it.

Beatriz smoked cigarettes in a long holder, so that her fingers wouldn't be stained yellow; and Sarah noticed how many more cigarettes she lit here in Miami than she had smoked in Managua.

"How are you, Doña Beatriz? Do you like living in Miami?"

"I like it well enough. At least I feel safe here. Armando hates it. I don't know how much longer he'll be willing to stay. He misses his friends and his routines and ... everything ... the country, the mountains, the lakes, the volcanoes ... everything."

"What do you miss?"

Doña Beatriz laughed and jangled her bracelets. "I miss speaking English. Everyone speaks Spanish in Miami. *Todo el mundo* (Everyone). Of course, it's Cuban Spanish." She wrinkled her nose at the word *Cuban* as if it smelled bad. "I miss my British and American friends here. It's ironic, isn't it, that I spoke more English in Managua than I do in Miami."

"Do you hear much from Managua? Do you get news about what's going on?"

"Oh, yes. More than I'd probably hear in Managua. There's another irony, my dear. We can speak freely here. None of Somoza's spies to overhear, although I'm still careful. The walls have ears, *¿verdad?* (isn't that right?)"

"What do you hear?"

"That Somoza, the bastard, is embezzling money from the international relief funds. You know he allowed medicine and antibiotics to go bad on the runways of the airport, because the *Guardia* (National Guard) was busy protecting his property."

"You'd think he has enough without trying to get more."

"It is never enough. For a greedy despot it is never enough. They say he controlled forty percent of the economy of the country. You get a clearer picture of things up here."

"How can he do it?"

"With the protection and blessing of the United States. You know Washington has sent the Marines back to prop up his regime, just like they did in the thirties."

"Why? How can they do that? Why do *gringos* do that? Why do we do that, Doña Beatriz?"

"Better the *bastardo* (son of a bitch) we know, as Roosevelt was supposed to have said about the Somozas back in the thirties, or something like that. But I don't think it can last. I think the people, the *campesinos* and venders in the *mercados* (markets), are beginning to see his true colors. He's no longer the savior, the great hero. Two years ago he would probably have won ninety percent of the popular vote legitimately, without rigging the ballots. But no more. When he turned the guns on the people to protect his property, to keep them from receiving the food and medicine that had been donated, they began to see who he was. I don't think he can last, even with the help of the Marines from *los Estados Unidos* (the United States)."

GUILLERMO HAD MARRIED IN June, as had been planned; but Sarah was not present for his wedding, and no grand party took place for the bridal couple at Quinta Louisa. Guillermo and Ana moved into the house at the back of the garden that George had built for Martín's family, and Guillermo began working at the coffee-processing plant in the job that George had promised him. Within a few weeks he was effectively managing the factory, and within the year he was officially recognized as the manager.

Martín had moved into the maid's room behind the kitchen at Quinta Louisa, and the cook who had occupied the maid's room since Flora's death moved back to the village and came to Quinta Louisa three or four days a week to prepare meals and do the laundry. (She greatly preferred living in the village. She'd never liked being isolated from her family and friends during the week.)

Pablo had graduated from the village school. Before the earthquake he'd shared a tiny apartment in the city with Guillermo in order to attend the school where George Rutledge had arranged for him to be enrolled. Once schools were reopened after the earthquake and Guillermo and Ana had occupied the little house behind the garden, Pablo lived during weekdays with some of his cousins near his school on the Masaya highway—George paid them a small stipend to cover Pablo's expenses. On weekends the plan was for Pablo to stay with his father in the servant's room behind the kitchen, but he often slept in the little house with Guillermo and Ana or stayed in the city or lodged with friends in the village or, as George Rutledge often said, "Slept God knows where. His father has no idea where." Martín's face contorted with an expression of pain and guilt, when he overheard George's words spoken in English, which he understood very well, although he pretended not to comprehend them and refused ever to utter a single word of English.

Armando Chulteco continued to long for his friends and associations in Managua, and after two years Beatriz stopped pleading with him to remain in Miami where they were safe. The Chultecos bought a small house in Los Robles, the middle-class neighborhood closest to the center of Managua that had not been leveled by the earthquake.

Sarah would not return to Nicaragua for over two years. Her father would fly up to see her two or three times a year. They would meet in Miami or visit her uncle's family on the farm in North Carolina. Sarah would always ask her father when she could come home to Nicaragua, and he would always tell her, "Not yet. Things are still too difficult. Perhaps next year."

She seemed to have lived during those years like someone in a coma, as if her life had been interrupted and put on pause. She went to class, visited her uncle and aunt, conversed pleasantly with acquaintances—she made no real friends and decided to occupy a single room, even at the extra cost that her father and uncle's family agreed that she needed after the shock of the earthquake. She took courses during the summer semester and found a job in a drugstore to help defray her expenses. The customers she saw every week and the customers she saw only once and her classmates at Elon all seemed the same to her: people with whom she could converse casually and pleasantly without really caring or remembering.

As the summer after her junior year approached, Sarah wrote her father that she was coming home. "I want to see Quinta Louisa and the people I love there. Please!"

George Rutledge agreed with his daughter that the situation had improved sufficiently for her to come home; but he warned her that everything would be different, that nothing would be the same.

LIKE MOST COLLEGE STUDENTS Sarah Rutledge hadn't thought seriously about what she would do after she graduated until the summer before her senior year, the first time that she would return to Nicaragua since the earthquake. Her academic record was outstanding—her lack of close friendships and absence of a serious romantic relationship had prompted her to seek refuge in books and her studies. Several professors had encouraged her to apply to a graduate school for a master's or even a doctoral program.

Sarah's only extracurricular activities had involved singing in the college chorus and tutoring children in the recently integrated public schools. She was drawn to the children, especially the black children, who reminded her of the *costeño* members at St. Francis. Perhaps she felt a kinship with them because they seemed to feel like visitors and aliens in the formerly all white schools. Sarah had written in one of her long, pensive letters to her father, "Living in the United States I feel like you said my grandmother felt in Nicaragua. You said she always called herself *a permanent visitor.*"

For Sarah the choice was greater than for most graduates, more dramatic than deciding between graduate school and employment. Even as her airplane landed in Managua she was stuck by the dilemma: would she come back to Nicaragua to live or would she look for a job in the United States? As she and her father drove from the airport around the ruined city, Sarah thought, "*This is no longer my home. There is nothing left here that I knew and loved. How could I possibly spend the rest of my life in*

Nicaragua?" But she also pondered, *"How can I abandon my father alone here? He will never leave Nicaragua."*

When the new Volkswagen beetle passed through the front gates at Quinta Louisa—George Rutledge had finally given up the old Austin and bought a new car—everything inside Sarah shifted, as if she were an empty bottle suddenly filled with rare wine. She was home. She tingled with more life, more peace, more hope, more joy than she had felt for two and a half years.

"Daddy, I'm home!" Sarah impulsively lunged across the gearshift and embraced her father and kissed him on the cheek before he could stop the car. They almost ran into a palm inside the circular driveway. George Rutledge began laughing. He couldn't seem to stop laughing. It was the first time he had laughed long and loudly for two and a half years.

The next day Sarah visited with Guillermo at the office of the coffee factory, and their conversation seemed as easy and natural as always despite Guillermo's having been married. Sarah told Guillermo that she wanted to meet his wife, and he suggested that she visit their cottage after Ana returned from her classes at the school one afternoon without *el viejo* (the old man) hanging around.

It was three days later that Sarah knocked at the door of the cottage behind the garden at Quinta Louisa where Guillermo and Ana had moved. She heard quiet footsteps inside, and it occurred to her that she should have brought them a wedding present. Perhaps her negligence in acknowledging their marriage was a reason for her delay in making Ana's acquaintance, or perhaps it was her reluctance to admit that Guillermo could no longer be her private confidant.

Ana didn't smile or invite Sarah inside as she opened the door.

"Bueños tardes (Good afternoon). *I am Sarah Rutledge. I wanted to meet you and . . . welcome you. Do you prefer Spanish or English? I know you are a bi-lingual teacher."* Sarah had initiated the conversation in Spanish.

"Could we continue in Spanish, if it is all right with you. I am more comfortable speaking Spanish, and your Spanish is perfect. Would you like to come in?"

"Gracias."

Ana was petite and pretty in a plain sort of way. Her features were well shaped and symmetrical, although none of them reflected a beauty that would inspire awe. Ana and Guillermo must have been about the same height. For the first time Sarah realized that she was several inches taller than Guillermo, and as she tucked nervously at her straw-colored hair, she thought how Ana's fine, shinny hair was exactly like Guillermo's. Sarah sighed. Was it inevitable that she was always taller than the men she liked?

"Please seat yourself."

"You teach in the village school."

"Yes, Doña Sarah."

"I've almost scalped Guillermo a dozen times for doña-ing me. You must not start, if we are going to be friends."

For the first time Ana smiled. *"I would like to be your friend."*

"I am very happy for you and Guillermo. Guillermo was one of my closest friends growing up . . . before I left for the university. I wanted to give a big party for your wedding, but after the earthquake . . ."

"Everything changed."

"I could still give a party for you."

Ana shook her head and frowned. *"No, Sarah. Everything is different now. We must accept that nothing is as it was before. Your father has been very good to us. He has helped us very much."*

"Not as much as Guillermo and his parents have helped us. I had to go away in order to understand just how much . . ."

"We help one another. That is what is important."

Sarah felt they were both embarrassed and trying too hard to be gracious to one another. She wanted to change the subject. *"I am thinking of teaching when I graduate next spring. I cannot decide whether to teach in the United States or here in Nicaragua. How do you find teaching in the village?"*

"Difficult. Very, very difficult. Most of the students are not interested in learning, and I have children of all different levels and abilities in the same classroom. With a degree from an American university you could teach at the American School, where you studied. That would be all right."

"You know where I attended school in Managua?"

"I know a lot about you. Guillermo has often spoken of you." Ana smiled

faintly again, shyly lifting her lips, probably as broadly as she ever smiled.

Sarah was struck by Ana's candor and honesty. *"I think we shall be great friends."* She believed her words and intended them as a promise, but she thought that she and Ana would never share the same kind of friendship that she had enjoyed with Guillermo. There would always be a wariness, a shadow of suspicion between them perhaps because they had met more nearly as equals while Sarah and Guillermo had struggled to find equality over many years and across the ravine of the caste and class that separated them. Sarah thought about the people she loved and trusted—her father, Aunt Beth, Don Martín, Doña Beatriz, Father Richard, and Guillermo. Only Guillermo was her contemporary, her own age. *"Oh, and Carlos Vargas Allen, from long ago,"* she thought. *"Whatever became of him, wherever he may be?"* She wondered if she and Carlos would ever meet again, whether they would have the same kind of understanding and confidence in one another that they had enjoyed as teenagers.

THE FALL SEMESTER AT Elon was both the happiest and the most anxious of Sarah's college years. She greatly enjoyed her courses. She found it easier to talk with other students, at least as casual friends, than during her first three years. At the same time she began to obsess about what she would do once she finished college.

Sarah spent the Thanksgiving holiday of her senior year on the family farm with her Uncle Walter and Aunt Beth, as she'd done every year during college. She laughed more often and more easily with her cousins than she did with any of her acquaintances and casual friends at Elon. She felt more relaxed at the farm than at the college, perhaps more relaxed than anywhere else in the world except at Quinta Louisa and really even more than on the *finca* since the earthquake.

As she'd done for the previous three Thanksgiving eves Sarah slept for almost ten hours—her longest slumber of the entire year—beneath the quilt that she'd been told was pieced together by her great-grandmother, in the wrought iron bedstead with flaking white paint; but even beneath her pleasant dreams and mingled with the delicious aromas that awakened her on Thanksgiving morning, she felt the anticipation of Friday, when her cousins would depart and she'd walk through the woods with her aunt. Since the summer she'd felt compelled to decide what she would do after she graduated from college. Almost all college students in the November of their senior year fretted about what they would do and where they would work. Only a few had jobs already lined up. Sarah knew she would teach languages, English and Spanish; but for her the decision was where, in Nicaragua or in the United States.

The pine needles cushioned their feet as Sarah and Beth walked through the trees the Friday after Thanksgiving. The weather was balmy and moist after the rain—Thanksgiving could be either hot or cold in North Carolina, and on the previous three years dry frozen leaves had crunched beneath their footfalls like crinkled paper.

"I really feel at home here on the farm. You've really made me part of the family. Roger and Lucinda seem like my brother and sister, and the boys really are like my nephews." Sarah stopped short of saying her Aunt Beth and Uncle Walter were like a mother and father to her, however close and comfortable she felt with Aunt Beth.

"You are family, honey. You always have been, since the day you were born. You just had to come and live up here with us for a while to find it out."

"I know. I'm glad. I'm so grateful, but . . ."

"What's eatin' at you, honey? What're you chewing over?"

Sarah laughed. "Left-over turkey and dressing, I think. I ate more for lunch today than I did for Thanksgiving dinner. I believe I love your turkey and dressing better than anything in the world, except for *nacatamales*." Sarah's laughter turned to tears and a quavering voice. "How do you always know what I'm thinking? You can read my mind."

"No, I can't. I can't do that. I don't have any idea what you're thinking, but I can tell when you're troubled."

Sarah laughed again. "It's choosing between turkey and dressing or *nacatamales*. I know I'm going to teach school somewhere after I graduate, but where? In Nicaragua or North Carolina? I don't think I could deal with the village school. I talked with Guillermo's wife about that last summer. I think I could get a job at the American School with Daddy's influence and his connections. I think I could find a position somewhere in North Carolina—I've done right well academically at Elon—so I could always get to the farm for Thanksgiving." Sarah laughed again, but her voice cracked and quavered. "Where am I going to spend the rest of my life, Aunt Beth?"

"You don't have to decide about the rest of your life right now. That's way too much. A long time off. All you've got to decide is what you'll do next year."

Impulsively, Sarah hugged Beth—Beth had usually initiated their hugs in the past. "Okay, what am I supposed to do next year?"

Beth was silent for a long time, as they continued walking toward the creek. "That's your decision, honey. I can't decide for you. What do you feel's right?"

"I don't know. I miss seeing Daddy more than two or three times a year, but I also feel I'll never really grow up if I live with him at Quinta Louisa, and I couldn't live anywhere else. When I was a little girl I promised myself I would help Nicaragua . . . give something back; but it's such a mess down there now and getting worse from all reports. I'm not sure I have anything to offer."

"What do you want for yourself?"

"I really don't know, Aunt Beth. I feel like I belong in two places—both of them are my homes."

"I know I said it's your decision, but my opinion is you should find a school up here for a year or two and then re-evaluate. It doesn't have to be forever."

"That's pretty much the way I'm leaning. The way things are in Nicaragua now, I think I'd be better off teaching in the States." But Sarah did not say what else she was thinking: that if she stayed for another year or two in the United States it might be forever. She would never return to Nicaragua except as a visitor, but would she ever be anything more than a *permanent visitor* in the United States, as her grandmother had allegedly called herself with regard to Nicaragua? Was having her heart divided between two homes anything different from having no home at all?

Sarah returned to Nicaragua for her first Christmas holiday at Quinta Louisa since the year of the earthquake—her father had joined her at the farm of his wife's family on the two previous Christmases. Her familiar world seemed to have shrunk to Quinta Louisa. Although George and Sarah Rutledge made several excursions to Masaya and the outskirts of the ruins of Managua, everything was different, as her father had written that it would be before her summer visit; but during the Christmas holidays everything seemed even more greatly changed. Sarah wondered if perhaps it were she who had changed and already left Nicaragua emotionally as she moved closer and closer to accepting a teaching position in the United States.

When Sarah and her father attended the Christmas Eve service at St. Francis, she felt at home once again; but most of the expatriate English-speaking members were strangers—the embassies and international companies had replaced the officers and families that had fled after the earthquake with new personnel. Sarah was able to chat for a few minutes with Father Richard at the reception following the service; but people kept interrupting them, so that she could never say anything confidentially to him; and Father Richard left to visit his family in the United States the day after Christmas. She never had the opportunity to engage in the kind of discerning conversation that might have offered her counsel and guidance about her vocational decisions.

Sarah was able to spend almost a whole day with Beatriz and Armando Chulteco in their cheerful little home in Los Robles. Although Armando relied more heavily on his cane with slower arthritic movement, he seemed his old self, joking and smiling and teasing Sarah. She lingered so that she could have a confidential talk with Doña Beatriz and began to wonder if Don Armando would ever give them any privacy. At last, just as Sarah was thinking about driving back to Quinta Louisa—her father had relented for the first time in her life by allowing her to drive by herself into the city—Don Armando left the house for his customary daily stroll through the neighborhood.

"¡Al fin! (At last!) Sarita, I thought we would never get him out of the house. Now we can talk cara a cara (face to face)."

"How are you, really, Doña Beatriz? How is it to be back? Are you happy?"

"Armando's happy, so I'm happy. *Claro* (To be sure), it's not the same. A lot of the world around us is gone, destroyed; but there are some good things left, even some new things."

"Such as?"

Beatriz laughed and jangled her bracelets and tugged at her earrings and spoke in her little girl voice. "The *supermercado* (supermarket). *Hay (there are)* more imported things now without as much *aduana* (tax)." She giggled.

"What about the political situation? You're the only one who will ever tell me the truth about that."

"Bad. Very bad, and getting worse all the time. The Sandinistas are fighting up in the mountains in the north. They're gaining ground. Who knows what will happen if they take over. It could be worse than Somoza. Did you ever think you'd hear me say that?"

"That bad? Really?"

"Weren't you a friend of the Vargas Allen boy? Nancy Allen de Vargas's son"?"

"Carlos! Yes, a good friend."

"The gossip is that his father is with Carlos Fonseca up in the mountains. I think Nancy and Carlos are in the States now. Are you still in touch with him?"

"No, I tried . . ."

"It's all very bad. *Pues* (well), what are your plans for . . . after you graduate?"

"That's what I wanted to talk about with you. I need to decide whether to stay in the States a while or come back . . ." she almost said *home* but couldn't bring herself to prevaricate ". . . to Nicaragua."

Beatriz was uncharacteristically silent for a moment. She usually responded immediately and assuredly, even when she was totally ignorant of the implications. "Stay, Sarita. Stay for the present. *Quizas* (perhaps) someday you can come back, come home, when things are different. ¡*Ojalá! Quizás.* (If only! Perhaps.*)*"

"I hate to leave Daddy alone down here."

"Sarita, George looks better than I've seen him since our *querida (dear)* Mary passed away. He has that new coffee-processing factory running, and it seems to be making lots of money. He looks ten years younger. He even pulls Armando's leg, as you *norteamericanos* (North Americans) say, and laughs at his jokes like the old days. Don't worry about George. We'll take care of him."

DOÑA BEATRIZ'S WORDS WERE affirmed by Sarah's observation of her father and Don Martín. They had settled into a relationship more like companions than master and servant. Sarah began referring to them as "the odd couple"—two grumpy old men who cajoled and corrected each other like schoolboys. "*Like the college roommate I never had,*" Sarah thought. Martín fretted when George came home late from the coffee-processing plant; and Sarah was aghast to witness her father dusting the parlor, because he believed that Martín wasn't able to see well enough to erase all the streaks on the wood as he complained about Martín with every swipe.

When Sarah came into the parlor from her bedroom three days before she was scheduled to return to North Carolina, she saw her father and Don Martín bouncing and almost dancing together around the room.

"*Great news!*" George Rutledge did look at least ten years younger than he had a year ago—Doña Beatriz was right. "*Guillermo and Ana are having a baby. It will be a little girl. They just told us. At last Don Martín will have a precious little girl running around his house for the first time.*"

"*Another precious little girl.*" Martín smiled and bowed toward Sarah.

The news prompted Sarah to go to Masaya—again her father allowed her to drive the car by herself—in order to buy baby gifts. She purchased a half-dozen baby dresses with the lovely embroidery in the uniquely Nicaragua styles. Then impulsively she bought a baby bracelet, made from the rose-colored gold that came from Nicaragua's Bonanza mine.

On the afternoon two days before she was to leave, Sarah knocked at the door of Guillermo and Ana's house beyond the garden. Sarah knew that she had been overly extravagant, but she hadn't given them a proper wedding gift and wanted to compensate. Ana's usually placid face rarely showed emotion, like the habitual stoic expression of Sarah's mother; but now it melted with pleasure and gratitude as she opened the gifts.

As Sarah was leaving Guillermo offered to walk her back to her door, a suggestion that Sarah found peculiar. When they reached the bench in the middle of the garden, Guillermo asked her if they could talk; and so they sat down in their usual place for meeting.

"*Doña Sarah . . .*"

"*¡Caramba! Guillermo, shit!*"

Guillermo laughed. "*Sorry.*" He'd been teasing her deliberately. "*But I wanted to talk with you, seriously. I am worried about Pablo. He is not attending classes regularly, and Don Jorge has threatened to stop paying his tuition. He is going to be home tomorrow. Could you talk to him and then maybe talk to Don Jorge?*"

"*I have not seen Pablo in ages. Years. I do not know what I could say to him. How old is he now, fifteen?*"

"*Sixteen. I am very worried about him, Sarah. I don't know what to do. Anything you say to him, anything you learn from him might help me understand . . .*"

"*Of course I will try, for your sake; and of course I will speak with my father about his tuition.*"

"*He can meet you here in the garden. At what time?*"

"*About eleven o'clock. I am going to be packing tomorrow for leaving.*"

"*Perfect.*" Guillermo reached over and took Sarah's hand in both of his hands and brought it to his chest. It was a gesture Sarah could never have predicted, and it surprised her and pleased her more than she would ever have imagined.

"*My true brother.*"

Guillermo looked down and spoke softly as if he might weep, but his eyes remained dry. "*My beloved sister.*" They rose and went back to the doors of their homes in opposite directions. They didn't embrace as they'd often done after intimate conversations in the garden in the past, not even with the accepted Nicaraguan custom of a quick, traditional *abrazo*.

SARAH WAS WATCHING FROM inside the French doors to the patio to see whether Pablo would actually come to meet her. At precisely eleven o'clock he strode into the garden, lifting his feet high, almost like a soldier marching, and swinging his hips like a pubescent rock star. He was by far the most handsome of Flora and Martín's sons. His fine features and perfect olive skin would have made him the ideal model for an Italian renaissance artist. He had obviously been working out—the muscles of his chest and arms and legs sculpted the fabric of his tight t-shirt and blue jeans. As Sarah approached him she noticed his expensive boots and wondered where he got money for his designer clothes.

"*Buenos días* (Good day), Pablo."

"Good morning, Miss Rutledge. How are you today?"

"I'm very well. Do you prefer to speak in English rather than Spanish?"

"It is good practice to talk in English. I talk Spanish with people of my own country."

Sarah decided to let the allusion to her as a foreigner pass without comment and came straight to the point. "Guillermo told me that you are not attending classes, and my father may cut off payments for your tuition."

"I am not wanting to go to *Instituto Téchnico* (Technical School). I am wanting to go to university, but your father not will pay."

"My father told me your grades were not good enough to be admitted to the university."

"If he pay, I could be admit."

Sarah paused, and Pablo glanced at her as if he were in charge of questioning her. "What do you want for the future, Pablo? How do you see your life ten years from now?"

"I want what belong to me. I want my share of my country as a man of Nicaragua, *un hombre verdadero* (a true man)." Pablo stared at Sarah. She was as much attracted by his beauty as she was repelled by his audacity.

"I see. I'll talk with my father. If your grades are good enough, I promise you that we'll find the funds to pay for your university tuition when you're old enough. But in the meantime you must go to class and make good grades at the *colegio* (secondary school) or else it's no deal. Do you understand?"

"No deal. I understand." Pablo waved his hands parallel to the ground and rose to leave. Sarah expected him to express gratitude with the florid phrases that Doña Flora had drilled into him, but he didn't even say "*gracias*". He said only, "*adios,*" at last breaking into Spanish.

George Rutledge was mellower and more compliant to Sarah's advice than he'd been four years earlier when he began paying Pablo's tuition after he'd graduated from the village school. He agreed to continue paying Pablo's tuition at the *colegio* (secondary school) unless he was expelled and even pledged to pay Pablo's tuition for the university, if he should be admitted and maintain a passing grade. "Although that's not a likely scenario," George muttered.

Late that afternoon Sarah knocked at the door of Guillermo's house. She hoped that Guillermo would have arrived home after his work at the coffee-processing plant and that Pablo would have returned to the city. Both of her hopes were granted, but she wondered if the bargain she had struck was a pact with the devil as she related to Guillermo the conditions of her negotiation. Guillermo expressed his thanks with the florid, elegant phrases that Pablo had spurned, but Sarah could read in Guillermo's face his doubt that there would be a happy outcome despite all their efforts.

IN SPITE OF THE references that Mary Rutledge had made to the "Negroes" she'd known growing up and the occasional slips of tongue she'd made calling the *costeño* members of St. Francis "Negroes"—much to her husband's chagrin—Sarah found it difficult to understand race relations in the United States. She didn't feel an emotional connection to the Civil Rights Movement. In Nicaragua people were divided into the rich and the poor, skin color didn't seem to matter.

Occasionally Sarah would deliberately choose to sit with the black students at Elon that always gathered together at a table in the cafeteria with two or three white student leaders of integration efforts at the college. Sarah was drawn to them because they seemed to be aliens in the student body, as she was, but she found the white student civil rights leaders even more unfathomable than the black students. They would often talk about race relations as if they were experts, while the black students maintained a respectful silence, occasionally raising their eyebrows incredulously. Sarah would ask the black students questions about how they felt as a minority at Elon and what it had been like when schools and public facilities were segregated, but their responses were tense and cautious, and she rarely gained much insight into their lives or their pasts.

THE FOLLOWING YEAR, AFTER she'd graduated from Elon, Sarah accepted a position teaching Spanish and English at a public high school in Greensboro, perhaps in part because she was still trying to understand the relationships of black and white people in North Carolina. The public schools in Greensboro had been integrated in 1971, just five years before Sarah began teaching. Her students, especially those in her Spanish classes, were eager to hear about her life in Nicaragua. She was drawn to her black students, especially the few who took her Spanish classes. As she came to know them and they came to know her, they became comfortable with one another. Gladys, a bright black girl, was unusually inquisitive.

"How'd it feel, Miss Rutledge, to be a foreigner in a Spanish-speaking country, to be part of a minority group?"

"I never felt like a foreigner. I was born in Nicaragua. My father had been born there, and my grandfather, too."

"Did y'all speak Spanish at home?"

"No, we spoke English most of the time." Sarah refrained from saying *except with the servants and workers.* "But we often spoke Spanish."

"Especially with Don Martín's family, with Guillermo and Carlos Vargas and Carmen and sometimes with Doña Beatriz," Sarah thought.

"Could you go anywhere you wanted to and get in and do things?"

"Yes." Sarah decided to be honest and say what she was really thinking. "In fact, sometimes we could go to places where lots of Nicaraguans couldn't go—private clubs and hotels and private parties and things like that."

"Just the opposite of the way it was for us, I guess."

Sarah's mouth gaped open in stunned silence. "Thank you, Gladys. Yes. Just the opposite. That's the first time I've been able to understand, I mean, how it must have felt to you."

Although Sarah had occasionally met Aunt Beth and Uncle Walter at the Presbyterian Church in Burlington and then joined them for Sunday lunch while she'd been a student at Elon, she'd more often attended the Episcopal Church of the Holy Comforter, on the occasional Sundays when she'd gone to church as a student. For several weeks after she began teaching she drove back to Burlington for church services on Sundays; but one Sunday she decided to worship at St. Francis, in part out of nostalgia, because of the name. It was a parish of over a thousand members, utterly different from her St. Francis in Managua; but on that Sunday the new curate, Brian Hayes, was introduced. He'd just graduated from seminary. He was blonde and blue-eyed and *tall*. Brian reminded her of the son of the British diplomat who had been a member of Father Richard's youth group in Managua. She felt the same fluttering excitement she'd experienced when she'd first seen the English boy more than a decade ago. By chance, or Sarah wondered if perchance by fate, they found themselves engaged in a long conversation during the coffee hour after the service when he discovered that she was a newcomer attending St. Francis for the first time on his own first Sunday there. Brian seemed fascinated to learn that she'd grown up in Nicaragua.

"I wonder if you'd like to have coffee or dinner, if you're free sometime . . . I mean, if you aren't engaged or with a seriously jealous boyfriend." Brian laughed.

Sarah felt herself blush deeply. She'd had fewer than a dozen dates during her entire four years at Elon, and she'd been taller than most of the men with whom she'd gone out. No one had ever asked her out when they'd first met. "I'd love to. I have no boyfriend, serious or otherwise."

"Wonderful! Nor do I. I mean, no girlfriend, serious or otherwise." Brian laughed again, and Sarah fell immediately and unequivocally in love with him.

BRIAN AND SARAH CONTINUED to meet for lunch or dinner throughout the autumn. When Brian asked her to go with him to a movie and later to a concert, Sarah convinced herself that they were dating. She liked him better than any of the "boys" she'd dated in college—she thought of Brian as a "real man"—and she rhapsodized about a deepening romantic relationship with him. She thought he refrained from intimate physical contact because he was a clergyman and was scrupulously moral rather than that he wasn't attracted to her. She hoped he wasn't being polite like the English boy in her high school youth group in Managua whom he greatly resembled.

When Sarah was honest with herself she admitted that Brian's passion focused more on his desire to lead a mission team to Central American than to engage in an *affaire de coeur* with her. As he talked about how she might help him arrange for a mission project in Nicaragua he waved his hands like a revival preacher (and not at all how he folded them sedately atop the pulpit when he actually preached at St. Francis.) Sarah promised him that she would explore various possibilities with Father Richard while she was in Nicaragua for Christmas.

ALTHOUGH SARAH ALWAYS VISITED Father Richard on her trips to Nicaragua, she saw him less often than in the past, usually only once during her stay in the country; and their conversations were increasingly brief, more perfunctory than the heart-felt confidences she'd shared during the first years after her mother's death. They now met in his office beside the chancel inside the church, rather than in the vicarage, as if Father Richard, like Brian, feared some temptation or scandalous gossip from being alone with a young woman.

As Sarah opened the door of Father Richard's office, she saw him inserting the little plastic tab into his clerical shirt that gave it the appearance of a cassock, as if he were formalizing their meeting into an encounter between priest and parishioner, rather than a meeting of old friends; but after the customary greetings and inquiries about health and well-being, Sarah found herself once again confiding her deepest thoughts and desires in the old familiar way.

"I think I'm falling in love. I'm more serious than I've been about anyone since I left Nicaragua . . . or ever."

"How grand! Is he another teacher?"

"No. He's a priest."

"My poor child! Couldn't you have done better than that? Found a real man?" Father Richard feigned appalled horror. "Episcopal, I trust."

"Of course. I wouldn't consider any other kind." They laughed together easily and freely as they'd often done when Sarah was a teenager and made some embarrassing revelation. Then they were quiet for a while before she continued, "His name is Brian Hayes. He's the Curate at St. Francis in Greensboro, where I started going because it's named St. Francis, although it's nothing like our St. Francis here. Brian really, really wants to bring a mission team to Nicaragua."

"And I hope that's not the only reason he's interested in me," Sarah thought, although she couldn't say that, even to Father Richard.

"How can I be of help?"

"I promised him I'd pick your brain for a project. Any thoughts?"

Father Richard glanced out the window and raised his eyebrows and rather self-consciously scratched his head. "The needs are enormous, especially since the earthquake. What does Brian have in mind? A medical team? And we also have a continuing need for water purification projects, especially in the rural villages, if he can assemble people with that kind of expertise."

"I think he'd like to bring a high school group, with some adult chaperones, of course."

"Ah, a construction project. I do have some concerns about taking jobs away from what local laborers can do better; and it costs three or four times more than what our locals would be paid, when you count the airfare and appropriate lodging and food and . . . if they'd only send us the money, we could do it for a fraction . . . but it does create advocates, especially with young people. They may become life-long supporters of mission. So, I suppose it's still worthwhile in the long run."

"Do you have any suggestions about what they might do, where they might work?"

Father Richard rubbed his forefinger back and forth across his lips as if pondering, although Sarah thought he was probably only delaying his immediate response for effect. "Why don't you look in your own neighborhood, close to Quinta Louisa? George has done some remarkable things in the village. We've started a clinic at the school about once a month—just basic health care and non-prescription medication and birth control for the women—don't dare let the Romans hear about that!" Father Richard again rubbed his lips, this time more obviously for dramatic effect at his ironic quip. "We need a place to store supplies and use for an office. A little cinder block building. Teenagers do very well constructing little cinder block buildings. They love it. They can see what they've accomplished at the end of the week, which is more than I can say about what I do most of the time." Now Father Richard looked morose, and Sarah knew his expression was not for effect.

"That's a wonderful idea! They could probably sleep in the quarters for the seasonal coffee pickers." Sarah could feel her enthusiasm rising almost to the level of Brian's excitement about a mission team.

"And you could supply auxiliary support from Quinta Louisa, for food and potable water and hygienic concerns. That's a very important consideration especially when you're dealing with teenagers."

"That's perfect! And maybe Brian could stay at Quinta Louisa or at least swap out with the other chaperones, so the adults could get a good night's sleep every other day or so."

Everything began to take shape in Sarah's mind, and before she left she confided her ultimate fantasy to Father Richard. "I've dreamed about how wonderful it would be if Brian decided to serve the church in Nicaragua. Perhaps he could even follow you at St. Francis, and we could live at Quinta Louisa. I mean many, many years from now after you retire." Sarah felt the rush of a blush on her cheeks even hotter, and she was sure, redder than when she'd first met Brian. She was afraid that she'd offended Father Richard by alluding to his age and retirement and doubly embarrassed at making the presumption of a marriage with Brian.

"Not so many years off, my dear Sarah. I'm seriously thinking about returning to the States for my final years in a parish. That's in the very strictest confidence. Age and infirmity are taking their toll. Since the earthquake it's been very ... Of course Brian would have to hear the call from above." Father Richard pointed toward the ceiling and lifted his eyes in an expression of simulated prayer, like the maudlin paintings of saints that adorned the walls of Roman Catholic churches in Nicaraguan villages.

"It's just a romantic notion. Brian and I aren't that serious, and I hope you'll be here many, many, many more years."

"In the meantime, my dear, let's promise to keep each other's fantasies to ourselves. Agreed?"

"*Claro que sí* (Yes, of course)."

"Oh, I meant to ask you if you'd heard about the death of Carlos Vargas's father? I remember you were close friends in high school."

"No! What happened?"

"He was killed just a little over a month ago with Carlos Fonseca up north in the mountains. A small Sandinista group was engaging in some guerilla activities, so they say. Things are becoming more dangerous even here in the Managua area. You'll have to take certain precautions to protect your mission team even ..."

Father Richard went on talking about the security measures that would be needed for a mission team, but Sarah did not comprehend what he was saying. All she could think about was Carlos. "*Poor Carlos! My beloved Carlos!*"

SARAH FLEW DOWN WITH the mission team the third week of June. Of the five boys and five girls, six were students from Sarah's school; four of them had taken her classes, including one black teenage boy who had been in one of her English classes. In addition to Sarah and Brian a young couple named Jerry and Norma accompanied them. They were the parish's youth advisors. Brian had probably asked them to be involved with the youth group because they were employed by a construction business. Jerry often supervised erecting small buildings, most often tool sheds in people's back yards in Greensboro. Sometimes Sarah wondered if Brian's enthusiasm about the mission trip was inspired by his devotion to the youth group or the youth group was mostly a means to enable his obsession about initiating a mission project.

Dozens of letters were exchanged between Sarah and Father Richard and her father as they planned the details of the project. Brian had suggested involving the youth group from St. Francis in Managua with the youth group from St. Francis in Greensboro during the ten days of construction; but Father Richard had discouraged the two groups working together. As Sarah recalled the passion that Father Richard had felt for organizing the parish youth group in Managua years ago, she was surprised by his negative opinion until she read further comments in his letter. "If the youth group from North Carolina only sees young people like themselves for two weeks, they won't gain much insight into Nicaragua. To be sure, it would be nice to have a shared social outing—perhaps to Pocho Mil or Jíloa. What would you think about your father involving some of the young people from the village, maybe some of the coffee factory workers' children in the day-to-day work?"

GEORGE RUTLEDGE HAD ARRANGED for the foundation of the building to be poured before the team arrived; and he and Father Richard had assembled most of the materials that would be needed for construction, paid for with money Brian had raised and sent ahead of the team's arrival. Father Richard had written Sarah that he'd seen too many mission teams spend their whole first week just assembling supplies and sitting around bored and helpless. "It's discouraging for any mission project but especially for teenagers," he'd written to Sarah.

The first several days the boys mixed concrete and toted cinder blocks and buckets of cement to Jerry and the local mason that had been employed to erect the walls. The girls painted the school and played with the younger children in the village. About a half dozen youngsters from the village worked with the team from North Carolina, often a different group every day. Most of them were several years younger or a few years older than the North Carolina teenagers, grade school age children or villagers in their twenties. Sarah was amazed how well they all communicated without speaking each other's language—she was the officially designated translator, but she was rarely summoned for interpretation.

One afternoon George Rutledge visited the village in order to see the progress in erecting the clinic's supply shed. "I see César has found himself a friend."

Sarah had noticed one of the younger boys from the village who came every day and stayed close to Henry, the black teenager from North Carolina, although Henry seemed annoyed at how the boy followed him everywhere and made hand motions to shoo him away with obvious frustration at not being able to express his displeasure verbally.

"You know that *muchacho* (boy)?" Sarah was aware that her father knew the names of all the adults in the village but could rarely recall who the children were or even to whom they belonged. She would often remind him of their names and parents and was surprised that he remembered one that she didn't know.

"That's César, Blanca's son. Don't you remember? Your mother picked him up off the street during the attempted coup of sixty-seven, ten years ago, and then insisted on moving the family to the village and insisted on giving his mother a job at the factory. Mary probably saved his life. One of the many things she did that I resisted. God bless her! He's a fine looking boy. Don't you remember?"

"I remember very well. So that's little César. He's grown so much! Don't chastise yourself, Daddy. You've carried on Mother's legacy very well. She was a good influence on both of us."

"Mary thought with her heart first and let the chips fall where they may, which they very often did. It's still hard for me." George shrugged, and Sarah circled her hand around his waist and put her head on his shoulder.

Sarah admired how Brian worked with the boys matching them in carrying bucket for bucket of concrete and hod for hod of bricks. At night Brian read passages from the Acts of the Apostles and gave devotions that drew parallels between the missionary adventure of the Apostle Paul and their experiences in Nicaragua. Sarah cringed at some of his references to how primitive and poor and ignorant the natives were. Some of the young people squirmed as he spoke, not quite sure why they were uncomfortable but perhaps sensing that the experiences they'd shared with the village children as equals didn't fit with his unintentionally condescending remarks. Even so, Sarah was delighted at the joy and love that radiated from Brian's face.

The health issues during the first week were minor, insect bites and sunburns and a few queasy stomachs. The St. Francis Managua youth group hosted the St. Francis North Carolina youth group at an outing to the beach at Pocho Mil on Saturday. The North Carolina teenagers were blissfully happy, almost ecstatic, after their hard week of labor. Boys and girls flirted with one another both within each group and between members of the two groups. Sarah was disappointed that none of the village children were present. Perhaps no one had thought of inviting them. As Sarah remembered huddling with Carlos Vargas in the *cabaña* after the thunderstorm years ago, she felt a pang of guilt at not being able to contact him in order to express her sympathy for the death of his father a few months ago. She'd made numerous, if sporadic, efforts to reach him, all of them futile.

The teenagers from North Carolina were more involved and attentive during the service at St. Francis on Sunday than they'd ever been in their own parish in North Carolina, according to Brian. But on Wednesday morning of the second week, shortly before Noon, a crisis came to the adults' attention, although the teenagers had been aware that it had been brewing for several days. Jerry's young wife, Norma, came to Sarah asking for her counsel and advice.

"Sarah, I need to talk with you about Henry."

"Is he sick? I didn't see him this morning."

"Well, sort of. Maybe. He's at the bunkhouse. He won't talk to anyone. He just lays on his cot and sleeps or reads one of his books. He says he isn't sick, doesn't need anything."

"Have you talked to Brian?"

"I wanted to talk to you first. I think he's catatonic. I think it's some kind of very severe culture shock." Norma had taken several classes in psychology before she'd dropped out of a community college to work as the secretary for the small construction firm where her husband was a foreman.

"Would you like for me to try to talk with him?"

"Would you? Please. You know what could be done for him down here or whether we need to get him on a plane back home. I hate to bother Brian about all this. I think this project is the most important thing in his life."

"I'm beginning to think you're right . . . about Brian, I mean. He'll have to make the final decision though. He's in charge. But I'll walk over and see what's going on with Henry. Would you like to come along with me?"

Henry was one of Sarah's favorite students. Perhaps she was drawn to him because he was black and reminded her of the *costeño* members of St. Francis. She held him in special affection as the only black student on the mission team. She'd thought he would fit in well and help the other team members identify with the darker skinned Nicaraguan children in the village.

It took them about a quarter of an hour to walk down the dusty road from the village. It would have taken them another half hour to continue on the road to the coffee fields, but Sarah led Norma through the forest. They hadn't allowed the students to take this shortcut for fear they would get lost. "This sure is pretty. I've never been in the jungle till now."

Sarah smiled. "It's one of my favorite spots. I don't share it with just anyone."

They found Henry curled up on his *tijera* (folding cot) reading a book.

"Henry?" He looked up at Sarah but didn't speak. "Are you sick?" He shook his head from side to side. "Are you all right?" He nodded but still didn't speak. "What's the matter?"

Henry looked back down at his book, as if he hadn't heard Sarah's final question. She didn't repeat it. She and Norma sat down on one of the other *tijeras* and were silent, although Norma glanced back and forth from Henry to Sarah with a worried frown. Finally, Henry said, "I want to go home."

Sarah didn't respond immediately, and Norma looked at them with increasingly anguished concern.

"I know what it feels like to be in a strange country and wonder if you'll ever get home again." Sarah paused once more, and Henry looked up at her with tears streaming down his dark cheeks. "The team will be flying back to North Carolina on Saturday. I don't think you should go back by yourself before then. I'll talk with Brian. You won't have to work in the village the last couple of days, if you don't want to. You can stay here and read. You've done a good job and made a real contribution to the project. It's all right."

As soon as Sarah told Brian about Henry, he returned with her to the bunkhouse. Brian tried to reason with Henry and cajole him into returning to the village. He talked about the importance of the project and tried to use guilt and incentives and shame to persuade Henry to go back with them. He talked and talked, and Sarah just wanted him to shut up. She knew how Henry felt. Although she had kept on going to classes and working and teaching, Henry seemed to manifest outwardly how she'd often felt inwardly for the last five years in North Carolina. Finally, she stood and walked over to Brian and put her hand on his shoulder. "I think it's better to let him stay here until he feels better. He can decide if he wants to come back to the village later. I told him he wouldn't have to work there the next couple of days unless he wanted to."

Brian looked up at Sarah. The expression of euphoric rapture that had adorned his countenance since he'd arrived in Nicaragua disappeared, never to return, as if the perfect world he'd conjured and created had been irreparably damaged, as if his Eden had been suddenly infected by original sin.

That evening as Sarah and Brian walked in the garden at Quinta Louisa after dinner, she said, "Henry will be all right. Everything will be all right."

"Thank you, Sarah, you really do understand." Brian wiped his eyes with his handkerchief. Then he kissed her and uttered the words for the first time that she had longed to hear. "I love you Sarah."

"I love you, too, Brian, very, very much."

THE FOLLOWING CHRISTMAS SARAH made her usual rounds of visits to Don Armando and Doña Beatriz and Father Richard, although she stayed at Quinta Louisa most of the time and didn't even go to Masaya shopping. Quinta Louisa was the only place in Nicaragua where she felt comfortable now.

Any telephone call from Nicaragua sent a chill of terror through Sarah. She always assumed it would be bad news, a death or a critical illness. She was relieved to hear her father's voice, and she knew if he were ill he would write her a long letter, not call her on the telephone.

His first words were predictable. "Sarah, I have some bad news."

"What's happened, Daddy?"

"Don Armando died this morning."

"Oh, Daddy! How awful! What happened?"

"A stroke. A cerebral hemorrhage. It was quite sudden. Very unexpected, although his general health has been compromised for some time, as you know. He didn't take care of himself very well." It was unusual for George Rutledge to babble with incomplete sentences. Sarah was aware that his awkward words were covering his emotions. This news so soon after visiting the Chultecos in December seemed almost surreal to Sarah, as if the people she loved in Nicaragua could not be changed or lost without her being present there.

"I'm so sorry. Shall I book a flight? It's going to be a little difficult for me to get away right before spring break, but I'm sure I can arrange . . ."

"No, no. You couldn't get here for the funeral. Into the ground or out of the country in twenty-four hours, you know." George forced an affected chuckle, again futilely attempting to disguise his feelings.

"I'm so sorry, Daddy. I know he was your closest friend. It must be hard for Doña Beatriz . . . and for you. How's she holding up?"

"Beatriz is a rock, as always. I think she's been preparing herself for this . . . for a long time. Write her one of your heart-felt, beautiful letters. That will mean the most . . ."

"Please give her my love and sympathy."

"I will, most assuredly. It's ironic, isn't it, Armando dying so soon after Pedro Joaquín Chamorro. They were pals from childhood, you know. Both dedicated to the old traditions and ideals, both leaders in the conservative movement. I suppose you heard about Pedro Joaquín's assassination in January. I'm not sure if I wrote you."

"I read about it in the newspapers up here. It was well covered by the American press."

"His assassination's given a new life to the uprising. I wonder if Somoza will be able to hold on much longer. Things are heating up again. I'm not sure you ought to come down this summer."

"We'll talk about that later, Daddy."

"It's so good to hear your voice. I do miss talking with you, even though you're a wonderful correspondent." It was unusual for George Rutledge to prolong an overseas phone call, but he didn't want to relinquish the sound of his daughter's voice.

"Maybe you can come up here during spring break. You know how beautiful North Carolina is in April."

"I don't think so, Susi. I've got to keep things together down here."

"Are you going to be all right, Daddy? I know how close you and Don Armando were."

"I'll be fine. Don't you worry about me. But I will miss him. He was one of the few people I could talk to and say anything and everything to . . . Armando and you and Beatriz to some extent and Martín, but of course it's different with Martín."

"I'm glad Don Martín is with you."

"Yes. I'd better be going. This call is getting right pricy. Do write Doña Beatriz."

"I will, of course."

"I love you, Susi." It was unusual for her father to say he loved her. He more often hugged her and gave her a kiss on her cheek, but hugs and kisses were not possible between Nicaragua and the United States, and words were poor, inadequate substitutes.

DESPITE HER FATHER'S WARNING Sarah returned to Nicaragua for several weeks during her summer break. She stayed on the farm almost every day of her visit and rarely ventured out from Quinta Louisa, because of the dangers of being attacked during the uprising or even more likely of being caught in crossfire. After the first few days she noticed an increased security even at Quinta Louisa and in the village and especially at the coffee-processing plant. Her father and Don Martín had guns strategically placed both inside the house and on the patio, always close at hand to one or both of them. The most trusted villagers and workers had been armed and guarded the coffee-processing plant day and night.

"Are we safe here, Don Martín? Are we in danger of being attacked in the uprising even here at Quinta Louisa?" Sarah hesitated to ask her father for fear her questions would upset him too greatly. As she'd done since she was a little girl, she went to Don Martín to learn the truth about the things her parents would not reveal.

"We will protect you, Doña Sarah. We will not let anyone hurt you. I will take care of you." Don Martín's firm, definite response assured her and gave her a degree of comfort.

Although Don Martín was not yet sixty years old, his gait had slowed, his eyes were dimmer, and his movements were stiffer. Sarah thought Nicaraguan *campesinos* often appeared twenty years older than people of their age in the United States. Hard work and less medical attention and tropical diseases aged them prematurely. Her father, who was close to Don Martín's age, also seemed older than his chronological years, much older than he'd looked a couple of years ago when he'd first opened the new coffee-processing plant and had seemed to be rejuvenated, before the uprising had become intense.

SARAH'S DESIRE TO VISIT Doña Beatriz and express her condolences for Don Armando's death face to face had been one of the primary reasons that she'd adamantly insisted on coming to Nicaragua, and her visit with Doña Beatriz motivated her only trip into Managua. For the first time in her adult life she didn't protest her father's insistence on driving her. As usual he attended to some business in the city while she called on Doña Beatriz in Los Robles.

Although Beatriz accepted Sarah's expressions of condolence and sympathy and gratefully and tearfully received her hugs, she was more anxious to talk about the dangers of her present situation than about her bereavement. "We thought the Somozas were horrible, but who knows what will happen to the country if the Sandinistas win the war. They may take everything. I don't feel safe even here in my own home, Sarah. I'm scared. I'm terrified."

"I'm sure Daddy would be glad for you to stay with him at Quinta Louisa. He'd really enjoy your company, and you'd be safe there."

"*Carita (Dear little)* Sarah." Doña Beatriz brushed away the tears that now flowed freely. "George is living in a fool's paradise."

Doña Beatriz's words so disturbed Sarah that she hardly remembered the rest of their conversation and visit.

ALMOST EVERY AFTERNOON SARAH strolled across the garden to visit with Ana and little Emalina after Ana returned from school and before Guillermo came home from the plant. She grew increasingly fond of Ana and adored playing with the baby, who was now almost two years old and babbled away with an infant's creative Spanish words. Emalina held Sarah's finger in her little fists and talked and talked, as if she were relating a long story.

One afternoon a few days before Sarah was scheduled to fly back to North Carolina, she noticed the swelling on Ana's abdomen. She felt she now knew Ana well enough to ask an intimate question. *"Ana, are you pregnant?"*

Ana blushed deeply but smiled and nodded. *"The baby is due early in the new year. I wanted to tell you, but I thought Guillermo should talk with you first."*

"Why Guillermo? You are the mother, and you are my friend, too, now."

"Pues (Well), not about the baby. I mean partly because we are having another child, but for other reasons, too . . . we are thinking about moving back to the village. I do not feel safe walking back and forth to school with the dangers now, and Emalina is getting heavy for me to carry and with the new baby . . . I want to be closer to people."

"Will you encourage Don Martín to stay in the house with my father? I would feel more comfortable if Daddy had someone in the house with him."

"Of course, Sarah. Of course, I will."

The next day Guillermo talked with George Rutledge about moving back to the village. After Sarah's father and Martín discussed the situation, George assured her that Don Martín would remain in the servant's bedroom next to the kitchen of the main house at Quinta Louisa. "We're kind of company for each other in our old age. For the present we'll just close up the little house. We may use it as a guest house in the future, or move someone in, perhaps, if there . . . seems to be a good reason."

Sarah knew that the words her father was thinking, in between the stumbling words he actually spoke, referred to putting an armed worker in the cottage for further protection; but she felt a great measure of relief that Don Martín would stay in the main house with her father. She'd seen the rifles propped in the corners of both of their bedrooms, and she knew that they would protect each other with any measures that were necessary.

GEORGE RUTLEDGE FLEW TO North Carolina for a visit with Sarah the following Christmas, but Sarah did not return to Nicaragua in the summer. Her father insisted that he was safe at Quinta Louisa, although he never ventured into the city and would be reluctant even to drive to the airport to meet her. He told her that he must stay in the country to protect their property and would not be able to visit her even for a few days during the summer. Sarah worried about her father, but she could not force him to flee to the United States as most of the other expatriates that lived in Nicaragua were doing. She could only pray, and she felt some comfort by repeating Father Richard's frequent quotation from Dame Julian of Norwich, *"All will be well, and all manner of things will be well."*

Sarah continued to go out with Brian every week for dinner often followed by a movie or a concert. In recent weeks he'd begun to kiss her more passionately and hold her more closely; and when she felt aroused, she wanted to go further, even to "go all the way" as the boys at Elon had put it. Although she wished that he would initiate a more intimate physical relationship, at least that he would touch her breasts with his fingers, she was not just imagining now that they were dating seriously. She continued to tell herself that as a priest, he had an inordinately high moral standard related to sex, but she was not always convinced by her own arguments.

THE NEWS FROM NICARAGUA was increasingly distressing as the summer of 1979 proceeded. In July Tachito, Anastasio Somoza Debayle, fled the country. Two days later Comandante Zero, Eden Pastorá, led the FSLN troops into Managua, and the city fell to the Saninista forces. George Rutledge continued to assure Sarah through their weekly shortwave radio phone-patch calls that he was safe and Quinta Louisa and the *finca* were secure.

ON THE FIRST FRIDAY in August Brian took Sarah to a somewhat more formal restaurant than he usually chose, especially on an evening when they'd planned to go to a movie after dinner. They'd both missed seeing *Norma Rae* when it had first come out, and it was being shown at one of the second-screening, reduced-price theaters in Greensboro. They lingered a long time in ordering and eating their entrees, and Sarah became anxious that they would miss the first part of the film. She knew that her panicked feelings originated with her anxiety about Nicaragua and her father and were transferred to little annoyances in her immediate surroundings, but she began to be agitated by Brian's dilly-dallying.

"Shall we order dessert, Sarah?"

"There's not time. We may miss the beginning of the movie as it is."

"We have time. I'd like some. I'm told they have really good chocolate mousse here."

"Not for me. I really want to see *Norma Rae*. We've missed it all year."

"Come on. You know your sweet tooth won't let you rest if I have something chocolate."

"Brian, what's going on?"

"Just this." Brian took a small velvet-covered box out of his coat pocket and opened it.

Sarah noted that the diamond in the ring was not large but not small either. It was beautiful. "Brian!"

"Sarah, would you consider being the wife of a clergyman?"

"Brian!" Then Sarah blurted out the thoughts that she'd fantasized about for over two years since they first met but had never spoken aloud to anyone except for Father Richard. "I've always thought that I'd go back to Nicaragua and live there for the rest of my life. My father is there. My mother's buried there. Our family has lived there for four generations. Have you ever thought about serving the church in Nicaragua? I know how devoted you are to foreign mission work. I mean . . . has the idea of serving the church there ever occurred to you? Father Richard plans to retire soon. We could live at Quinta Louisa and you could serve St. Francis. I mean . . ."

"Wow! You've already made a lot of plans for our future. Are they conditions for marrying me?"

"No. I mean . . . I don't know. No, not conditions. It's all something I have to think about. I hadn't expected . . . I mean . . . What do you think?"

"Sarah, it's not safe in Nicaragua now. I don't think even your father can continue to stay there much longer. You've said as much yourself. Things could change in a few years, and then . . ."

"And if they change for the better, could you see yourself serving the church and living in Nicaragua?"

"Frankly, no. I could see our making long visits and mission trips and staying at Quinta Louisa as our headquarters. Maybe letting the Episcopal Church use it as a retreat or conference center after your father dies when we're not in the country, if that would be financially feasible. I love short term mission work, but spending my whole career on the mission field? Frankly, no. At least that's how I feel now. I might feel differently in a few years."

"I see you've given some thought to long-range plans, too."

"I suppose so. Would you consider marrying me if I never wanted to live in Nicaragua?"

"I don't know. I can't give you an answer now. I'll have to think about it for a while. I probably won't be able to give you an answer for several days, maybe for a few weeks, not tomorrow." Sarah gently closed the box that was still in Brian's hand. "I love you, Brian."

Brian handed the little box back to Sarah. "You keep it until you decide. Perhaps that will help you to give me the answer that I hope for."

In the days that followed, as Sarah alternately pondered her answer to Brian and her worry about her father, she realized that Brian had not said that he loved her that night and had never said he loved her even before that night, except for the one evening at Quinta Louisa during the mission trip the summer before last.

SARAH WAS PREPARING TO leave for the Spanish class that she was teaching at the summer school session when the telephone rang. As soon as she heard Father Richard's voice on the long distance call from Managua, she knew that something was terribly wrong.

"Sarah, I'm so sorry to call you with this news. I tried to reach your young priest friend, but I wasn't able . . ."

"What's wrong?"

"Sarah, I'm so sorry. Your father had a heart attack."

"Is it bad? How is he?"

"I'm so sorry to tell you like this on the telephone. I'm so sorry . . . Your father didn't make it. He died late last night."

Sarah hardly heard anything else that Father Richard said, and she was not able to give Brian an answer to his proposal of marriage before she left for Managua the following day.

Socialism and Opposition

To Whom Do You Belong?

For days after her father's funeral Sarah experienced the same numbness that she remembered feeling after her mother's death. She'd shed more tears after George Rutledge's death than for her mother—not that she'd loved him more, just that she'd loved him differently and he was the last to die. A week after the service she recalled nothing except for a vague image of Father Richard at the altar in the white chasuble that he usually wore only at Christmas and Easter because it made him sweat too much in the tropical heat for use on regular Sundays.

Walking through the forest to the graveside cliff had inspired her clearest memory of her father. She'd taken Doña Beatriz's arm when she stumbled and had smiled in thinking how odd it was for her to support someone else rather than being supported. Julio had flown up from Costa Rica. Guillermo and Ana and Emalina and the baby had stood close to her. Ana was holding Emalina's hand, and Gullermo was holding the baby, and Sarah had reached out to grasp Guillermo's waist as they lowered her father's casket into the ground, and then she buried her face in his shoulder when she couldn't look down into the hole of black earth.

Her most vivid mental image was of Don Martín, bowed, as if broken, weeping even more profusely than she was—she'd never seen him sobbing openly before—as if he'd lost a member of his own family, even his own life. Doña Beatriz and Don Martín and his sons were truly her only family in Nicaragua now. Uncle Walter and Aunt Beth hadn't flown down for the funeral; but even if they'd come, they wouldn't be as much her family here as they were in North Carolina. Strangely, she couldn't remember seeing Pablo. Perhaps he was standing behind other people whose blur of faces she couldn't identify or remember now any better than the hundreds that had come to pay their respects after her mother's death.

Exactly one week after George Rutledge's funeral Sarah awoke and felt her mind clearing, as if a fog were lifting like the mists that rose revealing the shapes of the trees in the forest early in the morning. At almost the exact time that the service had begun at St. Francis seven days before, she telephoned Father Richard. "I need your help. Is there anything you absolutely have to do today?"

"Nothing that I can't put off, my dear. If I can help you work through your grief . . ."

"You can't help with that. I've got to do it for myself. Later. Oh, I'm sorry . . . I didn't mean . . . but I need some practical help."

Sarah heard Father Richard suppress a chuckle. "Of course, Sarah. Glad I can do something practical. We've always understood each other and been able to talk frankly. What do you need?"

"I want you to drive me into the city to see Doña Beatriz and help me decide what the hell I'm going to do, whether to stay or leave."

This time Father Richard was not able to stifle his chuckle. "What a way to speak to your priest!"

"I'm sorry . . . and for being so demanding."

"No apologies necessary. You don't have to make any excuses for at least a month after what you've been through. When do you want to go?"

"I'll be there in about an hour, if that's all right."

"That's fine. Is this a collared or a non-collared event?"

"Non-collared. It's practical advice I'm seeking, not spiritual comfort."

"To be sure." Father Richard chuckled again, and his laughter helped assuage Sarah's grief by his treating her as if she were sound and healthy, not on the verge of collapse, so fragile that she was about to break.

"No. No, wear your collar. It might help if we get stopped. God only knows what's happening now with the new government. Or is it just a lawless *coup*?"

"I don't know. I really don't know, but I'll wear my collar for whatever protection it may offer."

Sarah had telephoned Doña Beatriz to relate the basic decision she wanted to explore with her and Father Richard—whether to stay or to leave. In Doña Beatriz's inhaled wordless breaths, Sarah could already almost hear her advice, *Leave, Sarita, leave while you can*; but the words that came after a few seconds were, "I'll prepare a little *almuerzo* (lunch) for us. It may be just *arroz y frijoles* (rice and beans). I haven't been able to get out . . ."

"*Arroz y frijoles* will be marvelous. Just right."

Even before Sarah reached the vicarage she knew that she would return to North Carolina, not just to gather her belongings but also to live at least for several months. As the sun rose higher in the sky thoughts marched into her consciousness more and more clearly after her weeklong slumber of torpid bereavement. "I can't decide about Brian here." She spoke aloud to herself in the car. "I can't decide about living permanently while I'm here now. But how . . . ? How can I protect Quinta Louisa if I'm not here? Who'll manage the plant? Oh, God, how? How?"

Father Richard maintained a discreet silence as they began the discussion at Doña Beatriz's home in Los Robles, but Doña Beatriz began urging Sarah to leave—"Leave now while you can"—with the spoken words that Sarah had heard telepathically from her thoughts over the telephone.

By the time they sat down for lunch Sarah had told them about the decision she'd already made to return to North Carolina and her job at the high school for at least the first semester. (Doña Beatriz did indeed serve them rice and beans, a humble offering compared to her usual fare; but she had also warmed tortillas with the local white cheese and sliced a pineapple and some mangoes. Sarah thought how much more she enjoyed the simple food, especially today, than she would have liked Doña Beatriz's gourmet dishes.)

Then Sarah raised the issues that she really needed suggestions about how to solve. "What do I do about Quinta Louisa? I don't think Don Martín can stay there by himself. Who will run the plant? I think Guillermo can manage the machinery and the de-pulping and drying processes, but I don't know whether he can deal with the accounts and legal papers for import and export."

After pondering and discussing various possibilities, Beatriz jangled her bracelets and raised her eyebrows as she smiled, almost glowed, with a broad grin. "I have it! Wasn't Carmen Ruiz one of your friends at the *colegio* (high school)? She needs a job and a place to live. She needs to stay in the country a while for family reasons. She could keep the books and take care of the local *impuestos* (taxes) and papers. I'm not sure whether she would understand about the *aduana* (customs) and import and export licenses."

Father Richard suggested that one of the workers could move into the guesthouse with his family and guard Quinta Louisa. If Carmen took the job, she could live in the house with Don Martín. Before Sarah and Father Richard reached the South Highway on their drive back to the vicarage, Beatriz Chulteco had contacted Carmen Ruiz. The plan began to take shape in Sarah's mind. She believed it would work. She believed it would be practical and efficient and would allow her time to grieve for her father and make a final decision about where she would live for the rest of her life and what her answer would be to Brian's proposal of marriage. (Brian had offered to come to Nicaragua for her father's funeral, but Sarah had firmly discouraged him and told him that she would need him more later, which she fervently felt. She was a little disappointed, however, that he was so easily convinced that he didn't insist more strongly on joining her.) Now the next steps would be talking with Don Martín and Guillermo, but Sarah did not foresee any likely problems in eliciting the full cooperation of her surrogate—now her only—father and his son.

Two days later Carmen Ruiz telephoned Sarah. She seemed as eager as Sarah was to explore the possibilities that Doña Beatriz had outlined. Sarah hadn't seen her or spoken with her since they finished high school eight years ago. After junior high Carmen had largely dropped out of Father Richard's church youth group when she began dating before any of the other girls in their class and thereby had gained a scandalous reputation. During high school she and Sarah had spoken to each other only casually in the halls and in the classes they shared. Carmen wanted to meet Sarah in the city, but Sarah thought it would be important for Carmen to see Quinta Louisa and visit the coffee sheds and processing plant.

"I don't believe you've ever been to Quinta Louisa."

"I was up there once, a long time ago, when we were in grade school. On Halloween. When you were scared shitless, as I recall."

Sarah smiled, somewhat reassured that neither Carmen's candor nor her crude language had changed. It boded well that Carmen's honesty and distaste for obsequious flattery were also intact.

Neither of them was comfortable driving alone under the present tense conditions in the country, and Sarah agreed to pay for a taxi to bring Carmen up to Quinta Louisa at what she thought was an exorbitant cost, because she didn't want to ask Father Richard to act as a chauffeur again.

Sarah couldn't recall Carmen's acting nervous in any situation before, although she wondered now if her brash bravado might have been a cover for adolescent anxiety; but in the parlor at Quinta Louisa Carmen's head bobbed and her eyes flickered around the room like a newly captured bird. Her make-up was layered even more heavily than it had been in high school. Her eyelashes were so long that Sarah believed they couldn't possibly be real. She wore even more bracelets on both arms than Doña Beatriz did. Her skirt was so tight that it seemed impossible to take off and put on, but her fingernails were very short, unlike the tapers that extended for an inch or more past the fingertips of other Nicaraguan women who dressed as she did. Sarah had forgotten that Carmen bit and chewed her fingernails.

After they toured the processing plant and drying sheds and met with Guillermo and Sarah had introduced her to Don Martín, she offered Carmen the job, which Carmen accepted eagerly and gratefully, almost humbly. When Sarah showed Carmen the bedroom where she would live during the week, she noticed a tear forming on Carmen's mascara-ed lashes.

Although Sarah had mentioned her general plans to Guillermo before

Carmen's visit, they didn't sit down to discuss details until the next day. Their conversation began in the tiny office at the plant that Guillermo and her father had shared; but when they still had issues to work out, Sarah asked Guillermo to come to Quinta Louisa that evening in order to continue talking.

"Do you think it is going to work, Guillermo? Can we pull it off?"

Guillermo laughed at her sudden plunge into an English idiom. It was the first time she'd heard him laugh since she'd returned for her father's funeral. *"You know I will take care of things for you. I know how to operate the plant, and I understand the machinery. If it breaks, I know how to make it work or find the right man to repair it. I will do a good job for you."*

"I know you will. Not just for me . . . for us . . . for your family, too. We *are* in this business together." (Sarah again used an idiom in English as she spoke.)

Guillermo nodded. *"That is true, yes."*

"What do you think about Carmen? Do you think she can do the job for us?"

"I think so. Yes. She seems to know her way around the government offices." Guillermo pursed his lips knowingly.

"Can you work with her?"

"I believe so, yes; but you may have to explain things to Ana." Guillermo raised his eyebrows and laughed, then nodded solemnly.

"I will." They both laughed, and Sarah thought it was the first time she'd laughed since she'd learned that her father had died.

"There is one thing. I am not sure Doña Carmen understands the export and import licenses very well. She said as much to me."

"She told me the same thing. I suppose we can hire someone in the city to assist with that. Do you know anyone? Do you have any ideas?"

"If you will pardon me for suggesting it: Julio knows about all those things. He could come up from San José every month or two. He comes about that often anyway to visit Papá. He could take care of that. If Doña Carmen was not . . . doing everything quite right . . . I'm sure she would be honest."

"That's a wonderful idea! Do you think Julio would be willing to help us?"

"Of course. He would do anything for your family . . . for you."

"You really are my family now: Don Martín and his sons, my other father

and my brothers. By the way, was Pablo at the funeral, Guillermo? I didn't see him."

"No, Doña Sarah. He could not come. I apologize for him." The painful sorrow reflected on Guillermo's face was so grave that Sarah didn't ask him what had prevented Pablo from coming to the funeral and didn't even chastise him for the *doña*.

It had been difficult to talk with Don Martín since the funeral. For the first week he sobbed whenever they began a conversation. Sarah had never seen him weep before, even when he was in pain, even after Doña Flora's death, although he had not come to Quinta Louisa for a couple of weeks following his wife's funeral, so that Sarah told herself she'd probably missed observing the signs of his immediate bereavement then. Even after his tears dried, his eyes sank into desiccated sockets. He still carried out his routine daily tasks, but he looked like a dead man habitually repeating the movements that he'd practiced while alive. Sarah mentioned briefly the plans for the coffee factory and for Carmen's lodging at Quinta Louisa as they took shape, but the night before she was to return to North Carolina she asked Martín to join her on the patio, where she knew he would be more comfortable than in the parlor.

"Julio has agreed to come up every month or six weeks to sort out the import and export licenses and customs issues. I'm very grateful to him. It will be an opportunity for him to have a visit with you, too."

"That will be good. Very good."

"I know you'll take good care of Carmen, too, while she is living here. And thank you for finding a worker and his family to live in your old house that we have used for a guesthouse in recent years. He will be our guard at night, so you can rest."

"Of course. That is no problem."

"I am very grateful to you and Guillermo for taking care of everything and Julio also. You really are my family now. You are the only parent I have left. You and Guillermo and Julio and Pablo are my Nicaraguan family."

"Yes. Of course. It is true. But not Pablo. Never. Not Pablo."

Sarah wanted to ask Don Martín what he meant about Pablo, but the pain was so evident in his voice that she didn't question him, as she'd also refrained from pursuing the subject with Guillermo. Martín didn't weep again, but he seemed to shrivel beside her like an animal that was dying and losing its vital fluids. After a long silence, she said, *"I love you, my father Martín."*

"I love you, too, beloved daughter Sarita."

IT HAD TAKEN SARAH well into the second week following her father's funeral before she could make her way through the forest along her favorite trail to the family cemetery on the cliff overlooking the valley. Then every day until she left the country she visited her parents' graves and paused both on her way there and her way back to listen to the birds and spy on the monkeys and hope to see the quetzal that had eluded her for her entire life.

A FEW WEEKS LATER, when she returned to North Carolina, she couldn't understand a similar reluctance to visit the family farm. Although she had long conversations with Aunt Beth on the phone and also short conversations with Uncle Walter—as much as he ever talked on the telephone with anyone—she resisted their countless invitations to spend a weekend with them even after she began teaching again in September. The farm had no particular connection to her father; and her memories of the times they'd spent there together were rather vague, so her reluctance could not have been an attempt to avoid painful or even pleasant associations with her father. When Aunt Beth suggested in a somewhat wounded tone that Sarah was avoiding a visit with them because she was angry with them for not flying to Nicaragua for her father's funeral, she knew that she would have to schedule a weekend on the farm, whatever the real source of her unaccountable reluctance might be.

"It's not that I don't want to see you, Aunt Beth. I've just had so many things to take care of in Nicaragua, and it's not so easy, as you now, from up here, and I've had so many things to do with the start of school . . . I've had to *get my ducks in a row*, as you say . . . What about weekend after next?" Sarah could have gone just as easily the following weekend, but she would put it off as long as possible, and two weeks seemed as long as she could delay without deeply offending her uncle and aunt.

In the midst of their ritual stroll to the creek on Sunday afternoon—they hadn't insisted on Sarah's attending church services with them, for which she was grateful—Beth began her predictable homily on the virtues of settling in North Carolina. Sarah grasped Beth's arm and halted them in their steps.

"That's why I didn't want to come out here, Aunt Beth; I knew what you were going to say."

"I'm so sorry, honey. I didn't mean to pressure you."

"No, no, it's not that. It's just that I knew if I saw you it would remind me that I've got to decide, and I don't want to, but I have to decide before too long."

"There's no rush, honey, in spite of all my nagging. You could take the whole year to make up your mind. Longer if you need to. Like I told you a couple a' years ago, you don't have to decide about the rest of your life right away."

"But I do, Aunt Beth. There's something I haven't told you. Brian has asked me to marry him, and I want to. At least I think I do, but I don't believe he'd ever agree to live in Nicaragua. He asked me right before Daddy died, and I haven't given him an answer yet."

"Well, my goodness! Congratulations! The way you've been acting lately makes a whole heap more sense now."

"Thanks, but don't tell anyone else yet, not even Uncle Walter." They began walking down the trail again without talking. They watched some brown thrashers and rufous-sided towhees kicking up fallen leaves. Sarah saw an Eastern bluebird flit above their heads. As the prettiest bird in the North Carolina woods she thought it was the local equivalent of the Central American quetzal.

"Do you love him, honey?"

"Yes. Yes, I do." But Sarah didn't articulate the rest of what she was thinking: whether she loved him enough or even more crucially whether he loved her enough.

BRIAN HAD BEEN ATTENTIVE to Sarah since the day of her father's death.

He had driven her to the airport to leave for Managua and met her flight when she returned. He'd mailed her a long, beautifully comforting letter, which arrived miraculously before she'd left Nicaragua. He'd even attempted an overseas telephone call, which hadn't gone well because the reception had been too bad to hear each other clearly.

Since she'd returned to North Carolina Brian had telephoned her every day. He always said exactly the right things to comfort her, but at times Sarah wondered if he used the same words for all bereaved people, words he'd learned in seminary, words he honed to perfection during his experiences with grieving families in the parish.

Except for the weekend Sarah spent with Uncle Walter and Aunt Beth she was with Brian for several hours on Fridays and Saturdays, and he would have been with her on weeknights as well if she had not told him that she needed time alone to be quiet and mourn. He seemed to understand that as he'd said "she needed her space and needed him to be near her when she needed him" and then offered to be with her whenever she called on him. He never pressed her for an answer to his proposal; and when she brought up the subject—he never did—he encouraged her to take as much time as she needed to respond.

They kissed more passionately after she returned from Nicaragua. She believed that especially now with her emotions on a vulnerable edge she couldn't verbalize her physical desires to him. He held her in his strong but tender embrace for hours at the time, and she thought that if she could just sleep in his arms she might be rid of the insomnia that had plagued her since her father's death.

"Brian, I'm so sorry I can't give you an answer about getting married. Daddy's death has screwed up my life, and . . ."

"It's all right, Sarah. Take as long as you need. If it takes you a year . . . or more . . . that's all right. I'll wait." Somehow Brian's patience was not reassuring to Sarah, as if he didn't really care. "When are you going back to Nicaragua?"

"I'll have to go back sometime this fall. I'll have to take a few days leave or go at Thanksgiving. And maybe return during the Christmas holidays and once or twice more in the spring. I've decided to finish the school year here. I'll have to check on things until I . . ." Sarah couldn't form the words *sell Quinta Louisa*. "As long as I keep the coffee *finca* and plant, I'll have to make regular trips down there, even with all that Guillermo and Julio and Carmen are doing; and they're doing a wonderful job."

"Would it be helpful for me to go down with you sometime?"

"That would be wonderful! It would mean so much . . ."

"I don't think I could manage this fall. Maybe after Christmas or in the spring."

"Yes! Yes!" Sarah reached around Brian's neck and pulled his face to hers and kissed him furiously. "*That's the only way I'll ever be able to decide,*" she wanted to say to him; but as she'd done hundreds of times before she refrained from speaking the words that she wanted to say to him.

ALTHOUGH SARAH WOULD HAVE missed fewer days from teaching her classes if she'd gone to Nicaragua during the Thanksgiving holiday, she decided to make her trip in late October. She would have to pay for a substitute teacher for four days. Part of her decision was made because she wanted to coordinate her visit in order to confer with Julio on one of his trips to see his father and oversee the accounts. She told herself that meeting with Julio was the principal reason for making the trip in October, but she knew that Thanksgiving with her uncle's family on the farm had been an important part of her life for the past several years and was one of the few anchors of continuity for her life now.

Guillermo met Sarah's flight—she'd given him the use of her father's car while she was in North Carolina. She felt the tension in her body flow away as he gave her a traditional *abrazo* (embrace) with his huge smile. As he babbled about his family and told her about humorous incidents in the village and at the plant, she felt more physically relaxed than she'd been since her father's death. While Guillermo rambled on, she kept thinking, "*My Nicaraguan family will take care of me.*"

Sarah had been able to schedule her flight without an overnight in Miami by flying on TACA from New Orleans, but they didn't arrive at Quinta Louisa until mid-afternoon. Carmen was still working at the office in the plant. Martín was waiting on the front porch for them to arrive. He seemed to be in better health than he was when she'd left in August. He was plumper, less gaunt, less hunched and bowed over. He embraced Sarah and squeezed her hands. He seemed calm, almost serene; but it bothered her that he didn't smile.

As Martín took her baggage out of the bonnet and back seat of her father's VW beetle, Guillermo twisted his hands and his lips, as he usually did when he was hesitant about bringing up a problem. *"Where do you want people to sleep? When Julio came in September he stayed in a hotel in the city, because he had his own business to take care of there, but Carmen and I thought he would need to be closer to the factory this time, and . . ."*

"And Julio is too important now to sleep in his father's room or in your little house in the village."

"Exactly."

They both laughed. Sarah felt pulses of laughter rumbling through her body for the first time in three months. Then impulsively she gave Guillermo a big *abrazo* and kissed his cheek. He blushed, and they both laughed heartily again.

There were only three bedrooms at Quinta Louisa besides the servants' room and bath behind the kitchen where Don Martín lived now. *"I am sure that Carmen is settled in the guest room, and I am certainly not going to ask her to move. I want to sleep in my old room. Julio can take my parents' room. I suppose no one has slept there since Daddy died."*

"Of course not. Will it be all right? Will you be all right with that?"

"Of course. A little strange, but all right. That is how it must be. Things change."

Sarah was weary from her journey and greeted Carmen briefly when she arrived from the factory office and then shared a light supper with her and went to bed early. The next morning Julio arrived. He'd rented a large American sedan at the airport—a Pontiac, Sarah thought. Like all successful Central American businessmen he wore a *guayabera*—they never wore suits and ties—but his grey wool and silk slacks with a crisp crease were expensive and his hand-sewn Italian shoes must have cost over a hundred dollars. He had the good taste, Sarah thought, to refrain from putting the gold-link chains around his neck and wrist that often accompanied the outfit. Sarah had failed to notice at her father's funeral that Julio had grown plump, but now she saw how his stomach pushed out the folds of his *guayabera*. Guillermo still had an athletic, muscular build like his father. Until the last few years Don Martín would have been as trim and sinewy as any of the student track stars at her high school.

Sarah couldn't decide whether she felt more like a parent whose children had surpassed her knowledge level or a child who was incapable of understanding her parents' business negotiations as she sat in the corner of the tiny office at the coffee processing plant listening to Carmen and Julio discuss contracts and sales and balance sheets and import-export licenses. They always deferred to her for any major decision and frequently stopped to ask for her comments, which she usually deflected because she didn't know enough about what was at issue to offer an opinion. From time to time they would send someone into the plant to ask Guillermo to join them when they had a question about the machinery or the factory process, and Sarah was always impressed by Guillermo's knowledge and grasp of the whole system. Finally Sarah decided that she filled a role like some revered elderly chairman of the board who was retained out of courtesy and honorific esteem.

Guillermo brought the same cook from the village who had prepared meals several times a week for her father in order to serve dinner for Sarah, Julio, and Carmen. Sarah pleaded with Don Martín to eat with them. "*Will you not sit down with us and enjoy the visit of your son?*" She knew even before she'd spoken that it would be a losing effort.

"*I need to help Loreta serve and be sure she has everything she needs in the kitchen.*"

During supper Carmen and Julio regaled Sarah with stories about the outrageous actions of the Sandinistas and the new five-member directorate. Their commentary bounced back and forth between English and Spanish depending on which language conveyed best their alternating sarcasm and bitterness.

When there was a lull in the primarily two-way conversation between Julio and Carmen after dinner, Sarah remembered to ask the question that had occurred to her several times during the previous twenty-four hours. "Where is Pablo these days? What's he up to?"

The conversation halted, and a silence ensued as if a bomb had been dropped into the room. Finally Carmen responded. "I thought you already knew. I thought you knew that Pablo joined up with the Sandinistas even before they kicked out Somoza."

Julio scowled. "I hear he's joined *Comandante Cero's* gang. *Claro*, (Of course,) he did not find his place with them until after they had taken Managua. Typical. Typical of Pablo. Too little, too late, even when he is on the wrong side."

The references to Pablo turned the mood somber, and Julio and Carmen stopped their harangues about the Sandinistas and became solemnly quiet. Sarah decided that she shouldn't pursue the issues of Pablo any further or ask any more questions about him now. Julio used the excuse of his flight leaving early the next morning for San José to break up the conversation and bid them goodnight. Soon thereafter Sarah and Carmen also retired to bed.

Loreta had prepared enough food to last for the remainder of Sarah's stay, and the next evening she and Carmen were by themselves in the parlor after supper.

"I can't tell you how grateful I am for your help. I'm really impressed by how well you deal with the office and the bureaucratic crap." As she said the word *crap* Sarah felt a flush on her neck and cheeks and knew that Carmen had seen the familiar prominent blush that Sarah despised and had recognized Sarah's feeble attempt to match her racy language.

"It's me that's thankful. I have to be here to check on my parents. They won't leave and go to Miami like any sensible people would, like most of their friends. Maybe they're right to try and keep what they've put together over the years, 'though I think they'll lose it in the end anyway. I'm really thankful to have the job and a place to stay. If I had to live with them all the time I'd go out of my freaking mind."

"Have you found it very difficult dealing with the new regime? Do you think they'll let us continue our operation?"

"Some of your old friends in the new government are looking after your best interests. People are divided; families are cut in two. Some are sucking up to the Sandinistas; some are sticking to the stupid hope that Somoza will come back and take over again."

"Who are they? Who's helping us to stay in business?"

A panicked expression froze Carmen's face, as if she realized that she'd already said too much. "Oh, just some people who knew your family."

"Can you tell me some of their names?"

"They kind of all run together. I forget."

Sarah knew that Carmen was lying, and she couldn't imagine why Carmen would hesitate to tell her the names of the people who were promoting her best interests, but she decided that she shouldn't pursue the matter since she was here for only a few days, much as she'd ignored the implications about Pablo.

Carmen's father was a Nicaraguan, and her mother was a *gringa* of Mexican ancestry from Texas. Her parents had maintained only a tenuous relationship with the expatriate English-speaking community. Carmen and her brother Luis had attended the American School but hadn't gone to college in the United States. None of Sarah's American and British friends her own age had stayed in Nicaragua, and now few of her Nicaraguan friends were left in the country either.

"Didn't your family leave the country for a while?"

"Yeah. We went to Panama after the earthquake and then again during the shittiest part of the revolution. Except for Luis. He was always sympathetic with the Sandinistas until they actually won. Since the god-damned university he was nothing but a fucking communist. He still claims to be a Sandinista, but he's in Panama trying to get what we have left of the family business transferred down there. He likes to preach like a communist and live like a capitalist."

"Like Pablo, I guess."

"Sort of. They both got a bad sense of timing, as Julio said; but I think Pablo probably believes all that shit and lives for it. Luis is more an armchair socialist."

Sarah admired Carmen's honesty. She believed that she could trust Carmen, even though she wouldn't have been Sarah's first choice for a bosom friend under normal circumstances. She was almost envious of Carmen's filthy language and tight dresses and vulgar make-up that were all bold, defiant, and unapologetic.

"What about you? Do you plan to stay in Nicaragua for good?"

"Who knows? Probably not forever. Most of my friends have left, like yours. Depends if I can seduce a Sandinista *jefe* (chief)." Carmen winked.

"We thought Somoza was bad, but maybe he was better than what we have now."

"Hell, Sarah. You don't know the half of it. You don't know what went on. You never did."

"What do you mean?"

"Listen. I've been lucky. My family didn't have the kind of clout that yours did, but I didn't get raped, and I didn't get hooked on drugs. I can take credit for part of it. I've got enough sense and self-respect not to get myself all messed up. I always envied you growing up. I really didn't like you much, you know. You had a kind of security-your family's money and position. You never had to think about all the shitty things that could happen to people like us."

"Do things like that really happen to people without some complicity on their part?" It was her mother's word, her mother's voice. Words like *complicity* would keep vulgar women like Carmen at arms' length. Words like *complicity* would keep you from thinking about the horrible things that could happen, but Carmen knew where words like *complicity* came from, besides dictionaries, and could toss them away with a flick of her heavily mascara-ed black lashes.

"You never had to know about things like that hon'. But you can't be that naïve. Surely you hear some things. You know about Cynthia, don't you, the little English girl that used to come to Padre Richard's youth group with us?"

"I heard some rumors, but they seemed so exaggerated. I never knew how much truth there was to them."

"She started going out with one of Tachito's young cousins. We never had any love for the Somozas in my family. That's why I can stay on now—besides having little socialist Luis for a brother. She got on drugs and flew high with him for a while. He was just the greatest, she thought. Then he convinced her to open up a joint checking account. It was supposed to be so she could use his money. He was supposed to have gobs of money tied up in the family businesses. Then he drew out all her money and skipped out on her. The money she'd earned from nursing. That burns me up. The fucking bastard." Carmen screamed the words and stood up and paced around the room on her bare feet. Sarah was frightened because Carmen's outrage seemed out of character and unprecedented for her. "The nerve of that fucking bastard taking all her money—her little savings account."

"Whatever happened to her? I heard she'd had some emotional problems."

"She disappeared, and came back, then went to Nassau or wherever the hell her family came from years ago and came back again. She kept trying to see the little bastard. She went to his apartment and got in somehow. His father came in and found her. God only knows if she was drunk or on drugs or whatever. It doesn't matter, but his father came in and found her and raped her. That dirty fucking old cocksucker raped her. Those are the meanest words I know, sweet Sarah; and if I knew any meaner ones I'd use them. You shocked? Then her bastard boyfriend's brothers came in and raped her, too. Then that creep she loved came in and raped her, too, in front of them." Carmen sat down and wept until her cheeks were streaked in black, now more black than pink.

Sarah wept, too, as if she were a part of these people's lives for the first time—Cynthia and Carmen and even her brother Luis. "Oh, my God, Carmen. I didn't know. I didn't know that. I really didn't know. Where is she now? What's happened to her?"

"Nobody knows where she is. She disappeared. I'm not sure even her family knows where she is. They left Nicaragua, but my parents have kept in touch with them through friends in Panama."

"I can understand how people would rise up against Somoza after things like that."

"You think the Sandinistas are any better? I could tell you some other stories about them, too, hon'. But I hate the Somozas."

"That's terrible. I don't want to believe that things like that go on in the world."

"We never were able to take things for granted as much as you did."

"Maybe I can't again either. Nothing can ever be the same for me again. Not after what's happened in our country." As soon as the words left Sarah's mouth she realized the irony of claiming Nicaragua as her country as she used to do, as she hadn't done in recent years.

"I know. I'm sorry. I'm really sorry. There was a time when I wanted you to know what it's like to be scared walking down the street and coming home from school. I would've gloated over you finding out, but not now. If I could, I'd make you innocent and naïve and sweet all over again. But I'm sorry. It's shitty. It's a shitty, shitty world." Carmen sang to the Walt Disney tune of *"It's a small world after all."* "It's a shitty world after all; it's a shitty world after all; it's a shitty world after all; it's a shitty, shitty world."

Sarah and Carmen talked quietly the next night and shared stories and memories like sisters that had been reunited after having been parted for years. Sarah began to think of Carmen as her best girl friend in Nicaragua, however separated they had been in the past and however different they still were from one another. Now they were survivors who shared confidences and recollections that only they could know, as if they were the only two women left from a world that had passed away.

The next day, her last full day in Nicaragua, Sarah planned to attend the Sunday service at St. Francis and see Father Richard and then have lunch with Doña Beatriz. (Guillermo would drive her to Los Robles and come back for her. Although she invited him to eat with them, he was sensitive to her need to visit with Doña Beatriz by herself and made an excuse to meet with an old friend of his in the city.)

As was often true when Sarah hadn't scheduled a visit with Father Richard and hoped to speak with him privately on a Sunday after the service, she was frustrated in her attempt. After the last parishioners left the coffee hour in the church patio, her time was limited—she needed to go back to the village to meet Guillermo so that he could drive her into the city to Los Robles. Father Richard looked unusually weary-the

Sunday service always drained his energy and emotions, but today he seemed on the verge of collapse.

"I'm sorry there wasn't time for a visit with you on this trip. I'll be back after Christmas, and Brian is hoping to come with me. We'll need to talk with you and perhaps make some big decisions."

"I hope I'll still be here. I hope there's anything at all left for you here."

"What do you mean? Do you know that something else is about to happen?"

"Oh, no, my dear. I'm just tired and anxious from worrying about what I imagine might still happen. How are things going at the factory? Are your plans working out?"

"Splendidly." (It was her father's favorite word when all was going well.) "Carmen and Guillermo are managing splendidly with occasional help from Julio. I don't think they really need me at all." And suddenly Sarah also felt weary and anxious, as if she had contracted Father Richard's mood through some virulent contagion.

Her time with Doña Beatriz was also limited because she'd asked Guillermo to return at four o'clock so that they could arrive back at Quinta Louisa before dark. Doña Beatriz seemed to have moved in the opposite direction from Father Richard. She was almost serene, at least as calm as Sarah had ever seen her hyper, ever-active older friend. Doña Beatriz seemed to have accepted her limited options and limited possibilities. Her resignation seemed to have brought her a kind of peace. Perhaps by not having to worry about Don Armando she became content with what was left for her. She'd even abandoned her habitual harangue for Sarah to leave Nicaragua permanently.

"Do you still consider relocating to the States yourself, Doña Beatriz? Are you thinking about moving back to Miami someday?"

"No, no, Sarita. My life is here now, however much is left of it. I will enjoy what I have left, whatever they leave me."

"You seem *muy contenta, casi satisfecha* (very content, almost satisfied.) I'm glad. I'm happy for you."

"And what about you? Will you return, or will you make a new life up there? I would miss you terribly, but I would understand if you chose to stay in *Norte* Carolina." For the first time in the past several years Doña Beatriz seemed to be viewing Sarah's options equally, without a strong bias and recommendation.

"I don't know. That's what I'm trying to decide."

"And you must decide very soon *Cara* (dear) Sarita. You will have to decide very, very soon, *mi querida hija* (my dearest daughter)." It was the first time that Doña Beatriz had ever called Sarah *daughter*. Don Martín had used almost exactly the same words when he called her his daughter for the first time a couple of months earlier.

DURING THANKSGIVING DINNER AT the Lloyd farm Sarah told her family that she would need to return to Nicaragua for an extended time at the end of the school year in order to sort out property issues. She didn't tell them that she was still undecided whether her principal residence would be in Nicaragua or in North Carolina. She'd also asked Aunt Beth to keep her marriage proposal confidential because it was too complicated to explain to Uncle Walter, much less to her cousins.

"Won't the communists take everything away from you?"

"Or kill you?"

Her cousin's little boys had grown into big boys and obviously parroted the perspectives and statements overheard from their parents.

"That's what I have to go down and find out. Nothing's very certain. It's all kind of a muddle."

"But we don't want them to hurt you, Sarah. We love you." The youngest boy's face contorted in alarm, and Sarah got up from the table, walked around to his chair and gave him a hug.

Aunt Beth was not feeling well on Friday. Either she prompted her husband to offer his companionship for the traditional after-Thanksgiving Day walk to the creek, or he sensed for himself how important it was for Sarah. Their walk was mostly silent—Uncle Walter couldn't supply Aunt Beth's continuous repartee however attuned he was to Sarah's need for succor. They had almost reached the creek when Walter broke the silence. "It's not up to me to tell you what to do, Sarah. Just remember you always got a home here, and wherever you're at, you belong to us."

Sarah gave her uncle a hug and was startled by how strongly he embraced her. In the past he'd rarely done more than shake her hand or pat her shoulder.

"Wherever I wind up living, I hope I can always get back here to the farm for Thanksgiving."

"Long as I'm alive I'll try to see to that. You can count on it."

SINCE SARAH PLANNED TO return to Nicaragua on a semi-permanent basis after the school year ended, she decided that one trip at Christmas would suffice until then. Carmen and Guillermo and Julio were managing the factory well without her, and she probably couldn't contribute anything to their efficient work. She had an even stronger yearning to be in Nicaragua at Christmas than she'd felt for visiting the farm in North Carolina for Thanksgiving. Brian couldn't leave before Christmas, of course, with his liturgical duties in the church; but he reaffirmed his intention to join her on December 27 and return with her on Wednesday January 2, so that she could begin teaching for the second semester at the high school.

Although Sarah wished that Brian might share her bedroom and her bed, she knew that his strict moral code would not permit him to make such a concession. It was perhaps stretching his sense of propriety even to be in the same house without proper chaperones—Don Martín and Carmen hardly qualified for the role.

As Brian moved through the gate at the airport in Managua with his blonde hair glowing like a halo around his blue eyes and pink lips Sarah thought that he looked like a god towering over his darker Latino traveling companions. Below the sleeves of his sport shirt his bare arms, rarely visible in his clerical garb, were chiseled with the elegant muscles of a renaissance statue.

During their week together at Quinta Louisa Sarah thought almost constantly about how she would answer Brian's proposal of marriage. They made the usual courtesy calls on Father Richard and Doña Beatriz, but none of their visits helped to clarify Sarah's thinking. Don Martín had brought Loreta from the village to prepare their food; and although Carmen ate dinner with them every evening, she excused herself as soon as they finished their meals in order to leave them alone. Don Martín was gracious and uncharacteristically obsequious with Brian; but because Brian spoke almost no Spanish, their relationship was limited. Even Guillermo, who spoke fairly good English, was self-conscious around Brian and never seemed to relate to him personally.

One morning while Brian was shaving, Guillermo was on his way to the factory and brought some papers by Quinta Louisa for Sarah to sign. When she asked him what he thought of Brian, Guillermo hesitated and didn't answer her.

"What is the problem? Why do you not answer my question?"

"I believe that you love him more than he loves you, and that bothers me."

Sarah thought that Guillermo had taken on even more completely the role of her older brother and protector who would never consider any man good enough for her.

CARMEN DECIDED TO SPEND New Year's Eve and New Year's Day with her family in the city. Sarah asked Loreta to leave some food partly prepared so that she could cook the meals that she and Brian would share on their last two days together at Quinta Louisa by themselves. Loretta was grateful to be able to return to the village for the holiday celebrations. Guillermo even persuaded Don Martín to spend the night on New Year's Eve with his family at his home in the village. Sarah wondered how Brian would respond to being completely alone with her in the house, but he seemed to accept the situation as a necessary suspension of propriety due to unforeseen and unavoidable circumstances.

Sarah wanted to serve Brian the traditional festive Nicaraguan *nacatamales* on New Year's Eve. She had prepared some *ceviche* with fresh red snapper as a hors d'oeuvre and had asked Guillermo to purchase a bottle of sparkling wine for them while he was in the city on business. Brian was exquisitely polite in complimenting the *nacatamles*, although Sarah knew that he would have preferred other food and liked them far less than dishes they'd shared in the past, much less than she enjoyed them as her favorite cuisine in the whole world.

After dinner they sat on the patio as the rising moon's beams began to glisten on the palms like Christmas tree lights. Sarah knew that the time had come for them to have a final conversation about marriage and for her to give a definitive answer to Brian's proposal.

"Do you believe you could ever live in Nicaragua or at least spend some time every year for our vacations here? I might have to come down several times during the year to see about the factory. The system seems to be working remarkably well—I'd say almost miraculously well—thanks to Guillermo and Carmen along with Julio's help."

"The question is whether you would be content as a priest's wife in the United States. I think you'd make a wonderful clergy spouse, but it would be a full-time job, and when we had children . . ."

"You want to have children, Brian? We've never really talked about it."

"Of course. I assumed you knew that."

"So you want a clergy spouse and a mother for your children, but do you really want me as your wife?"

"Of course. What a strange thing to say."

"It bothers me that we haven't become more physically intimate after all the months we've been together."

Brian didn't respond for a long time, and Sarah refrained from her impulse to elaborate. "I do want you to be the mother of my children, and we would certainly have conjugal relations after we're married, but . . ."

Again Brian paused, and this time Sarah couldn't stop herself from speaking. "But what, Brian?"

"I've never been that interested in sex. I would try to please you in bed . . . after we were married . . . but it's never been a big deal for me. I think maybe I enjoy social intercourse more than sexual intercourse. I like interacting with people, both women and men, and I enjoy working off my physical energy playing sports."

"I see."

"I would try to please you, Sarah; and I think I would perform pretty well . . . in bed, I mean."

This time Sarah was silent for a long time. She thought of many questions she would like to ask Brian, but they seemed irrelevant now and would be posed only from prurient curiosity. At last she did understand, although she couldn't fully shape her understanding into words and concepts. She knew now that she didn't belong to Brian and so Brian could never belong to her, as much as she had thought she wanted him to be her husband. She told him that she believed they wanted and needed different things in their lives. She took the box with the engagement ring out of the pocket of her dress. (She didn't usually carry it. She usually left it in the drawer of her dresser in the bedroom both in North Carolina and in Nicaragua.) She had thought that tonight she would hand the box to Brian to remove the ring and place it on her finger, but she returned the box and the ring to him forever.

"I hope we will still be friends, Brian. I know people always say that, but I think it's really possible for us."

"I believe we really can, Sarah. I'll always be your friend."

"I'm sorry I took so long to give you an answer, and then . . . had to tell you . . ."

Brian took her hand. "It's all right. It was a risk I was willing to take. I still think you would have made a perfect priest's wife."

Even then if Brian had told Sarah that he loved her, she might have reconsidered her decision; but Brian never spoke the words; and Sarah realized that he could not say them, because he did not love her in the way that she had hoped and needed.

On Saturday morning the second week of April, the week after Easter, Sarah received a frantic telephone call from Doña Beatriz.

"How soon can you come down Sarita? They are beginning to take property away from foreigners to give to the *campesinos*—or so they say. After *Obispo* (Bishop) Romero's assassination in El Salvador last month the Sandinistas are increasing pressure on everyone. They're afraid the opposition will try to take control again. You have to come down and prove you belong here. It doesn't matter enough now that your family has lived here for four generations. You must be in the country yourself to fight for what is yours . . . or you may lose everything. Your friends in the government cannot protect Quinta Louisa any longer if you are not present here in Nicaragua."

"Who are these friends of mine in the government, Doña Beatriz? Who has been protecting me?"

There was a long pause, as if Sarah had interrupted a well-rehearsed speech or even a sermon in a sacred place with some boisterous outcry. Finally Doña Beatriz answered in her little girl, silly voice, not the grave tones that she had used in her eloquent plea. "Oh, you know: people who were acquainted with your family and respected you." Sarah could hear the bracelets jangling even over the static on the telephone as Doña Beatriz shook her arm nervously.

"But who are they? What are their names?"

"I can't recall their names just now, but you must come soon, Sarita, or they will take everything." Doña Beatriz uttered the same evasive words that Carmen had used to deflect Sarah's inquiry.

"Who are my friends in the government? What were their reasons and motives for protecting me?" Sarah thought.

"I have to finish the school term. I promised, and I've signed a contract. I'll be there in a few weeks, a little over a month from now. I hope nothing happens until then."

"¡Ojalá¡ (May it be so!) Let us hope you come soon enough."

Expropriation and Rebirth: 1980–1981

What Belongs to You?

A lthough Guillermo greeted Sarah at the airport with his habitual broad smile and virile *abrazo* (embrace), he was uncharacteristically quiet as they drove out of the city and ascended into the hills. Sarah was grateful for the silence. She was arriving neither for a visit nor for a permanent homecoming but rather for an extended residence, and she was exhausted from the efforts of packing and sorting and storing her things before she'd left North Carolina. The thoughts about what she might confront in dealing with the Sandinista government and the uncertainty about how long she would need to stay in Nicaragua added to her weariness.

The houses and little stores were gradually replaced by green forests beside the road, the smell of the city by crisp floral fragrances, the noisy traffic of Managua by the voices of animals and birds, dust and smoke by clean, clear air. The car slowed after kilometer thirty, but Guillermo sped down the dirt road toward the village and the factory much faster than he usually drove, bumping over the ruts and trailing a cloud of dust that boiled up to the tops of the jacaranda trees.

Finally Guillermo spoke, as if he'd waited as long as he possibly could delay before they reached the village. *"There are some problems I need to tell you about."*

"What has happened? Are the Sandinistas already trying to take Quinta Louisa away from us?"

"I do not know anything about that. There are rumors, but these are different kinds of problems, very little problems." Guillermo held up a space between his thumb and forefinger and looked over at her as he flashed his familiar grin.

"Such as?"

"Lots of changes. Nothing too bad, but you need to know." Guillermo hesitated as if he were trying to break bad news as gently as he would to a child who couldn't understand the implications.

"Tell me about them."

"Loreta's husband and daughter are sick again, and she needs to take care of them. Papá has hired Isabel to come and cook for you, just as she has done before . . ."

Sarah understood Guillermo's reluctance to speak about the last time that Isabel had substituted for Loreta in the kitchen. *". . . as she was doing when my father died. Perhaps I can talk with her more about that. She was so upset last August that I could not ask her much about it. She was the one who found him, is that not true?"*

*"¡Cómo no! (*To be sure!)

"What else?"

"José wants to move back to the village. He and his family miss being with their friends."

"Like you and Ana."

*"¡Como no! (*To be sure!) *That is no great problem. They do not have to leave right away, and Papá can find someone else to come and guard the quinta at night, but no one may stay very long. Campesinos (*peasants) *like us do not like to live apart from other people."*

Guillermo glanced at Sarah again and grinned, and she punched his shoulder with her fist. *"You are no more a campesino than I am, my brother. Is that all? Those things do not seem too serious."*

"Unfortunately no. It is a pity, but Carmen also wants to leave. She will be harder to replace. She has done a very good job."

"Why does she want to leave?"

"She says she needs to help her family get ready to move to Panama."

Something in Guillermo's choice of words and inflection implied that there were other reasons for Carmen's departure, but Sarah thought it would be better not to press him for an elaboration now. Sarah didn't respond until they'd almost reached the factory where she would drop Guillermo off before driving herself to Quinta Louisa. *"I will be here for several months. Perhaps I could do some of Carmen's work. I will need something to occupy me every day."*

"Marvelous!" Guillermo took both hands off the steering wheel and pretended to fleck sweat off his forehead. *"That would be perfect! Julio and I can show you anything you need to know."*

"Careful, Guillermo! Or the factory will lose both a foreman and a new business manager at the same time. You will kill us both!"

Guillermo broke into English. "No way. Every little thing is good. You solve all our problems, Doña Sarah."

Sarah punched his shoulder again, this time with the sharp jab of a boxer and responded in Spanglish.

"Don't you start *doña-ing* me, *hermano* (brother)!"

They both laughed, and Sarah felt that she was now back home with her Nicaraguan family that would take care of her.

Sarah screeched to a stop as she approached the wall around Quinta Louisa and almost hit the Sandinista soldier who stepped through the gate in front of her holding a rifle flat against his chest with one hand on the trigger. *"What are you doing here?"*

"My colonel told me to guard this house. Please get out of the car."

Sarah was furious. In the rear-view mirror she saw her pale blue eyes glowing like ethereal ambers. Her fine brown hair sizzled around her face like flames, and beads of sweat on her neck began to break and run down her back. *"I certainly will not get out. This is my home. Now you stand aside, or I will run over you."*

The little soldier might have shot her, but she was too angry and tired and frustrated to observe any of the careful maneuvers that they'd rehearsed over and over through the years for dealing with the military.

Sarah thought that he was a teenager who had probably been picked up barefooted out of the *campo* (countryside) and had a rifle shoved into his hands and sent out here with precious little training. She'd seen boy soldiers about his age for years in Somoza's *Guardia* (National Guard), sometimes twirling their loaded rifles like majorettes' batons, sometimes firing them by accident and killing people, sometimes shooting at the slightest provocation.

He lifted the rifle slightly. He could as easily have shot her as not, but then he relaxed his arms and lowered the gun. Remarkably he never pointed it at her. *"My orders are to guard Quinta Louisa."*

"If your colonel tells you to guard my house, you may have to obey his order; but you can stand on the road. You must not stand inside my wall. Do you understand me?"

The soldier might call his colonel and initiate a power play with a whole troop assigned to stay in her garden, and there would be no getting them out for a month or forever if it became a matter of the colonel's pride, but the least likely of all possibilities happened. The boy stepped aside and meekly retreated outside the gate. Her angry bluff had worked in spite of all predictions, even her own if she'd taken the time to think instead of acting on her feelings of the moment.

Sarah looked in the rear-view mirror again and fluffed her wispy, brown (almost red) hair around her ears. The splotches on the sides of her neck, just below her ears occurred only in the tropics. The dark lines under her eyes on her thin face had appeared for the first time after her father died. She was pretty, if a little too thin and much too tall; but her father had believed she was beautiful, *his English porcelain doll*, he'd called her, with her pale creamy complexion the color of old English stoneware tinged with pink here and there.

She called from the driveway before she entered the front door. *"Don Martín, I'm home."*

"Doña Sarah! Welcome!" Only their shoulders and arms touched in the embrace, still given the formal way, unlike Guillermo's vigorous *abrazo*, even though she probably loved the short aging man with ginger-colored skin better than anyone else in the world now that her father was dead.

"How are you? How is everything on the finca?"

"Everything is fine. I am fine, too; but you are very thin. It is good to have you back home. We will give you some good food to make you fat again." Don Martín formed facsimile breasts and buttocks with his hands in the air.

Sarah blushed but didn't respond to his familiar risqué gestures. *"How long has that soldier been in the yard?"*

"He arrived just this morning."

"They always know our comings and goings, is it not true? They must have known I was arriving today. Well, they are not going to intimidate me. Did he say anything about why they sent him?"

"He said the quinta must be guarded until the government decides what to do with the property." Don Martín looked down and shuffled his feet. He was wearing straw slippers and machine-made work trousers, his best clothes in honor of her homecoming.

"Do not give him anything to eat or drink. Nothing. And if he comes inside the gate, let me know immediately."

"Of course, señorita. Shall I get your suitcases?"

Guillermo could readily call her his sister *(hermana)*, but Don Martín could not call her his daughter *(hija)* in their everyday discourse. He had spoken the word only once to her. Sarah hoped he might repeat it again more often, more habitually in the coming days.

"Just put them in my bedroom when it is convenient. I want to stretch my legs and walk around a while. There is no hurry." Sarah slipped the white sheet off the Sheridan settee brought from England by her great-grandmother Louisa, the matriarch for whom Quinta Louisa was named. The settee was badly worn and frayed, even ripped along the front edge; but Don Martín still covered it every morning as he'd been taught to do by her mother and her grandmother. She sat down with the sheet bunched up on her lap. It was the most uncomfortable resting place in the house, where people never sat, away from the conversational groupings of chairs and tables, away from the lamps for reading. From that position she could see the place beside the front door where her father had collapsed and also the view toward the kitchen where the terrified cook and her nine year-old grandson had stood and caught

the first glimpse of George Rutledge lying motionless after his massive heart attack.

Martín struggled through the front door carrying more suitcases and boxes than he could easily manage. *"There is no hurry. I do not want to unpack right away."*

After Martín finished unloading the car, he went into the garden and began the afternoon watering of the flowering plants, done every day especially at the end of the dry season for them to survive, done every year for decades and decades. Sarah walked to the patio door and watched him. Bougainvillea still covered the stone walls at each side of the house. Just beyond the limes and papayas and avocados at the back of the garden Sarah could see the coffee bushes under the big trees and beyond them the mountains. Her great-grandfather had put out the coffee plants nearly a century ago, side by side with his workers under the tropical sun. The native laborers had laughed at his painfully red, blistered skin, which was the same pale color as hers, she had been told. She'd heard her father tell a hundred times how his grandfather had slept for the whole first year in a hammock slung between two mahogany trees.

"Oh, Martín. Oh, Martín dear, do not forget the roses." She laughed, and he slapped his thigh and also laughed at her mother's words, intoned almost in her mother's voice and Southern accent that had even penetrated her Spanish. Don Martín seemed to have recovered from the morose bereavement that had afflicted him for months after her father's death. He looked like his old self, although now older and slower.

Roses didn't grow well in this climate, but Mary Rutledge had never stopped trying to make them bloom for over three decades, until her death twelve years ago; and Martín still maintained the futile effort of nurturing them. Was it possible that her mother had been dead for twelve years and her father for almost a whole year? Sarah still felt that if she called them from the patio at Quinta Louisa they would answer her and perhaps even come outside to greet her.

SARAH WANTED TO SEEK Father Richard's counsel before she contacted the authorities about the guard that had been posted at Quinta Louisa.

As she drove through the gate she saw the little soldier slumped down against the wall over the road holding his rifle that was supported from the strap slung around his neck and resting against his bare shoulder and stomach between the folds of the unbuttoned shirt that was draped over his back and arms. One leg was on the ground, the other knee hiked up on a rock. He stumbled to his feet and pointed the gun at her. She refused to look at him. Her lips were tight, pulled inside her teeth; and she felt the hot and cold places on her neck, so that she knew the red splotches had appeared again. Sarah nodded her head as a signal that she was would not stop and that he would not interfere with her unless he intended to shoot her. This kind of intimidation had happened before, under Somoza, when there was the threat of a coup or an uprising. Then the guard would usually disappear in two or three days. Foreigners were always suspected of some kind of collusion with the enemy. The excuse for sending a guard was always to protect them. She knew that the real motivation now was the expropriation of her property, and the clear, although unstated implication was still intimidation. Pointing a rife at her today was the last straw, even if he had been startled by the noise of the car engine and roused from a siesta and had responded in fright. He might have killed her.

"How do you feel about having a guard on your gate, courtesy of the new regime, my dear?" Father Richard Sims often affected her father's British accent when talking with her, without any intentional parody. He even assumed George Rutledge's mannerism at times. Her father had been his closest friend in the country. He'd been admired, almost idolized, by the missionary priest in spite of their different political perspectives.

Sarah's head snapped toward Father Richard, and her lips disappeared inside her teeth before she spoke. "You know damned well how I feel. I told Don Martín not to give him anything to eat or drink. Thought I'd starve him out; but I relented and told Don Martín to see that he had plenty of water. I couldn't let him suffer from thirst."

"Of course you couldn't, Sarah; it's not in you." His chuckle annoyed her. "Is there anything I can help you with?"

"You can get that damned soldier out of the driveway for me."

"I'm afraid that's not in my province. Anything I can do in the realm of the possible?"

"Just support me while I'm in the country. Let me come and talk with you and vent my emotions every few days."

"How long are you going to stay here, Sarah?"

"I want to stay at least until I get the property matters settled one way or the other."

"You know your chances of holding onto the Quinta Louisa are very small indeed." He took off the thick spectacles with their square lenses and thin silver frames and wiped them. His uncovered eyes look blinded.

"Do you really think so, padre?"

"You're playing by a set of rules that are no longer observed. Citizenship is obsolete for foreigners in Nicaragua now, my dear. Respect for nations has been replaced by an adoration of ideology."

"You sound bitter. I've never heard you talk like that before."

"No, no, not bitter, just disappointed. I thought there would someday be justice and prosperity for the poor of this country. It really is a different world now, Sarah. How ironic! I'd hoped for over a decade that there would be more economic equality among people in Nicaragua, and your father opposed the whole idea. Then, when the revolution purported to embrace those ideals, I hated what was happening; and George was better prepared to accept the changes than the rest of us. He just wanted to live out his life at Quinta Louisa in his own house and garden. God knows I wish you could keep Quinta Louisa. It's the most beautiful place on earth to me, but everything's different now, and there's no hope of maintaining it as you've done in the past."

"I'm going to see that it stays the same. I'm going to keep it exactly like it was before Daddy died, for as long as they'll allow me to."

"And just how do you plan to go about accomplishing that, my dear?"

"The first step is going to the Ministry of Justice tomorrow morning and trying to find out just what my situation is . . ."

"Good luck with that."

". . . and getting that damned little boy soldier off my gate."

"And more good luck with that, my dear."

SARAH DISLIKED HAVING TO take Guillermo away from the factory, but she was wary about driving herself into the city. Although Don Martín and Mary Rutledge had alluded several times to the attack on her grandparents as they drove back to Quinta Louisa late one night along the Panamerican Highway, Sarah had learned the details only during her senior year at Elon, when she'd met her father for a visit in Miami. Her grandparents had hit a calf, and an angry mob had dragged them from their damaged automobile and beaten them on the side of the road. *Campesinos* often responded violently to automobile accidents, usually only if a local pedestrian was hit by a foreigner's car on a darkened road. For her grandparents it had involved just a calf. With the tensions following the revolution, Sarah thought she was even more vulnerable than they had been almost a half a century ago.

Guillermo agreed with her that it was important to have their property rights clarified, although he shared Father Richard's skepticism that she would receive many answers. As they left the office at the factory and got into the car Guillermo asked her, *"Have you talked with Carmen? I mean about her leaving?"*

"No. One thing at a time."

"Maybe that's just as well. Let her bring it up."

"Your Spanglish reminds me of my students, but they jump into English because they can't remember the Spanish words. You're perfectly bilingual, but you just throw in English when it suits you."

"Whatever works best."

They laughed. Sarah always laughed more with her brother Guillermo than with anyone else.

Since the earthquake more than seven years and eight months ago, trips into the city affected Sarah with sick despair. As they circled the ruined blocks almost nothing looked familiar. She couldn't determine where she was when they paused at an intersection, and she wondered where they were headed. Then she peered through the weeds that grew shoulder high through the cracks of a paved strip that had once been a street and saw a part of a marquee on a crumbled building and the broken ticket window of the theater where she'd first seen *The Sound of Music*.

Guillermo left Sarah in front of the Ministry of Justice while he went to buy machine parts for the factory. Inside she was confronted by the familiar fetid, musty smell of a public government building in the tropics, and she felt that she had found her way again and knew where she was, who she was. The yellowed brown of the walls painted a generation or more ago was the color of old public government buildings all over the world. The flabby, baggy-eyed man with rumpled black hair and a rumpled white shirt resembled the functionaries of the Somoza regime. His eyelids drooped as if he were dozing, about to drop off to sleep while an elderly woman obviously not from the city but from some distant rural village wrung her hands and asked him about her missing son. He replied disdainfully but politely that he had no knowledge of her son and told her to try again next week and to move along because others were waiting.

Only Sarah was waiting and said, "*That is all right. I am not in a hurry.*" The old woman stood transfixed for a moment. "*When did your son disappear, señora?*" Sarah emphasized with the grief and pain of losing a son as she thought of losing her father.

"*A year ago in June.*"

Sarah was stunned. She'd thought he might have been missing for a few days or a couple of weeks from the expression of raw agony in the woman's terrified eyes and trembling lips.

"*She comes every week.*" The bureaucrat spoke in a disgusted tone without any sign of emotion, not even contempt. "*I even sent her to the Human Rights Commission.*" He now spoke as if it were an act of heroism and extraordinary courage—perhaps for him it was, perhaps even the petty bureaucrat had to assuage his personal guilt in some way. "*Now get out of the way, old woman.*" His eyes opened; his face brightened somewhat; and he more nearly approached a wakeful, conscious life as he looked up at Sarah. For him she was still special, favored, and privileged. He hadn't been quite able to transfer his habits of flattery to Russians and East Germans. Expatriates from the United States and Europe still commanded a respect that had been ingrained in his behavior for decades. "*What can I do for you, young lady?*"

He listened laconically to her complaint about the soldier at her

gate and took out a pad, rumpled like his shirt, and jotted notes about
the name and location of the *finca*; but in spite of his obsequious tone
and deferential manner, his prescribed advice was the same for Sarah as
for the old peasant woman—to come back later. *"The Minister will not
be in today. The vice ministers all have appointments, and they will have to
consider your request before they can make any recommendation. I will pass
your request on to them, señorita."*

Sarah knew that her complaint would never be heard by anyone else if
she left. This old bureaucrat was a specialist in absorbing the grievances of
distressed people. He could listen all day, day after day, without ever being
affected by people's anguish and then could prevaricate week after week
about what was being done, so that the important officials were spared
from listening to the problems of individual people. It was still typical of
Nicaraguan bureaucracy, typical of the way things had been done under
the Somoza regime, typical of how little things had changed. She would
have to get beyond him if anything was ever to be accomplished. *"I will
wait until I can speak with one of the ministers. I can be very brief."*

*"That will not be possible today. Perhaps if you would come back tomorrow.
Thursday or Friday would be even better."*

*"I will wait now, and I will come back every day if I have to. I imagine
one of them will walk through the lobby eventually."*

*"Señorita, please be reasonable. You must follow the proper procedure.
Nothing can be done for you if you do not observe the regulations."*

Suddenly the little man stood and became as erect as his flabby, stoop-
shouldered body would allow. A chill ran through Sarah as she turned
and saw the tall man dressed in khaki and boots wearing sunglasses in
the dimly lit corridor with a pistol in a holster on his hip. Even though
she had never met him before, there was no doubt that she in the presence of Castillo López, a hero of the revolution, one of the five members
of the Directorate, and now the Minister of Justice. He removed the
mirror-plated sunglasses, but his eyes seemed to be made of the same
kind of one-way glass. He looked out; but no one looked into his soul, if
there were any soul inside him. Castillo López seemed to embody power
without any feeling, bloody violence without any mercy, efficient force

without any compassion; and Sarah sensed that he was everything that he seemed to be.

Sarah instinctively assumed the character that she had often observed in her mother. Mary Rutledge could translate even into Spanish the pose of a North Carolina belle that often threw the old Somoza officials off guard whether they respected her or not. *"Señor Minister, would you be so gracious as to give me two or three minutes of your time?"*

Castillo López stared at her without speaking or moving for several moments. Sarah looked directly at him and remained quiet and still and relatively serene, although she could feel the hot and cold places on her neck. Then he nodded curtly, and she told him succinctly about the situation with the soldier at her gate.

"Who are you?"

"I am called Sarah Rutledge Lloyd."

"Your father operated the coffee plantation and factory at Kilometer Thirty."

"Yes. Since the death of my father I have become the owner of Quinta Louisa and the Rutledge coffee finca and factory off the South Highway."

"One of our vice ministers has taken a special interest in your finca. I will send him out to talk with you tomorrow. I will see that the soldier is removed at once. With your permission, señorita." He turned and walked away briskly, and Sarah shivered as she realized that he already knew all about her *finca* before she told him who she was.

Less than two hours later when she reached the gate at Quinta Louisa after dropping Guillermo at the factory, the soldier was already gone. A shudder ran through her exactly as it had when she'd talked with Castillo López in the lobby of the Ministry of Justice. She hadn't expected that communications and actions would be so swift in the new government that action would be taken immediately. She paused just inside the gate with the motor running and looked at her home and front garden. She'd felt enormous relief that Quinta Louisa had been spared when the earthquake demolished the city. Managua had never been as important a part of her life as Quinta Louisa was. She didn't grow from the city as a plant grows in a garden. She didn't feel personally stripped and bruised as many of her friends who had grown up in the city felt after the earthquake, like roots and branches that are torn away from the place they had lived and borne fruit. She felt that Quinta Louisa was utterly different from Managua, from the rest of Nicaragua, from anywhere else in the world. She lived on the *finca* and perhaps also in North Carolina now and only visited Managua. For her Managua had always been a place to be visited, not a place to live, not a place that was a part of her life. She vowed that no one would take Quinta Louisa away from her without a fight, not even Castillo López. If God had spared Quinta Louisa from the earthquake, surely the revolution could not despoil it and wrench it from her; but again a chill ran through her body.

THE SHERIDAN SETTEE WAS draped with dozens of old dresses, skirts, blouses, and nightgowns that had been her mother's. As she sewed Sarah looked at her hands, the parts of her body she was most ashamed of, too small for playing the piano, not even able to stretch over an octave. Her fingers folded together when she relaxed them like unopened buds of a lily, not splayed out like those of other people. Fortunately her mother's clothes would fit her. She didn't know how long she would need to stay in Nicaragua; but however long it was, she would require more clothes to wear than she'd brought from North Carolina. There were enough dresses to make do and have something appropriate for almost any occasion. She heard a car, and she recalled Castillo's promise that someone from the Ministry of Justice would be coming today.

Martín wouldn't allow anyone inside the house without first announcing them, except for Father Richard and Doña Beatriz and one or two other friends that seemed almost like members of the family. *"Señorita, there is a man from the Ministry of Justice here to see you."*

"Ask him to come in." Martín hesitated. *"What is it?"*

"He is someone we know. I thought you might have forgotten his name. He is Carlos Vargas."

"My God! Carlos Vargas Allen . . . at the Minstry of Justice! Thank you, Don Martín. Ask him to come in."

"Sarah."

"Carlos Vargas Allen."

"Carlos Vargas. I'm using only my Spanish name most of the time these days."

"I'm so sorry . . . about your father." They said the same words simultaneously and smiled at how they still finished each other's sentences just as they'd done as children long ago despite the sad sentiments they were both feeling about grief for their fathers.

"I tried to call you several times in the States but wasn't ever able to reach you."

"I know. I got some of your messages, but when I tried to call you back . . . you seemed so far away. I wasn't in the country when your father passed away; and after I returned to Managua, you'd already left, and then . . ."

"Yes, we've been far apart. It's been so many years, Carlos, since we read each other's minds." For several moments they were silent and stared down at the floor. They reached out to each other as if they wanted to embrace, but they never touched, not even their fingertips.

"So many years . . ." Carlos lowered his head. Time rolled back like a breaker at Pocho Mil that left tiny shells and ocean plants on the black volcanic sand of the beach, where they'd laughed and teased and whispered and sat huddled under a blanket when the storm blew up. Then like a wave that rolled in and covered the wet sand of memory with its oddly shaped pebbles, Sarah's mind returned to the present; and they were standing in the parlor at Quinta Louisa again.

"Please sit down." Sarah scooped up the dresses from the settee and flopped back the dust cover. "Let me get these clothes out of the way."

After Carlos sat down across from Sarah they were both silent again for several moments and didn't look at each other. His eyes were still dark, penetrating but no longer afraid. As a boy he had slick, smooth dark skin. Now he had thick hair on his chest. (Hair on the chest was the old standard for suffrage centuries ago under the Spanish to prove European blood.) His skin still glowed suggesting the luminous Mayan gold just below the surface. His guayabera was unbuttoned below his breastbone in typical Nicaraguan fashion; and he wore a thick gold man's bracelet, Nicaraguan style, and a thin gold chain choker around his neck, gringo style. Sarah smiled at her bemused recollection at being glad that Julio hadn't adopted what her mother would have called tacky *macho* jewelry. Sarah thought that the gold of his skin was far more beautiful than the gold chain around his neck and the bracelet on his wrist.

"I never really knew your father, Carlos; but please know how very sorry I am . . ."

"Maybe we never know what our friends' fathers are really like, but I admired your father. He was a good man. I was a little jealous of how much attention he paid to you. My father was never around much."

Sarah was astounded at how loquacious Carlos had become. As children he'd spoken to her only in short sentences, not in paragraphs. She wanted to leave the topic of their fathers. They were feeling each other's pain too acutely, and opening each other's wounds was more than she could bear now. "And how is your mother?"

"She's in Miami. Like so many expatriates now. We don't agree about politics. I don't talk with her about my work in Nicaragua."

"And when did you come back to Nicaragua?"

"About six months ago to live here for good. I've come and gone over the last four years . . . since my father was killed, trying to help the revolution, sometimes in Nicaragua, sometimes abroad. I wanted to finish his work or at least try to carry on some of the hopes and ideals he died for."

"And you work for the Ministry of Justice now."

"¡*Cómo no!* (To be sure!). I'm a vice minister, more out of the leaders' homage to my father than because of anything I've ever done."

"And you're the one who's been protecting me, just as you used to do."

"*Quizás* (Maybe). Mostly I've been delaying any decision until you arrived. I haven't asked for any special treatment or unusual favors for you. That wouldn't be fair."

"And it's fair to expropriate the *finca* that our family has owned for four generations?"

"We've all had to make some hard choices." He looked at her as if he expected her to understand, as if they could pick up their rapport and sympathy from the past decade, as if nothing had happened since they were children.

"I know it's been hard. My father died of a heart attack probably caused by the strain and tension of this revolution."

"He was a good man. I am very truly sorry."

"I would have thought the Sandinistas would be glad to be rid of him without having to execute him as an enemy of the new regime."

"They . . . we don't do things like that. They're not like Somoza. They don't kill people who oppose them. They don't have them killed. They've been extremely conciliatory toward their enemies. Even most members of the *Guardia* (National Guard) were pardoned. Very few people were jailed, only those truly dangerous to the government. They were very conciliatory toward their enemies."

"There are about two thousand people being held at the prison at Tipitapa, I've heard . . . besides those who were killed."

He pushed his fingers back through his hair. It had always been black but curly, unlike the straight hair of most Nicaraguans. "I know this is a tough time for you, but I want to help you."

"I certainly need some help. What do you suggest that I do?"

"We need to begin working on your appeal. They're talking about instituting a new policy called a *solvencia* that will allow people to stay on their property and manage it until a final decision is made."

"You wouldn't betray me, would you, Carlos, just to pacify me and keep me from fighting for what belongs to me while the Sandinistas are taking Quinta Louisa away from me?"

Sarah saw Carlos's cheeks flush and anger rise in his face. He wouldn't cower before her insults and try harder to please her as he had done when he'd played with the big husky gringo boys on the beach. His expression changed. Then she saw the face that Carlos had never revealed to any other friend in their group, to no one except to her, a vulnerable, kind face but not afraid now.

"I'm worried about you. I care about what happens to you." He dropped his eyes almost as the shy boy had done years ago; but Sarah wondered if he were only posing now, using a sincere expression from their childhood to manipulate her now.

"I wonder if you don't care more about moving me out of Quinta

Louisa so that government can take it over than you're concerned about my personal welfare."

His black eyes blazed with a fire of passion. "You fool! Don't you know the government could move you out and take over this *finca* any time it wanted to? Just like that." Then he tried to snap his fingers, but they still bumped gently together. Sarah almost giggled in spite of the tension between them, as she remembered how he'd tried to make his fingers snap, how he'd practiced and practiced to no avail; but she told herself that she must not rely on childhood reveries of vulnerability and kindness until she'd decided whether she could trust him now as a grown man.

"So the government can do anything it wants to me. I don't have any rights now. Is that it? Seems there isn't even the hope of getting justice in Nicaragua any more under the communists. Isn't that what you're saying? All I want is what's fair. I just want what is just and right." If he had come as a stranger, if he had been cold and hard like Castillo, if he were not handsome beyond even the adored idols of her dreams, if they hadn't once been the closest of friends, she wouldn't feel such fury now, she wouldn't speak with such intemperate folly and say things that could be used against her later.

"Now there's real justice and equality for all the people, not just for the wealthy and for foreign capitalists and colonial exploiters. There's opportunity for the poorest *campesinos* (peasants). It's not like the days under Somoza. You're being allowed to stay on here because the government hasn't decided if you deserve to keep the *finca* or not. If they decide you've got to leave, they'll throw you out and turn it over to the workers."

"You call that justice? People on the streets and in the villages look poorer than ever to me. They don't even seem to have enough to eat. What has the new government done for them?"

"Haven't you heard how many people are being taught to read for the first time? Hundreds of thousands."

"Oh, I've heard; and that's very commendable, I suppose. And hundreds and thousands of Cuban and East German communists are here to teach them. I've heard that, too."

"Many Cuban young people came to help. Others came, too. We

needed all the help we could get, and we asked for help from everyone. Some people came from the States. Not many. The U.S. government sent a little money at first. We had to accept help from wherever it was offered. Yes, from East Germans and Russians, too. There are still many problems, many enormous needs. Somoza stole millions, billions from the people and then smuggled the nation's assets out of the country."

"Why did you come out here? To lecture me on the revolution?"

"I wanted to see you. To express my condolences about your father."

"Thank you. I accept your condolences. I believe you're sincerely sympathetic about Daddy's death. We have some good memories together from the past, but we don't have anything in common any more, Carlos." Sarah was as much afraid of her attraction to the man, no longer a boy, as she was afraid of the contempt and rage she felt about his involvement in the revolution.

"I have to return every week to see about the *finca*. It's part of my responsibility."

"So you're here as an agent of the government after all. That's why you really came, isn't it?"

"I asked to be assigned because we were once friends." He turned to leave and then faced her again. "Would you prefer to have someone else? Someone will have to come. Someone has to check on things until the issue of the property is settled."

"I don't really care whether it's you or someone else. What difference does it make?"

"Then I'll see you in a few days unless you request someone else."

Carlos seemed hurt and offended by her cold rebuff, and Sarah wondered if he really did still care about her and sincerely wanted to help her. "Would you really try to help me keep Quinta Louisa?" She began weeping. She detested her tears even more than she detested Carlos for representing everything that the revolution might do to her, everything that was being threatened in her world and taken away from her.

"Of course I would." He stepped toward her but then turned away as tears began to form in his own eyes. He left quickly, and she heard the engine crank and the wheels throw up gravel in the driveway as he sped away.

THURSDAY AFTERNOON SARAH SAW a Land Rover come through the front gate and guessed that it was Carlos Vargas, even though she hadn't seen his vehicle on Tuesday.

"Come in, Carlos. I didn't expect you back so soon. Are you going to check up on me every other day? Did you think I might transport the *finca* across the Costa Rican border?"

"I had a chance to read all the reports about Quinta Louisa at the Ministry yesterday, and I thought you might be interested in knowing just how things stand. I promised to be honest with you, and I'll keep my promise. If you want to hear about them ..."

"I'm sorry, Carlos. Yes, of course I do. I'll try to be civil. It seems strange to think of you as my enemy. I can't forget how close we were as teenagers."

"I'm not your enemy, Sarah. I'm still your friend."

"The government is trying to take everything away from me, and you're part of that government." Carlos looked at her with soft eyes and a benign smile like Daddy and Don Martín had looked at her when they treated her like a five year-old child; but she wouldn't accept such treatment from him and would not tolerate his attempt to confuse her memories, even her very sense of who she was.

"The government isn't your enemy. We're trying to be fair. We're considering all the large portions of property held by single families and how they were obtained and the families' association with Somoza. Land held by foreigners is an especially difficult issue."

"What's your policy going to be? What standard are you using to see if I qualify ... for what my family has owned and looked after for more than a century?"

"There's no agreement between the leaders, just a lot of discussion so far. There aren't any guidelines from the past. Of course, nothing that was done during the oppressive years under the Somozas can be used as a precedent. And it's been so long ... since the thirties. They're trying to be just and fair, but some innocent people will probably suffer losses. It's inevitable in times of great change. I'd like to keep you from getting hurt, from losing everything, if I can. But a lot of things have to be considered—the rights of the poor, who've suffered so much over the years, the rights of workers. Still, you've got several things going for you . . . in your favor."

"Please tell me what is in my favor. Tell me what's going for me, Carlos. Please."

"The length of time the *finca's* been in your family. That's in your favor. Your father had no direct ties with Somoza. I think that can be established. He had a good reputation as an honest, compassionate man. He treated his workers well and made significant improvements in their housing and health care in the village."

"That was mostly Mother's legacy." Sarah spoke without thinking. "I mean she had the inspiration first, but Daddy carried it out. He once said it was the most important thing he ever did."

"As long as they don't consider him along with all the other great landowners, his friends and associates, the people in his class . . ."

"It's so typical of Marxists to condemn people by their class. Evil by association is a terrible fallacy in all socialist propaganda."

"Not all the Sandinistas are Marxists. Not all of us . . . Your nationality is against you more than anything else. If you were a Nicaraguan . . ."

"I won't give up my American citizenship. I wouldn't stop being an American, even to keep Quinta Louisa."

"I didn't think you would. Of course, Nicaraguans are Americans, too, Central Americans."

"You know very well what I mean."

"The very size of the *finca* is against you. The long, long inequities between the very rich and the very poor . . . the revolution was based on changing that evil, on bringing justice and hope and opportunity to the poor, on letting the people of the country determine their own destiny and be justly rewarded for their labor."

"We weren't exactly filthy rich, Carlos. I don't suppose Daddy ever cleared twenty thousand dollars a year. Sometimes he hardly broke even. And he always gave his workers better than average wages. He certainly paid them a hell of a lot more than the Nicaraguan landowners *in his class*, as you say."

"It's strange you talk about dollars instead of *córdobas*. This is Nicaragua, not the States; and we have to work things out according to the realities that exist here now."

"I really don't want to argue with you, Carlos. It's pointless. Our values and beliefs about what's just and right are hopelessly opposed."

"We both still believe in the value of human life, in the basic goodness and honesty of ordinary people, don't we?" He popped his knuckles as he always did when he felt shy and uneasy with her. His hands were much larger now, with the black twisting hair on his fingers down to their first joints, like a strange esoteric script of some forgotten civilization. She wished he hadn't matured into such a handsome man. She detested being attracted to him. Their friendship in the past had been brotherly, sisterly.

"Carlos, I'm not sure what I believe any more. People seem so different here now. Even people in the village act strangely toward me."

"*Only Don Martín and his family, my family now, only they haven't changed,*" she thought.

"The difference may be the revolution. Everyone went through a lot. Everyone changed. We all did. We learned a new kind of fear, to be silent in a different way."

It was the latent accusation that she was not there, that she didn't participate or suffer during the revolution, that she could never understand their experiences or be a part of their lives again after the trauma. "You'll let me know if you learn anything, anything at all, won't you?"

"Of course. I'll call you and try to come back over the weekend."

"Oh, do they make you work on weekends, too? That doesn't seem like a very democratic regime."

"Damn it. I thought I might have some news for you. I'll see you officially next week then." Sarah had finally raised his ire. Carlos was truly hurt and angered by her sarcasm. Suddenly she was sorry, and he was leaving, but she didn't want him to think that she was repentant for the things that she had said about the revolution. She only regretted hurting him, and she was suddenly afraid that he wouldn't return.

"Please come this weekend if you can. It would be nice to know that you're here just as a friend, not in any official capacity."

"I'll stop by if I can. I can't promise."

Part of her fervently hoped that he would visit her during the weekend, but another part of her thought that perhaps it would be better if he never came again, if she never saw him again. She believed that now they belonged to different worlds and that the attachment from their past could cause only more arguments and more anger and more pain.

On the Sunday evening of Sarah's third week back in Nicaragua, Carmen returned from her usual weekend visit with her parents in the city and finally brought up the issue of leaving her job as they sat down for dinner together.

"There's something I need to talk with you about."

Sarah smiled, aware of what Carmen was about to say. "What's that?"

"I'm gonna have to give up my job at the coffee factory. I really hate to do it."

"Why's that, Carmen? Are you unhappy with our arrangement?"

"No way. I've had a ball working at the factory and living here. I hate to lay this on you. I really do." Carmen lowered her eyes in the way that Sarah had learned indicated a prevarication, at least a shading of the truth. "My parents need me to help them make their final preparations for moving to Panama. I have to move back to their house in the city right away to help them pack up."

Sarah refrained from asking if there were other reasons for Carmen's leaving, as Guillermo had implied, as she sensed now. "I'm truly grateful for what you've done. It's been an enormous help. I'll probably stay on in Managua for several months, at best. Maybe I can take on some of your work until we can find someone else. I know I can't do everything you do. No one could do the job as well as you. Will you be able to stay a few more days—at least the rest of this week—to show me the ropes?"

"¡*Claro*! (Surely.) I can get Luis to drive me to the factory to work for the rest of this week, maybe even a few days after that."

"Are you moving to Panama, too, or leaving the country to go somewhere else?"

"I'm not sure. Probably not Panama. Probably not right away, but yeah, probably eventually."

"I hope we can get together while you're still in Managua. I really enjoy talking with you and getting reacquainted."

"Yeah. Me, too. We'll have to meet for *almuerzo* (lunch)." Carmen dropped her eyes again so that her long false lashes completely hid her irises from view. Sarah understood that whatever Carmen's reasons for leaving besides helping her parents might be, they involved something between the two of them and that Carmen had no intention of meeting with her regularly nor perhaps even on an occasional basis.

OVER THREE WEEKS HAD passed since Sarah returned to Nicaragua, and she had not talked about her father's death with Isabel. She had put off the conversation in part because she didn't want to recall the gruesome details about how he was found but in greater part because she dreaded throwing Isabel into the kind of emotional frenzy that she'd exhibited in August. Just before she was about to leave on Saturday in order to be with her family in the village, Isabel was humming and occasionally breaking into soft singing in the kitchen, and Sarah thought it was a good moment to question her.

"Isabel, do you mind telling me again how you found the body of my father? We were both so upset last year that I could not comprehend everything you told me."

"¡Oh, Doña Sarah! Isabel began to weep, and Sarah wondered if she would ever be able to talk with Isabel about how her father's body was discovered. *"He was just lying there, right beside the front door, so still, and I knew he was dead, and Manuel was frightened—he was only nine years old, you know—but I was glad he was with me because I was so scared, too, especially after the raid the night before when I thought Don Jorge was going to have a heart attack right then because he was so angry and I think maybe he was scared, too . . ."*

"What raid? I have never heard about any raid before."

"¡Oh, Doña Sarah! I am so sorry. I was not supposed to tell you about that. Don Martín said I was never to mention it. He said it would upset you and

add to your grief and made me promise, and I am so very, very sorry."

"That is all right, Isabel. It was good not to tell me everything right after my father died, but I need to learn all the details now. It was very good for you to mention it. Tell me more about it."

Isabel wrung her hands. She was trembling, even though she'd stopped weeping. *"Don Martín will be very angry with me. He made me promise never to tell. He ran outside with the gun and shouted at them, and I heard the gunshots, and they all ran away. I could not see any of them—I only heard their voices-and Don Jorge ran outside without a gun and when he came back inside—Don Martín stayed outside—I thought Don Jorge would collapse and die right then, but before I went to bed he seemed to be calm, and I thought he would be all right. I should have stayed to take care of him."*

Sarah gave Isabel a hug, more a true hug than just an *abrazo* (embrace). *"You have taken good care of us. You could not have done anything to help my father that night. I will speak to Don Martín. He will not be angry with you. I am sorry you have shared so much of our grief. You must not blame yourself."*

SARAH DECIDED TO SPEAK with Guillermo before she talked with Don Martín about the raid that had been kept a secret from her, and she waited until they were together at the factory on Monday rather than going to the village during the weekend and making a huge issue of it.

"Guillermo, did you not know there was a raid at Quinta Louisa the night before my father died? Surely you knew about it."

Guillermo pursed his lips, first pulling them down, then up, then to the left, then to the right, before responding. *"Yes, of course, I knew about it. Papá made us swear not to tell you. You know how stubborn and tough Papá can be and how we have to obey him when he gets like that. He made us swear not to tell. How did you find out? Did Isabel tell you? She promised never to tell."*

"She let it slip. You must not blame her. Who else knows? Your brothers?"

"Julio was not here. We have never told him. I told Ana about it, and she has *kept her ear to the ground, as you say, to find out if anyone mentioned it at the school. I do not believe anyone in the village knew about it. I do not*

believe Isabel has told anyone in the village about it. Papá put the fear of God into her, *as you say."*

Even in the tense conversation Sarah was amused by Guillermo's Spanglish, switching back and forth mid-sentence from Spanish into English. *"I will discuss this with Don Martín later. I have not mentioned it to him yet."*

"I hope you will not. I beg you not to. It will throw Papá back into that . . . way he was right after Don Jorge's death. He believes he should have protected your father better. He believes if he had protected him better Don Jorge would not have died."

"Guillermo, what burdens you carry! What a load you carry for me!"

"No, no, Sarita . . . we carry for one another."

Sarah gave Guillermo a hug like the one she had given Isabel, more than an *abrazo* (embrace). *"I love you all very much. I will not speak to your father about it . . . at least not for the present."*

CARLOS VARGAS CONTINUED TO visit Quinta Louisa at least twice each week. He and Sarah alternately argued about their political differences and reminisced about their childhood friendship, and Sarah was alternately annoyed by their different philosophies and confused by her attraction to him. She had once been a head taller than he was. Now he was several inches taller than she was even in her two-inch heels—because of her height she never wore heels higher than two inches. He may have been the tallest man she had seen in Nicaragua since she returned, and he was certainly the most handsome.

One morning she saw the Land Rover pull through the gate and felt a little girl excitement as she walked out to meet Carlos. She could almost see herself walking toward him as if she were in a movie with the gentle wind blowing her skirt against her legs as it tossed the palms above her head and made a sound like rain in the morning light. She had watched from the front door as her mother would walk across the same lawn to meet her father and embrace him and kiss him. The hair on Carlos's chest and arms glistened with sweat after the hot drive from the city, and she could smell the male scent of him.

That afternoon the Land Rover had trouble starting, and Carlos asked Sarah if he could work on it in her driveway. He stripped off his shirt, and his beltless jeans slipped so low on his hips that she thought he wasn't wearing underpants. She'd never seen his adult torso naked before, although the triangle of skin between the suggestively unbuttoned shirt had been more titillating than his bare chest. He still thought of himself as a runt, haunted by the taunts of his childhood tormentors. She liked to watch him from the window, spying, assured of not being seen by him, as they'd watched a migratory painted bunting once long ago from a window at the American School. He was unaware of his sexuality, as natural and beautiful and lush as the fruits and flowers of the garden.

Carlos's luminous golden and bronze skin was unlike Guillermo's earthen, hairless Indian body that was nonluminous even under the glistening sun and film of sweat. The heavy hair on Carlos's chest knotted and curled tightly from his neck down over his navel to the top of the pants that covered the bulge of his manhood. His forearms weren't shaped like Don Martín's and Guillermo's and seemed small below his big shoulders and biceps. His hands also seemed somehow delicate with unusually thin long fingers, not like a peasant's hands and wrists.

He was wearing a pair of old grey hushpuppy loafers, unlike Guillermo's tattered sneakers, unlike her father's sensible oxfords. He was neither Caucasian nor Indian, neither pure Nicaraguan nor pure European. Her father had never worked outside without wearing a shirt because of his fair reddish-blonde English skin. She'd seen her father without a shirt only three or four times in her life. In the garden her father had moved efficiently and deliberately to accomplish tasks reasonably and rationally. Guillermo worked with a natural grace, instinctively, rhythmically, like the wind tossing the fronds of the palms. Carlos wasn't like either of them as he worked under the hood of the Land Rover with methodical precision.

Sarah tucked her head and looked down at the white skin of her chest; then she unbuttoned the top of her blouse and looked down at her breasts, small and flat and wide and round but with unusually large, very pink nipples. She went into her bedroom and put on the caftan that her mother had bought years ago in Panama. It had been made of real silk imported from the orient. Without underclothes she felt her skin, especially her nipples against the silk, and enjoyed the nakedness of her body as Carlos was enjoying the nakedness of his body feeling the sun and sweat and tropical breeze on his skin like the silk on hers.

She called out to him, "How about staying for dinner? Can you have a little *cena* (supper) with me before you have to get back to Managua?"

"I'd love it! Thanks. I've almost finished with the car. You sure it's not too much ..."

"*Bueno* (good)." She caught herself just before she said, *it's a date.* "*Está bien* (It's fine)."

While Carlos was finishing his labor under the hood of the Land Rover Sarah slipped out into the garden and cut flowers for the dining room table. Tonight she, not Don Martín, must put the flowers on the table, as her mother had done every evening before her father came in from his daily tasks. She found another of her mother's dresses, all cotton, faded blue, with several rows of lace and a very low bodice. It would never do to wear anywhere in public; but it was too pretty to throw away, even though it was faded and old-fashioned. Luckily she and her mother had worn the same size. A button was missing at the top so that her breasts would have been exposed; but she fastened the cloth with a Nicaraguan filigreed gold orchid pin, made by a craftsman in Masaya who probably never realized the value of his talent. The English dress showed to good effect the skin of her pale, white English bosom. Her Nicaraguan sandals were made from delicately carved leather, found only rarely among all the handmade things of the Masaya market in the past, never seen now. In the old days beautiful things like her sandals would sometimes appear among the rank-smelling vegetables and fly-covered meat and piles of trashy straw and wood and leather geegaws.

Carlos flung his shirt over his shoulder—the shirt he'd used all afternoon for a rag to mop sweat from his face—and went around the side of the house and then came back. "Would it be all right if I washed up in your bathroom? I have a spare shirt and pair of pants in the car."

"Of course. Come on in."

As Carlos came through the front door Sarah pointed him toward the bathroom. "It's in kind of an odd place, off an alcove on the back hall."

"I know the way."

"Really? Were you in the habit of coming inside the house on your surveys for the ministry before I returned?"

Carlos looked shocked, as if he'd been caught in some obscene act, like a boy startled by a parent while he was masturbating. "Oh, no. Of course not. I remembered from when we were children."

Now Sarah was surprised. She couldn't recall any occasion when Carlos had been inside the house at Quinta Louisa, not even during the dreadful Halloween party of despised memory.

Carlos dressed in clean chinos with a white shirt like a vest that fastened with only a strap at the bottom. It resembled Guillermo's peasant work shirt but was stylized and elegant, made for the beach on a hot, tropical day or for relaxing at home. The shirt slipped up over his waist when he raised his arms and was unbuttoned at the top. His tan skin and black chest hair seemed even darker against the white cloth, unlike the white skin of Sarah's bosom that looked even paler in the dim light.

Father Richard had given Sarah some Danish cheese from the American commissary that had been a gift to "the Padre" from the American Ambassador. She served the cheese with some cold chicken and local fruit on a big blue platter that also held tortillas. Nicaraguan tortillas were not like the thin Mexican ones, but were thick, made with coarser corn meal. The rest of the meal consisted of a big bowl of rice and refried red beans and a small bowl of white, dry Nicaraguan cheese.

"You are very pretty. Your dress is beautiful. I like it."

"It was Mother's." Then she realized that she'd never seen her mother wearing it. It would have been old-fashioned and inappropriate for almost every occasion even during the years of her mother's adult life; and she suddenly wondered if her mother might have worn it when she became engaged to her father in order to look both English and casual, to accept the proposal of an Englishman. Whether it was true or not, she would believe her fantasy.

After dinner they sat on the back patio just as Sarah had lingered with her mother and father after they'd finished eating every night and then alone with her father after her mother's death. Sarah and Carlos seemed like an old married couple at ease with one another, and she couldn't suppress her fantasy of being married to Carlos. Tonight the bonds of their childhood friendship seemed to outweigh their ideological differences.

"I suppose you'll go back to the States after you get a property settlement."

"Wouldn't you be glad to be rid of me, not having to come out here every few days?" She lowered her head and detected a tearful catch in her voice that she hoped Carlos hadn't heard.

"You know I wouldn't." Carlos looked angry and frustrated. He clenched his teeth, and she saw the muscles moving in his jaw.

"Have you ever thought of living in the States? I could help you get a job in North Carolina. I know a lot of people there now through my family and those I've met."

"There are things I have to finish here. I can't leave now. I can't run out. I've made a commitment to the revolution."

"Is the revolution really that important to you? Couldn't you be satisfied as a decent, honest man with a wife and a good home and a job in a country that offers some real freedom and a chance to be fairly rewarded for your labors?"

"But what will happen to Nicaragua then and to all the other places in the world where people are struggling to overcome poverty and tyranny, if everyone takes the easy way out?"

"Oh, Carlos! This revolution is a farce. It's just a mirage. You overthrow one tyrant and have a big parade, and everybody believes there will be a new life of justice and equality the next morning, but you can't change a country overnight. The revolution has brought as much misery and ruin as it's taken away." She'd already heard disillusionment whispered among people in the village as they murmured about having even less now than they'd had under Somoza. If Somoza had been an evil tumor in the country—and she was willing to believe that he was very evil—removing the tumor had only spread cancerous growths throughout the land. Poverty and disease and ignorance were worse than ever along with the same old greed and corruption and injustice.

"I can't be a comfortable leech living in security and material wealth while my country suffers. Maybe it's still possible to be a decent, honest man and live comfortably for a little while longer in the States, as long as you look away from the rest of the world, until the rest of the world crowds in on you. Maybe it used to be possible in Nicaragua . . . in your father's time. But it's not possible for me. That's what you want, isn't it? You want me to be a decent, honest person like your father and forget about what happens to the majority of the population of Nicaragua."

"Daddy didn't ignore the problems of the world. He certainly didn't live off the blood of the poor."

"I never said he did, Sarah."

Carlos slumped into his chair and bowed his head and held his temples between his palms. "Maybe that's the best I can do. Maybe that's all I'm good for, too."

"Carlos, no . . . I didn't mean . . ." Sarah reached over between their chairs and grasped his arm. She felt the muscles contract, not relax at her touch, and almost pull away from her.

"You don't know what a coward I've been. During the first part of the revolution I was in college in the States. Oh, I wrote pamphlets and letters, especially after my father was killed; but even after I finished college I never made a guerilla raid or really did anything. I raised money and tried to explain things to reporters and diplomats. They said I was being the most help that way. I accepted it because I didn't really want to be in danger. I didn't want to risk my life. Now I have a soft job at the Ministry of Justice. It's the people who risked their lives and made sacrifices for the revolution that should be in charge now, people like Castillo López . . . I can't even wear khaki clothes without feeling like a complete hypocrite. It would just be a mockery of those who suffered and fought, those who gave their lives."

His expression reminded her of Don Martín's forlorn face in the days after her father's death. She couldn't touch the hurt with her fingers or reach the shame with her words.

"You're an honorable man. However much we may disagree, I admire your integrity. You'll do more in the long run than people who brought all this violence and killing . . . taking things away from some people but giving almost nothing to the poor."

"It will take time, Sarah. We have to keep on trying." He shrugged free from her hand on his arm and rose from his chair. His face was contorted in pain. He walked to the door leading into the dining room with his back to Sarah. He held his hands behind him, popping his knuckles.

"It's not what you do, it's who you are deep down that counts. So much of what we do at any given moment is determined by chance and circumstance."

"You make it sound very easy. Don't you want more out of life than just being comfortable and secure? Isn't life something more for you than just having material things?"

"You're beginning to sound like Father Richard. You may be right. I've thought a lot the last few weeks about the workers' houses in the village. It was my mother's passion . . . and my father's cross, sometimes."

"I wish we could believe in the same things and work for them together like we did when we were kids. You gave me a kind of special courage when I was a little boy. I never was so afraid when you were around. I felt brave and special, like I could lick the world."

"I remember, Carlos. You even said you loved me and tried to get me to say I loved you, too, over and over."

"And you never would."

"Maybe it's time to ask me again." She wondered if she had spoken too soon and had taken a foolish risk and exposed her secret fantasies and desires for nothing.

"It's not so simple now. Wouldn't it be wonderful if things were as simple and uncomplicated as they were when we were just kids?"

"Were they ever that simple and uncomplicated? I don't think so . . ."

"It's getting late. I better get back to Managua. It's a long drive." Sarah was aware that Carlos was avoiding further conversation with her. "The roads are still dangerous at night, even for a vice minister of the government." The tone of his voice mocked himself, and he slumped into the insecurities of his boyhood that Sarah remembered both painfully and fondly. "Are your plans working out at the factory?" Once again he abruptly changed the subject in his attempt to regain his adult control and self-assurance.

"Yes. I'm able to do most of Carmen's work, and Julio can take care of everything else when he comes up every few weeks. I do have one little problem to solve. It's nothing major. José and his family want to move back to the village. We need a guard at night. I don't want Don Martín to have the whole responsibility twenty-four-seven. I guess he can find someone else. I don't suppose you'd be interested in moving into the guesthouse?" Sarah laughed at what she imagined was an absurd suggestion.

"Are you serious, Sarah?" Carlos came back from the door and sat down beside her. "Are you really serious?"

"I wasn't. It was meant as a joke, but if you'd consider . . . Oh, Carlos, it would be wonderful! I'd feel so safe, and having you across the yard . . . Would you really consider it?"

"Of course. *Ciertamente* (certainly). I've wanted to live at Quinta Louisa my whole life. I've dreamed about it. This is the most beautiful place in the world, the most perfect . . ." Sarah thought how he echoed Father Richard's words of praise for Quinta Louisa. Carlos reached over and took Sarah's hand in his. Her tiny hand that felt almost deformed to her seemed perfected, restored in his strong grasp. His long, thin fingers wrapped around her hand almost like coils, and she felt safe, even secure, for the first time since her father's death.

"When can you move in?"

"As soon as you'll let me."

"*El próximo sábado* (Next Saturday)?"

"*Perfecto.*"

DURING THE SECOND WEEK of July the telephone rang early on Tuesday morning; it was a familiar pattern in Nicaragua—nothing seemed to happen for weeks, and then things happened so quickly that there was no time to consider their implications. The strange voice introduced himself in Spanish as Ernesto Andrejo Sánchez, another vice minister at the Ministry of Justice. His voice was husky with a slur of casual dissipation unlike the slur of peasant inflections in the voices of some revolutionaries, who might be well-read and well-educated but were the first literate generation in their families. He wanted to meet with Sarah privately but not at the ministry office. He implied that he wanted to come to her home some evening.

"Señor Carlos Vargas Allen is staying here to guard the property and protect me."

Ernesto Andrejo Sánchez knew, and he didn't want to encounter Carlos. Their meeting must be strictly private. He wondered if she couldn't arrange for Carlos to arrive late one evening, so that they could talk privately. She began to get the picture of sexual favors being given in order to expedite the process of her settlement—another familiar tactic under the old regime, although rarely proposed in the past to expatriates of her class who were permanent residents in the country. *"Some things change, but others are nauseatingly familiar after the revolution,"* Sarah thought. If a carnal liaison was what he had in mind, she didn't want to encourage him.

"I would be afraid of being alone on the finca at night, even for a few minutes." She lied. She was becoming adept at lying. Carlos was rarely at Quinta Louisa on Saturday nights and often arrived late on weeknights when he had work to do at the ministry office. *"Perhaps I can tell Señor Vargas about our meeting and arrange for him to leave just as you arrive and then return at a specified hour a short time later."*

Vice Minister Andrejo was adamantly opposed to Carlos knowing anything about the meeting. She must not mention it to anyone, to no one at all, especially not to anyone from the ministry, above all not to Carlos. He had a proposal, but it was very important that it be discussed in complete confidentiality and secrecy if there were to be any possibility of its succeeding. It was a very sensitive issue and must be handled with great delicacy.

"Perhaps we could meet in a restaurant."

It would be too public.

"I could arrange to use the home of a friend and have the family remain in the back, out of sight." Sarah thought of Doña Beatriz's house in Los Robles.

Her friend's home would not do either. No one, absolutely no one, must know about their meeting.

Sarah was determined that she would not allow him to find her alone at Quinta Louisa; but if the Ministry of Justice was about to propose a secret settlement, if the meeting did hold the possibility of a legitimate offer, she must not let the opportunity slip by. Then the whole proposal for a settlement might be discarded, and she might lose forever any possibility of getting a clear title to Quinta Louisa. Perhaps it was being kept from Carlos because Castillo López knew about their friendship and didn't want him to be involved. Father Richard and St. Francis occurred to her. Perhaps Andrejo would agree to meet her in the sacristy.

"We could use the American Church, St. Francis, at kilometer seven and a half on the South Highway. I could arrange to get a key from the priest, and he wouldn't have to know your identity or anything about the nature of our business. I could tell him simply that it was a legal matter. Actually it would be more private than my home, because the cook and gardener could not observe us there." But Father Richard would be just across the driveway, and she could scream for help if Andrejo tried to assault her. He would probably be restrained from making indecent overtures, perhaps even from making indecent proposals, if he possessed the common Nicaraguan superstitions about churches.

Andrejo wanted to see her as soon as possible.

"I think I can arrange it for tomorrow night. Wednesday. At what hour?"

It must be well after dark, perhaps eight o'clock. He gave her a telephone number where he could be called tomorrow afternoon, but she should call only if she could not arrange the meeting at the church, and she must not discuss the matter or reveal her identity over the telephone. She should simply say that she could not meet him. Sarah recognized the number as one of the telephones at the Ministry of Justice from the list that Carlos had given her in order to reach him in case of an emergency.

"I promise that I will not tell anyone, especially not Señor Vargas Allen. I will tell him only that I am going to a meeting at the church, and I will not tell the padre anything about the nature of our meeting or your identity."

When Sarah called to make arrangements with Father Richard, he offered to come out for her and drive her to the church; and she agreed. She remembered when she had felt safe driving into Managua by herself at night, to a friend's home or to the movies, although her father had always disapproved, even after she returned as an adult during vacations. In the past the slight feeling of danger had given her a pleasant thrill, but driving at night frightened her since the revolution. She didn't want to be alone at night without someone she knew nearby, not on the *finca*, not in the city, especially not on the road, not even at the church.

SARAH LEFT THE DOOR of the sacristy ajar, so that Vice Minister Andrejo could see that she had arrived. Father Richard was in the vicarage just across the driveway, but she still felt alone and afraid. Nowhere was lonelier than a church at night, especially in a room like the sacristy at St. Francis. God seemed to go away with the people. The ceiling of the sacristy went all the way to the roof of the chancel, as tall as the nave. It would have been a large room if it were laid down on its side; but as the room stretched upright, the small red tiled floor was completely filled by the crude desk and five folding chairs, the same chairs that had been used for her confirmation class over a decade ago. Across one wall the built-in cabinets for the vestments and church linens were locked. She'd taken things out of those cabinets hundreds of times when she'd helped her mother set up the altar. She'd dressed in the sacristy as an acolyte with the boys—she was usually the only girl. Allowing a girl to serve as an acolyte was one of Father Richard's liturgical innovations, to which her father had vehemently objected.

Sarah didn't think much about God outside the church building, except in times of terrible need and pain—when her mother had died twelve years ago and when she'd first returned after her father's death in August, almost a year ago, when she'd hurled angry curses up to heaven. God once seemed very real to her. As a little girl, even as a teenager, she could talk to God; and when she'd worshipped in the church, she'd felt as close to God as to her father as she cuddled on his lap.

Sarah hoped that Vice Minister Andrejo would arrive soon. She flipped through an old copy of *TIME*. The only sources of news in English from outside the country for years had been *TIME* magazine and *THE MIAMI HERALD* newspaper, delivered weekly or daily by air. For years there had rarely been even a mention of Nicaragua in *TIME* until the revolution, except for the coup of 1967 and the earthquake nine years ago; but now almost every issue contained articles about Nicaragua, stimulated by the phobia of the United States about communist nations on its doorstep.

Then light spilled out into the driveway; and a car drove in very fast, squealing at the turn, blowing up dust into the open doorway of the sacristy. It was an old Mercedes, like all the government officials used to drive. (After a few years they became taxicabs. Managua must have been the only poor capital in Latin America with as many Mercedes taxis. Somoza had held the Mercedes import license himself.)

Sarah heard footsteps crunching on gravel in the driveway and felt her heart pounding. Hands appeared before a face as Andrejo caught the threshold to pull himself up the steps into the room. Seeing his strange hand first was more frightening than his face might have been. He wore three large rings; and his meticulously well-groomed fingers reminded her of government officials before the revolution who had their hands manicured almost every week. Her heart pounded even more rapidly than it had on the morning when she first visited Castillo's office. She reminded herself over and over that Father Richard was in the vicarage just across the driveway.

"Señorita Rutledge Lloyd?" Andrejo's English pronunciation was good. Rutledge often came out in a variety of ways: Root-*lay*-ha, *Ru*-lay, sometimes it sounded like "rude lady." Lloyd, her mother's family name, was an utterly impossible combination of letters for most Nicaraguans to pronounce. Visual appearances were almost always different from how voices were imagined, but Ernesto Andrejo Sánchez looked like his voice. He was short, fat, middle-aged, and wearing an open-necked white shirt, just as she'd pictured him from their telephone conversations.

"*Sí, Señor. Come in, Señor Vice Minister.*" Sarah decided to speak to him in Spanish. He could direct the conversation into English if he so chose. He gazed up toward the high ceiling of the tiny room, and Sarah saw in his face the fear he felt of losing his pride and losing his control. He must want something very badly from her, something more than going to bed with her, to risk meeting her here.

"I have never been in this church before. I have passed it many times of course and noticed it from the highway. It is a charming building." He continued to speak in Spanish; thus he didn't want to flatter her, better done in English if he had the command of the language that she imagined. What he wanted to say must be expressed with great delicacy, a delicacy not possible for anyone in a second language, however well learned.

"Yes. This church embodies many memories for me and my family over many, many years. We love it very much."

"And do you plan to stay in Nicaragua, to live here for your lifetime?"

"My plans are indefinite." An ambiguous phrase once shaped becomes easier with each repetition. She didn't think that her face betrayed her true feelings.

*"I knew your father. He was a fine gentleman. Muy simpático (*very charming). *I am deeply sorry for his tragic death."*

"Thank you. Did you know my mother, too?"

"No, I did not have that pleasure, but I did visit your finca several times. I knew your father through business. I was engaged in importing and exporting for many years." He had probably been involved in smuggling and helping people to skirt the law and evade customs and import taxes. *"What a charming place Quinta Louisa is! It is surely one of the most beautiful fincas in the country. I can understand why you might want to spend the rest of your life there."*

"It was a wonderful place to grow up. I have many happy memories."

*"¡Como no! (*As you say!) *But it might be sad for you to live there with the many memories of your childhood, now that you have no family here, now that your parents have died. You must have thought of some of the difficulties of remaining at Quinta Louisa. It would be very difficult indeed for a young woman to maintain the finca and the factory by herself."*

Sarah could see his purple colored lips moving with a salivation of greed, like a hungry gourmand prevented from consuming a feast that was set in front of him. She felt a rage toward Chief Minister Castillo López. First he'd sent Carlos, an old friend, to coax her away from Quinta Louisa. Now he was trying to intimidate her through Andrejo Sánchez.

"I am aware of the difficulties." She would make him play the role of

the cat and hold a mouse just beyond his grasp, but she must be careful and watch out for the claws. The tamest pussy could become a wild ocelot with a half-dead, bloody mouse dangled wriggling before its nose. *"I know that I may not be able to stay indefinitely at Quinta Louisa."*

"If you should decide that you cannot remain as a permanent resident in Nicaragua, it would have a great influence on the settlement of your claims to the property. Ascertaining your intentions, one way or the other, is vital for the ministry."

"So I have been told before. Part of the difficulty seems to be that I cannot really make my own plans until I know what the disposition will be of the factory my father built, and it seems that the government cannot make decisions until I make my plans. It seems to be impossible, a catch twenty-two, *as we say in English."* Sarah arched her eyebrows, her schoolmarm's countenance, waiting with a staged silence for an answer. It was an amused and slightly intimidating expression, a little scene played out self-consciously by every schoolteacher.

"Perhaps I can help. I shall have to receive your vow of complete confidentiality. If you should repeat what I say to anyone, to anyone at all, it could be very harmful for both of us."

"You have my pledge, Don Ernesto." She used his first name deliberately, calculatedly, with the old honorific "don."

Andrejo fidgeted with his thumb until the cuticle began to bleed around the nail. He was the epitome of an overly anxious student. *"It is my opinion that the government would not pay you much for your father's coffee processing plant and almost assuredly not for shares in the coffee exporting brokerage. Things have already been organized differently in order to export our national products. I speak with some certainty, because I am privy to the decisions of the government regarding imports and exports. Without the factory and access to the export market, it would be very difficult for you to operate the finca profitably. This must all be in the strictest confidence, you understand."*

"Of course. I understand."

"If you should decide to sell the factory and also your finca, I would have a great personal interest in attaining them. I think that you can appreciate how my personal interest might be misunderstood by some people in the government."

Sarah nodded solemnly but did not speak.

"If you were inclined to sell the finca, I believe I could arrange for a clear title in your name. Of course, the payment would come directly to you from the government, and I might be rewarded with an option to bid on it, you understand."

"¡Cómo no! (As you say!). *I understand perfectly, and I will consider your suggestions very carefully, and let you hear from me."*

Some things had not changed since the revolution. Even the manner of proposing a corrupt deal had not been altered. Sarah smiled as she thought of Adolfo Castillo López's self-righteousness and Carlos's pious words about justice and equity. She thought how outraged her father would have been. He had always been offended by such proposals, even though he often had to deal in a manner like this, with people like Ernesto Andrejo. From Andrejo's implications Sarah gathered that her father had very likely dealt with Andrejo himself on some occasions in order to gain an export license or an import permit. She had given her word, and she would not betray this contemptible man, but now she would have to decide. Now she would have to deal with the issues of staying or leaving. Dishonorable men force choices upon you. The ideals of honorable men could delay interminably the difficult decisions of life, because no perfect answer could ever be found; but for dishonorable men there was always a simple answer to be given—yes or no, to accept or reject their bribes.

Sarah couldn't be sure whether Andrejo's plan had been an official proposal for settlement from the Ministry of Justice or simply an invention of his own avarice. Was he acting on behalf of Castillo López? Was this Castillo's trick to deceive her and cause her to expose her intentions? Andrejo had been more cunning than Sarah in their cat and mouse game after all. Now she was the cat, and the mouse was being dangled in front of her. Even the wildest ocelots became almost gentle at the end of the dry season when they would creep into the back of the garden seeking water and food and would let you watch them, call to them, walk close to them, before they ran away. Wild creatures can be tamed by desperation, and tame creatures can become wild in their fear and panic.

Father Richard told Sarah that he would be glad to drive her back to Quinta Louisa, but she insisted on calling Carlos and asking him to come for her at the vicarage. Father Richard didn't object strongly. Even he was becoming wary of driving in the countryside at night. He looked down at the floor and pushed the palms of both hands firmly over his short-cropped hair, pulling his scalp back so that his eyebrows moved into the middle of his forehead.

"Did you learn something about keeping your property tonight? I don't mean to pry. You said it was a confidential meeting."

"You're right—it did have to do with the property settlement, but that's about all I better tell you now. Oh, Padre, I don't think I could endure losing Quinta Louisa after losing Daddy."

"Perhaps that's how missionary priests are different from everyone else in the world. You feel you have so much to lose, your houses and lands, all your material possessions." There was a bitter hardness in his voice that Sarah hadn't heard before.

"Don't you share that sense of loss? Are you really different from the rest of us?"

"I wouldn't suffer any material loss at all. This furniture doesn't even belong to me. If I should leave Nicaragua tomorrow, I'd be blessedly relieved of those dreadful orange drapes that the women of the parish put up." He looked at the burnt orange drapes with disgust. Sarah remembered with some satisfaction that her mother had objected to them as much too hot a color for the tropics when the women of the church were redecorating the vicarage. "I've lost only my dream of doing something worthwhile in the world, of building some little corner of a more righteous society, of moving a few people just an infinitesimal part of an inch closer to the Kingdom of God. That's what I've lost."

"But you've helped people. I've seen the love and hope you gave people when I went with you and Daddy to visit in poor villages. It's impersonal governments that do bad things to people. Individual people are usually the ones that do what's right and good."

"Do they? Do they indeed? I saw cases of medicine from the States spoil in the sun at the airport after the earthquake because an individual official in the government wasn't interested in medicine for the poor. I've seen food that was supposed to be given away to poor people sold by an individual government functionary. I've seen a strong individual taking a few *centavos* from a weak individual even at the very lowest, poorest level of the country. The poor are not always very blessèd, you know. Even when things were distributed by the church, the only way they'd get to the *campesinos*, I've seen a greedy individual village leader grab the food away from babies. But I've also seen children who would've died live because they did get some of the medicine provided by government agencies, however impersonally. I've seen people kept from starvation by the churches' social programs. But it wasn't enough. In the end, it didn't work. It all failed." In his tone of voice Sarah heard him also saying, "*And I failed, too.*"

Sarah had never seen Father Richard weep in the poorest villages holding babies whose bellies puffed out like birthday balloons with parasites or giving communion and anointing old people whose feet were too swollen for walking and whose tongues were too swollen for talking. Then he had done what needed to be done, what could be done under the limitations of the situation. Now he was weeping for himself, feeling sorry for himself. He lacked the hard compassion and stern mercy for himself that he'd prescribed for others.

"God hasn't finished with you yet. God still has some things He wants you to do." Sarah was astonished at the words that came out of her mouth. What a travesty, if not downright blasphemy! She had most assuredly heard no voices from heaven.

"So the Lord is speaking directly to you now, eh, Sarah?" Father Richard snickered in his habitual way that often made people distrust misjudge him. Then he began laughing, as she hadn't heard him laugh since her father's death, as she hadn't ever heard him laugh except when he had joked with her father.

"Don't make fun of me. I certainly haven't heard God whispering in my ear, and I don't ever expect to."

Suddenly Father Richard's face became serious. "Sometimes we do see God's face and hear His voice, usually echoed in another person's words and reflected in another person's face."

Then they heard the Land Rover in the church driveway, and she stood to go out, but the car door slammed, and she heard footsteps drawing nearer to the vicarage. Carlos would come in, of course, in order to speak with Father Sims. However much Carlos had rejected his mother's religion, he retained both the sense of personal caring he'd learned from his American mother and the ornate civility he'd inherited from his Nicaraguan father.

"Good evening, Father Sims. Are you all right? I hope you had a good meeting tonight."

"I'm quite well, thank you." Padre Richard glanced at Sarah to make a reply about the meeting. His face was still somber after his despondent conversation with Sarah. "We'll know whether the meeting was worthwhile until later, I suppose." Perhaps he thought it was better to avoid telling outright lies whenever possible in order to save them for occasions of absolute necessity.

"I think the meeting was productive. I learned some things." Sarah tried to cover Father Richard's obfuscation with her own dissembling as she walked over to the table where she had laid her sweater and a scarf. She never carried anything in the daytime, except an umbrella during the rainy season; but living up in the hills outside the city had ingrained the habit of always having a sweater and scarf at hand in the evenings when she went out. The night air in the higher elevations was always cool, and a sudden wind off the lake could bring a chill at night even in the city.

"Won't you sit down? I'd be delighted if you could stay for a while."

"For a few minutes, if that's all right with Sarah."

"Of course, Carlos."

"Are you saving many souls these days, Padre?" Carlos was relaxed now, casual, cocky in Father Richard's presence. His legs were crossed loosely, and his right arm was draped over the back of the couch. He no longer squirmed in discomfort while talking with the priest. He was no longer torn by conflicts of faith and doubt, of sin and righteousness, at least not as expressed and defined by religion.

Father Richard Sims's eyes brightened. He detested being asked the inane question about how many souls he'd saved, but he thoroughly enjoyed verbal jousting with a born-again agnostic. His self-pity and morose feelings were swept away by the challenge of some good religious thrusting and parrying. "We've had to leave most of the evangelizing up to you folks in the government since the revolution. About all the church can do is to help fill people's stomachs."

Carlos blushed. He recognized the challenge, and his eyes also brightened, as he decided to join the duel with his opponent. "Too bad the church didn't come up with that idea a long time ago, Padre. Maybe the revolution wouldn't have been necessary."

"Churches have done some bad things in the past, just as governments have. But governments and churches are both necessary in some form or another."

Sarah recognized Father Richard's familiar parry. He would offer an apparent truce; and if Carlos were distracted he would lose his balance and be tipped over.

"I suppose religion can help to unify a country, and every nation needs that. One of the things Nicaragua needs most now is a unified culture. I suppose the church could help with that."

"Ah, a unified culture . . . that is one of the great goals of the revolution, isn't it? But, you see, true faith respects the diversity and dignity of varying cultures."

Sarah glanced at Carlos and realized that he was unaware that Father Richard had subtly shifted the focus from the church and religion to faith. "There were fewer and fewer remnants of uniquely Nicaragua culture even before the revolution. I used to go from a Carib village to a Mesquito village over on the East Coast and in doing so move from one world to another. I suppose the revolutionary government wants to make even the turtle fishermen on the Pearl Lagoon just like the city dwellers in Managua. You're going after a great homogenized blob of a country, aren't you?"

Poor Carlos was smiling with a relaxed grin, as if he didn't realize that he was about to be thrown down into the dust in their joust.

"Of course not, but I suppose you'd like for the people on the Pearl Lagoon to be as good Christians as those in Managua, just as our new government would like for them to have equal justice and equal opportunities with the city dwellers."

Sarah's mouth gaped open in amazement. Carlos had responded as quickly and adroitly as her father might have done in an argument with Father Richard.

Father Richard smiled at his young opponent. "As long as you haven't forgotten what it means to be a Christian, Carlos, we have nothing to argue about."

Carlos grinned broadly and nodded his head as a sign of submission. Neither of them had been humiliated, and perhaps they would meet again in another tournament. Father Richard beamed. His pleasure seemed to come from gaining something far more precious from Carlos than scoring a victory in a verbal match. He had found an opponent almost as worthy in debate as his friend George Rutledge had been.

WHEN SARAH HEARD THE Land Rover come to a stop beside the guesthouse, she called to Carlos from the front door of the main house. "Want to have a little *cena* (supper) with me tonight? I have some cold chicken that Isabel roasted yesterday and some cheese-stuffed *chayotes* (vegetable pears)."

"I need to talk with you. Are you busy right now?"

"Not at all. Come on over."

"*Gracias.*" As he came into the parlor Carlos ducked his head and lowered his eyes in the way that Sarah remembered he'd always looked when he was especially troubled. At first he remained standing.

"Won't you sit down?"

"Sure." When he sat on the edge of the settee, he didn't lean back and didn't look over at Sarah, who sat opposite him on the little Guatemalan midwife chair, the only other piece of furniture in that part of the room beside the front door.

"What's wrong?"

"I really do want to be your friend and help you keep Quinta Louisa if I can, and I really do appreciate living in your guesthouse, but . . ."

"But what, Carlos?"

"I don't think we should get romantically involved. Things seemed to be moving that way the other night, and I don't think the time is right . . . right now, I mean . . ."

Sarah thought that her heart stopped beating for a moment and felt that her breath had left her body, as if her spiritual essence had been sucked out the open front door like a ghostly vapor dissolving into the hot afternoon air. She remembered her confrontation with Brian in this same spot, just past the place beside the door where her father's corpse had lain. She wondered if every man she loved would leave her here.

"I see."

"I really, really do care about you, Sarah."

"We were like brother and sister . . ." Sarah searched for words that would cover her embarrassment, her disappointment, her painful dejection, so that she wouldn't cry.

"And since neither of us has a brother or sister . . ." Carlos also seemed to be struggling to find words.

"But I do have three brothers now, Don Martín and Doña Flora's sons. They are my true family now."

"*Claro que sí* (Of course)."

"You're still welcome to stay for supper if you want to."

"I think it's better not to, not tonight. *Quizás* (perhaps) another time when we've sorted . . . things out."

"Perhaps so."

"Should I move out of the guest house? Do you want me to leave Quinta Louisa?"

"Of course not. Don't be absurd . . . unless you want to. You're doing me a huge favor by spending the nights here for our protection."

"*Gracias*, Sarah. It means a lot to me. You know I'd rather live here than anywhere else in the world."

LATER IN THE WEEK Sarah watched Carlos park the Land Rover in the driveway; but she jumped back from the window because he didn't go inside the guesthouse to douse his face and hands with water as he usually did when he'd just arrived home but rather walked directly toward the main house, toward where she was peering out the window at him. She had wanted to observe him without his noticing her, especially now. She could see the beads of sweat on his upper lip and forehead and the dust in the hair on his arms and chest. He frowned. His eyebrows were drawn together, and his eyes searched the ground as if he'd dropped a coin; but Sarah knew that he was searching for words, trying to decide if he would tell her something. He'd buttoned up his *guayabera* after she'd teased him about trying to look *macho*, but the thick hair on his chest and neck still showed around the collar and made him look just as masculine, just as handsome and desirable as he'd looked when his chest was exposed.

"Sarah, did you have a private meeting with Ernesto Andrejo Sánchez?"

"Whatever are you talking about Carlos?" How delightful to have a secret from him, a secret that annoyed him, a secret that he'd partially discovered. They'd kept secrets from one another as children and tried to discover them; but now it was not a game.

"When you said that things might be working out for you to get title to the *finca*, I thought Castillo López had been in touch with you. I asked the minister today, and he didn't know anything about it, but he wanted to know if Andrejo had contacted you."

"My dear Carlos, I appreciate your help, your kindness and solicitude." She teased him with a touch of anger and resentment in her voice. "But I don't have to tell you all my business."

"You listen to me. Castillo has reason to believe that Andrejo is involved in graft, and that's the last thing we need. You better tell me all about it."

"What right do you have to lecture me? I have no idea what you and Castillo López are planning. I still wonder whether you're really on my side."

"You know I'm not that kind of man." There was fire in his eyes and fire in his voice.

"I have no idea what kind of man you are. I don't know whether I can trust you or anybody else. I don't know who I can trust anymore." She'd assumed that Andrejo was acting out of personal greed, but she sometimes wondered if he might be the agent of a ruse by Castillo López to trick her into revealing her plans and making her throw everything away. She wanted to believe that Carlos was on her side, but she feared that Carlos's hero worship of Castillo was greater than his loyalty to her. Sometimes in her paranoia she even suspected that Carlos might have come to stay at Quinta Louisa in order to watch her every move and carry out some plot devised by Castillo.

"Sarah …" The plaintive tone pleaded and promised to give her an answer to anything she might ask. The gold American style chain was gone from around his neck, perhaps as a final rejection of his American identity; but she could see the gold Nicaraguan medallion on the longer chain beneath the cloth of his shirt, quivering between his breasts that trembled with little muscle spasms. "This business with Andrejo might lead to a real settlement. If you're willing to talk with Castillo, he may come to a decision about the finca, a real decision. A lot of things could be settled in the next few days for you … and for me, too."

"What do you want me to do about it?"

"The minister would like to see you privately in his office."

"*Muy bien* (very well). I just want things to be completely settled once and for all, for good."

"You're going to get some answers very soon, Sarah, if not final and complete answers, at least some of the answers you've been waiting for." He smiled without grinning or leering, with a tender gentle expression, a brotherly expression, Sarah thought. What more could she expect from him? All the rest had been merely her imagination. The more her passions had become inflamed by Carlos, the less she'd thought about her loyalty to her father's heritage. The mixture of lust and anger about Carlos had burned out some of the grief and hurt about her father's death. She must regain her focus on retaining her father's property. If she left Nicaragua, she would be able to forget about Carlos. Perhaps she had no one to blame but herself for her assumptions and desires and now for his keeping her at arm's length. "When would you be willing to meet with Castillo López? He'd like to talk with you as soon as possible. What about *mañana?*"

"Tomorrow is as good as any other time for me. I want to get everything settled as soon as possible and be finished with it. *Mañana* will be just fine, as early as possible." And then she could go home, back to North Carolina where she belonged, and put Quinta Louisa and Carlos behind her forever.

On Tuesday Sarah chose to drive herself into Managua despite her enormous fear about going into the city alone. She didn't want Guillermo to learn about the meeting and the possible sale of the factory. She didn't want to ask Carlos for any favor or help. She no longer believed that she would be given anything substantial for Quinta Louisa. She wanted to be finished and done with it, as she'd told Carlos last night. She glanced at the mountains and the lake, but they didn't reach into her feelings as they usually did. They looked to her like the faded backdrop at the Academy of Arts where she'd studied ballet years ago, just accustomed scenery. Things on the outside didn't matter when she seemed dead on the inside. She felt like a camera without any film in it, unseeing, uncaring, unremembering, as if she were slipping through days that leave no impression, no mark, no record, no memory. For the past week Sarah had done only the things that needed to be done each day from dawn until she went to bed and then forgot everything that had happened during her waking hours. This day seemed indistinguishable from any other day, without even the variations of temperature and seasons that made each day in North Carolina distinct and individual by saying it had rained or was unusually cold in the morning or unusually warm at Noon. Her spirit was ground down, wrung out, exhausted. Her face looked like the faces of people after the earthquake, drained of any emotion. Her soul was a mummy, wrapped to preserve it intact for eternal death or else bundled like a cocoon to metamorphose into some new and strange creature for a different life.

As Sarah entered the office of the Chief Minister of Justice, Adolfo Castillo López, on August 26, 1980, she spoke even before he addressed her.

"*Carlos Vargas Allen said that you wanted to see me, and I also hope you can do something for me.*"

"*Bueños dias* (Good morning), *Señorita Rutledge Lloyd. Please have a seat.*"

"Gracias." Sarah sat in one of the straight wooden chairs without an armrest.

"What do you want me to do for you?"

"I want to get a final decision about the disposition of my property."

"Do you plan to stay in Nicaragua permanently and live on the finca (farm), *or do you intend to sell it and leave the country?"*

Weariness overcame Sarah. She could no longer pretend and deceive Castillo, perhaps because she could no longer pretend and deceive herself with tentative possibilities and illusions of happy resolutions. She had already collapsed and given up within herself, and there seemed no reason to maintain any outward resistance to the government's program of confiscating foreigners' property, no matter how much they might protest.

"When I came back to Nicaragua, I did not think I would stay permanently. After the revolution and the death of my father it has been difficult to operate the finca and the factory; but since I have been back, almost three months now, I have found it hard to think of leaving for good, forever. This is my home. I am a citizen of the United States, but I have always thought of Nicaragua as my real home. Quinta Louisa has been the home of my family for almost a century. I have not been able to decide whether to sell it and give it up or to stay. Right now I think I will leave, but I just do not know."

Against her will Sarah was forced to dab away tears from her cheeks. Castillo's face softened, almost as if it might show a human expression. She thought that telling the truth moved him more than her tears. His lancing stare had penetrated to the center of her ambivalent sentiments.

"If it is difficult for you to decide, you can imagine that it is also difficult, much more difficult, for the government to decide what is right in these matters. In times of great change not all matters are easily adjudicated fairly and justly."

"What do you think my chances are for keeping Quinta Louisa at this point?"

"I cannot speculate. It will be decided on the basis of what this ministry and other officials think your true rights are. Some people want to curry the good favor of the United States government and make that a part of the issue. I do not personally think the issues of property settlement should be influenced by the international climate. I believe each case should be decided on its own merits."

"Even if I decide to leave Nicaragua, surely I have the right to receive something in compensation for Quinta Louisa."

The cold mask returned to Castillo's face, and he made no reply. Sarah understood that rights and values were defined differently in the two worlds in which they lived, one socialist and the other capitalist.

"I believe Vice Minister Vargas has told you that we need your help to learn if there is a problem of dishonesty and corruption within our ministry. If you help us, it will not influence the final decision about the disposition of the property; but I will make an effort to expedite that decision . . . if you agree to help us."

"What sort of help do you mean, Comandante Castillo?"

"We have reason to believe that you met privately with Vice Minister Andrejo Sánchez. I would like to know about that meeting."

"I assumed that the meeting might have been planned with your knowledge. He asked me not to mention anything about it to anyone else at the Ministry of Justice, especially not to Carlos; but he left the impression that he had the authority to work out an agreement with me."

"And did you work out some agreement?"

"No. He said that I would have to give up Quinta Louisa, that I would have to put the finca up for sale before a clear title could be arranged. I have not been able to make that decision. His proposal—it was never spelled out—was contingent on my relinquishing the finca."

"And if you should decide to give up the finca, the government would reimburse you for it; but the property would pass in some unspecified manner to Señor Ernesto Andrejo Sánchez, is that not true?"

Sarah didn't respond. Adolfo Castillo López's eyes pierced her, but she dropped her head. *"I feel that I am in a trap. Someone is lying to me, but I do not know who. I am not able to trust anyone."* When she looked up, she was again aware of tears in her eyes. She tried to conceal them by blinking. She didn't want Castillo to see her weep and show weakness. Certainly *Comandante* Adolfo Castillo López wouldn't be moved by her pain. She didn't want him to think that she was attempting to play on his sympathy. *"My family has lived through many regimes, long before the Somozas. We did business in other countries of Central America, too. The proposal of Señor Andrejo did not come as any great surprise. It is not an uncommon way of doing business in Latin America."*

"Even after the revolution our country is not completely free from corruption. There will always be dishonest men in the world, and they seem to be especially attracted to the functions of government. I cannot be sure that Ernesto Andrejo has done anything wrong, but I plan to find out, and I would like for you to help me. You can be certain that if you make any agreement with him that is not in the best interest of Nicaragua, it would not be upheld by this ministry."

"I only want to settle things honestly. I only want what is fair, what is just and right."

"As I said earlier the vice minister was correct in one thing. Your personal plans are involved in the disposition of the property. Once again I ask you, are you planning to live permanently in Nicaragua?"

"I have not made a final decision. It would depend to a great extent on whether I am assured of keeping our property permanently. That is why I have not made any response to Señor Andrejo. And I do not have a definite answer to give you either." Something inside her would not collapse completely, would not give up and give in, would not stop fighting, would not stop hoping. *"Carlos says you are an honest man, even if you are a communist."* Sarah spat out the words. She'd be damned if she'd let him condescend to her and make her give up without a fight. She wouldn't roll over and collapse without a scream of protest.

A faint smile crossed the minister's lips, almost a human expression on the cold mask of his official face.

"I may not be as much a communist as you think, but I am inclined to believe that you may be honest. We both probably have some integrity, Señorita Rutledge Lloyd, whatever our other differences. That may be rare. I have some suspicions about Vice Minister Andrejo, not just from your case, but also from some others as well. I need to find out the truth. Will you help us determine whether he is abusing his office and perhaps also breaking the law?"

"Why? Why in the name of God should I? You are threatening to take away everything that my family has worked to build for almost a hundred years. You leave me dangling in frustration. Why should I help you? To be perfectly candid, what would I get out of it?"

"I will not make any deals with you about your finca in exchange for your

help. That would not be any better than what we suspect Vice Minister Andrejo Sánchez of doing. I will try to expedite the decision about your property, if you come to a decision and tell me with an oath of truth, with every honest fiber of your soul, whether you plan to remain in Nicaragua and live on the finca and operate the factory, or not. After we have dealt with Señor Andrejo, I will give you one week to decide whether you are staying or leaving, and then I will try to have a decision in about one month. All I can promise you is a prompt decision. As promptly as possible. Will you help us to determine whether Señor Andrejo Sánchez is a man to be trusted or not?"

"Why should I, when you may take Quinta Louisa away from me the next day? You are giving me no assurances at all that . . ."

"Because I believe you love Nicaragua and do not want robbers to run the government, even if you do not like some of our principles. You would do it for Nicaragua and for what is right, not for yourself. I hope I have made that clear. I think you love this country whether you decide to stay and live here or not. From what I have heard about your father, he would have helped us deal with dishonest officials, whether he approved of our regime or not."

In their own strangely different and similar ways, Castillo López and her father were both Nicaraguan patriots. Something about Castillo reminded her of her father more than anyone else in Nicaragua. He would not put his own welfare and personal desires over the good of the nation. Whether it was a clever manipulation or an honest gesture of good will, Castillo's appeal to the memory of her father had convinced her that she would work with him.

"Muy bien (very well). I will help you. And I will give you a reply about my plans for the factory and my permanent residence after we have dealt with Señor Andrejo."

TEN DAYS ELAPSED AFTER Sarah agreed to participate in Castillo's plot to trap Andrejo in his fraud. She had heard nothing more from the Ministry of Justice. She no longer rushed to the front door when she heard the Land Rover pull into the driveway at dusk, and she no longer even looked out the window to see Carlos enter the guest house. One afternoon just after she heard the Land Rover stop beside the guesthouse, she heard a soft tap on the front door. Carlos knocked tentatively, as if he almost wished not to be heard, as if he didn't want to be discovered there.

"Come in, Carlos." During the past couple of weeks they had rarely spoken and even then with only polite, civil greetings. They hadn't shared any meals since his rejection of her as a potential lover. She vowed she would not ask him to eat with her again now, even though Isabel had prepared sufficient food for both of them that evening. She gestured for them to sit in the main part of the room, beside the patio door, where the more comfortable chairs would accommodate only one person. She could not bear to sit beside him on the settee by the front door. The physical discomfort of the settee would not have compared to the emotional anguish of sitting there beside him.

"Adolfo Castillo López has set up the arrangement for trapping Andrejo. I'll drive you to the place where you will call him on the telephone tomorrow evening. Castillo will talk with you about what you should say when we get there."

"I see." Sarah never took her eyes off Carlos's face, but he looked down at the floor, never meeting her eyes. "What do you think my chances are of keeping Quita Louisa?"

"You'll get something, I believe. If you don't leave the country, you might be able to get more . . . or keep some of it for yourself."

"Will you be with me when I do whatever Castillo wants me to do to trap Andrejo?"

"*Claro que sí* (Of course)."

"I'm glad you'll be there with me."

They sat without saying anything more to each other for several minutes. Then Carlos rose to leave. They didn't bid each other goodnight. They didn't even say, "*I'll see you tomorrow,*" at the front door.

IT WAS ALREADY DARK when Sarah and Carlos joined

Castillo López at a government office in Managua. It was not the Ministry of Justice office, and Sarah didn't ask where they were. They met in a large room with very high ceilings and a skylight that cast strange shadows on their faces. It reminded her of the gymnasium at the high school where she taught in North Carolina. Sarah fluffed the hair around her ears, first one side and then the other, and thought how Guillermo teased her about the nervous habit.

There were several desks in the room with old-fashioned telephones on stems sitting on them. Only a few of the telephones had dials for calling out. She would have to speak into the bell on the top of the stem and take the receiver shaped like a black ice cream cone off the hook and hold it to her ear in order to hear the conversation and then turn the dial on the base of the phone for making the call. It was all very awkward and required her to stoop toward the desk.

Sarah, Carlos, and Castillo were alone in the huge room. Carlos and Castillo listened on the extension phones without dials when she turned the numbers on the round circle to connect her to Ernesto Andrejo Sánchez at his home. Castillo had prepared certain subjects that he wanted her to raise in the conversation. Ernesto Andrejo didn't seem surprised to hear from her. He expressed some astonishment that she hadn't called him sooner.

"It has taken me a while to make up my mind, but now I am certain that I should not stay in Nicaragua. I am afraid it is no longer a place for North Americans to live." She could speak sincerely because a large part of her believed the words. Sarah looked at Carlos, propped by one haunch on a desk across the room from her, with one foot on the floor and his left hand over the telephone receiver. He looked down at his other dangling, swaying foot. Her words had been framed by Carlos and Castillo, even though she was replying to Andrejo's questions; but she hoped Carlos believed her vows to leave Nicaragua and never see him or think of him again.

Andrejo congratulated her on her wisdom and courage. He pressed her to confirm her intention to sell Quinta Louisa, all of it, the homestead as well as the farm and the factory.

"I feel I have no alternative. I would prefer to leave the country in a couple of weeks. What can you offer me?"

He stalled, telling her that these things take time in order to determine how much the property would bring in the present unsettled conditions.

"*I must have some indication about how much the government can give me.*"Sarah glanced at Castillo, who would make the real settlement, either to allow her to keep the *finca* or to give her some payment or cheat her out of everything. Castillo glanced at her without blinking or changing his expression as he stood holding a telephone receiver without touching the desk across from hers except for the fingertips of his left hand making a compulsive circular motion beside the base of the telephone.

Ernesto Andrejo told her that the value of things was quite different now than before the revolution. He would try to arrange for a substantial payment, but she must realize that it would not represent the real value of the *finca.*

"*About how much do you think?*"

He mentioned perhaps as much as half a million *córdobas.* He would certainly not be able to get more than that.

"*That is impossible. That doesn't represent a quarter of the value of the finca, not even in the present market.*" Castillo nodded rhythmically, like the motion of his fingertips, like the swinging of Carlos's foot. Then he smiled slightly, encouragingly, to let her know that she was performing well in his drama, that she was reading the lines he'd written acceptably. He never turned his eyes away from her face.

Andrejo said that he was aware that it was only a small payment; but if she waited even a few more days, she might receive nothing. The government would soon confiscate her entire holdings, and she would be left without anything at all. He assured her that the moment she left the country everything would be taken. Perhaps it would be taken even before she left. He assured her that she wouldn't receive a better offer. Something in his words sounded sincere, as if he told at least part of the truth from some specific knowledge, as if he knew that Castillo had already made his decision about her property, even before hearing Sarah's response to him about her permanent residence.

"*Córdobas will not do me any good. I cannot spend them in the United States. And I must have more money. If you can get a hundred thousand dollars for me in cash, I will consider the offer.*" Castillo had told her to negotiate for dollars in order to make the proposal seem serious. Now Castillo smiled with open lips at her for remembering the plea about dollars. He raised his left hand from the desk and gave a single wave, like a casual salute. The accessibility to dollars would give him an indication of whether large foreign interests were involved with Andrejo.

Andrejo said that dollars were very difficult to obtain.

"I must have one hundred thousand dollars. American dollars. And I must have the payment in cash within two weeks, so that I can leave the country."

Andrejo said that a number of other people would be involved and must be consulted. Some of the payment might be needed for "fees" to pay certain government officials.

"Whatever bribes are required must be your doing, Don Ernesto." She used the old patronal title, "Don", deliberately, ironically, to mock both Andrejo and Castillo and to indicate how far "Don" was removed from the artificial "comrade" of the new ideology. *"I need to have no less than one hundred thousand dollars free and clear."*

Andrejo didn't believe that he could come up with that amount, especially in dollars, but he didn't dismiss her offer completely.

"What would the procedure be?" It was another of Castillo's questions prepared for her to ask. *"To whom would I transfer the title?"*

The government would buy the *finca*, and it would be strictly a governmental matter. Andrejo hoped that he might be allowed to purchase a small portion of the *finca* after making an acceptable arrangement with her, that he would be given some consideration for having settled the matter amicably. He also hoped that she would find comfort in knowing that someone who loved Quinta Louisa would be living there and taking a personal interest in it.

Carlos's foot stopped still. He took his hand down from his face. She saw his lips drawn together in an expression of disgust and contempt, as if he'd bitten into a green banana.

"What arrangement will be made for transferring the title?"

The papers would be handled by a lawyer. The title would be transferred to the Nicaragua Development Company, S. A., a governmental agency.

Castillo and Carlos looked at each other and nodded, like men giving the signal to move toward the quarry in a hunt; and Sarah saw from the expressions on their faces that Ernesto Andrejo Sánchez had made his fatal mistake. He'd assumed that a foolish young *gringa* would accept the Nicaraguan Development Company, S. A., as a governmental agency with its official sounding name. Sarah would have known better, even if Carlos and Castillo López were not listening to the conversation on extension telephones, especially from the initials S. A. (*Socieded Anónima* i.e., Incorporated) attached. Perhaps Andrejo wasn't concerned with whether Sarah realized how illegitimate the procedure was. Other foreigners had probably accepted whatever they could get from him in their panic to leave the country.

Andrejo said that he would call her in a few days to let her know what kind of payment could be arranged.

Castillo held up his hand in alarm when Carlos replaced his receiver on the hook beside the bell before Sarah had put hers down. After all three receivers were back on their cradles, Adolfo Castillo gave Sarah directions for her next lines and scenes in his drama. He asked her to wait for the call from Andrejo and to make a definite appointment to see Andrejo's lawyer, so that they could seize the papers and perhaps learn the identity of the other parties involved in the transaction.

Castillo turned to her, almost casually, as he was locking the office. *"Have you made your real decision about staying in Nicaragua or not?"*

"No, Señor Castillo. I will let you know next week, if possible."

Carlos looked pained at her answer. The negotiation about leaving Nicaragua between Sarah and Castillo López had not been revealed to Carlos by either of them.

"And I will try to give you a final answer from the government by the last week of November. I am grateful for your help in dealing with this disreputable official; but I must tell you again that as much as I value your assistance, it will not influence the outcome of the decision of the government about the disposition of your property. That matter will have to be decided on the basis of its own merits."

On the way back to Quinta Louisa in the Land Rover Carlos asked Sarah about her negotiation with Castillo. "Can you tell me what you were talking about?"

Sarah was delighted with her secret and with hearing the pain in his voice. Even if he didn't love her, he did love Quinta Louisa; and she still had the power to take Quinta Louisa away from him as well as to sever it from herself forever.

"I've got to decide within the next few days whether I intend to stay in Nicaragua permanently or return to the United States. The minister has promised that when I inform him about that decision, he'll ask the government for a final settlement on the property."

"Do you know what your decision will be . . . regarding leaving the country?" Carlos's face was squeezed in anguish, as if it were fleshy dough kneaded by invisible hands, not shaped by its own will but rather twisted by things over which he felt he had no control.

Sarah remained silent. She hoped that her face was hardened and impassive like the official face of Castillo. "No. I just want a few more days to think about it."

"Please don't decide anything finally until the weekend. I want to talk with you about something, but I have to wait until the weekend."

"Very well, Carlos. I'll wait . . . for old time's sake." She would wait. She didn't think it would make any difference. Carlos could surely no longer be a part of her future, but why else would she delay making a decision? Her promise to Carlos was as good a reason as any to delay making the final decision that she feared and dreaded. She hated her heart for pounding, as if it still hoped for Carlos to love her. Surely Carlos couldn't hear it in the darkened car. He turned his head away from her. If it hadn't been such an awkward, unusual position, she wouldn't have looked so carefully at him that she saw the tears in his eyes reflected in the green light from the dashboard.

Sarah and Carlos said nothing else to one another on the drive up into the hills until they said goodnight properly, formally, almost coolly at the front door of Quinta Louisa; but she could see in his face that he was not cool inside. He was as distraught as she was. She was delighted by a little revenge in making Carlos feel badly.

CARLOS TELEPHONED SARAH ON Sunday afternoon to tell her that he wouldn't reach the guesthouse at Quinta Louisa until late that night. He wanted to be sure that Don Martín would be with her—occasionally Don Martín spent Sunday night with Guillermo's family in the village. Sarah wondered if her cool response after his rejection of her romantic overtures had initiated a cycle of resentment and hurt between them that would lead to more and more estrangement.

Sunday night was hot and muggy, even up in the hills. Sarah tossed in bed and slept fitfully. She could feel the damp places on the sheets where she lay when she turned over. She awoke bathed in her perspiration. Then she heard voices coming from the road in front of the gate, talking loudly and shouting. She wondered if it might be a drunken mob coming back from a wake or a fiesta until clanging and banging against metal drowned out the voices.

Then she realized that the lock on the front gate was being pounded by rocks, as if the raiders didn't care how much noise they made or who they aroused, as if they knew the house was unguarded and unprotected with only a young woman and an old man inside. When light flickered across the hall through the front windows, Sarah ran from her bedroom in the back of the house to look through one of the windows in front.

Just as she peered out, the lock gave way and the gate opened and a dozen or so men cheered and rushed in holding flashlights and waving staves and machetes in the air. Scenes from Sarah's nightmares after the ill-conceived Halloween party of her childhood flashed through her mind. Then she heard Martín trying to unbolt the front door. She hurried toward the parlor. Had he forgotten the old rule never to unbolt the door when there was trouble? Surely Don Martín knew better.

Don Martín held a rifle in his left hand as he struggled with the bolt. *"Do not unbolt the door. Do not go outside. They will kill us."*

"I will protect you. I will chase them away."

"No! They will only kill you if you go outside."

"If I die, then they will leave. Hija (daugher), *you cannot stop me."* He had called her *daughter* only once before as they'd grieved together for her father. Sarah caught his arm, but he pulled away from her so forcefully that she fell against the wall behind her. For a moment she was unable

to move from her loss of breath. Then she dove toward him and tried to hold him around his chest, but he flung free with a strength many times greater than hers. Previously, only the gentlest and most tender touch had ever passed between them.

Once more she tried to stop him by clutching his shirt in her fists like an angry baby, but he gripped her wrists and tore away her hands and shoved her against the wall so powerfully that a sharp ache shot from her shoulder down across her back to her coccyx. She thought that all traditional order and decency in the world were breaking down. Every expression of meaning in relationships between people was being reversed.

"Don Martín, you are hurting me." She whimpered, and he finally stopped pushing her away from the bolt. *"Please do not go outside. If they break down the door, they can kill us both together."*

"They will kill you if they come inside. Stay here. I have to stop them. You stay here. I could not save Don Jorge, but I will save you."

Don Martín ran toward the kitchen, and Sarah heard the kitchen door open and close. In a few minutes the voices moved away from the front door toward the middle of the yard and became quieter, talking with one another in questions and answers and conversations; but Sarah couldn't understand their words. Then the voices became loud again but different from before, no longer cheering with jubilant shouts, now angry with accusations and screams of quarreling protest. A rifle shot rang out. For several moments there was a silence even more foreboding and threatening than the noises had been. She heard the voices again, at first almost in whispers, then growing gradually louder in a babble and din of confusion that seemed to swirl together.

Sarah rushed back to the same front window where she'd first looked out at them breaking the lock. They were tumbling through the gate, scurrying as closely together as they'd come in. They were carrying someone on their shoulders, and Don Martín was following them.

Then the Land Rover swung through the gate almost as if it were part of the same motion, and the men seemed to dissolve in the beams of its headlights. All was quiet and still and dark except for the lights of the Land Rover parked where it had lunged to a halt just inside the gate with the motor still running.

A voice cried like a child's after a terrible dream. "Sarah! Sarah! Are you all right? Please, Sarah, be all right."

"Yes, Carlos. I'm fine. I'm all right. Were you hurt? Have the robbers gone? Did they hurt you?"

"I'm fine. Let me in."

It took both her hands to push back the bolt that had resisted Don Martín's efforts; and even then all her strength and weight had to push against it to move it, so that it left a pink and blue impression, almost like a bruise on the heel of her palm. A loud clang rang out as she finally jerked it back, louder sounding inside the house than the clanging and banging that had broken the lock on the front gate.

Until Sarah heard the bolt open and touched the sore place on her palm, she'd felt no fear, only great confusion; but now terror rose through her like ice water splashing over her legs and seeping up around her stomach. The tingling rose to her heart and accelerated its beat into a rapid pounding that seemed to shake her whole body. She became dizzy and slightly nauseated with a sweet sick taste in her mouth that was almost pleasant, like a narcotic given after an illness. She blinked away the faintness and red haze over the objects around her and steadied herself by propping with one hand against the wall at the spot where Don Martín had shoved her. Her mouth was dry. Her lips felt as if they were being pulled inside her teeth.

She was still breathing heavily when Carlos opened the door and grasped her. They embraced and held each other so tightly that she could hardly breathe. She could feel his body sensually, sexually against her, every curve and muscle, every hard and soft place. She wanted him never to take his arms from around her. She wanted to hold her breath and barely catch enough air to live while he held her. She moved her face toward his to kiss him, but he turned his head away and buried it in her shoulder.

Sarah pushed back from him. "Where's Don Martín? Did they kill him?"

"No. I saw him carrying a rifle and chasing the raiders down the road toward the village as I pulled in the gate. I am here to protect you now."

"So he's not dead. Thank God!"

"I was not here when you needed me."

Sarah grasped him again and pulled him closer. His manhood was aroused against her stomach, and against the small of her back she felt the butt of the pistol that he'd held in his hand since he'd come into the house. Her breasts were firm and her nipples taut. Her skin tingled as it touched the silk of her nightgown. She wanted Carlos to make love to her.

They released each other, and Sarah closed the door and pushed back the bolt. She was surprised how easily it moved into a locked position. Then she gently took the large pistol out of Carlos's hand and laid it on the table beside Don Martín's bowl of flowers. She pulled him, stumbling down the hall toward her bedroom. At the doorway he seized the jam as if he couldn't resist her strength by his own power.

"Sarah, no. It's not right. Not now. Not yet."

With both hands she pulled his head down and forced his lips against hers. On her bed they pulled off and pushed back clothes, seeking handholds of flesh like wet, shivering, drowning people trying to wrap themselves in a dry blanket and find warmth to save their lives.

Sarah experienced almost nothing during the brief moments of copulation, less pain, less pleasure, fewer sensations of any kind than she had perhaps ever felt before, as if it were something they must do and get through; but afterward they held each other, and she felt calm and peaceful and safe in their tight embrace. They moved their hands from one another only long enough to brush away the tears from their cheeks that continued to stream from their eyes quietly like springs that ooze out of the mountainsides for days after a great storm.

"I love you, Sarah. I always have, but I never thought it would be . . ." As Carlos spoke she thought it seemed as if they hadn't yet made love, as if it were still only a possibility, something that might happen to them sometime in the future.

"I love you, too, Carlos. I love you very, very much."

Then they fell asleep, exhausted by the emotional storms of fear and love.

Perhaps if Don Martín had not called, they might have made love again, as if for the first time.

"Doña Sarah? Are you all right?"

Sarah stood and pulled her nightgown back over her head and walked toward the bedroom door without panic or embarrassment, almost deliberately and comfortably. They hadn't even closed the bedroom door into the hall.

"I am fine, Don Martín. I will be there in just a moment." Sarah kissed Carlos lightly, primly, on the cheek. "I really am all right now, Carlos. Don't worry."

"I know. We're going to be all right. I love you."

"I love you, too." Sarah glanced back and saw Carlos still untying and lacing back the shoes that he'd pulled off still tied. She wondered if Don Martín would accuse and condemn her with words or censoring parental scowls, but he glanced down and bowed his head as if he were the one caught in a great shame. His hands were clenched tightly around the rifle, but his arms were limp.

"Are you all right? Why on earth did you run out there? Why did you chase them?"

"I thought I might scare them away and save you."

"I heard a shot. Was anyone wounded?"

"Everything is all right now. I do not believe they will ever come back again."

Sarah glanced at the clock on the dining room sideboard. It was almost five o'clock, almost dawn. She and Carlos had slept together for more than three hours after the raid, after making love.

Carlos joined them in the living room. He touched her hand gently, shyly. From the way he looked at her and took her hand reassuringly Sarah knew that he would not take advantage of her because of what had just happened between them. Don Martín was too distracted and disturbed even to have noticed that they'd both emerged from her bedroom.

"Let me get dressed, and then I will prepare breakfast for us."

DON MARTÍN WAS SITTING on the edge of the patio looking at the garden when Sarah came into the kitchen. She found a can of mushrooms that must have been in the pantry for years, since long before the revolution, and impulsively began cooking a large breakfast—cinnamon toast and a mushroom omelet and slices of papaya drizzled with juice from limes, both grown in the garden at Quinta Louisa, and her father's coffee, made with the special grinder and pot that her grandfather had developed. She believed that there was no other coffee like it in all the world.

Carlos came into the kitchen rubbing his eyes and his chin, but he was fully dressed. "Where's Don Martín? Did you find out what happened?"

"He's out on the patio. You may get more out of him than I would." The *macho* fraternity: some things you don't talk to a woman about.

When Carlos returned from the patio, Sarah raised her palms and her eyebrows for an answer. "Well?"

"He said the raiders cut the telephone line to the house. I'll get someone out to repair the line today. And he said he'd called the police, for whatever good that would do. There's no point." His face filled with disgust and contempt. The familiar ineptitude of the police to do anything following an attempted robbery seemed to shake his faith in the revolution for a moment; and everything in him seemed to give way, give up, surrender, like his face on the beach long ago when three American boys all twice his size had held him down and bent back his arms until the pain could no longer be endured—"*Now you'll give up; now you'll do what we say, you little Nica punk.*"

Sarah was tempted to take Carlos back to her bedroom, to absorb his hurt and ache as he had done for her, to wrap him in her flesh; but it would be wrong now, inappropriate, too easy, too cheap a release and reassurance. "It's all right, Carlos."

"I'll tell Castillo about it. Maybe the ministry can do something . . . find out something."

"Let's have breakfast. I've cooked something special. Tell Don Martín to come in and get a plate." Sarah thought that it was strange that Don Martín had not already come inside to help her in the kitchen. He'd remained sitting in the same spot on the patio as if he'd suffered a stroke.

After Martín came inside and greeted them with his customarily formal, ornate politeness, he took his plate and coffee back to the patio.

For a moment Sarah wondered if the puritanical old man's sadness might have resulted from an awareness of what had happened between Carlos and her in her bedroom, but he'd been strangely oblivious to them when he'd returned to the house from the village. In the past there had been robberies and raids along with threats and dangers; but Don Martín had never been affected like this before her father's death. Now his face darkened as it had looked for weeks following George Rutledge's death. In previous crises Don Martín had been strong and brave and defiant, even when the other members of his family and the members of her family were frightened and confused. Now he appeared lost, as if his world had crumbled.

Carlos put down his fork and seemed to find it difficult to swallow.

"Don't you like my breakfast? I prepared it 'specially for you."

"It's a feast, but how can I enjoy it? You don't seem to take what happened last night very seriously."

"They were just robbers. Just hoodlum robbers, weren't they?"

"No. That's what they wanted you to think. Maybe that's why they came, to make you think that. Maybe they didn't mean to hurt you, just scare you; but we can't take a chance. Not now."

"What do you mean—they weren't robbers? It seems to me like they were robbers. It's happened before. They were wearing *campesino* clothes and barefooted, carrying clubs and machetes."

"You didn't get as good a look at them as I did. They were a little too perfectly made-up. The way they moved, the way they walked especially. It wasn't hard to see through the disguises up close."

"I couldn't see them very well in the darkness. Was one of them hurt? I thought I saw them carrying someone as they ran away."

"I just got a glimpse. I think one of them may have gotten shot. Maybe one of them had a rifle and someone was caught in the crossfire with Don Martín."

"Do we need to talk about what else happened last night . . . between just the two of us?"

"Not now, Sarah. Please. I want to, but not now, not yet. Very soon. Is that all right?"

Guillermo always arrived at the coffee factory every morning before Sarah came to the office. He was usually there even before the first workers appeared in order to check out the equipment and plan the day's schedule and review any papers that needed Sarah's attention. Even though he reserved his *abrazos* for special occasions, every morning Sarah could count on his broad smile and cheerful mood, often accompanied by a quip or a joke, to brighten the beginning of her day.

After the raid Guillermo seemed to have caught his father's morose mood. Following her father's death Guillermo had sustained his usual cheerful countenance in contrast to Don Martín's gloom and depression, but now they reflected the same joyless melancholy. Sarah credited their dark expressions to their anxiety about her safety; and even though she appreciated their concern, she tried to assure them that Carlos would protect her personally and also alert the Ministry of Justice officials to discourage any future raids. Guillermo might smile faintly at her reassurances, but his lips would droop within minutes into his recent dejected countenance.

Although it had been ten days since the raid, when Sarah arrived at the factory office on Tuesday morning, Guillermo seemed especially disturbed.

"*What is going on, Guillermo? Is there more bad news?*"

"*We knew it would happen. Doña Carmen is moving to Panama for a while to live with her parents. She came by early this morning. She asked me to give you her regards. She was sorry to miss you. She could not stay to see you. It was even before the workers arrived.*"

"*We will miss her. She helped us very greatly, and I will miss her as a friend. We became good friends while she was working with us.*"

"*Yes, it is very true. I could always rely on her to help me, even after she left the office, when I needed for her to look over some papers or tell me where to go for assistance in the city.*"

"*I am surprised that she is moving to Panama. She once told me that she would never live there with her parents.*"

"*The same thing (Lo mismo) she said to me.*"

"Her work was so helpful, so efficient and productive . . . Did anything ever happen at the factory to upset her?"

"No, not here. Not at the factory."

"Was it something in the house? Did she and Don Martín have a disagreement?"

"Not a disagreement. You should ask Papá about that. I cannot tell you. I do not know if he will tell you about it. You know how he keeps secrets to protect all of us and makes us keep his secrets."

Sarah intended to talk with Don Martín about Carmen that evening, but she was so preoccupied with the conundrum of her conflicted feelings about Carlos and her own continuing anxious memories of the raid, despite her reassuring words to others, that she forgot to ask Don Martín about Carmen until much later.

ALMOST TWO WEEKS HAD passed, and Carlos had never mentioned having made love to Sarah the night of the raid. She could have rationalized that it had been only a visceral response to their fear and tension, if they had not also declared their love for one another. The professions of love bothered her more than the sexual encounter, which had been brief and somewhat physically painful, not the glorious ecstasy that she'd imagined in her virginal state. She didn't really blame Carlos for taking away her virginity—it had to happen sometime—it had almost happened a few times in college, and she had hoped it might happen with Brian. She blamed Carlos for saying he loved her if he did not really mean it, perhaps for saying it only to seduce her and satisfy his male craving and stoke his macho image. She began to imagine that he had sinister motives. Although when she was brutally honest with herself, she acknowledged that she had seduced Carlos more than he had seduced her; but such an interpretation only increased her resentment of him. He didn't have to tell her that he loved her. She felt a sense of despair about what she perceived as the growing distance between them once again.

CARLOS TALKED WITH MARTÍN even before he told Sarah that he would need to be away for a couple of days on government business. He wanted to be sure that Martín would be in the house and even asked him to hire a guard from the factory to spend the nights at Quinta Louisa for additional protection. Sarah thought he was being overly protective of her, but she appreciated his concern for her. When she heard on the morning of September 18th that Anastasio Somoza Debayle had been gunned down in Paraguay, she wondered if Carlos had been involved in planning the plot against him or even in the assassination.

After Carlos returned to Quinta Louisa three days later, Sarah questioned him about his absence. "Did you have anything to do with Somoza's assassination, Carlos?"

"You know there are some things I can't talk about, Sarah. Some things are better for you not to know."

THE DAY BEFORE THE second week anniversary of the raid Sarah awoke on Saturday morning and heard the banging and clinking of metal and was reminded again of the raid. The room was bright with sun, and she resolved to get blackout shades or heavy drapes if she should stay permanently at Quinta Louisa. She'd grown accustomed to sleeping late on Saturday while teaching; and the habit persisted, even here, where every day was the same length from dawn until dusk. She pulled the sheets and pillow over her head. They were soft and slightly dampened and warm from her body during the night; but the clanging, however faint, roused her from dozing.

Don Martín usually respected her Saturday morning laziness; he must have forgotten what day it was. He was growing old and forgetful, but he rarely forgot courtesy and kindness. Personal consideration would be the last thing he would lose in senility. She got out of bed and walked toward the front door barefooted, not even bothering to put on slippers and a robe, to call to him and ask him to stop so that she could rest. The tile floor on the soles of her feet seemed bitterly cold, painfully cold, the coldest thing in Nicaragua, colder than North Carolina snow and ice, she imagined—how quickly her body was tuned to the sensations of the tropics. The hood of the Land Rover was raised, and Carlos was piddling with pliers and screwdrivers. He must have been unable to start the motor again. Anger and sour bitterness rose to her throat because it was Carlos who was interrupting her Saturday morning sleep. She was glad to have something specific to blame him for.

She went back to her room and put on her slippers and robe. She didn't want him to see her today in her nightgown, to be able to see her breasts through the sheer nylon. She made coffee and toast and took them grumpily to the opposite side of the house away from Carlos, to the patio, which was far too bright and hot in the mornings to be pleasant and was never enjoyable until the middle of the afternoon.

After the clanging and banging stopped for fifteen or twenty minutes she tiptoed to the front door as if it would be shameful to be seen by Carlos or even be caught by Don Martín looking out at him. The hood of the Land Rover was down, and she heard a faint snip, snip, and turned to see Carlos clipping vines in the corner of the wall behind the guest house.

Sarah put on the ugliest housedress she could find for Saturday, for work, for Carlos, in order to show her contempt, her lack of concern and interest that he was stranded with her for the weekend. He couldn't borrow her car. She wouldn't take him into the city. Let him walk as her father used to make Guillermo walk to catch the bus. Guillermo deserved respect and thoughtful effort from her, not Carlos. He wouldn't dare ask her to give him a ride or borrow her car today. If he asked her, she'd tell him exactly what she thought of him. Her chest seethed inside and prickled outside with anger.

Half an hour later he was oiling the hinges on the gate. Sarah tried to read. She would have to offer him lunch, as she'd given water to the Sandinista soldier boy. (Then he'd pointed a rifle at her.) When she looked out the front door again, he was taking tools back to the garage where her father's car was parked. "Car won't start?" She put her hands against the middle part of the screen door, holding it closed, barring him from daring to enter; she would ordinarily have opened the screen door to talk with him, to see him better, to be seen and heard, to have nothing separating them.

"No. It's okay. I was just tuning the engine."

"You want some lunch?"

"No thank you. I've got to go into the city in a few minutes." Carlos walked toward her. She reaffirmed her intention not to allow him to come inside the house. She pressed against the door. "But I would like to have dinner with you tonight."

"I don't know. It's the cook's night off. There's nothing but leftovers or whatever I can scrape up. I don't usually have much to eat on Saturday night. Maybe you'd better eat something in town."

"I'll take care of dinner for us tonight. I'm going to pick up something special in Managua."

"If he brings back nacatamales, I'll puke all over the dining room table," she thought. "Oh, I think I have enough for us. I'll find something."

"I'll treat you tonight. It's something I'd really like to do."

Perhaps it was a peace offering. After all, he would stay on the *finca* tonight, on Saturday night, presumably to protect her, although he usually stayed in the city on Saturday nights; and she would feel safer especially because the raid had taken place only two weeks ago. "All right, if you really want to."

"It may be late in the afternoon before I come back. Can Don Martín stay until I can get back?"

Sarah remembered how Carlos had disappeared during the time that Tachito Somoza had been assassinated in Paraguay and wondered if he might be involved in something else that was about to happen.

"I'll be fine. Don't worry about me."

"Sarah, please don't give up on me."

Sarah nodded. He'd used the same words before, after leaving Castillo's office, in the same tone of voice, as if pleading, as if it were important, as if it mattered to him, as if it could really make a difference for them.

Martín often went into the village on Saturday evenings. Of course he hadn't left her alone since the raid. He might like to visit Guillermo's family tonight if Carlos were with her, but if Carlos thought that he was going to seduce her again on a Saturday night with Don Martín out of the house, he was badly mistaken.

When Carlos returned about five o'clock Sarah was still wearing her ugly Saturday work dress. He called to her from the front door. His arms and hands were filled with several bundles of groceries, so that he couldn't knock. She would have to let him in now, of course.

"Can I put some things in the refrigerator? Don Martín is going to grill a *lomo* (tenderloin) for us and then go see his family in the village."

"Oh, is he really? How interesting."

"Can you stay out of the kitchen for a while? Dinner will be a surprise."

Sarah thought that he was being childish and foolish if he thought she would fall into bed with him again tonight. *"¡Como no!* (As you say!)"

"Just put on a pretty dress, and I'll call you about seven-thirty."

"This one won't do?"

"No. I want you to put on something pretty."

The audacity of his telling her what to wear! How could she ever have been smitten with this demanding, macho, rude Latino?

The clattering and banging from the kitchen was both louder and more annoying than his work on the Land Rover had been during the morning. The smell of the tenderloin being barbequed on the patio was one of her favorite aromas; but tonight she hated it, mocking her and promising joy and pleasure when bitterness and pain were now the realities of their relationship. Sarah closed her bedroom door and tried to read. Soaking in the tub provided her only a few moments of pleasure as she rubbed the pink skin of her body with soap suds and thought of preparing herself for some man, sometime, somewhere, but not Carlos, not here, not tonight.

She decided to wear a bright, elegant sundress with a Guatemalan hand-woven stole and play the seductive *señorita*. She put on her largest, gaudiest Nicaraguan earrings, a gold stalk of bananas, which had been the subject of jokes at parties over the years: *"Can you hear me, Sarah? You've got a banana in your ear."*

Impulsively she pinned her hair up. She didn't like herself with her hair pinned up. Her neck was too thin, her hair too fine and not long enough, so that it fell down around her face in wisps like an old woman's, accentuating her thinness and frailness. Tonight it suited her mood, a mixture of frivolity and despair.

Carlos rapped gently on her bedroom door. When she opened it, he was standing in the hallway dressed in a black suit and white shirt and blue tie. The sleeves of his suit were too short and the pants too tight around his waist and thighs and were baggy at the seat and loins. He'd gained weight and filled out since he'd bought it, perhaps years ago. It was his *wedding and funeral*, as they said in Nicaragua, referring to the only times anyone would wear a suit of any kind in the country, certainly the only times to wear a black suit. He was holding some small, fragile, waxy, fragrant mountain flowers from the forest that Sarah was sure Don Martín had gathered for him. He handed them to her.

"May I put them in my hair?"

"Please do."

She went back into the bedroom and stooped to see herself in the dim light of the old dresser mirror. Her face was white and her eyes and hair and lips were pale. She thought that she was almost beautiful in spite of being too thin, with too long a neck, and of course, always much too tall to interest most suitors.

The beauty of the dining room in the candlelight almost broke her control. Of course they'd always had candles close by to use when the electricity went out—at least once every month—but not arranged in brass candlesticks on the table except for special evenings at Christmas or on birthdays, with the lamps in the living room turned low.

Martín's *lomo* (tenderloin) was served on the big blue English platter that her Great-grandmother Louisa had brought from England as a bride. Her grandfather's carving set was beside the meat, probably sharpened surreptitiously during the week by Martín in his secret planning and plotting with Carlos. Don Martín was an innocent accomplice for this night, planned to bring her joy but rather giving her only pain in acknowledging that Carlos had no serious interest in sharing her life.

The fruit salad was garnished with strawberries probably imported from Costa Rica. They used to cost a small fortune, and now would surely cost a large fortune. They were arranged in the cut-glass and sterling silver bowl that her father had given to her mother for their tenth anniversary. The silver had been polished. *"If Don Martín only knew how he's hurt me with his great labor and great efforts!"* she thought.

The beautifully shaped croissants were one of her favorite foods. No bakeries were left in Managua now to make bread like that. They were covered by her mother's most beautifully embroidered *panera* (roll cover) from Masaya. All she could think of to say was "Where did they come from?"

"A friend got them for me. Flown in from Panama."

"They're lovely."

"I never saw you with your hair up . . . in a dress like that."

"This is what I used to wear for special family dinners. I certainly never saw you in a suit before. A black suit! Is it for a wedding or a funeral?"

He bit his lip before he replied. "I didn't mean for it to be a joke." He served her plate with several slices of the beef. "Damn! *Mantequilla.* I forgot the butter."

"I'll get it. I know just where it is."

"No. I'll be back in a moment." She heard him rattling through the cabinets in the kitchen trying to find a dish. The glow from the kitchen lights fell into the dining room and dispelled the romantic candlelit scene. She giggled and told herself that her infatuation with Carlos had been a foolish notion. Carlos finally returned with the butter on a rather chipped and faded old yellow saucer. "Butter." He looked triumphant and proud.

"Parkay," she thought and suppressed her giggle but held it nearby as a comfort and security. She hadn't even noticed the wine on the sideboard in the darkened room. They hadn't served wine even before the revolution except for special anniversaries and birthdays, or when someone from the diplomatic community gave them a bottle from the commissary for Christmas. She wondered if it was the rot-gut from Guatemala, but it was French. Carlos filled their glasses.

"*¡Salud!* (Health!)"

"*¡Pesátas!* (Wealth!)." She felt the word stick in her throat, but now she'd have to finish the traditional toast. If only she'd replied *salud* and stopped, simply and cordially. "*¡Y amor!* (And love!)."

Finally he laughed, and then she laughed, too. It was strained but didn't seem too forced. She lifted her fork high with amused, exaggerated ceremony to indicate that he could eat. "The *lomo* is delicious."

"Thanks to Don Martín."

"Umm. And the salad and bread."

"Thanks to me." They ate for a while without talking. The food was delicious, and the room was beautiful, as everything used to be on special occasions with her mother and her father. Sarah wanted to cry. She told herself that she must not cry.

In the candlelight Carlos's face seemed to be reflected in an old mirror, like her face before supper in the dark mirror of her dim bedroom, as if the light came from within their faces rather than from a source outside them in the room.

Sarah tried to think of something frivolous and unthreatening to talk about that would be appropriate and gracious for all the trouble Carlos had taken. She thought of Nicaraguan birds, an interest they'd shared as children and renewed during the last few weeks. They discussed the seasons of migration and varieties in the tropical jungle and those in the lake regions and those on the Caribbean lowland and finally those in the central mountains. "Did you ever see a quetzal, Carlos?"

"No. I always wanted to, almost more than anything."

"Me, too." Now she hoped to see the quetzal someday with Carlos. The tender, loving feelings had returned because of his kindness and awkward, boyish chivalry and great effort to please her. Perhaps he could still be like a brother to her. Perhaps they could see the quetzal together before she left the country. "They're very rare now, but Don Martín says a few still come back to nest."

"Their habitat is being destroyed. They can't possibly last much longer. There's no place for them to hide in the forests any more, and for years they've just barely survived. Now civilization is destroying them." Despite his somber words, Carlos smiled at her.

"*Like Doña Beatriz and Father Richard,*" she thought. "*There's no place for them any more in the new Nicaragua, amid socialist reform and techno-logical progress.*"

"Maybe we'll see one while we're still together at Quinta Louisa. It's getting close to the time when they come to Nicaragua for breeding in a few months. They arrive in such splendor with tail plumes longer than their bodies like blue and green tropical ferns, the color of emeralds and sapphires. Then after they nest, they go back to Guatemala in a horribly bedraggled state. Poor dears." She meant to be light and charmingly entertaining; but even the talk of birds felt serious and sad, as if she were talking about other things that she couldn't express or even understand.

"Who would've thought you'd like those gaudy pagan birds—bright red and green and blue. Seems to me they dress in very bad taste." He gently mocked her concern for tasteful combinations of colors and laughed, and Sarah smiled, but she couldn't join his laughter. She thought of how the quetzals were dying in the country she loved. She thought how someday very soon there would be no more quetzals in Nicaragua, perhaps none left in the world; and she wanted to weep. Her sadness felt overwhelming; but she was able to conceal her despair, because they'd finished eating; and Carlos was preoccupied with completing the feast according to his meticulous plan.

He cleared the table and brought the coffee and cake with considerably more ease than he'd found the missing butter. Martín had prepared the dishes carefully in the kitchen for this transition before he'd left for the village. Then Carlos brought in two dishes on a silver tray held above his head like a flamboyant waiter. He swept the tray down and quickly, ceremoniously set a dish in front of Sarah.

"Ice cream! It's real ice cream! Where on earth did you get it? How on earth did you keep it from melting?"

"In dry ice. I was scared all afternoon it would melt. It used to be your most favorite thing."

". . . in the whole world." She began crying.

"Don't you melt, too!" Now he laughed, easily, gently, delighted with himself and his surprise and Sarah's happy tears that he believed sprang from the pleasure that he'd produced. "Eat your ice cream."

"We never could get real soda fountain ice cream from the city without its melting on the way home. Daddy tried and tried on my birthdays, year after year. He finally gave up."

"Tonight we did it. Now eat it for Pete's sake."

She dabbed her eyes with the corner of her napkin, because she'd forgotten to put a handkerchief in the pockets of the old sundress. Then she ate it. All of the birthdays and all the little girl excitement from each of them poured over her: all the special birthdays, when she was six and her father had brought monkeys and a pony that Guillermo led around the garden for all of her friends to ride, when she was twelve and Doña Beatriz had arranged for a juggler and a magician to come to Quinta Louisa, when she was sixteen and her friends had sat together in the dining room for a formal dinner. Carlos's face glowed like a celestial angel as he watched her eat. He didn't touch his ice cream.

"Carlos, yours is melting."

"That's o.k."

When she finished, he took away her dish and put his in front of her. "Have mine, too."

"I can't eat your ice cream!"

"Are you full?"

"No, but it's not fair. You must have some, too."

"Please. Pretty please. Let me watch you eat another dish. It's much more fun to watch you than to eat it myself. He laughed, and his eyes sparkled as if she'd made him sublimely happy. He began thumping his fingers together in his spastic attempt at snapping. "Now eat up-hup, two, three four." Carlos's English was perfect, but occasionally the hint of a Spanish accent infected his speech with a delightful distinction almost like a faint lisp, as when he said *hup* with a resistance to the "h" and a softening of the "p".

"All right, if you're sure." Sarah finished the second dish and folded her napkin. Carlos's elbows were on the table, and his chin rested in the cups of his hands. He was still smiling, glowing at her. "That was delicious. It was marvelous and beautiful and wonderful. Thanks you, Carlos. *¡Mil gracias!* (A thousand thanks!) What can I say? Real ice cream at Quinta Louisa!"

Carlos took a small velvet box from his coat pocket. Once it had been pale blue. Now it was mostly grey. "I love you, Sarah, and I want you to be my wife. Perhaps you'll say it's impossible, that our lives are too different; but I had to tell you how much I love you and how much

I want you to marry me." He opened the box and held it out to her. The beautiful Colombian emerald was surrounded by small diamonds. "I asked my mother to send the ring from Miami. She said years ago that I could have it to give to the woman I asked to marry me."

Sarah wondered if Carlos had deferred talking with her about a long-term relationship for the past two weeks and even for weeks before the raid because he was waiting for the ring to arrive in the country. She didn't take it out of the box or touch it or even touch Carlos's hand holding it. She couldn't answer. She didn't know what to say. Dozens of thoughts seemed to flow into her mind together. Where would they live if she lost Quinta Louisa? Where would they be married?

"I don't even know if I'll be able to keep Quinta Louisa."

"I wanted to ask you before you knew for sure. You'll have a better chance of keeping the *finca* if you marry me. I'm a Nicaraguan citizen, and I joined the Sandinistas a long time before the revolution. I even got a scar on my only raid in the jungle—my badge of honor." Carlos laughed, cynically, still believing that he had behaved cowardly during the revolution, as he touched the little white scar on his neck.

A chill passed through Sarah. She wondered if he wanted to marry her because he really loved her or only because he wanted to have Quinta Louisa for himself, but then she thought her demeaning idea was unworthy of his character and dismissed it.

"I love you, Carlos. I loved you like a brother when we were children. I've wanted to make love to you since the first afternoon you came out to the *finca*. But it's all so new and strange. I can't give you an answer tonight. There's so much that separates us."

Carlos knelt and began kissing her hands, washing them like a puppy with his lips. She ran her fingers through his thick curly hair, clutching it and pulling her fingers through it. She'd wanted to feel and fondle it since she first saw him in the doorway of Quinta Louisa.

"Sarah . . ."

"Everything is all mixed up inside me. I'm so confused, but I do love you, my *guapo, macho, simpático querido* . . . (my handsome, manly, soul-mated beloved . . .)"

Their lips touched. She held his head between her palms, as he knelt in front of her while she was still seated in the chair, until she slipped down beside him. For a long time they kissed each other's faces and caressed each other's bodies with their fingertips, not afraid or ashamed to touch anywhere, not embarrassed or guilty at being touched anywhere. Their bodies were comfortable, entwined in desire but at ease together, unlike the way they had panted and grabbed at each other after the raid two weeks ago.

"I'll wait a little while for your answer."

"Please let me have tomorrow completely by myself. . . to go to church, to think and pray."

"Trust me. Don't give up on me."

SARAH RETURNED TO QUINTA Louisa from the vicarage earlier than she usually did on Sunday after her weekly visit with Father Richard following the service. About two o'clock as she glanced out the window over the patio she saw Carlos working in the garden. When she'd left for the church, he'd probably still been asleep; there had been no sign of him moving around in the guesthouse.

Carlos came inside before the sun went down, so that they could share the sunset together on the patio. She hadn't told him what time she expected him. She loved him for choosing the right moment.

"I came casually, no *wedding and funeral* tonight."

"*Perfecto.*"

"Have you made any decision? About us, I mean."

"Ssh. Don't talk." She put her right index finger over her lips and her left index finger over his lips. The words and gestures they'd used when they saw a special bird as children, so that it wouldn't be frightened away. "We'll talk about it later."

"How long will you keep me waiting for an answer?" His tone was jesting, teasing.

"You must be patient until after dinner. We have just enough wine left from last night for a toast on the patio as we watch the sun go down." She giggled and cursed herself for it silently.

Carlos giggled, too, with unpleasant spurts of sound like her father's laughter. She hadn't heard him giggle since she returned, and it surprised her. They watched the motmots with the disks on their tails and the scissor-tailed flycatchers clipping their long feathers together as they flitted back and forth across the sky. Sarah and Carlos both knew almost certainly what her answer to his proposal would be but were perhaps afraid to have it spoken lest its magic be spoiled.

Even after their feast on the previous evening, they were hungry again and ate heartily. She served his fruit, left from last night, making a miniature arrangement on his plate with little rosettes. He rolled pieces of tortillas around the beans and dry cheese and fed her bites as she served their plates with the cold slices of tenderloin that were left. They talked very little but looked steadily at each other, without shame or embarrassment, without lust or seduction, but never taking their eyes from the others' face and body, unafraid to stare for any length of time, allowing their eyes to go and rest where their hands had been on the night of the raid, almost everywhere their hands had been, as if they already belonged to each other. Sarah thought that she already loved and cherished Carlos's face and body much more than her own. Perhaps that was what it meant to be married.

"Your dinner was very good."

"It wasn't extra special, like yours. Someday maybe I'll make you a dinner like that, but I won't ever find such wonderful surprises. Ice cream! The wine! The strawberries! And the rolls! Where did you ever find the croissants?"

Sarah's eyes dropped, unable to hold the steady gaze into Carlos's face, ashamed to let her eyes remain on his body, his torso and loins any longer. Then Sarah was able to look at him once again without having to glance away. "You're wearing the American chain around your neck again."

Carlos lifted it with the little finger of his left hand. "You like my little *gringo* chain?"

"I noticed when you stopped wearing it. You seemed to take it off so deliberately that you were declaring to the world, *I'm not a North American*

*anymore and never will be a North American again. I won't have anything
to do with the States or Americans again.*"

"Clever girl. You were right, but I put it back on for you, my little
gringa."

"I hated those chains when men started wearing them in the States.
They seemed to advertise that their bodies were available and that they
were on the make. But I love it on you tonight." She giggled again. "And
your tight white chinos and your vest that shows your bellybutton and
your tiny acorn breasts."

Carlos's face became serious but never took his eyes away from her
face. He reached up and unpinned the gold orchid. The front fell open
on the blue-grey dress with rows of lace, the same dress she'd worn when
she'd prepared a dinner for him, the dress she'd imagined her mother
wearing to accept her father's proposal of marriage. Carlos looked at
her breasts. Then he kissed each one, only once apiece, and very gently
pulled the material together and fastened the pin again. "Do you have
any answer for me yet?"

"Now stop it, Carlos." She hadn't resisted his unpinning her dress or
kissing her breasts, but she would not allow him to change her agenda
for the evening. "Don't you try to trick me into giving you an answer
before the sun sets."

"*Querida mía* (My beloved), you even want to make the sun fit your
schedule."

"That's not really true." But she could try to make her life fit the rising
and setting of the sun and gain the greatest possible advantage from its
light and seek protection from the worst of its heat.

"You have only a few more minutes until it's dark. Then I'll demand
an answer."

"Like the cruel tyrant that you are."

"Like the cruel tyrant that I am."

The sunset was as beautiful as she'd hoped it would be, as if she'd
planned it, too, as if she'd ordered its colors for the evening. The dust of
the dry season filled the air with particles that reflected reds and purples
and blues, yellows and ambers, crimsons and pinks, oranges and lavenders.

They stood on the patio watching the sky and sipped the last of the wine. "Yes, Carlos, I want to be your wife. I love you."

"Sarah." His voice was plaintive and frightened as it had been last night after he'd proposed to her, as it had been when he'd called her name from the yard on the night of the raid. "Sarah, I love you." He sounded like a little boy at bedtime, just before his eyes closed in sleep. They were still standing at the edge of the patio with their arms around each other when he took the empty wine glasses from their hands and laid them on a chair. Then they sat down on the edge of the patio where she'd often sat with Guillermo. Their bodies nestled together as they'd huddled under the blanket on the beach at Pocho Mil many years ago, comfortable and secure in each other's embrace until the sky darkened into indigos and blacks ornamented by the white twinkle of stars and pale glow of the moon. "On what conditions?"

"There mustn't be any conditions for us. We'll promise to love, honor and cherish each other as long as both shall live whether I get to hold onto Quinta Louisa or not, without promising we'll stay in Nicaragua or go to the States to live eventually. I do want to keep my American citizenship. Oh, I'd like for Father Richard to marry us, even though you don't believe in religion, if you don't mind. We don't have to have the wedding at St. Francis, if it would be wrong for you. But please, soon. Very, very soon."

"I don't think we can do it before tomorrow."

"Carlos, please don't tease me tonight."

"I'd like for Father Richard to perform the ceremony, too, as a dear old friend, whatever I believe about religion. How soon? Next week?"

"As soon after we get an answer from Castillo López about Quinta Louisa, as soon as possible."

"*Bueno* (good)."

They talked long into the night about how Sarah would make her appeal to Castillo López for keeping Quinta Louisa and what he might say to her. They talked about how they would operate the *finca* and what they wanted to do for the workers, how perhaps they could even turn portions of the land over to the workers little by little and let them buy their own little plantations.

"Carlos!"

Carlos jumped at her sudden loud exclamation of his name. "What is it? What's the matter? Have you changed your mind already?"

"What would happen if I deeded the factory to the workers for a cooperative? I would want Don Martín's sons to have a major stake. They could even take over the export business. Maybe I could still help with that. It all makes sense. It's all coming together in my mind. Isn't that the sort of thing the government is proposing? Cooperatives? Isn't that the kind of thing that fits your ideals and hopes? It's the kind of thing Mother—and Daddy, too, after a while—wanted and worked for in the village. Do you think Castillo López might let us keep Quinta Louisa and the coffee farm if we donated the factory?"

"That's brilliant! Yes, yes, I do believe Castillo López would agree to it. It's all perfect. I believe . . . Yes. How did you ever come up with . . . ? Is that what you really want to do? Are you sure?"

They found themselves in perfect agreement, amazing agreement even about politics and economics as they talked about what should happen to Quinta Louisa. She knew that all their plans were as fragile as the flowers that they'd seen at sunset in the garden, now covered by darkness. The flowers would be withered by sunrise tomorrow; but tonight Sarah and Carlos couldn't disagree. Tonight their hopes seemed as certain and fixed in their courses as the moon and the stars above them.

SARAH DECIDED THAT DOÑA Beatriz would be the first person she would tell about Carlos's proposal of marriage. Father Richard would raise too many serious questions and concerns for her to celebrate with him. Don Martín and Guillermo wouldn't understand her hesitancy to accept his proposal but on the other hand might consider any man unworthy of her. Doña Beatriz would giggle with her and clap her hands in excitement before they began discussing plans for her wedding.

Sarah believed that she loved Carlos, but she couldn't test the words just inside her head and her heart. She must say them out loud to another person in order to know if she truly believed them or not. Perhaps *love him* would sound silly as soon as it was uttered in someone else's presence.

Doña Beatriz would help her sort through her feelings and handle them gently but lightly, with amused little jokes but not with weighty disparagement. She'd told Doña Beatriz about her boyfriends as a teenager, and Doña Beatriz had kept her confidences and her anguished infatuations a secret and had helped her embroider her fantasies of romance, and of course Doña Beatriz had shared the sad conclusion of her involvement with Brian.

"My dear, you look a thousand times better than you did a few weeks ago after that terrible *ataque* (attack) on Quinta Louisa. You're almost glowing. Some good news? Have you learned something about your property settlement?"

"I'm afraid not, Doña Beatriz. My news doesn't have anything to do with the *finca*. It's something personal."

Doña Beatriz jangled her bracelets and smoothed her hair back toward the bun at the nape of her neck. "Are you in love again?" Yet, she showed no joy. There was no exulting excitement in her voice. Sarah wondered what had happened to her mother's best friend, the confidante of her youth, her conspirator in innocent romance.

"You don't seem overjoyed."

"Tell me about it. Who is he?"

"Doña Beatriz, I wanted to share my happiness with you. You sound like an angry stepmother giving me the third degree after the ball."

"Maybe you need a stern stepmother, now that your own mother is gone—may she rest with the angels. You're not sixteen anymore and excited about some cute boy that you just met. Who is it? I pray *Dios* (God) it isn't Carlos Vargas Allen."

"Yes, but how did you know? I didn't even suspect that I'd fall in love with him when I talked about him after he first came out to Quinta Louisa. He was still just a goofy boy I knew as a child, the son of my mother's friend that I never took seriously except as a good friend, and I hated him for getting mixed up in the revolution. I certainly wasn't in love with him then."

"So you said, but when there's that much emotion expressed . . . I could see the signs . . . in your eyes, in your words, your smiles and frowns.

Oh, Sarita, I should have warned you. You have to break off with him immediately. Nothing good can come of a relationship with him. Please do exactly as I tell you and break off with him and ask me no questions."

"Why? For what reason? What has he done, Doña Beatriz? Is it because of his involvement with the Sandinistas? We've talked about all that. I think we can live with those differences. Carlos has asked me to marry him!"

"*Por amor de Dios* (For the love of God), no, no, no! It's not the revolution, as much as you really should consider that. No, no, no! You must not marry him!"

"Doña Beatriz, why? Why? What's the matter?"

"If I make you hate Carlos Vargas, you'll hate me, too. You're like a daughter to me, and . . ." Doña Beatriz shook her head and tried to smile but failed. Sarah wanted to ask a hundred questions, but she remained silent and waited for Doña Beatriz to continue. "I should have never recommended Carmen Ruiz to you. I should have known it would be a disaster. I'm so very, very, very sorry. *Perdóname* (Please forgive me)."

"Carmen? What does Carmen have to do with it?" Almost before she spoke Sarah knew the answer to her question and hoped that Doña Beatriz would not confirm it in actual words.

"She is his mistress, my dear. Haven't you wondered where he goes on the weekend? The mistress comes before the wife."

Sarah remembered that Carlos had always given Carmen a ride into Managua ostensibly to visit her family on Saturday afternoons and that he did not return on Saturday nights. They had been fucking throughout those Saturday nights. "Oh, oh!" Sarah began weeping. She wondered how Doña Beatriz knew about Carlos and Carmen; but she recalled that even in a big city like Managua, everyone in the expatriate community and all their Nicaraguan friends knew everything about everyone else.

Doña Beatriz stood and began pounding Sarah's shoulder as she spoke. "Never, never forget that the mistress is chosen first. She is loved first. She has first place. Carmen has been his mistress for several years. How it hurts me to tell you! But it's better for you to know, even if you hate me forever. I should have told you. I never thought that Carlos would become involved with you at Quinta Louisa. I should have told you about them as soon as he moved into the guesthouse. I'm sorry. Please forgive me. Think very carefully if you want to share Carlos with Carmen Ruiz for the rest of your life. She'll get the better part of him." Doña Beatriz's face was angry and her voice was bitter. Don Armando's mistress had been a part of her life for over a quarter of a century. She spoke out of the anguish of her own experience.

Sarah had thought that Carlos had come to Quinta Louisa as a friend and in his official capacity as an agent of the government would warn her if the *finca* was about to be confiscated. She'd been grateful to him for his protection on the night of the raid. After they made love, he'd treated her with kindness and respect; but he shouldn't have pretended to care about her. He shouldn't have told her that he loved her. She despised him for being kind to her, for responding sympathetically and warmly to her grief about her father's death, as if he really did care about her. She hated him for needing to be with Carmen more than wanting to protect her on the weekends. His lust and his addiction to getting laid every weekend were contemptible. Now she detested his kindness. She could see his kindness and feel his kindness, even taste his kindness, like a dark, filthy sweet-smelling rag that was choking her and trying to kill her. Above all Sarah detested his audacity in asking her to marry him.

Doña Beatriz's revelation about Carlos and Carmen seemed to unleash a deluge of her own bitterness and anger. Sarah hardly heard her as she related for the umpteenth time how before the end of the revolution the *Guardia* (National Guard) had stopped her one night on the South Highway and dragged her out of her car and thrown her to the ground and frisked her. Never in all the years under the Somozas had such a thing happened to her. Then wealth and position were always respected, even though she and Don Armando belonged to the old Conservative Party that opposed Somoza's ironically named Liberal Party.

She told Sarah again about the events that led up to losing their home in the earthquake—the failure of the cotton markets and the debts that were suddenly called in all at once, all together, and the rush of the government agencies and banks to foreclose immediately, rather than granting them time to work things out as they'd always done before. "The banks could have ruined Armando dozens of times, hundreds of times in the past; but that's not how business was ever done in Nicaragua. They knew they'd get their money with plenty of interest to boot. And what did they accomplish? After the earthquake they ruined all the little farmers with twenty or thirty hectares of cotton that relied on Armando as their broker." Doña Beatriz jangled her bracelets as she thrust her arms into the air and turned completely toward Sarah on the couch. "They crushed them, the little people that the glorious revolution was supposed to help. Armando always said that the emerging middle-class, like the little cotton farmers that used his brokerage, were the real hope of building a modern economy in the country. And they suffered dreadfully, even more than we did, if that's possible. They lost absolutely everything. They were totally devastated."

Sarah had heard about the Chultecos' sufferings many times in almost exactly the same words; but she was furious that Doña Beatriz chose this moment to reiterate all her wrath, when Sarah wanted solace and comfort for her own pain at the news about Carlos and Carmen Ruiz. *"How can Doña Beatriz be so insensitive that she can't feel my anguish?"* Sara thought. She tried to remember all the gracious and good things that Doña Beatriz had done for her and for her mother over the years and not feel such great resentment now.

"I'm sorry, Doña Beatriz, for both of us."

"Don Armando had many mistresses over the years. Many, many *putas* (whores), but we had our business and a good life . . . my parties, my friends. I've never said these things before, not even to your mother. But I expected some other compensation in my later years. Things were supposed to turn out differently in the end. You make certain compromises with life, and you expect certain compensations. You make your bargain with life . . . When I had a lovely home and servants and friends, it was a bearable life."

Sarah was stunned that Doña Beatriz would even allude to things never mentioned before, even among the closest of friends. Now, Doña Beatriz should be coming into her reign of power; but she had been cheated out of the advantage of aged matriarchy in the Nicaraguan culture, at the age when Don Armando would have tired of his whores and his mistress. The mistress would have retired with a little pension to an apartment and called on only occasionally. Don Armando would have returned to live quietly at home. Intimacy would have been shared again with his wife who would finally dominate their family and even take charge of his money and business due to his guilt, his price for a quiet and peaceful old age; but the business had been lost, and Don Armando had died.

"Don Armando was such a genial host. He made everyone feel at home, even when we were children at the Christmas parties." Sarah tried to dampen Doña Beatriz's diatribe against her deceased husband. She believed that Doña Beatriz would regret her words later and be chagrinned at having spoken them to Sarah. Don Armando had always accompanied his wife to the parties on holidays and was present at family gatherings and in times of emergency. As an honorable man, a gentle and compassionate man in terms of the mores of his society, Don Armando had treated his wife with respect and even reverence; but Sarah wondered if his real intimacy and passion had been reserved for his whores and his mistress. The Chaltecos had no children, and the code was especially strict when there were no children between the husband and the wife. A man must have many, many women to prove his manhood, his machismo, over and over. Yet, Don Armando had been a model of proper behavior, as defined by his place and rank in the society.

"There's nothing left for me in a communist society. Do you understand?"

"I think so."

"Do you understand why you must never marry Carlos Vargas Allen?"

"As I said, I believe that I understand." Sarah at last saw the connection between the incompatibility of the new social order and the old ways of marital infidelity that were still in force. Doña Beatriz wanted to save Sarah from the fate that had befallen her. Sarah stood. She wanted to say something to relieve the awkwardness of her despair after Doña Beatriz's outburst in contrast to her initial excitement about Carlos's proposal. It was as if they had intruded into the private parts of each other's lives that should never have been entered and thereby had committed some shameful, unpardonable act. "It's nice to have someone to talk to me as my mother would."

"I can never take Mary's place. I can't do what Mary would do or say what she would say. She was an American, and I'm a Nicaraguan. That's the way it was, and that's the way it will be, always. But I do miss her so. I loved her best of all my friends. No one can take her place."

"We all miss her, terribly."

"She never really adjusted to Nicaragua, you know. Over a quarter of a century she lived here, and she never understood Latin America. She always thought there was only one good way to live your life, only one right way to do things, the North Carolina way. She always thought she could do all sorts of things for herself that women, certainly women of her position, simply couldn't do in Nicaragua. You're very much like her, you know."

"Most people think I'm more like my father."

"Yes, you're like your father, too; but I see more of your mother in you. Still, you're very different from both of them. I think you might have been the first of the Rutledges after four generations to be a true Nicaraguan, in the old Nicaragua, of course. None of us can have any real life, any good life here after the revolution, unless the country is liberated from these Marxists and restored to us."

"Mother and Daddy remained rather American and British, I suppose, in a lot of ways. Certainly Mother and Daddy enjoyed an American marriage, as foreigners living with their own customs and values in a strange land."

"How I envied Mary for that! Find an American boy, Sarita. Don't marry Carlos Vargas Allen."

Sarah tried in vain to change the subject again. "I thought you were happier now. I thought you'd sort of adjusted and accepted . . ."

"Accepted? Yes, I suppose. Given up. Given in. This is all there is. This is all I have left." Doña Beatriz waved her arms and jangled her bracelets but not in her customary exuberant excitement, now in despairing resignation. There was thick dust on the tables, in the corners, even in rolls and puffs. Sarah was hardly fastidious about housekeeping, but it seemed incongruous, even a sacrilege in Doña Beatriz's parlor.

"I'm so sorry, Doña Beatriz."

"Promise me that you won't marry Carlos Vargas Allen. Promise me solemnly."

"Of course not. I don't want a Nicaraguan marriage." Her words were harsh and deliberately insensitive as if she wanted to hurt Doña Beatriz as much as Doña Beatriz had hurt her. She wanted Doña Beatriz to feel the same degree of pain that she had inflicted by her revelation about Carlos.

It was time to leave. They bade elaborate goodbyes at Doña Beatriz's front door in the old way, by touching cheeks while their noisy kisses were made into the air. They embraced by holding each other's arms so that their bodies brushed lightly together but never pressed against each other, conveying deep affection without passion. It was another ritual whose time had probably come to pass away.

Perhaps they both understood that the relationship they'd shared for many years had been irrevocably damaged. They would continue to see each other and remain friends, but they were saying good-bye to the intimacy they'd known together but could never share again. As Sarah drove away from Los Robles she felt a deeper sadness for the loss of her bond with Doña Beatriz than for the destruction of her fantasy about marrying Carlos. At that moment she was angrier at Doña Beatriz than she was at Carlos.

CARLOS CALLED TO SARAH from the driveway after he arrived from the Ministry and asked about getting together, but she feigned a headache—what she really experienced was a heart ache—because she was not yet ready to confront him. The afternoon with Doña Beatriz had left her numb, drained of emotion. She felt neither angry nor belligerent toward Carlos, just disappointed. She wondered if she would ever find a man to love her, to belong to her. Brian didn't like women enough, and apparently Carlos liked them too much.

Sarah needed to urinate in the middle of the night—an unusual requirement for her—and as she moved around the awkwardly angled, almost hidden wall of the little alcove that led to the bathroom, she suddenly remembered how Carlos had found it immediately without her directions and seemed uncomfortably embarrassed by his knowledge. "*The bastard. He was fucking Carmen right here at Quinta Louisa,*" she thought as her numbness turned to fury and contempt.

The next morning Sarah asked Don Martín if Carlos had spent the night in the house with Carmen while she was in North Carolina.

"*Sí, Señorita.*"

"*How often?*"

"*Many times.*"

"*Why did you not tell me?*"

"*It was not my place, Doña Sarah. It is better to leave some things unspoken.*"

"*Let us have no more secrets, my father. We are one family now. I do not want you to protect my feelings any longer. Perhaps you will not be so sad now at having to keep a secret from me.*"

"*Perhaps, hijiña* (little daughter), *but there must be some secrets even in families.*"

Don Martín's calling her daughter for the third time, this time using the affectionate diminutive, brought her only moment of joy during those bleak hours.

SARAH COULD NOT PRETEND to be ill after two more days lest Carlos seek medical attention for her. She would have to face him and return his ring, as she'd been obliged to return Brian's ring for very different reasons.

Carlos was almost leaping and skipping for joy as he came in the front door. "Good news! Castillo has approved our plan for the *finca*. He was impressed with the idea of the cooperative, and your marriage to a Nicaraguan sealed the deal." He put both hands on his chest, pointing to himself proudly.

"There will be no marriage." Sarah dissolved into a flood of tears.

Carlos moved toward her alternating between an impulse to embrace her and a fear of touching her. "Why? What do you mean?"

"I know about you and Carmen."

"I was going to tell you about Carmen. I thought I needed to be honest, but I wanted to wait until . . ."

"Not now. Not yet." Sarah sarcastically mocked the words Carlos had often used.

"Yes. I had to get things settled with her . . . even before I asked you to marry me. And then . . . I wanted for us to have some time to make our plans." He was popping his knuckles.

"Can you deny that you were fucking her while you were flirting with me, almost trying to seduce me from the moment you walked into this house?"

"I can't deny anything, but you've got it all distorted." Carlos was popping all his knuckles so compulsively that Sarah thought his hands would become completely disjointed like a puppet that was being pulled apart. "I'm sorry. I didn't think you would ever be attracted to me. You never were, even though I've loved you since we were children . . . not as just a brother. When we snuggled under the beach towel at Pocho Mil just before I left . . . I wanted you . . . so much . . . even then, but I thought you only wanted to be friends . . . even after you came back a couple of months ago."

"But you were making love to Carmen the whole time, from the beginning."

"Sarah, I have been with many women . . . since I was a teenager. I am not a virgin."

"I was . . . until the night of the raid."

Now Carlos dissolved into tears and held his face in his hands. "Oh God, Sarah, I am so sorry. I never wanted to hurt you. I am so sorry."

"What makes me the most furious is your fucking her here at Quinta Louisa. This house is sacred to me. In my bed . . ."

"No. Not in your bed. Only in the guest room. Carmen's room."

"Would you have married me just to claim Quinta Louisa for yourself? Is that why you came here in the first place—to finagle a way to get Quinta Louisa for yourself, what you call the most beautiful place in the world, the place you'd rather live than anywhere else in the world?" Sarah's voice was angry and bitter.

"That would make me worse than Andrejo. Surely you can't believe that about me." Now Carlos was wounded, and Sarah was delighted that at least she had hurt him almost as deeply as he had hurt her.

"Did you plan to keep Carmen as your *querida* (mistress), your *puta* (protitute) after we were married?"

"No, no. That is why I waited . . . to settle things with Carmen. We never intended to be serious. We were a comfort to one another in difficult times. We knew it would not be permanent."

"Some other *querida* then, like your father."

Now Sarah knew she had wounded Carlos at the core of his being. He seemed to collapse in his chair.

"Not like my father. I would have kept my promise to be faithful to you, to never be with another woman."

"And Carmen? Did she understand that?"

"It was very hard for her. She cared more for me than I realized. That's why I had to wait and not take advantage of you. That's why she left for Panama."

"Here's your ring."

"Is there no hope? Couldn't we talk about . . . ?"

Sarah paused because she couldn't speak. She felt she could hardly breathe. At last she said, "I don't know," because she could think of nothing else to say.

"Please." His voice was so desperate, so pleading, so full of pain that Sarah almost wanted to hold him in her arms.

"Maybe we can talk later, but I don't have much hope."

"If you want me to marry you . . . if it will help you keep Quinta Louisa, I will marry you and never live with you, never live at Quinta Louisa, give you a divorce when things are settled. Never see you again, if it will help you keep Quinta Louisa."

It was perhaps the only thing Carlos could have said that would have convinced Sarah that there was hope. In spite of everything, she knew him well enough to see that he was sincere and completely honest in his offer and that she still loved him.

"JESUS CERTAINLY WOULDN'T QUALIFY as a modern feminist," Sarah thought and smiled as Richard Sims read the Gospel. He'd walked farther down the aisle than he usually did, and the sun was in her eyes as she stood and turned toward him behind her pew. She squinted. "Everyone who looks at a woman lustfully has already committed adultery with her in his heart."

"What about a woman looking lustfully at a man? Jesus probably hadn't ever thought about a woman's lust," Sarah reflected and recalled how often she'd lusted for Carlos in her heart and committed spiritual adultery, or more precisely, spiritual fornication with him. The memory of her sexual fantasies now accused her and mocked her with both guilt and rage. Few people had even talked about feminine lust before a decade or so ago. It was still taboo in the Church.

Sarah helped Father Richard disrobe in the sacristy. It was the first time she'd assisted the priest after the service since her return to Nicaragua, the first time she'd been in the sacristy since the night she'd met Ernesto Andrejo Sánchez and the first time she'd folded the white amice and alb and washed the silver paten and chalice since her father's death. Her mother had always assumed that she would assist with the altar and had never given her any choice in the matter nor allowed any discussion about it. Altar duty hadn't seemed an issue onerous enough to cause a major argument and estrangement between them.

After her mother died Sarah had thought she would never prepare the altar again, as part of her oath never to be like her mother. Perhaps it took twelve years to do such simple things again for herself, neither in acquiescence to her mother nor in rebellion against her, but because they were routine and helpful, because she knew more about altar work than anyone at St. Francis and did it better and more easily than anyone else after her years of apprenticeship to her mother.

"Guess what, Padre? Carlos Vargas has asked me to marry him."

Father Richard pursed his lips and searched the top of the table with his eyes and hands for his pipe. "Congratulations." He spoke dryly, as if he already knew about Carmen Ruiz. He showed no shock, not even surprise.

"That's only half the story. He's been …" Sarah started to say *screwing Carmen Ruiz* but despite the candid, almost obscene language she often used in speaking to Father Richard, she couldn't use those words with him here in the sacristy, in part because she still respected his role as her priest, in part because it sounded too much like Carmen's vulgar chatter. ". . . sleeping with Carmen Ruiz, apparently for several years . . ."

"My dear, I'm so sorry."

". . . even at Quinta Louisa."

"Sarah." The utterance of her name conveyed even more compassion than his words of sympathy.

"Ironically the Ministry of Justice has just agreed to our plan for keeping Quinta Louisa, contingent on my marrying a Nicaraguan, that is, Carlos Vargas Allen."

"Sarah." It would not have seemed possible for Father Richard to express even greater pity in uttering Sarah's name for a second time, until he did.

"Carlos has even offered to marry me just so I can keep the *finca*, and not live with me and divorce me later if I want to . . ."

"And you're considering it?" Now his tone was appalled.

"Not really. But it makes me think there is a tiny possibility . . . just this big . . ." Sarah held up about a two-inch gap between her thumb and her forefinger in a gesture she'd adopted from Guillermo. ". . . that I might . . ." She would not articulate her actual thought—*might actually marry him*. The idea was too painful, too remote, too preposterous.

"And just what is this possibility?" Father Richard imitated Sarah's gesture with his thumb and forefinger.

"You know the odds of marrying across cultural lines. Carlos is more a Nicaraguan than he's an American. I don't think his parents had a very good marriage, and that's a bad precedent. Men tend to act like their fathers did as husbands, don't they?"

"So some psychologists suggest, I believe."

"Even under the best of circumstances marriages between a Nicaraguan and a *gringa* are usually unhappy. Carlos's mother always struck me as being very unhappy in her marriage."

"Nancy Vargas was a rather sad woman, I fear."

"Even if Castillo López gives us title to Quinta Louisa, how can we be sure of keeping it with the turbulence in the country now? The way things are developing in El Salvador, Carlos might be involved in a war there too. The United States may suspend diplomatic relations at any moment. What kind of life would we have?" Sarah heard the echoes of Doña Beatriz's warnings in her words.

"That true, very true. It couldn't be a more difficult sort of political situation for you and Carlos."

"The odds of Americans ever being able to live comfortably and securely again in Central America are overwhelmingly against us."

"Oh, most assuredly. The odds are very much against you." Father Richard stood and paced around the table, almost as if he were acting out a part in a little Sunday School charade and was required to pace a bit at this point. "Any couple that marries in this day and time celebrates a wedding in the face of the probable destruction of the whole human race through a nuclear disaster. There are thousands of reasons for not getting married at all in the last decades of the twentieth century."

". . . besides all the differences of two cultures that divide us and the problem of where we'll eventually live and how we'll manage economically."

"Quite so, my dear." She hated his British imitation in the non-committal phrase *"quite so"* learned from her father.

"You know that Carlos is not even a Christian. He's a communist. Our beliefs are diametrically opposed to one another." Sarah fluffed her hair around her ears and thought of how Guillermo always teased her when she fussed with her hair.

"Do you really think so? I'm not as quick to judge as I used to be—who's a Christian and who's not. He has a passion for justice and righteousness, and I've never known anyone who had that kind of passion who didn't find God's grace and mercy along the way. Sometimes I think Carlos may have a much greater capacity to be like Christ than I do." Father Richard laid down his pipe and quickly brushed back his short-cropped hair in nervous rapid movements with the palms of both hands.

"Quite apart from having Carmen as a mistress, I'm sure he probably started going to *putas* (prostitutes) when he was barely pubescent in typical Nicaraguan *macho* fashion."

"Are you afraid that Carlos won't be faithful to you?"

"No, I don't think Carlos would sneak around. I believe he'd keep his vows. I know that's incongruous, but I believe he'd be faithful to what he promised."

"That's the impression I have of the boy I knew growing up here at St. Francis. What else is bothering you, Sarah? There's still something else, isn't there?"

"It's the deception. Why didn't he tell me about Carmen before he asked me to marry him? Why did I have to find out from Doña Beatriz? Why didn't he tell me before he moved into the guesthouse?"

"Why indeed?" Father Sims waited for Sarah to formulate her own answer.

"Quite honestly I think he didn't tell me because he really loves me and didn't want to jinx it all before . . . I wonder if it still might work, in spite of everything."

"But do you love him, Sarah? Do you love him enough?"

Sarah withered inside, as if he'd asked some grossly unfair, obscene question.

"Last night I read through the marriage service several times in the Prayer Book. It has more about covenants and vows and honor and promises and faithfulness than about love. And trust. That's Carlos's big word, *trust.*"

"Those are all crucially important things for a marriage, my dear; but you still haven't answered my question. Do you love him?"

"Damn it. Of course I love him. The issue is not whether I love him. The question is whether I should marry him, whether I can forgive him." She blushed and felt her anger directed back at herself more than at Father Richard or even at Carlos who lay at the core of it. She wanted Father Richard to make explicit all the reasons that a marriage with Carlos was impossible, to make Father Richard responsible for her not being able to marry him. "Oh, Padre, tell me what to do. Please just tell me what to do."

"So that you can get your dander up? You want me to present all the reasons for not marrying Carlos so that you can defy me and feel right and justified. You want me to argue against Carlos so that you can defend him, but I won't do it, Sarah. This time you've got to make up your own mind and search the reasons out of your own heart. I know you, Sarah; and I love you too much to give you an excuse for doing something out of sheer rebellion. It wouldn't be fair to you."

"Why can't Father Richard be subtle and sympathetic and kind and understanding? Isn't that what priest are for? Isn't that what priests are supposed to do? How can he be so brutally and painfully honest with me?" Sarah thought. "But I need you to put into words all the reasons that I know deep down in my own heart why I shouldn't marry Carlos, even though I may love him." Sarah wanted to cry; but for once the tears wouldn't come to her eyes where tears usually came easily, as if Father Richard had quenched the anger that was the source of her tears. She couldn't have wept even if she'd tried. "Oh, Father Richard, I'm so frightened."

"Just what are you afraid, of Sarah? Not communists and revolutionaries, I think. Not even cultural differences and Latin machismo, though you may have convinced yourself those are the real problems. What are you really afraid of, my dear?"

"Failure. I'm so afraid of failing. I love Carlos. I really do, but I'm not sure I can forgive him for . . . what he did with Carmen. Half my friends who have gotten divorced say they still love their husbands and that the sexual part is still good. We've got so much against us. I want my marriage to be perfect. I don't want it to fail."

"It wouldn't be perfect, and you would fail, of course. Everyone fails, and that's the first thing you've got to know about a marriage. The question is whether your failure will be redeemed by God's love and grace."

"If God would only give me a sign and tell me what to do. You sure as hell won't!"

"Have a little patience, Susi. God may yet give you some sign, so you'll know the truth in your own heart."

Sarah thought that Father Richard was not even aware that for the first time in her life he'd called her by her father's pet name.

"I do love Carlos, and I do love Quinta Louisa, but I can't make a trade-off of one against the other. They have to be separate. Separate decisions. I can't marry him just to keep Quinta Louisa."

"Life rarely has such distinct boundaries, my dear. The human heart cannot be divided. Certainly your heart can't."

Almost every day for over a month Sarah had noticed that Don Martín had taken flowers from the garden and carried them past the trees and through the first rows of coffee bushes toward the cemetery on the cliff overlooking the valley. Sometimes he'd cut blossoms, even some of the straggly English rose buds that her mother and grandmother had tried in vain to nurture. At other times he'd dug up plants, both domesticated perennials and the native wild flowers from the jungle.

Years ago Sarah's mother had given Don Martín permission to transplant flowers to his cottage in the village, and after Doña Flora's death Sarah's father had encouraged him to move any plants that he chose to the cemetery and place them around their wives' graves without even asking. Even so, Sarah had never observed the daily procession to the graves before the past few weeks, not even following her father's death when Don Martín had been emotionally devastated. Sarah wondered if he was observing some peculiar anniversary season for Doña Flora. In addition to the formalized Roman Catholic celebrations, mostly familiar to Sarah because of their similarity in the Anglican religious calendar, there were local rituals that *campesinos* (peasants) like Don Martín took even more seriously. Perhaps some kind of novena had occurred completely unknown to Sarah. She hesitated to question him, lest he think she was accusing him, but eventually curiosity overcame her.

"Don Martín, I have noticed that you are taking flowers to the graves very often, and . . ."

"Please excuse me, Doña Sarah. I do not intend to remove more out of the garden than I should. I will take no more."

"Do not be absurd, Papá. You can always take as many as you wish."

"Your mother and father told me to get them whenever I wanted."

"Of course. You can take everything, even the rose bushes." Sarah attempted to make him laugh at their running joke about the futility of growing roses in Nicaragua, but Don Martín didn't even smile. *"I only mentioned it because I was afraid that I had forgotten some anniversary or novena."*

"No, no. That is not the reason." Don Martín twisted his fingers together in a strangely uncharacteristic gesture, almost as if he were imitating his son Guillermo.

"Are you taking them to the graves on the cliff?"

"Yes, yes, señorita. They are to cultivate at the cemetery."

Once again Sarah was astounded by Don Martín's sophisticated vocabulary and perfect grammar, although she shouldn't have been surprised after years of hearing him speak.

"Please take all you want. I only mentioned it because I thought I had been unaware of some anniversary."

Don Martín nodded and continued to twist his fingers together in a way that Sarah had never seen before. She thought that he was concealing the true purpose of his project from her, perhaps to surprise her with a new garden where her parents were buried, but she soon forgot all about his strange behavior and laconic responses.

SARAH PULLED HER KNEES onto the seat of the Land Rover so that she could face Carlos. She'd decided to ride with him into Managua. Gasoline was more and more difficult to obtain every day; and it was with great trepidation that she'd begun to drive by herself into the city again, and even then she'd tried to keep trips to a minimum.

"You said Castillo López will be fair."

"When I said he'd be fair, I meant he'd treat you the same way as other people and wouldn't treat you any worse than anyone else. He's a good man, one of the best officials in the government."

"You mean he won't hold it against me because I'm an American and my family owned a lot of land?"

"Castillo spent half his life fighting the great land owners for control of this country; and he doesn't have a very good impression of North Americans, whether they live in Washington or in Managua; but I think he'll try to put his prejudices aside and treat your situation on its own merits, especially since you helped him expose Andrejo."

"Anything I can do to improve my chances?"

"Sarah, you know the answer to that question. The settlement was predicated on the assumption that we would be married . . . that you'd marry a Nicaraguan and . . ."

Sarah stretched out her legs onto the floorboard. "I'm sorry, Carlos. I just don't know . . ."

"Like I said before, I'll marry you and never . . . live with you if that's what you want me to do. It would seal the deal. I promise I won't try to take Quinta Louisa away from you, not anything away from you. I promise solemnly." Carlos looked as solemn as his words and the tone of his voice.

"I know, Carlos. I can't ask you to do that . . . to lie. I know what it would cost you, how much you'd hate the deception. Anything I should especially avoid saying to him?"

"Just be yourself. Don't try to fool him." Carlos turned toward her with a forced smile. "The minister's always suspicious of being deceived. You can't live like he did—ten years in exile under terrible conditions, lacking the basic necessities of life, putting himself in constant danger on guerilla raids—without a touch of paranoia."

"I'm not afraid of him."

"Maybe you should be. Like King Saul, *Comandante Cero* (Edén Pastora) may have killed his thousands, but like David, Castillo has killed his ten thousands." Carlos remembered the Bible stories from his youth even now in his professed agnosticism. "Of course, if you became a Nicaraguan citizen . . . it might be . . . as good as a marriage."

"If I could have dual citizenship . . ."

Carlos was silent for several moments. "Even if you could, you'd have to choose eventually, sooner or later, and then you might be even worse off . . . lose everything."

"I'm not giving up my U. S. passport."

"I know."

From certain curves at the top of hills Sarah gazed over miles of countryside at vistas that she could see only in snatched glances when she was driving herself. They were same scenes that she'd often viewed while riding with her parents as a child. She'd accepted them as a child without comparison or admiration or analysis. Now she looked at the volcanoes and the tortured, rough landscape rent and torn by nature.

Like its people it was a land prone to violence and passion from within itself, and it burst open in earthquakes and volcanic eruptions that left scars on the outside. Yet, it was also a land beautiful in a way that serene landscapes cannot be truly beautiful, as people who have not suffered cannot attain a certain kind of beauty.

Then they saw a pair of scarlet macaws flying over the valley. Carlos pointed toward them without speaking. Macaws were occasionally spotted in the hills. They weren't as common as green parrots but certainly not as rare as quetzals. They weren't Sarah's favorite birds, not even on her top ten list, perhaps because they were too squawky or because many people kept them in captivity. Even Doña Beatriz and Don Armando had imprisoned a pair in a big cage in their back yard when they'd lived in the mansion in the city before the earthquake. Sarah thought of scarlet macaws either as prisoners or as fugitives about to be captured, and so they always made her sad.

Sarah was far more frightened now in Carlos's Land Rover than she had been on the night of the raid. Only things that are anticipated can cause true terror. Carlos didn't try to make further conversation. He respected her feelings with silence.

When they arrived at the office of the Ministry of Justice she could feel her heart pounding, an even more rapid pounding than the day she'd landed in the country after her father's death.

"Can you stay with me until Castillo López calls me in?"

"I don't think that would be quite appropriate. I need to get started on my own work."

"*¡Como no!* (As you say!). *Claro* (of course)."

"But I'll come back and go in with you to see the minister if you want me to . . ."

"Yes, please, Carlos. *Por favor* (please)."

Sarah waited in the makeshift lobby where Carlos left her in order to check messages in his office. She looked at the lighter squares on the dirty walls where the pictures of Tachito Somoza had been removed. The crude, rough chairs and tables were the same ones from the offices of the old regime, only the people looked different. Most of the men dressed in the obligatory khakis of the revolution now instead of *guayaberas* or white shirts and dark ties. It seemed strange that Carlos still wore *guayaberas*, not the khakis of his beloved revolution. The women were even more greatly changed, now with simple dresses or slacks (worn only by prostitutes in public formerly) instead of tight-fitting dresses above the knee and gathered at the waist. Neither did they wear heavy eye make-up and bright lipstick like the secretaries in the old regime; but they still wore their gold earrings and bracelets. Even for Marxist revolutionaries there was still security in gold, where the poor and middleclass in Latin America had always invested their meager savings.

Finally a secretary called Sarah's name. Adolfo Castillo López rose as she entered his office, perhaps more to intimidate her than to show respect. In his forties he was tall and very thin with hard, sinewy muscles and not an ounce of fat, with a strength that might bend or twist or strangle, not the heavy strength for crushing like the old generals. His eyes, like the grey eyes of a hungry wolf, would have been strange in any country, but here in Nicaragua, in a Latin American face, they seemed an aberration of nature, like the wild canine eyes of a hungry beast sometimes docile but unpredictably vicious. The paunchy old ministers had glanced with evasion from oozy eyes set in pink bags and dark lines of dissipated yellow flesh. Castillo would use his clear sharp eyes to focus directly on his prey.

"Please have a seat, Señorita Rutledge Lloyd."

"Gracias."

Castillo turned to the secretary that had ushered Sarah into his office. *"Please ask Vice Minister Vargas to join us and then leave us alone without interruption."*

Carlos came into the office immediately, almost on tiptoe, as if he were trying to slip around the fierce wild beast without being seen.

"Bueños días, Señor Minister."

"I believe congratulations are in order for your forthcoming marriage. The documents are prepared for you to sign. When is the wedding to be solemnized?" Castillo patted the thick legal folder on his desk. His face softened almost into a smile.

Carlos spoke quickly, as if to shield Sarah from embarrassment. *"We are trying to work some things out. We don't have a date set.*" Carlos popped his knuckles and glanced at Sarah nervously. He was not accustomed to lying, especially not to Castillo López.

"*Is it true (¿Es verdad?). Then have you decided to become a Nicaraguan citizen, Señorita Rutledge Lloyd?*"

"*I have not decided about that* . . ." Sarah glanced over at Carlos. "*. . . either . . . yet.*"

"*Then we shall have to delay a final decision about your property.*" Castillo López scooped up the sheaf of papers, opened the top drawer of his desk, placed them inside, and slammed it shut and then lifted his hand as if to dismiss her, as if he had nothing more to say to her, as if annoyed that she'd wasted his time for nothing. Sarah stirred angrily to respond, to fight back, as a helpless trapped bird fights and flutters before a snake. Carlos reached toward her to calm her, trying to prevent her from speaking.

"*I should not have to jump through all these hoops to claim what belongs to me. You did not know my father. He was a man who was honest and hardworking. He treated all his workers fairly and went out of his way to take care of them. He loved Nicaragua. He was a credit to this country. And my grandfather and my great-grandfather were, too. They were a credit to Nicaragua for almost a century.*"

Adolfo Castillo López responded with a cold anger utterly different from the heated anger in Sarah's voice. "*We know only that he was a member of a class that prevented the people of Nicaragua from claiming their basic rights—to education, to liberty, even access to decent health care and food. He stood with those who supported the tyranny and injustice of the Somoza regime.*"

"*He never supported the Somozas. He never approved of the evil things they did.*"

"*Perhaps. But he never spoke out forcefully or tried to stop them, and he was a part of the system that supported them and kept them in power. His friends and business associates were part of the network integrally linked to the Somozas.*"

"*He was a good man.*" Sarah could feel hot tears in her eyes.

"*And what about turning the factory into a cooperative owned by the workers. I suppose you are still deciding about that, too.*"

"*No. I shall turn the factory and the brokerage over to the workers and to the family that has worked for us for three generations. I shall do that whatever you do . . . whether you take my home away from me or not. That will be done.*" Sarah's eyes were flashing and for the first time since she entered Castillo's office her voice was firm and authoritative, the tone she used in her classroom to quieten rowdy students.

"*We shall be fair. We are not seeking revenge.*"

"*I only wish that you could have known my father.*"

"*It is more important that we know you, señorita. We shall deal with the past as little as possible. The future is our concern now. We need to ascertain what role you intend to play in the future of our nation.*" The grey animal eyes flickered away from her for an instant, as if for the briefest few seconds Castillo was unsure, uncertain of himself. Then they peered at her, as if trying to decide whether to strike, whether to kill, whether to devour her. "*We shall talk again soon. You have shown good will in your decision regarding the factory. Perhaps that will be enough, even without the issue of citizenship. I will need to ponder and consult with other members of the government. Now you must give me a few more days.*"

AFTER SARAH'S EMOTIONAL AFFIRMATION to Castillo López that she would turn the coffee factory into a cooperative for the workers, she felt a strong desire to tell the workers about her intentions, so that her promises would buttress her resolution. The first person she wanted to tell was naturally Guillermo. She restrained her eagerness to disclose her plan until after they'd finished going over the bills and orders late in the afternoon when all the workers had left the factory.

"*That's everything.*" Guillermo dusted his palms together. Some gesture with his hands accompanied almost every phrase of his lips.

"*Not quite. Please sit down. I have something else to talk about with you.*"

"*It sounds serious. Is it bad news?*"

"*Serious, yes. But good news. I believe we are close to getting a property settlement with the government.*"

"Bravo!" Guillermo rose from his chair and moved toward Sarah as if he intended to give her an *abrazo*, but he raised his hands in the air and did a dance around the desk, swerving his hips with the spontaneous sexual insinuation that always made Sarah blush.

"Sit down before I forget what I was going to say."

"¡Cómo no! (As you say!), *Doña Sarah."*

"Guillermo, shit! This is important! Part of the agreement involves turning over the factory to the workers. It will become a cooperative. It is something I had wanted to do anyway. Each of the workers will get a share. I plan for you to have five shares for all you have done and your position at the factory, the same number of shares that I shall reserve for myself. Julio will receive three shares as thanks for his help. And Pablo will get two shares as a member of the family, even though he has not been involved in . . ."

Suddenly Guillermo sat down and looked as if he might weep. He placed his hands over his face. *"No, no! Not Pablo! Never! He cannot . . ."*

"Guillermo, I know that Pablo has caused you grief, but he is your brother, a member of the family, Don Martín's son, like you and Julio, my family, too . . . my brother."

"No, no! It is too much. You must not do anything until I talk with Papá. I must talk with Papá first. Then I will talk with you . . . after I talk with Papá." Guillermo rushed from the office and left Sarah sitting utterly confused with mouth wide open.

She wondered if she should have spoken to Guillermo concerning the extra shares with greater tact rather than immediately blurting it out after telling him about turning the factory over to the workers and creating a cooperative. She couldn't understand his reaction. Perhaps he interpreted her generosity as condescension. Perhaps he thought of her good news as a remnant of colonial grandiosity. She felt deflated and a little angry that he hadn't been happy and excited.

Sarah still felt it would be good news for the workers. Her conception of the plan had brought her great joy, and she wanted to share it with someone. She decided to stop by Blanca's cottage on her way home to Quinta Louisa. César's mother held a special place in Sarah's affection. After Mary Rutledge had rescued little César on the night of the attempted coup and brought Blanca's family to the village and given her a job in the factory, Sarah had always associated Blanca and César with her mother's other projects in the village. They symbolized for Sarah her mother's passion for proving a better life for the workers.

Blanca was drying her face and hands after washing them following her day's work in the factory when Sarah knocked on the door of her cottage.

"Doña Sarah, is something the matter?" Blanca looked almost as distressed as Guillermo had been.

"No, no. I have some good news to share with you. May I come in?"

"Claro (of course). *Please come into the house."* Blanca began to take some of the children's clothes and books off one of the four straight wooden chairs in the room so that Sarah could sit down. *"Please have a seat."* Blanca remained standing in front of Sarah like a pupil sent to the principal's office.

"Will you sit down with me?"

Blanca began moving more clothes and magazines off the seat of another chair for herself. *"Is it César? Is he in trouble again?"*

"No, no. I wanted to share some good news with you. We are turning the factory into a cooperative. You will receive a share along with all the other workers."

"Doña Sarah, how wonderful! You have been so good to me."

"And I want the people in the village to own the houses that we rent to them, like the others who already own their houses, like the family of Guillermo. You will become the owner of your cottage (casita) little by little, if you continue to work at the factory for three more years."

"Doña Sarah, you have always helped me so much. Your family has been so good to me and helped us so much and given us so much . . ."

"Now you will have to help yourself. You will have to maintain your cottage. You will have to pay for the electricity, but it will be yours. That is how things should be now after . . ." The word almost choked in Sarah's throat. *". . . the revolution. I think that is what my mother and father were moving toward doing, although they never thought that it would happen in quite this way. It is a different world from what they ever imagined, especially that my mother . . ."* Sarah realized that she was babbling about things that Blanca could not understand and that Blanca had begun to cry.

"Doña Sarah, I do not believe . . ."

Sarah thought that Blanca was afraid of taking on responsibility for her house and did not understand what a share in the coffee cooperative would entail. *"It is all right, Blanca. I will still help you if you need something, if you get into trouble. We are all together now. We will work together for . . ."*

"No, no, that is not it. Doña Sarah, I am so sorry. I am so ashamed of César. You have been so good to us, and I apologize for what he did."

"What do you mean? What did he do?"

"You know. The raid. The raid on your house. I know that Don Martín recognized him and called him by name. I am sure Don Martín told you, and you are still so good and kind to us. It was just a prank for César. He did not intend to do any harm. It was that Pablo. He has so much influence over the boys in the village, the boys in their teens. They follow him like he is a little colonel. That Pablo is bad, very bad. I told César he could have nothing more to do with him."

"I do not know anything about that. Don Martín never told me." Sarah wondered why Don Martín had not told her about César, and then she realized that Don Martín would also have been compelled to tell her about Pablo's involvement. Now she understood why Don Martín had been morose and dejected since the raid, from embarrassment, from shame, from his concealed humiliation about his youngest son.

"Pablo has not been back to the village. Maybe he is still injured. César said he was hurt. They had to carry him to the house of Guillermo."

It was more than Sarah could comprehend. She was shaken, sickened and gradually becoming very angry. She spoke a few polite words of goodbye on leaving Blanca's house quickly as she assured Blanca that she would not take any punitive actions against César for his involvement in the raid and would not hold any grudges against Blanca's family for what he had done.

As Sarah left Blanca's cottage she didn't know where she would go, what she would do, to whom she could talk. She felt dizzy, as if she might faint. Then she knew she must talk with Guillermo, confront him, learn about Pablo's involvement and get a full account of the raid. She didn't think she could focus on driving. She left her car in front of Blanca's cottage and walked down the main dirt road of the village toward Guillermo's house. She moved so rapidly that she kicked up dust like someone running.

Before Sarah had even knocked the first time Ana opened the door. *"Come in. I saw you trotting down the road."*

"I need to talk with Guillermo." Sarah didn't even greet Emalina and Enrique when they ran up to her and she tousled their heads. *"It is important."*

"He is not here. I think he may have gone to your house to speak with Don Martín. He said he would not be home until tonight. What is wrong?" As Ana spoke she found a rag doll for Emalina and a set of plastic rings for Enrique and settled them in a corner to play.

"I have been to Blanca's cottage. She told me about the raid . . . about Pablo."

"Finally! Thank God! I have told Guillermo every day that he must talk with you, but he is afraid of what his father would do. And he is so devastated himself."

"Where is Pablo? Blanca said he was hurt."

"Sarah . . . so you do not know. I am not sure that I know everything. Pablo is dead. He was killed in the raid."

Sarah sat in stunned silence for the third time that afternoon. It took her even longer now to speak. *"How?"*

"He was shot in the crossfire . . . or that is what they say. They brought him here . . . to our house, where he died. Guillermo and his father took his body away at night and buried him beside his mother on the cliff. The people in the village do not know he is dead."

"Oh, my God! My God! How awful!"

"Sarah, what can I get you?"

"A glass of water, please." After Sarah sipped the water in silence, Emalina came up behind her chair and stroked her hair. Sarah pulled her around in front of her knees and hugged her and held her around her waist. *"Who shot him?"*

"They say he was killed in the crossfire. That is what we tell Don Martín. I do not know if he believes it. The boys from the village that went with Pablo, César and Alejandro, say none of them had guns. Only Don Martín."

"So Don Martín killed his own son." Sarah released Emalina and put

her hands over her mouth. For an even longer time she was silent. *"He killed his own son to protect me."*

Now Sarah understood everything, and having understood everything she thought that she understood nothing. It seemed to her that everything she had understood in the world before this moment was now lost to her understanding.

"Please do not mention any of this to Don Martín until after you have talked with Guillermo. I will make him come to see you tonight."

"Of course not."

Ana held Sarah in a tight embrace at the door, and the children ran over and hugged the calves of their mother and Sarah, both reassuring them and seeking reassurance as children do when they do not understand the distress of the grownups they love.

FROM OUTSIDE THE PATIO door Guillermo silently motioned to Sarah to follow him to the back of the garden, to the place where they had often sat and talked, so that his father would not know that he had come to Quinta Louisa after dark.

"Sarita, I am so sorry. I am so ashamed. Forgive me."

"Hermano (brother), *you should have told me."*

"I could not. I wondered if Papá would die of shame. And I thought I would die . . ." Guillermo began to weep as Sarah had never heard him weep before. *". . . die from shame. I am so sorry. Forgive me."*

"You are not responsible for your brother . . . our brother. Your father shot him to protect me, although he may not know . . ."

"He knows, and he does not know, does not want to know."

"Of course. Ana told me everything. Now I know everything."

"Not everything. Even Ana does not know everything. I have not told her. Pablo also led the first raid . . . with some of his rebel friends from the school. The village boys were not with him on the first raid . . . when Don Jorge died. Your father was so angry . . . that night he collapsed. Papá believes that Pablo killed Don Jorge. That is why he fired the gun to scare them away from you. He could not let Pablo kill you as he had killed Don Jorge . . . as Papá believes . . . I should have told you. I am sorry. Forgive me."

"So you and Julio are the only ones who know everything about both raids."

"No, not Julio. He knows nothing. We have not told him that Pablo was involved in the first raid, and he does not know that Pablo led the last raid. He does not even know that Pablo is dead. We have told him only that Pablo is missing. Julio has so much contempt for the Sandinistas . . . and for Pablo."

"Oh, hermano (brother), *you carry such heavy burdens."*

"Do you forgive me for not telling you?"

"Of course, but I cannot forgive Pablo. Not yet. Perhaps never . . . Guillermo, please hold me."

For almost half an hour Guillermo and Sarah held each other as brother and sister and discussed how they could protect and take care of the only parent they had left, the shell of what was left of the strong, honorable man they now both called Papá. They heard the symphony of birds and tree frogs and insects as the moon cast the shadows of the palms wafting in the night breezes over their faces.

SARAH WANTED TO TALK with someone about the raids and Pablo's death. Doña Beatriz was out of the question, not only due to her tirade when she'd told Sarah about Carlos and Carmen but also given her sentiments as a aristocrat *(dueña)* about peasants *(campesinos)*. Doña Beatriz would have little sympathy for Don Martín's plight and would trivialize Sarah's attachment to him as a surrogate father. Eventually Sarah would talk with Father Richard, but now she couldn't bear his perennial habit of rational analysis or his more recent perspective of pessimism. Above all, Sarah wanted to talk with Carlos. In spite of everything Carlos was now the only person to whom she could open her heart and express her confusion and anguish.

As if she'd summoned him she saw him walking toward the front door of Quinta Louisa late in the afternoon the day after her evening conversation with Guillermo in the garden. Before he knocked she opened the door.

"Come in. I'm so glad to see you."

Carlos looked puzzled by her warm welcome. "I'm glad, too. Do you know why I'm here then?"

"*Claro* (of course). You must have sensed you're the only one I could talk with."

Carlos smiled and looked even more greatly puzzled. "I have a draft of the property agreement from Castillo López. How did you know?"

"I didn't. I have something even more important to tell you."

Carlos's expression changed from confusion to distress. "What could be more important than that?"

"Sit down." Sarah gestured to the midwife chair beside the door as she sat down on the Sheridan sofa. She relayed the whole narrative of the raids as if she were reading a lengthy novella without interruption, especially lingering on the details of how Don Martín had shot and killed Pablo. She included every word of her conversations with Blanca and Ana and Guillermo and expressed all her feelings of distress and anger, her love for Don Martín, and her anxiety about what might happen to him.

When Sarah finally paused, Carlos moved to the settee beside her and took her hand. "Sarah." Only Carlos could say her name in a way that brought her such great comfort and understanding that she believed everything would be all right. "I'm so sorry, so very sorry. What can I do for you?"

"Would you really marry me just so I could keep Quinta Louisa?"

"You know I would. I've told you many times I would, but you may not need to marry me now . . . just for that reason. Castillo has drafted an agreement. I don't think he would go back on it even if we were not married."

"Now that Quinta Louisa is not part of the equation, do you still want to be married, really married, really husband and wife?"

"*Claro que sí* (Of course). Are you really considering it? Why?"

For several moments Sarah didn't respond. Then she said, "When I learned about how Pablo was killed, I realized I had to tell you about it. You're the only one I could ever talk with about things like that."

"Sarah, I love you. I want you to be my wife more than anything else in the world."

"Well then, you can go over to the guesthouse and get the ring and put it back on my finger . . . if you'll still have me."

"Sarah." Only Carlos could say her name in a way that brought her such great delight and joy that she believed everything would be good and happy. "Do you forgive me then?"

"Yes. There's nothing to be forgiven for your relationship with Carmen. That started before I was in the picture, although it does still give me pain. For the days you deceived me . . . after . . . yes, I forgive you for that. I forgive you, but I still need some time to get over it. I can't marry you quite as soon . . . as soon as I thought. I need a little more time, but I want to marry you, if . . ."

Carlos stopped her words with his kiss.

After he returned with the ring, they cuddled in each other's arms. They decided they couldn't concentrate on the details of the property settlement then, but after dinner Carlos went through every paragraph, every sentence, every word of the draft agreement, and raised every possible implication that he could imagine. He cautioned Sarah to be aware that the agreement would not be binding until it was approved by all the members of the Directorate and was then legally certified; but he believed the other four members of the ruling junta would approve anything that Castillo López strongly recommended.

"Carlos, I want to wait until the decision about Quinta Louisa is finalized and binding before we are married. Can you understand that? Can you accept that? If something should happen and the agreement is scuttled and I lose Quinta Louisa, I still want you to be my husband, but I want them to be separate, two separate things. Do you understand that?"

"Not really. But I love you, and I accept your conditions unconditionally."

They laughed together for the first time in many days. They laughed at each other, and they laughed at themselves, and they laughed at the absurdity of their lives now and the prospect of their lives in the future. Then they kissed and cuddled for a long time. And then they laughed again at the blessing of their lives now and the hope of being blessed in the future.

It was late at night when they turned their attention away from themselves and began to ponder what needed to be done for Don Martín. Carlos told Sarah that because so many people had disappeared and been killed during the battles of the revolution, little attention would be given to Pablo and few questions would be asked. (Sarah recalled the troubled mother in Andrejo's office on her first visit to the Ministry of Justice.) Carlos asked her permission to solicit Castillo López's perspective and advice. With some reluctance Sarah agreed for him to consult with the minister, but she pleaded with him to be discreet and cautious in what he said. Although they could make plans to avoid any criminal offense that Don Martín might face, they did not have any idea about how to bind up his emotional and spiritual injuries.

As SARAH ENTERED THE vicarage she held up her left hand so that Father Richard could see the emerald ring on her finger. "It's back on, Padre. We'll have to plan a wedding."

"So, you've made your peace with Carlos."

"I've forgiven him for deceiving me, and I sort of got over my pout about his relationship with Carmen. I really do love him."

"Forgiveness is the essence of love, my dear."

"I'm not in as big a hurry for the wedding to take place. I want to get everything settled first. The property agreement's been drafted, but it may be December or even into the new year before it's certified."

"There's something I need to tell you, my dear. I'm planning to leave right after Christmas. I'm going back to the States permanently."

"Father Richard!" Sarah thought first about how her vision of her wedding would be jeopardized by Father Richard's absence. Then she scolded herself when she imagined the pain he must be experiencing in making such a decision. "I know you've thought of leaving before, but . . . I never expected you to . . . Your ministry in Nicaragua has been your whole life . . . everything you've done and planned and hoped for . . ."

"Indeed. But the world has changed. Nicaragua has changed. The church has changed. Everything is different now from what I imagined. The church needs to be led by Nicaraguans now, not missionaries from Britain or the States. There's no place for me any . . ."

"That's not true. You've done so much and accomplished so many things. And you wanted to do so much more."

Father Richard slumped in his chair. He ducked his head, and rested his cheek against his fist. "*Quizás* (Perhaps). But this is not the time for foreigners. I'll always be a foreigner here, just a *gringo* priest. Sometime in the future foreigners may come back to Nicaragua, to live, to help and contribute. But not now. Not me."

"And what about me with a British father and an American mother?"

"You're more Nicaraguan than you are British or American. Your father stayed more British than Nicaraguan till the day he died, and your mother . . . well, Mary never really left North Carolina in her heart. God bless them both. But you are Nicaraguan. I saw that when you were a little girl. You belong here no matter what your passport says."

"Doña Beatriz said something like that to me once, that I was the first Nicaraguan Rutledge in four generations . . . But Padre, this is your home, too."

"No, Sarita, this was my dream, and dreams often have to die when the world changes."

"But you have to marry us! You have to stay that long!"

"Then you'll have to plan to celebrate your wedding before Christmas or very shortly thereafter."

"Surely you can stay until Epiphany. Surely I can get a final certification by the first of the year. Would you be able to stay until the first couple of weeks of January?"

"For you, my dear. For you, I'll stay through your favorite festival of the church. But no longer. Not beyond the Feast of the Epiphany."

By mid-November the property agreement had still not been approved by the five-member Directorate that ruled the country. Carlos told Sarah that Andrejo had elicited some of his old cronies to work secretly in the government against Castillo López for having exposed him and removed him from office and threatened him with prison. The disposition of Quinta Louisa was caught up in their disputes. As much as Sarah wanted to visit the Lloyd farm in North Carolina for Thanksgiving, as she'd promised her Aunt Beth and Uncle Walter she would always try to do, Carlos again advised her not to leave the country until a final legal settlement for the property was approved. She had wanted to tell Aunt Beth about Don Martín's sacrifice to protect her. She needed to tell someone. She could not talk to anyone in Nicaragua, not even Father Richard, until she was sure that Don Martín would not be accused of murder and tried for the crime.

Without telling Carlos, Sarah had driven into Managua and left a copy of the property agreement with an official at the American Embassy to be reviewed in order to be sure everything was legal. Carlos had encouraged her to tell Castillo López the full story of how Pablo was shot by Don Martín in the raid and to ask for his counsel and help. Carlos had talked in hypothetical terms to him without revealing any specific names. On the way to the Ministry of Justice Sarah stopped by the American Embassy to pick up the papers and receive an opinion about the agreement.

The new American Embassy, built after the earthquake, was located outside the city. It looked like a U. S. government building that had lost its way and gotten plunked down in the middle of the tropics. It aroused none of the old fear and pride that had been associated with the yellow stucco compound on the lagoon, located halfway between the parliament building downtown and Somoza's presidential palace on the hill. The inside of the new embassy building also looked like a piece of U. S. governmental bureaucracy transplanted to the middle of Central America, accented with Nicaraguan secretaries and janitors, tropical plants, Nicaraguan tables and chairs, and even boxes of cookies with snack wrappers in Spanish from the Central American Common Market.

Sarah had expected to talk only with a secretary, but she was told that the Ambassador had asked her to come into his office. Ambassador Warren's secretary was an American; and as she ushered Sarah into the ambassador's office, Sarah wondered if Nicaraguans were ever allowed to enter and tread on the dark blue, plush-piled carpet. Ambassador Warren's private inner sanctum was a perfect replica of an American executive's office. The heavy dark blue drapes were drawn against the bright sun and light blue sky, keeping out any glimpse of the tropical birds and flowers and the dry brown hills of Nicaragua. His desk and chairs had been made in the United States and upholstered in the United States with American fabrics. The room might have been in Washington or New York or North Carolina. Nothing within it would suggest that it was located in Nicaragua except for the Nicaraguan flag standing in one corner behind the desk, opposite the stars and stripes in the other corner.

After the revolution, an appointment as American Ambassador to Nicaragua was no longer a political plum. Now the Ambassador's role was an onerous, thankless, dangerous task. Ambassador Warren seemed to be a sincere and capable man, neither to be envied nor to be ridiculed.

"The document seems to be in order. I had several of our staff look over it, but let me give you a piece of free advice, strictly off the record. As soon as they make a formal offer, take it, even if it's not everything you'd hoped for. The new government is still trying to curry favor with the United States; but all that could change very quickly, especially with the Reagan administration coming in and threatening to cut off foreign aid. I believe that our relations are very tenuous. We could be out of here, for all practical purposes, in a very short time."

Sarah wondered what Ambassador Warren's specific fear might be as he twirled his pencil and pulled his earlobe and shifted things around on his desk. Although rumors were rife on every street corner in Managua, was the Ambassador privy to some secret intelligence? At least the former ambassadors often possessed an ignorant, almost regal serenity, even on the eve of cataclysms.

"I understand, and I deeply appreciate your candor. I will certainly respect your confidentiality."

Whatever troubled Ambassador Warren, Sarah believed that it reflected a change of mood in the United States, a national phobia about small, strange, unknown, threatening nations that had once been looked upon with disdain. Perhaps American ambassadors now represented the mood of the United States far more accurately than they represented any intentional rational policy.

Sarah drove straight from the American Embassy to the Ministry of Justice. Unexpectedly she also walked directly into Castillo's office as if he were expecting her, as if half of Nicaragua weren't waiting to see him. Perhaps she had arrived at a calm moment between other events.

The chairs were covered with stacks of files and piles of papers. Several empty boxes had been dumped haphazardly at the side of the room. *"What is the matter? Has Andrejo threatened you?"* Castillo López's forehead was wrinkled in an unusual expression of concern for her.

"Well no, I had not even thought any more about him."

"You must watch out for him. He may try to hurt you. Let me know if he makes any contact with you. What is it then? What is bothering you?" They were both still standing. Sarah glanced at an almost empty chair, so that he'd know she couldn't be dealt with cursorily, abruptly. *"Please sit down."* As Blanca had done in her cottage, Castillo took the papers out of the chair for her and sat down himself across from her behind his desk. A slight nervous tic around his lips revealed an uncharacteristic expression of fear. *"Are you all right?"* He sounded protective, as if she were someone he actually cared about.

Sarah told him about Don Martín shooting his son Pablo in the raid to protect her. She told him how Pablo had grown up at Quinta Louisa, how her father had helped him get an education, how he'd rebelled and begun drinking and using drugs. Through the whole narrative she looked down at the floor, and her eyes filled with tears. When she looked up at Castillo López, his face had relaxed with an expression of relief that her distress wasn't related to anything he'd done, that it had nothing to do with him. He stood and took out his handkerchief from his back pocket and handed it to her, as if he'd read in one of his manuals that such an act was comforting when a young woman was disturbed. It would have been almost impossible for him to touch her consolingly, and his coolness made it easier for Sarah to continue.

"He is a prime example of how your revolution affects a troubled, naïve idealistic young man." Now she knew that she'd come to see Castillo partly to blame someone for the horrible atrocity, so that it could be explained and understood. She'd been unable to focus anger and grief even on Pablo. It was like trying to hate an earthquake or a flood or a fire. He was just an instrument of evil through his revolutionary delusions. He was nothing more than a side effect of the revolution. *"The revolution is to blame for this tragedy more than Pablo."*

"The Pablos of this world justify what they do in the name of Sandino or Marx or Jesus Christ; but if the revolution had not come along, he would have found some other excuse, I imagine." Something about Castillo was reminiscent of her father—his clarity of expression, the way his mind worked, his certainty of a precise moral order in the world, his competence, his rationality, his ability to assume responsibility, and his calm assurance that everything was under control. As much as she feared his ruthless power she felt more at ease with him in some ways than she'd been with Ambassador Warren, whose responses she could predict.

Sarah began more contritely to make her request that Castillo López use his influence and authority to spare Don Martín from being interrogated by the police, to spare him from a public trial and the publicity it would generate, so that he wouldn't have to answer accusations, so that his secret wouldn't be exposed to the world and known to his friends in the village.

"What is it you want from me? Do you want me to lie for you?"

"Yes, as I lied for you to Andrejo. I am just trying to protect an old man who has suffered enough. Does Pablo's body have to be exhumed? Can we at least avoid that, please?"

"You're quite certain that the grave is Pablo's and that everything happened exactly as you told me?" The grey animal eyes bore into her, searching her, stripping her soul like the glaring lights on a corpse in a morgue.

"Absolutely certain."

"Then I will write a report that will close the matter once and for all, if that is your wish." Insofar as a face can show an affectionate sneer, Castillo sneered affectionately at Sarah. *"I can do that much for you—just one favor while it is still possible for me."*

"And you will leave Don Martín out of it? He does not have to be involved in any way, does he?"

"I understand, Sarah." Castillo López had never called her by her Christian name before. *"Now you must practice telling your story many times, over and over again, until you almost believe it yourself, to create an official version of the truth."* He smiled. He was an expert interrogator who could ferret out every answer and every shred of evidence as well

as a brilliant strategist who could devise a tactic for any problem.

Sarah nodded. She admired Castillo for having the genius to discover answers and propose solutions, but she also pitied him as if some vital quality were missing from his nature, as if he were incapable of understanding a deeper level of truth. *"Thank you, Mr. Minister. I shall look forward to seeing you at my wedding."*

Again the tic appeared around his lips, and his face contracted around his eyes with a tension something like fear, as if she'd distracted him from his own concerns for a few moments but then reminded him of them. *"Perhaps. Perhaps so. I hope so, Señorita Rutledge Lloyd. The Contras are becoming very organized again. We may have a civil war. It could be very bad, especially if the United States arms them against us."* He reached out tentatively to take his handkerchief back from her as a shy person often reaches out awkwardly for warmth and kindness. *"Adios."*

SARAH ALSO WAITED UNTIL mid-November, several weeks after Guillermo had told her about Pablo's death, to talk about it with Don Martín and even then it arose by chance. She had asked him to sit with her on the back patio late one afternoon in order to talk with him about her wedding.

"You know that Carlos and I are planning to be married in a few weeks."

"¡Cómo no! (As you say!), *I am very pleased for you. He is a good man. He will be a good husband for you."*

"I would like for you to be a member of the wedding party, Papá. Will you walk me down the aisle? You are my only parent now."

The breath seemed to leave Don Martín's body. He turned away from her. *"No, no, Doña Sarah. I cannot. I cannot be a member of a sacred ceremony. I have done a terrible thing. It would not be right. I am cursed."*

Sarah knew that he was referring to Pablo's death, but she believed that she must not reveal her knowledge of the event to him. It was several moments before she spoke. *"Why not? I really want you to take the place of my father at my wedding."*

"Because I cannot wear shoes. I have not worn shoes for more than thirty years. Everyone will be wearing shoes."

"Is that all?"

"*No, Sarita. You know the other thing. You know that Pablo was killed.*"

"*How did you learn that I know about his death? Did Guillermo tell you?*"

"*No, Guillermo has said nothing. He is too afraid. I know from how you look at me and from what you do not say to me.*"

"*Guillermo told me several weeks ago.*"

"*Claro* (Of course). *I thought that he had told you, but I was not sure. It is good that he told you.*"

"*He said Pablo was killed in the crossfire by one of his companions.*" Sarah ventured to express the contrived version of the story in order to reassure Don Martín.

"*Yes, that is what they say. Do you also know that Guillermo and I buried him on the cliff without asking for your permission? Please forgive me.*"

"*I know, and I am glad you did. You should have buried him there. You did not need any permission. The cemetery is for our family, all members of our family. That is why you took flowers from the garden to put on Pablo's grave.*"

"*Please forgive me for that, too.*" Martín began to weep. Sarah moved beside him and sat on the arm of his chair. She put her arms around him and cuddled him like a baby, as she'd never held him before, the way that he had held her thousands of times over the years when she'd been hurt or sad or lonely. She could feel him quivering inside and shaking outside. Some of his tears fell on her arm like the first large drops of rain before a storm. "*It will be all right. Do not worry. Everything is going to be all right. I am going to take care of you. I love you very much.*"

"*There is one more thing I must ask you to do for me. Prayers have not been said over the grave of Pablo. He was my youngest son, my little boy, our baby. I loved him, too. Would you ask Padre Richard to say the prayers over his grave?*"

"*Of course. We can do it right away, as soon as you would like. Perhaps next week.*"

"*No, no. We must wait. We must wait for Julio to come for your wedding. He does not know that Pablo was killed. We could not tell him on the telephone. When he comes for your wedding, we will tell him everything. Then we will have the sacred rites, and Pablo will rest in peace.*"

Sarah wanted to thank Don Martín for protecting her, for shooting the gun that he believed he had to fire in order to save her, for killing his beloved son for her sake; but she could not now nor would she ever be able to express her profound gratitude to him. They could never tell each other the secret that both of them knew. It must forever remain unspoken, and they must forever pretend that they did not know what each of them was aware of that the other already knew.

"I will ask Padre Richard to have the service whenever you want it to be."

"Gracias. And I will ask Guillermo to buy me a pair of shoes to wear for your wedding."

"We will see (Vamos a ver). We will think some more about that."

When Sarah called her uncle and aunt to invite them to her wedding in Managua on January 7, Aunt Beth told her that Uncle Walter was not in good enough health to make the trip. They mutually lamented that Sarah hadn't been able to visit the farm for Thanksgiving. Although Sarah had not received a certified copy of the property agreement, Carlos had learned that the Directorate had signed it. Sarah had felt more comfortable about making definite plans for their wedding.

Carlos also believed that the arrangement with the government was now certain enough that it would be safe for Sarah to leave the country for a few days, and on impulse she had decided to fly to North Carolina to see her mother's family for a few days after Christmas. Carlos teased her about being the *coolest bride in the hemisphere* by leaving the country only a few days before they were to be married. She told him that it would be a very small wedding, more due to the circumstances of her family and the political situation than her choice and preference. No one from her family would be present, except for her surrogate family, Don Martín and his sons. Almost all of her friends had left the country either after the earthquake or during the revolution. Carlos would be better represented by his Sandinista comrades and government colleagues.

"Would you like for me to fly up to North Carolina with you? I'd like to meet this Uncle Walter and Aunt Beth and the cousins you talk so much about. I'd like to get to know some of your family, and since they can't come to the wedding . . ."

"Oh, Carlos, that would be wonderful! And you could see the family farm, and we could walk to the creek. North Carolina is so different from . . . but you know that."

"I can't take more than two or three days . . . a couple or three nights away at best. We could fly up together, and you could stay a while longer."

"I can't spend more than three or four days either. After all, I do have a wedding to prepare for." Then Sarah suddenly thought of Carlos's mother in Miami and wondered if she would be coming to the wedding. "Should we stop over in Miami for the night and visit your mother?"

"I don't think so. Besides, you'll see *mi madre* (my mother) at the wedding. She'll get here just after New Year's Day. You'll have plenty of time to visit . . . maybe too much time."

"You never told me she was coming."

"I just assumed . . ."

"Is she okay with your marrying me? I know you've had your differences the last few years."

Carlos laughed and kissed Sarah's forehead. "She's delighted. Doña Nancy has fond memories of you . . . and your mother. She believes you'll save me from the godless communists."

"*¡Ojalá!* (Would it were so!)"

"Oh shit!"

"What?"

"Where's she going to stay? I don't think with me in the guesthouse."

Sara hesitated for a moment. "Let me work on it. I think . . . Let me feel out Doña Beatriz."

"I thought you were on the outs with her."

"She was very insensitive when . . . several weeks ago. But *forgiveness is the essence of love.*"

"Thus sayeth Padre Richard."

"Oh, my God, Carlos! Oh, my God!"

"What now?"

"She will have to fill the role of mother of the bride. She's the only one . . . the only one left. Mother and Doña Flora are dead . . . Aunt Beth can't come. Doña Beatriz is the only one left."

WHEN SARAH CALLED DOÑA Beatriz to ask her to take the place of the mother of the bride, she didn't mind also asking her to recommend a seamstress to make her wedding dress. As much as Doña Beatriz had objected to Sarah's marriage to Carlos Vargas Allen, once the decision was made she accepted it and moved on as if it were a glorious occasion, just as she had done throughout her life.

Sarah had delayed the fitting for her wedding dress until a few weeks before her wedding as if it represented the act from which she could not turn back. She could give Carlos the ring back again; but once the wedding gown was stitched, the marriage would be as final for her as signing legal paper for Quinta Louisa or registering the nuptials in dusty books at the American Embassy.

"Why don't you tell me more awful things about Carlos so I can get out of this wedding." Sarah smiled. Her words were more to patch up the estrangement between her and Doña Beatriz by making light of their very serious conflict than finding a reason to cancel the wedding.

"You have cold feet? Ah, that's a good sign. *Pues* (Well), there's no backing out now." The woman who had once objected most strongly to Carlos now became the most ardent defender of the marriage after the decision seemed to be irrevocably made. *"Octavia? Octavia, come in here and take her measurements."*

Octavia was probably an eighth child, born after her parents had exhausted their supply of names. Sarah hoped it wouldn't be a portent for her own family. At least as an agnostic revolutionary, Carlos was favorably disposed toward birth control measures, unlike the majority of *macho* Roman Catholic men in Nicaragua. Octavia had a flat Indian face without a profile as if her features were painted on an ancient clay pot that hardly showed the bulge of a nose or eye sockets.

Sarah stood, and Octavia measured her. *"Please turn, señorita. Gracias."* Octavia seemed limited to a vocabulary of a dozen polite words, like a foreign tourist with a guidebook.

"You need to get another measurement between the waist and the bust. Now get one down the back from the waist." Doña Beatriz wouldn't have chosen the girl unless she was the best seamstress in Managua, any more

than people in the United States would allow inferior appliances in their kitchens and bathrooms.

"*Sí, señora.*"

Doña Beatriz rapped Octavia sharply on her head, and Octavia whimpered slightly. "*You stupid girl, you wrote that length incorrectly. You imbecile!*" Sarah cringed at Doña Beatriz's harsh words and humiliating treatment of the little seamstress. Then Doña Beatriz gave Sarah a soft, loving pat on her arm. "She's almost finished. I hope you're not too un-comfortable from having to stand still so long."

Sarah glanced down at Octavia scooting around the tile floor on her knees. She could see the pain in Octavia's face when she moved after having crouched so long on her knees.

Octavia was relegated to the kitchen again so that Sarah and Doña Beatriz could discuss the wedding dress privately. "Now, my dear, I think I know more or less what you want. Here are a few sketches—simple straight lines, but I think you'll need a sash of some kind around the middle." She showed Sarah several of her sketches. Doña Beatriz had been hard at work. Sarah had forgotten what a talented artist Doña Beatriz was until her hand sped over her drawings with a piece of art gum and a pencil, adding lines here, changing lines there. Then she remembered other fittings for parties and special occasions. Doña Beatriz had designed her dresses when she'd graduated from high school and left for college.

"I like this one, but I'd rather have a kind of scooped neck instead of the square neck. And sleeveless or very short sleeves."

"Exactly. And you said a shoulder length veil. See what you think of this. I remembered a friend whose daughter married just before the revo-lution. You're welcome to use this if you like it. No *problema* if you don't."

"It's beautiful. I love it. I really do. It's so pretty."

"Now for the *pièce de résistance*." Doña Beatriz jangled her bracelets high in the air like some musical instruments in the finale of a symphony and brought out a sack from beneath her chair. She deftly slipped the paper away and produced a bolt of exquisite white silk.

"Where on earth did you get it?"

"I've saved it for your wedding . . . for many years. I put it away, just in case. It's survived the earthquake and . . . everything else. And I'm paying Octavia for your wedding dress. It's my wedding gift to you."

"I couldn't accept . . . I really couldn't let you . . ."

"You said we were family now, and I'll sit in your mother's place in the pew. That's what families do. Perhaps the greatest joy I've had in life is giving people beautiful things. I can't do that very often any more. This will be one of my last gifts, perhaps my last really beautiful gift. It will be a great joy for me. You must not deny me that."

Sarah remembered that her mother had taught her that gifts offered in love must never be refused, even when the donor couldn't really afford the sacrifice.

"I'm overwhelmed . . . but if you really want to . . . *Mil gracias* (A thousand thanks). Thank you with all my heart."

They hugged with a closer, more physical hug than she'd ever received from Doña Beatriz. Sarah felt Doña Beatriz's breasts as if she were lying against large pillows. They were comforting and reassuring; and they made her feel happy, as if her own mother were with her, as if her mother were tucking her into bed for the night just before an important event. "I'm so glad that you're helping me have a beautiful wedding. I never thought I could have a beautiful wedding now with all that's happening in the country, and I wouldn't if you weren't making the gown and giving it to me. You and Mother were so close. It's almost like Mother were here, doing it for me through you."

Doña Beatriz held Sarah's head with one palm against her cheek, nestling her against her large breasts like a suckling child, like the baby she never had. She stroked Sarah's hair with her other hand. "My dear sweet child. My little girl. I love you very much. I do hope it will be all right."

"Then I have one more favor to ask."

"*Cualquier* (anything)."

"Would it be possible for Carlos's mother to stay with you? She's coming on January second and leaving on the eighth, immediately after the wedding. I know it's a lot to ask, but there are such limited possibilities in Managua now."

"*¡Claro!* (Of course!) I'd be delighted. I'm very fond of Nancy."

"One thing I insist on doing. I want to pay a woman from the village to come and clean and cook while she's here. She's our old cook, Loretta. She's agreed to come and stay with you. You may remember her. She left before Daddy died to take care of her family, but she already offered to help me with the wedding in any way she could. This is my non-negotiable ..." Sarah hoped that Doña Beatriz did not suspect that a part of her motivation was cleaning the filth from Doña Beatriz' house that seemed almost a violation of her former self.

"Muy bien (very well). You know I am not a good housekeeper."

Sarah believed that she had pulled off her legerdemain without offending Doña Beatriz and that Doña Beatriz would enjoy having a maid and cook again that she could order about and supervise as the aristocratic *dueña* (mistress).

Carlos settled into his place in the Lloyd family from the first moment he stepped through the front door of the farmhouse. Sarah and Carlos arrived early enough the first day for a walk to the creek together. They spotted an Eastern bluebird that Sarah had designated as her personal icon for North Carolina. Carlos was delighted to see a bluebird for the first time, but he seemed even more fascinated by the mallards at the edge of the pond in the cow pasture.

On their second day in North Carolina, their first full day on the farm, Sarah's cousins arrived. Roger spoke more words to Carlos than Sarah had ever heard him utter to anyone. Even Aunt Beth noticed that he was "positively chatty" with Carlos. Lucinda and Harry, Uncle Walter and Aunt Beth's daughter and son-in-law, both commented on what a perfect match Sarah and Carlos were; and during the afternoon Carlos tossed a football with their sons in the back yard. Sarah's little cousins obviously adored him.

On the afternoon of their third day, the last full day on the farm, Sarah asked Carlos to stay with Uncle Walter so that she could make her traditional walk with Aunt Beth. Walter told Carlos the history of the farm and the genealogy of the Lloyd family. Then he related the seasons for planting and harvesting and told Carlos what crops had been raised in former generations before most of the farm was converted to timber and cattle after he was too old to propagate row crops and his children had left the farm and he couldn't hire farm workers any longer because they could receive better wages in the city. If Carlos didn't listen carefully to every word, he gave a good impression of rapt fascination.

Sarah and Beth took their familiar trail toward the creek.

"I can't believe how much at home Carlos is here on the farm, Aunt Beth."

"He seems real comfortable in his own skin, honey. I think he'd make hisself at home, wherever he was."

"Carlos seems to really like all the family. You like him, too, don't you?"

"He's trying real hard to get us to like him. Course we do, but not mostly 'cause he's workin' so hard at it. We like him mostly 'cause he loves you so much. That shows without him trying at all."

"We have lots of differences, lots of things we need to work out."

"Most couples do. You'll find your way."

"I think we'll be able to keep Quinta Louisa, at least for a while. I don't know whether I can prove it belongs to me if the government begins expropriating even more property."

Aunt Beth caught Sarah's arm. They'd reached the place overlooking the creek that Sarah had once called their *truth spot*. "The important thing isn't what belongs to you, it's what you belong to. You belong to Nicaragua, to the *finca*, as you call it, just like I belong to North Carolina and this farm. I could see that years ago when you first came to visit us. You were like a tourist that loved coming out here, but it wasn't home to you. I wish it could be. You and I can talk more heart to heart than I can talk even with my own daughter. Oh, I love Lucinda dearly, but you and I are sort of soul friends. We think and feel on the same wavelength. I wish you could live closer by so we could see you more often, but I know Nicaragua will always be home for you. Even if you have to leave someday, it will still always be home for you. One of these days Walter and I will have to leave the farm and move closer to one of the children, but this farm will always be home to us, just like Nicaragua will always be home to you, whether you're living there or not."

Late that afternoon Walter and Beth left to meet their children and grandchildren in Raleigh for their traditional trip to see the performance of *A Christmas Carol*. Beth had tried to buy tickets for Sarah and Carlos when she'd learned they would be coming for a visit, but the play was completely sold out. Beth then tried to persuade Sarah and Carlos to go with her cousins and take Walter's and her tickets, but Sarah adamantly refused.

"This is your family tradition. Besides we need to pack and rest for the trip tomorrow." Then Beth and Walter offered to stay home and keep Sarah and Carlos company, but Sarah insisted that they go on to the play. Sarah had her own ulterior motives for wanting to be alone with Carlos on the farm that evening.

After eating the food that Aunt Beth had meticulously prepared and left for them, Sarah dropped to her knees in front of Carlos. "I want you to make love to me here on the farm. Tonight before Aunt Beth and Uncle Walter come back. There's an ancient religious custom for couples to make love just before their wedding and then have their union blessed by the church. I want the first part of our marriage to begin here on my family's farm and then continue with the wedding in Nicaragua."

"Are you sure?"

Sarah never spoke but led him to her bed. She ran her fingers through the thick hair on his chest and then through the hair around his navel and on his legs and around his penis. He kissed her lips and then her breasts and then her stomach. When he entered her body she experienced the ecstasy and pleasure that she'd always imagined. It was utterly different from the pain and numbness she'd felt on the night of the raid, the only other time their bodies had been linked together.

When they made love for the second time Sarah experienced the same ecstasy; and as they held each other she felt a joy deeper than she had ever known before, as if all would be well, whatever might befall them in the future.

By the time that Walter and Beth returned from Raleigh Sarah and Carlos were sitting together fully clothed in the living room sipping apple cider. On the airplane the next day on their way back to Managua

Carlos asked Sarah about the religious tradition of making love before having their union blessed by the church.

"I never heard that before."

"That's because I just made it up."

Carlos laughed in the deep tones he'd enjoyed since he was a boy. "I like it. Maybe you can get it instituted into canon law."

"Everything has to be reversed for us, our honeymoon before our wedding, the consummation before the consecration. It's how it has to be in our situation."

"Speaking of the wedding ... who have you invited? Do you think anyone will show up since we didn't send out any formal invitations?"

"I called a few people at the Embassy. I don't know if Ambassador and Mrs. Warren will come or not. Father Richard announced it to the congregation at St. Francis, and I invited all the factory workers and the villagers. I'm not in touch with the people who went to high school with me. I don't even know where their families are now, except for Carmen. How about you?"

"Some of the people from the Ministry are coming. I'm not sure about Castillo López, if he's in town or not ... and some of my friends from the party and the army."

"Sandinistas at St. Francis. That'll be a picture."

"I know you asked Don Martín to walk you down the aisle and Doña Beatriz to sit on the mother's pew across from *mi madre* (my mother). Is anyone going to stand up with us? Aren't you supposed to have a best man and a maid of honor or something?"

"I guess I would've asked Carmen until ... you told me. I still think of her as my friend, but I don't want her at our wedding."

Carlos blushed. "I don't either. I think it would be more embarrassing for me than for you."

Sarah grasped Carlos's arm and almost jumped up from her seat beside him on the airplane. "Ana! That's it. I do want someone to stand beside me. I'll ask Ana if she would be my matron of honor. *¡Dios mío!* (My God!) She'll need a dress. I'll have to see if Doña Beatriz can get Octavia to make one. She can probably put something together in a couple of days, if Ana doesn't have anything appropriate to wear. I hope Ana will agree to do it. What about you? Do you want a best man, a colleague from the Ministry or a comrade from the party?"

"*Mi madre* would die of shame. You're supposed to save me from the godless communists, *¿no es verdad?* (isn't that true?) What about Guillermo? Do you think he would do it . . . keep it a family affair?"

"Oh, Carlos!" Sarah twisted toward him in her seat and raised herself high enough to kiss his cheek. "Oh, Carlos, that would be wonderful! But you shouldn't do it just to please me."

"I'm not. I truly believe he is the best man, probably one of the best men I've ever known."

"Maybe Emalina and Enrique can be the flower girl and ring bearer. They wouldn't sit in the pew by themselves and that way they could have some reason to stand with their parents. Is the ring ready?" Carlos and Sarah had engaged a jeweler in Masaya to make a wedding band out of Nicaraguan gold for her. She had wanted for him to have a ring too, but she agreed that the custom of husbands in the United States wearing a wedding band was anathema to Nicaraguan men; and she accepted Carlos's desire not to have one, although he'd offered to wear one for her sake.

"It will be ready. What will I wear, my *wedding and funeral?*"

"Please no! It doesn't fit you in all the right places." Sarah put her hand over Carlos's crotch, and he blushed again. "Besides, I promised Don Martín that he could wear sandals. Why don't all the men wear sandals and *guayaberas?*"

"Suits me."

"Do you want me to ask Guillermo for you?"

"No, I'll ask him. After all, he's supposed to be my best man."

"I'll ask Julio to usher, if you don't mind. He'd be gracious showing people to their seats, rather informally, of course."

"So it really will be a family affair. All the siblings for two only children."

NANCY ALLEN DE VARGAS arrived in Managua on January second, five days before the wedding. Carlos and Sarah both met his mother's plane and took her directly to Doña Beatriz's house in Los Robles to rest. The following day Carlos brought his mother to Quinta Louisa during the mid-morning and returned to his office at the Ministry of Justice in order to complete some paper work. Nancy wanted to see the home where her son would live with his bride. In spite of playing bridge with Mary Rutledge and seeing her often at social events and charitable activities sponsored by expatriate women in Nicaragua, Nancy had never before visited the *finca*. Sarah found her future mother-in-law even quieter and more taciturn than she'd been a decade ago when Carlos and Sarah were in high school.

"Would you like anything to drink? Some tea or a soda?"

"I'm good, *gracias.*"

"We really appreciate your coming down for the wedding. I know it must be hard after . . . Colonel Vargas's death . . . to be in the country again."

"I wouldn't miss my only son's wedding, even though we don't agree about a lot of things these days."

"We don't either, you know."

"I know. That's what I'm counting on." For the first time since arriving in Nicaragua, Nancy smiled, somewhat faintly. Sarah had never heard her raise her voice or display any dramatic facial expressions, positive or negative. Like many blonde women she didn't show many signs of aging. Her features faded rather than wrinkled, and her light brown hair thinned rather than grayed.

Nancy asked Sarah if she might look around the house where her son and his wife would live. Sarah chose not to follow her but encouraged her to spend as much time as she liked and go wherever she pleased in the house. Nancy stayed for ten or fifteen minutes in each room, although she never touched anything. After lunch Nancy asked Sarah if she might rest in the guesthouse where Carlos had been living. To Sarah's great relief Nancy stayed in the guesthouse for two hours, almost until the time that Carlos returned to drive her back to the city. Sarah imagined that Nancy was breathing the scent of her son from whom she'd been almost estranged for several years and feeling the presence of the one she loved best in all the world, as Sarah had done on occasions when she'd slipped into the guesthouse while Carlos was working in the city during the days when they were bitterly parted. To Sarah's even greater relief Nancy wanted to spend the following day, Sunday, with Carlos in the city, just the two of them, mother and son.

JULIO DID NOT ARRIVE until Monday, only two days before the wedding; and he brought his wife and three children with him. Sarah had not imagined that Julio's wife with whom she was hardly acquainted would come to her wedding, nevertheless that Julio's three children, ranging in age from nine to fourteen, would be present. Mercifully, Julio planned for his family to stay at the Intercontinental Hotel, one of the few buildings near the old city center of Managua that had not been destroyed in the earthquake. Julio still did not know about Pablo's death; and although Guillermo had urged Julio to come the previous week on the pretext of preparing for his role in Sarah's wedding, Julio told his younger brother that he didn't think showing people to their places in the pews at St. Francis would require a long rehearsal.

Fortunately Julio came to the factory on Monday afternoon to look over legal and financial documents, and Sarah was able to excuse herself and leave the brothers alone in the little office. Guillermo told Julio about the raid, the shooting, and the burial; and they left immediately to see their father. Sarah tarried at the factory so that she wouldn't intrude on the conversation between the father and his two surviving sons at Quinta Louisa; but about an hour after Julio and Guillermo had left the factory, Julio telephoned her and asked if she would contact Father Richard about having a funeral service at Pablo's grave the next day. Julio planned to return to Costa Rica immediately after Sarah's wedding, and he didn't want to change his plans lest it arouse his wife's suspicion. Julio did not want his family even to know that Pablo was dead.

"I do not know. Tomorrow is the Feast of the Epiphany, and Padre Richard has a service and my wedding the next day and the day after that he is leaving the country."

"It would have to be very early in the morning, so we do not arouse attention. I understand that the people in the village do not know he is dead."

"Yes, Castillo López has advised us not to draw any attention to his death."

"I am so very sorry, Sarah. I regret that this has happened to you. You do not deserve this calamity." Julio's sincere apology and concern for Sarah seemed to be more deeply felt than his grief over the death of his brother.

"I have already asked Father Richard to say some prayers at Pablo's grave. I know how important this is for Papá and Guillermo . . . and for me, too. I believe that Padre Richard will help us if he can, even on a very busy day."

Guillermo told Sarah later that he'd never told Julio about Pablo's involvement in the first raid on the night that her father had died. Guillermo had also given Julio a rather expurgated version of the raid when Pablo was killed. He had said that Pablo was caught in the crossfire, the contrived official version of events. He had not told Julio that his father almost certainly possessed the only gun in the garden that night and therefore had killed his own son. Julio was a successful businessman. He had accumulated great wealth. He knew much about the world, but he did not have the personal strength of the brother he regarded as somewhat naïve and uncouth, and so he was not able to bear a deeper truth. As Don Martín had told Sarah, some secrets are necessary even within families in order to preserve them from coming apart.

Sarah drove immediately from the factory to the vicarage without stopping at Quinta Louisa. In Father Richard's study she recounted a more complete narrative of Pablo's misadventures and death, including his involvement in the first raid the night that George Rutledge had died. Father Richard reacted in shocked disbelief, running his fingers over and over across the short-cropped hair atop his head.

"This is the last straw. It's the abomination of desolation. Surely these are the final days for Nicaragua." Then Father Richard laughed dryly and bitterly, almost as if he were coughing up something that was choking him. "What a fitting end for me, for my final days here."

"I'm sorry, Padre. If it's too much . . ."

"Of course not. I'm being egocentric and mean-spirited. Of course I'll do it. You're the one who's suffered so much . . ."

"Not me as much as Don Martín, Papá, and Guillermo and perhaps Julio, too, when it finally sinks in for him."

After further discussion they decided that Father Richard should spend the night at Quinta Louisa in order to attract as little attention as possible and walk to the cemetery as discreetly as possible before the sun rose. Father Richard would sleep in the master bedroom. Julio would drive up from the city in the early hours of the morning. Guillermo and Ana would slip away early from their cottage and walk to Quinta Louisa. Julio would tell his family that he needed to help with some preparations for Sarah's wedding; and if the people in the village should notice the unusual activity on the *finca*, they would also assume that it had something to do with preparing for Sarah's wedding, perhaps some pre-nuptial celebration.

WHEN THEY GATHERED IN the parlor early on Tuesday morning, only Sarah and Martín had flashlights. Father Richard said he had one in his car, and Carlos had one in the guesthouse. They went out the front door to pick up the flashlight from the padre's car and the one from the guesthouse and walked the long way around the house listening to the palms creaking and moaning like mourners in the wind. Then suddenly the fronds splashed together in the breeze like breakers at the ocean. The black velvet night was jeweled with pearls from the reflection of the moon and stars on the glossy leaves and damp rocks, but in the forest the darkness was black and thick. Everything was still and frightening like a haunted, petrified jungle of stone frozen by a witch's curse as the beams of their flashlights rippled over shapes along the trail and the faintest whisper of leaves rustled overhead like devils flying through the nether regions. No one said a word.

The trail to the right led to the coffee; the steep trail to the left led farther into the forest. As the path became rougher, steeper, and rocky and difficult to climb, Martín kept the beam of his light just ahead of Father Richard, so that he wouldn't stumble. Sarah and Carlos walked with their arms around each other's waists as did Guillermo and Ana, who had left their children with trusted friends in the village. Julio carried the priest's flashlight and books, because he had to hold up the skirt of his cassock; but Father Richard held the little vial of sand himself, as if it already held consecrated earth.

The light became delicate, filtered through the leaves but still soft, not yet bright from the blazing sun that would envelope everything like the air itself, but now bright enough to bring the trees and flowers and ferns and vines and bushes to life, as if waking them. A few birds came out and flew from limb to limb, not yet high up into the sky or into the tops of the trees. They sat on the branches, blinking and ruffling their feathers.

Flowers were planted at the edge of the cemetery close to the tangled bushes where the land hadn't been cleared. Sarah recognized some plants that Don Martín had taken from the garden at Quinta Louisa, even varieties of the roses that her mother had tried to grow. The huge trees arched with mossy limbs over the hills and rocks and ridges and furrows of the graves, different from the flat garden at Quinta Louisa. Until that moment Sarah had believed that no garden could be more beautiful than the garden behind her home, but this was even more beautiful than the garden at Quinta Louisa. She saw a cross at the edge of the precipice. It was made of mahogany intricately carved with flowers and vines. Martín had been secretly shaping the cross for many weeks but had not placed it on Pablo's grave until after Sarah learned about his death and burial. Inlaid in the center of the cross was a heart made of dark crimson rosewood, the color of dried blood. Below it was carved in crude letters, PABLO HIJO AMADO (Pablo Beloved Son).

"You can start as soon as you have enough light to read, Padre. I know you have to be back at St. Francis to prepare for the Epiphany service."

"No, no, Sarah. This comes first. It's too important to rush. We won't hurry through it." Those were the only words they'd exchanged since they'd left Quinta Louisa. The sky became paler and paler grey, and finally the first red glow of the sun appeared like a torch being lit far away.

Sunrise was sudden and brief, and they could see the flowers clearly for the first time, with a beauty beyond the measure of words or pictures or even thoughts, like an imagined vision of paradise, like Eden might have looked to Adam and Eve before the Fall. Father Richard stared at Sarah and Carlos still nestled together with their arms around each other.

Without any announcement or indication from Sarah, Father Richard began reading from his prayer book. As he walked toward the head of the grave he muttered in his broken Spanish, almost incoherently in a raspy whisper. *"I know that my Redeemer liveth, and that he shall stand at the latter day upon the earth; and though this body be destroyed, yet shall I see God, whom I shall see for myself and mine eyes shall behold, and not as a stranger."*

Then Padre Richard took a deep breath and dove into the funeral service with its archaic Spanish words. He spoke very slowly and precisely; but when he came to *misericordiosamente*, he couldn't get it out. He tried a second time and a third, then shrugged and went on. He stepped forward and almost seemed to lean on Don Martín's carved cross without touching it. The others formed a semicircle around the foot of the grave, Julio beside Guillermo and Ana on his right, Sarah and Carlos facing him, Don Martín on his left. *"We are more than conquerors. For I am persuaded that neither death, nor life, nor angels, nor principalities, nor powers, nor things present, nor things to come, nor height, nor depth, nor any other creature shall be able to separate us from the love of God, which is in Christ Jesus our Lord."*

Richard Sims fumbled awkwardly with the vial of sand trying to get it positioned between his fingers for pouring out while holding his prayer book with the other hand; but he read boldly, confidently from the Psalm. *"I will lift up mine eyes unto the hills: from whence cometh my help? My help cometh even from the Lord, who hath made heaven and earth."* Then he stooped and scattered the sand over the grave. *"Dust to dust, ashes to ashes . . ."*

Sarah felt a sharp pain in her chest, as if the rational, Christian words were being pushed away exposing an ancient, brutal, pagan rite underneath them. Carlos was still holding Sarah's hand; and suddenly he lifted their hands together and pointed with his forefinger to a branch above Martín. The quetzal flew from a hidden perch, then it swooped down almost touching Martín's head before it disappeared into the forest. Martín never turned around; but he smiled, as if he knew that the quetzal was there even without seeing it. His back was to the precipice with the rising sun behind him; and his face became brilliant, as if it radiated with a divine light. Sarah saw Father Richard's eyes filling with tears as though the bright light in Don Martín's face had blinded him.

Sarah remembered the legend of the quetzal that Don Martín had told her as a child. She seemed to find as much truth and comfort in the myth as in the words of Christian scripture, but neither of them gave her any final answers. Through her tears Sarah could still see Don Martín clearly, and she could feel his presence filling her with his light.

DOÑA BEATRIZ MADE SARAH put on her wedding dress an hour earlier than was necessary, like a good parent. (Her mother and father had also prepared her too early for important occasions to be sure that there would be plenty of time.)

"Please pin this brooch on the strap of my dress."

"Sarita, why do you want to put this on? It's just a cheap silver pin, and it's a little tarnished."

"It was my mother's"

"Your mother had some lovely jewelry. Surely you could find something else . . . Besides, it's Guatemalan, not even Nicaraguan."

"She bought it during her honeymoon in Guatemala." Sarah didn't tell Doña Beatriz that the little quetzal pin carried another meaning from the distant past, from when Don Martín had told her the legend over and over as a child, and a very recent significance from only yesterday on the Feast of the Epiphany when she had seen a quetzal for the first time in her life as it flew over Pablo's grave. She knew that Doña Beatriz would accept the sentimental association with Mary Rutledge's honeymoon. The other reasons for wearing the quetzal brooch would remain Sarah's secret.

"Very well, *carita* (dearest). I suppose you must . . . Let me see if the padre needs anything."

Sarah stood in Father Richard's guest bedroom at the vicarage looking through the blinds and watching people arrive at the church across the parking lot. Father Richard flitted like a boat-tailed grackle from the church to speak with Doña Beatriz and back to the vicarage and then to the church again, making certain that the candles and the altar hangings and the flowers were in place, fussing over every detail.

Ana was lovely in the blue dress that Octavia had made for her. Sarah was glad that she'd asked Ana to be her matron of honor. If Nicaragua could become a young woman, it would be Ana standing beside her with its strangely ravaged beauty, its luxuriously rich poverty, its fearful, terrified hope, it unsettled, unformed fate.

"Sarah, this note came for you. I don't know who sent it. The boy who delivered it said it was important." Father Richard poked his hand through the door and averted his eyes. The manila envelope had been hand delivered and hand addressed with a flourished, old-fashioned script to *Señorita Rutledge Lloyd*. A small white envelope was taped to the front of the larger tan envelope, and the flap of the creamy linen stationary popped up without having to tear the paper. Inside were three lined pages torn out of a *Cuaderno* notebook like the ones that Nicaraguan children use in school. Sarah unfolded the note to the read the signature on the last page and see that the letter was from Adolfo Castillo López, Minister of Justice.

Dear Señorita Rutledge Lloyd,

Attached you will find a certified copy of the property agreement. Guard it well. It is my wedding gift to you and Carlos Vargas Allen. I took some pains to secure it for you.

Difficult days may lie ahead for you and for all of us. Our informants in Washington have learned that the incoming Reagan administration will begin funding the Contras if we do not agree to cease allowing the transport of arms to the freedom fighters in El Salvador. Of course, we cannot stop the support of our brothers there. It may result in civil war for Nicaragua.

I regret writing this to you on your wedding day. I am sorry not to be with you for the celebration. Due to the events noted above, I must make a trip outside the country.

One more piece of advice: beware of Andrejo. If we do not succeed, he will seek to do you harm.

My thoughts and best wishes for your marriage and future life together,
With great respect,
Adolfo Castillo López
Minister of Justice

SARAH FOLDED THE PAGES and put them back inside the smaller envelope and moistened her forefinger with the tip of her tongue and rubbed it against the flap and tried to seal it back. Then she slipped the whole parcel under a book on the table in Father Richard's study next door to his guest bedroom, where she believed it would be more secure.

Ana looked concerned when Sarah returned to the bedroom. *"Can I do anything for you, Sarah?"*

"Go check on Carlos and Guillermo and be sure they are dressed and ready in the sacristy. Please do not tell them anything about the envelope that arrived for me."

Sarah watched Father Richard flit around the church appearing again like a gangly black bird as Ana walked toward the sacristy where Carlos and Guillermo were waiting. Perhaps it was absurd to be married in an Anglican chapel in Nicaragua, an anachronism even in the United States, perhaps even in England itself, and most assuredly an anachronism in Nicaragua. The officiant would be Father Richard Sims, who was also an anachronism, utterly irrelevant to the future of this country. Yet, Padre Richard and St. Francis Church preserved the spiritual meaning of life from her past in Nicaragua. Sarah wondered if real meaning, deep meaning could ever be preserved apart from anachronisms.

When Ana returned from the church, Sarah was smiling, as if she'd forgotten Castillo's letter, as if her wedding with its joy and hope had displaced all her concerns and worries.

"Are Carlos and Guillermo ready?"

"They are both dressed and waiting. Carlos keeps pulling up the collar on his shirt to hide the little white scar on his neck. I think he is just nervous." It was the scar that he'd received on one of the few Sandinista raids that he'd made. It was both his badge of honor and his emblem of shame, sometimes displayed, sometimes concealed. Sarah felt a tingling between her legs as if she could sense the banquet of their bodies pressed together—Carlos's darkness and her paleness, his hardness and her softness melding, transforming each other; but now she was content to be dressed in her beautiful white gown, to touch the silk, to look at how it fit around her breasts and hips like a flower perfectly formed around her body, keeping all her best and most beautiful feelings secretly inside, hidden, waiting

for Carlos. As she took a few steps she felt how the dress flowed away like petals unfolding around her.

Sarah peeked out between the slats of the Venetian blinds again to see Don Martín standing with Julio at the front door of the church. The old *campesino* (peasant) was awkward, ill at ease, out of place, like a slightly mis-sized, stiff mannequin in the doorway waiting for her. The radiance had faded from his face now, but Sarah remembered the holy light she had seen in it yesterday on the mountain. His face would always hold a saintly beauty for her, even when he was proclaiming his prudish strictures or making his bawdy gestures, even now as he looked afraid and embarrassed by the strange, formal ceremonies and the well-dressed, condescending people.

Ana crowded beside Sarah to look out between the splayed slats that she held open.

"Your guests are beginning to arrive."

The Nicaraguan members of the congregation, the *costeños* (people from the East Coast), were walking the driveway from the bus stop. Taylor was dressed in his overly large brown suit like a molting thrush as he helped Miss Ann up the steps, climbing with her left foot and cane and then dragging up the right foot.

"Here come his Excellency the American Ambassador and Mrs. Warren. My wedding must be considered a state occasion. Dueña (Mistress) *Elizabeth is carrying her white gloves."*

Some of Carlos's revolutionary comrades from the Ministry of Justice drove up in a military jeep wearing their obligatory khaki clothes, but one of them had a ridiculous black bow tie clipped to the soldier's collar that made Sarah laugh when she saw it. Then Sarah saw Doña Beatriz walking across the yard, as fast as her slow, gouty, arthritic gait would allow, in her best, most elegant and beautiful, out-of-style, old dress. She had spent everything she could afford on Sarah's wedding dress. Nothing was left even for a simple new frock for the woman who had always cherished her stylish clothes above everything else. Doña Beatriz was coming to escort Sarah to the church door, to her wedding, to Carlos, her beloved. Tears were already forming in Doña Beatriz's eyes. Sarah glanced at Ana. Her eyes, too, were misty and blinking; but Sarah shed no tears, not even a hint of tears.

The young revolutionaries and the old aristocratic *dueña* (mistress) met as they passed each other in the churchyard. It was a parable of the transition from the old life of the country to its very different future.

Doña Beatriz handed Sarah her bouquet at the head of the aisle. Only Sarah and Don Martín knew that the little pink roses were clipped from the bushes at Pablo's grave. Not even Carlos was aware of their origin.

Nancy Allen de Vargas turned to face Sarah with the other people in the congregation. Her yellow suit had been tailored for the mother of the groom in Miami. She wore a corsage of white roses that obviously were not grown in Nicaragua.

Don Martín was trembling as he escorted Sarah down the aisle. She supported him and was afraid he might faint before they reached the altar.

Father Richard began with the archaic English words of the *Book of Common Prayer*. "Dearly beloved, we are gathered together here in the sight of God, and in the face of this company to join together this Man and this Woman in holy Matrimony . . ."

Later he would read some passages in Spanish, but every word of the Anglican ritual would be spoken in English. "I require and charge you both, as ye will answer at the dreadful Day of Judgment when the secrets of all human hearts shall be disclosed . . ."

"Who giveth this Woman to be married to this Man?"

"*Yo la entrego.* (I deliver her.)"

Sarah kissed Don Martín on his cheek. "*Thank you, Papá, for giving me away.*"

Don Martín sat down beside Doña Beatriz. He seemed to relax, to Sarah's great relief. Doña Beatriz smiled at Don Martín and took his hand. It was perhaps her greatest gift to Sarah, sitting beside an old *campesino* (peasant) as an equal, as Sarah's other surrogate parent. Perhaps this scene of Don Martín and Doña Beatriz sitting together holding hands was a picture of the new Nicaragua even more vivid than Doña Beatriz's crossing paths with the Sandinista soldiers in the churchyard.

Although Father Richard had quite willingly agreed to use the older liturgy of matrimony, the rite that had solemnized the union of Sarah's parents, rather than the revised service authorized during the previous decade by the Episcopal Church, he wanted to include a reading from scripture, as prescribed in the newer service. Sarah chose the thirteenth chapter of First Corinthians, "Love is patient and kind . . ." She also asked Father Richard to read the whole passage by Dame Julian of Norwich from which he often quoted. For Sarah it represented not only the hope and promise for her marriage to Carlos but also hope and promise for their life together in Nicaragua.

AS TRULY AS GOD is our Father, so just as truly is God our Mother, and he revealed these sweet words where he says: I am he, the power and goodness of fatherhood; I am he, the wisdom and lovingness of motherhood; I am he, the light and grace which is all blessed love; I am he, the Trinity; I am he, the unity; I am he, the supreme goodness of every living thing; I am he, who makes you to love; I am he, who makes you to long; I am he, the fulfilling of all true desires. And from this foundation in substance we have all the powers of sensuality by the gift of nature, and by the help and furthering of mercy and grace.[1]

It is behooved that there should be sin, but all shall be well, and all manner of thing shall be well.[2]

AFTER THE SERVICE EVERYONE enjoyed a piece of wedding cake, also arranged by Doña Beatriz with a bakery in the city, and a cup of lime-ade slightly flavored with Nicaraguan rum and white wine. A couple of *costeño* members of St. Francis played guitars on the outdoor brick patio between the church and the cabañas where children gathered for Sunday School, where the coffee reception took place every Sunday after the service. Even in the tropical heat almost everyone danced, even Miss Ann hobbling beside Father Richard. Guillermo danced with Ana and

---

1   *Julian of Norwich: Showings,* translated by Edmund College, *OSA,* and James Welch, *S.J.,* Paulist Press, 1978, ch. 59, pp. 295-296.

2   *Julian of Norwich, Revelations of Divine Love,* Christian Classics Ethereal Library, ch. 27, p. 55.

then with Sarah. Even Don Martín danced with Sarah. During the last dance as Sarah and Carlos held each other, she whispered in his ear and told him about the wedding gift they had received from Castillo López. She told him she had hidden the property agreement under a book in Father Richard's study and asked Father Richard to keep it safe for them until after everyone else left the reception; but she did not tell him about Castillo's accompanying letter with its dire warnings.

Nancy Allen de Vargas was the last person to leave the reception. She apologized to Sarah for taking Carlos away early the next morning after their wedding night in order to see her off at the airport.

"Not at all. We're so glad you came back for our wedding. If I can manage to get up out of bed . . ."

"Would it be too selfish of me to ask for tomorrow morning by myself with my boy?"

"It would be perfectly natural . . . and very, very kind."

They both laughed and hugged each other.

"I can understand why you love Quinta Louisa so much and want to stay here. I hope you can, but in all honesty I have to tell you I pray every day that Carlos will change his mind and see through these Sandinista illusions that killed his father and that you'll both come back to the United States to live." It was perhaps the longest and most well-rehearsed speech that Nancy had ever made.

"I understand, and I promise we'll visit you in Miami often, at least every year."

The next morning Carlos left, as planned, to take his mother to catch her flight to Miami. Because Father Richard Sims was flying through New Orleans on TACA later in the morning, there was not enough time for Carlos to return from the airport to accompany him. Sarah and Guillermo would drive to the vicarage in her car—she still thought of it as her father's "new" Volkswagen beetle, of which he'd been possessively proud. Guillermo would then drive Father Richard's car, which he was leaving for his successor, a Nicaraguan priest, to use at St. Francis. Father Richard was shipping more luggage and boxes than could be carried in either of the cars separately. Carlos would meet Sarah and Father Richard and Guillermo at the airport.

At the vicarage Father Richard had packed his car leaving only room enough for the driver. He rode to the airport with Sarah in her car.

"I can't believe you're leaving Nicaragua, Padre. It will never be the same here without you."

"As I told you some time ago, there's no future for me here, Sarita."

"And what kind of future is there for Carlos and me?"

"At least in Nicaragua you can see how fragile, how besieged, how threatened human life on the earth is today. You'll be alert and aware of constant danger. You won't be drugged and mesmerized into a feeling of false security like people in the United States."

"You know all this, and yet you're leaving!"

"There's no place for me any longer, my dear. I hope I can remember what I learned here and be an advocate in the United States . . . for Nicaragua . . . for justice. But you still belong here."

". . . if I can hold onto Quinta Louisa."

"Remember that Quinta Louisa is only loaned to you for a time . . . like all the parts and pieces of the earth, all the *fincas* and gardens and nations. We borrow them for a while during our sojourn of life. They are only loaned for our human use, regardless of the political regime in power, no matter who sits upon the throne. My time here is over, but your time has not yet run out. You still belong to this place."

Sarah thought that Father Richard's speech had been even more carefully planned and rehearsed than her new mother-in-law's yesterday. It was almost like one of his sermons.

"But for how long? When will my time be over here, too?"

"Don't forget to say the prayer I taught you as a little girl. Say it every day. *Grant us not to mind earthly things, but to love things heavenly; and even now while we are placed among things that are passing away, to cleave to those that shall abide.*"[3]

At the airport Carlos and Guillermo took Father Richard's posses-

---

3   Collect for Proper 29, *The Book of Common Prayer*, p. 182.

sions that were to be shipped. Sarah and Padre Richard sat together and observed long periods of silent understanding interrupted occasionally by exchanged pleasantries. They had said everything that they needed to say to each other in the car. When Carlos and Guillermo returned from the shipping area, more pleasantries and good wishes were exchanged, some in English, most in Spanish.

After Father Richard walked through the gate for his flight, the three of them went upstairs to the observation window and waited for the airplane to take off. Carlos put his arm around Sarah, and Guillermo, standing beside Carlos, reached his arm all the way around both of them.

Sarah's voice was trembling as she spoke. *"It is so sad. Father Richard is the last gringo friend of my parents to leave. As he told me on the drive to the airport, there is no place here any more for foreigners who love Nicaragua."*

Guillermo squeezed Sarah's waist with his fingertips. *"But you are not a foreigner any more, mi hermana* (my sister).*"*

"De veras (That's true). *"But Father Richard will never come back."*

The rays of the morning sun splashed under the airplane ascending off the runway into the sky with a red glow like the belly of a quetzal flying away.

Carlos kissed Sarah's cheek. *"Do not be too sure, my love. Remember the quetzal did return despite all predictions that it had left Nicaragua forever."*

Acknowledgments

The narrative of this novel was complicated by its setting in Nicaragua and the United States over the span of two decades more than three decades ago. A number of people helped to verify locations and events: Harry Strachan, Alice Pfeiffer, and Jonathan and Lyana Drewry in Nicaragua and Julie Lellis and Bill Blanchard at Elon College. Luz Helen Robinson and Richard and Lonna Harkrader provided information about coffee production in Central America. A book about Nicaraguan birds published by Timothy Sedgwick-Jell as a teenager was often consulted. Shanee Yvette Murrain located citations for several religious references at the Duke Divinity School Library.

Joel Sanders edited this book, as he did my previous book, and brought greater clarity, fewer contradictions, and an improved tone to its final draft. My wife, Rilla, proofread several drafts and was especially helpful with suggestions about Spanish usage. The image of the author on the book cover by my photographer daughter makes me look better than I deserve. The Writers' Group at Fearrington Village, North Carolina, listened patiently and offered helpful advice at gatherings for more than two years as portions of the narrative were read.

A great debt of gratitude is owed to Richard (Rick) Mills who graciously provided the painting for the cover, as he did for my previous novella and short story collection.

Finally, all of my books were published only through the kind and thoughtful encouragement of Randall Williams and the staff of NewSouth Books in keeping with their high standards of print and design.

www.ingramcontent.com/pod-product-compliance
Lightning Source LLC
Chambersburg PA
CBHW030347020726
47493CB00003B/730